The God Gene

by

Jaymie Simmon

TELEMACHUS PRESS

Cover designed by Princess Iris
irisbookdesigns@gmail.com

Cover art Copyright © Jaymie Simmon

Published by Telemachus Press, LLC
http://www.telemachuspress.com

Visit the author website:
http://www.thegodgene.com
http://www.thestarrymessenger.com

ISBN# 978-1-937698-47-8 (eBook)
ISBN# 978-1-937698-48-5 (paperback)

Version 2012.07.24

Printed in the United States of America

10 9 8 7 6 5 4 3 2 1

What others are saying about *The God Gene*

"Compelling! A page turner that pays off, and an astute allegory for the moral confusion of our times." –James Riordan, Author of *Break On Through: The Life & Death of Jim Morrison* and *The Coming of the Walrus*

"Simmon's brilliant first novel is cleverly-crafted; part weird science, part social satire, totally entertaining." –Gary W. Moore, Author of *Playing With the Enemy* and *Hey Buddy*

"As a scientist, I loved the accurate descriptions of DNA with Simmon's added twists. Exceedingly clever story line and fascinating characters—a fun read!" –Donna Decker, Senior Research Technician, University of Chicago

Acknowledgements

To all who gave a word of encouragement and/or critique, thank you. I love you all. With apologies to anyone I may have inadvertently left out, I wish to especially thank:

Donna Decker of the University of Chicago for her expertise, creativity, and friendship.

For generously sharing their time and expertise: Dr. Ann Sperling and Dr. William Buikema and their associates at the University of Chicago, Professor Melvyn Duvall of Northern Illinois University, Judge Clark Erickson of the 21st Judicial Circuit of Illinois, Jeff Yordon of Sagent Pharmaceutical, Jim Fatz of Northern Illinois University, Sumit Sehgal of George Washington University Hospital and Sarah Smith of KMBC in Kansas City.

Dr. Leland Kaiser, Kevin Kaiser and Leanne Kaiser Carlson for their inspiration.

Frank Fetters and Bob Tamasy for their thoughtful editing and critiques.

Mallory Simpson for her support, logistical help, and friendship.

Dr. Dan Boone for his inspiration, encouragement and friendship.

Jessica Simmon Bullock of *re:think studios* for the book cover and photo.

Mable Dankers, who taught me reverence for language that inspires me to this day. RIP Mable.

For their love and constant encouragement: Dad, Willy, Jess, Brian, Jackson, Grant, Nicole, Grace, Nyla and Cindy Lou.

Most especially, my wonderful husband, Harry. You know who you are and you know what you did. None of this would have happened without you.

Above all, thanks to God, from whom all blessings flow.

For Mom

The God Gene

Part I
Witness

Chapter 1

ROSALIND EVANS CAREFULLY laid bound copies of her slides on the conference table. In less than fifteen minutes, Alan Dyer, the CEO of PharmaGen, would walk through the door, blue-suited and impeccably composed, expecting to hear that six months of top-secret genetic research was finished, that her analyses were brilliant, and that PharmaGen now had the tools it needed to develop a new generation of targeted leukemia therapies. Fair expectations, given that he was the guy paying the $15 million bill. As Principal Investigator on the project, Rosalind could be forgiven for gloating; the project was nailed on time, on budget, and her analyses were beyond brilliant. But there was no urge to gloat in her. It was more like an urge to run outside and throw up. She fought back niggling doubts about what bit of data she might have left out, what erroneous conclusion might leap out of her mouth, what stupidity she might betray that would blow the whole thing. She told herself that her insecurity was heightened by the lack of sleep the night before. But it wasn't true. Sleeplessness had nothing to do with it. She was an expert at sleeplessness. She hadn't had a good night's sleep in over a year and a half, not since Claire's diagnosis. She didn't even curse that reality anymore. She just endured long nights meandering through the dark places of her soul, and then stumbled into pre-dawn consciousness with a dry mouth and a vague sense of disconnectedness. Dead tired was the new normal. At least the nightmares were gone, but she wondered whether they weren't preferable to endless mucking around at the edges of sleep. It didn't matter.

In the end, no pill, mantra or strong drink could overcome the reality: Since Claire's death, Rosalind Evans was, like Jacob Marley, doomed to wander. Only when she walked into her lab at the Clearbrook Institute each morning did she feel human, or as close to it as she believed she would ever be again. Get over it, she told herself, your insecurity isn't caused by fatigue; it's your obsessive fear that you could still blow this.

She forced herself to focus. All that was left to do before Dyer arrived was to hook up the projection system and run through the slides one last time. Her stomach was doing flip-flops, and in her ravaged brain state, she couldn't make the slides come up on the screen. She tried plugging and unplugging wires, but still the screen was dark. She had hard copies of everything just in case, but she knew the presentation would be much more effective up on the screen. She threw the wires down on the table in frustration, picked up her iPhone, and called the one guy she thought could fix her problem.

In the basement of Clearbrook Hall, Mick 'The Tech' Morrison was in his office shuffling through a stack of work orders, slurping the last of a protein shake before his first service call. Even though campus was pretty well shut down, Information Services was in full maintenance and upgrade mode. The summer lull was anything but for Mick the Tech. It was his busiest time of the year. Major systems needed to be taken apart, upgraded, and put back together again in the relative quiet of summer, before the fall semester began.

Mick smiled. The one bright spot in this insanely busy day would be a service call in the University President's office. He didn't give a rip about The Man; it was The Man's assistant he was after. He looked at his watch. This little hottie was always glad to see him, and the earlier in the day he dropped in to see her, the better his chances of scoring. He had a full-length mirror on the back of his door for moments like this. He checked his reflection, taking his time, giving due diligence to every nuance of hair, smile, and belt positioning. As he was taking it all in, he had a sudden flash of enlightenment: If you took all the males at Rutherford University and stacked them one on top of the other by looks, he would be on top.

He walked across the hall and stuck his head into the bullpen where the other I.S. technicians, grad assistants, and interns sat in their cubicles, sipping their coffee before the day's madness began. His presence attracted the attention of absolutely no one. He sat on the edge of a desk shared by his two-grad assistants, Danny Wu and Sammy Kew. He leaned down close and fanned his stack of work orders in their faces.

"Everybody wants me," Mick said, a smile spreading across his chiseled face. "I can resuscitate a crashed hard drive just by breathing on it, and I can tell a Trojan from a worm by smell. I am the magical, mystical wizard of tech." Wu and Kew said nothing. Mick flipped his long blonde hair over his shoulder and raised his voice so all could hear. "When the pediatric unit at University Hospital crashed last week, I had it back up, plus nailed the head nurse, in under half an hour. The boss says I have an intuition for non-obvious solutions, and that ain't all I got. And that, my bros, is why you are all in here, and I have my own office."

"That's not an office, it's a closet," a voice came from behind a cubicle wall. "You didn't earn it, you stole it."

"*Was* a closet. It might be small, but it has a private door that leads into the ANSR 1000. You got a door that leads to the ANSR 1000?"

"Your office is a hole," the unseen voice said.

"Yeah? Better to have a small hole than no hole at all, I say. Now if you'll excuse me, duty calls." The President's office was all the way across campus, and the hottie was waiting. He leaned down and spoke quietly to Wu and Kew. "Why don't you two kids hustle on over there and clean my office? You never know when I might have company coming."

Wu and Kew looked at each other. Kids? This guy was beyond imbecilic. But he was their supervisor this semester, incomprehensible as that was, so they had no choice. They shook their heads, amazed once again at the cruel irony that they, brilliant computer geniuses who were about to rock the world, had to bow to the likes of Mick the Mistake Morrison.

Mick bounded up the steps and out into the sultry July morning. As he started across campus, his cell phone rang. He looked at the caller ID. Well, well, he thought, this should be interesting.

"Good morning there, Dr. Evans."

"Mick, I have an incredibly important presentation this morning, and I can't get the projector to work. I need your help."

"Well, what seems to be the problem?" She sounded breathless. He tried to imagine what she was wearing.

"I can't get the projector hooked up to my laptop. It's on some kind of a toot."

"Toot. Hmmm. Could you be more specific?"

"No I can't!!"

He looked at his watch. "Well, OK, then maybe we could try a couple of things over the phone to get you up and running." Yeah baby, he thought, I got a couple of things I'd like to try with you over the phone. The sound of silence on the other end was ominous.

When she finally spoke, it was in measured tones. "Mick, let me ask you something. Has someone you loved ever had cancer? Suffered, wasted away and died? Have *you* ever had cancer? Because some day you probably will, and you will vomit blood and die because there is no cure. Oh, there would be; I'm very close to finding it you know, except that I can't, because I don't have anybody to help me with my *computer*!!!"

That was it. Hottie or no hottie, you couldn't rub the exalted Dr. Rosalind Evans the wrong way, oh no. That was a career-ender. "I'll be right up."

Mick smiled confidently as he sauntered into the conference room. His hair was tucked behind his ears, and the way his shirt and jeans seemed to haphazardly hug certain parts of his body had actually been carefully orchestrated for maximum impact. "Nice to see you Dr. Evans," he said, extending a strong, capable hand. Her laptop was sitting on the conference table covered in a tangle of wires.

"Let me see what I can do here." For several minutes, Mick rolled his fingers over the computer keys like a pianist, making images appear and disappear on the screen, calling up messages from deep within the system. Rosalind paced behind him, willing him to finish before Dyer got there. She didn't want him thinking she was some stupid female who couldn't hook up a computer.

He plugged and unplugged wires and turned around occasionally to smile at her. He thought she seemed tense, and the longer he thought about it; the more ideas took shape in his mind about how, given the chance, he could make all that tension go away. Hooking up her computer should have taken ten seconds, but he wanted to take plenty of time, so that his aura would penetrate deeply into her consciousness. After a few minutes, he turned to her.

"There you go, my lady." The images were bright and clear on the projection screen. He stood looking at it for a moment. The slide was filled with strings of letters. "What the heck is that, word puzzles?"

"It's translation code, the readout of sequenced DNA." Rosalind saw by the look on his face that he didn't understand and didn't care. She took the remote and scrolled through the next several slides. She smiled. They were beautiful.

"What does it say?"

"You wouldn't understand."

"I bet I would. I'm really good at word-find puzzles." Mick said.

A game, she thought. I studied my whole life to embrace and understand the complex layers of meaning revealed in translation code, and you think it's a game. This is the answer to why my baby girl died. Or half of it anyway. She quickly shoved the thought out of her head. "Then go find yourself a word-find puzzle. That's not what this is."

"OK. OK. Come on over here and I'll show you how to set up the projector so you can do it yourself next time. Here, lean up close so you can see." She leaned in closer to him. He casually tossed his hair and flexed his oversized bicep. "First, you put the USB cable in this hole right here. See? Now you try it. Good. Then you put this end in this hole. Good. Then you press F7. And *that*, little lady is what I'm talkin' about." He turned and tossed a crooked little smile at her. He was surprised that she seemed not to notice. That almost never happened.

"I have a big favor to ask," Rosalind said. "I really need you to stay while I make this presentation, so that if anything goes wrong, you'll be here to fix it for me. Can you do that?"

Ah, the damsel-in-distress gambit. He'd seen it before plenty of times. Now he was pretty sure she was attracted to him. The whole F7 thing usually worked pretty well. But the President's hottie … she was still waiting.

"Sorry, I can't. We're taking down the security camera system for maintenance."

"This won't take long. Please?"

The exalted Rosalind Evans, begging. He loved it. "Alright. But only if you pay me back. How about you come down to my office and give me a few decorating tips?"

Decorating tips, she thought. Right. Who let this guy in? But she didn't have time to argue. "We'll see. Where is your office?"

"Basement. Turn right off the elevator. My name is on the door." He walked up close to her. "I have my own entrance to the ANSR 1000. I can give you a private tour." He knew that a private tour of the most powerful computer on earth was bound to strike a chord somewhere south of her sweet little navel. He raised one eyebrow and winked at her.

Rosalind looked around the conference room. She didn't want this guy in the room when Dyer arrived. There were two doors, one in front and one at the back. "Stand outside that back door," she said. "I'll call you if I need you." She turned and busied herself with the computer.

Mick picked up a set of handouts and lumbered out the back door, feeling a bit deflated. He wasn't used to being relegated to the hallway, especially by a woman. He slumped against the wall and glanced at the handout of the slides. There were thirty pages, some of them pictures and charts, the rest word puzzles. He stuffed them into his backpack. He opened the door a crack and focused his gaze on her, thinking about what moves he would use once he got her into his office.

At precisely 8 a.m., Alan Dyer walked into the room, followed by his Director of Research, Peter Gleason. Immediately behind them was Benton Bradshaw, the Director of the Clearbrook Institute. Bradshaw was holding a champagne bucket and four glasses.

"Behold the second chromosome!" Bradshaw said, pouring champagne and gesturing at the drawing of the x-shaped blob of DNA on the screen. "It's too bad we can't invite the whole world to this momentous celebration! Of course we can't, not yet, but one day soon the world will celebrate with us!" He raised his glass. "Today we celebrate the completion of phase one of the PharmaGen revolution in genomic medicine!"

Alan Dyer did not seem to share Bradshaw's giddy enthusiasm; nevertheless, he clinked his glass and took a sip. "Let's proceed," he said.

Bradshaw stood as tall as his five feet four inches would allow. "Gentlemen, never in my career at the Clearbrook Institute have I been more proud. Rosalind Evans and her team have done a comprehensive analysis of the genetic variations that contribute to adverse reactions to many cancer drugs. Just six months ago, custom drug therapies for leukemia were only a dream, Alan. Today, you are a pioneer who is about to revolutionize cancer treatment through targeted therapies. Congratulations!"

Dyer leveled his gaze. "It's a long road, Ben. This is just the first step. We're a decade away from bringing any new drugs to market."

"Come on Alan, you are the first to complete basic research. Who could possibly beat you now? Let's celebrate!" Bradshaw said.

"We'll celebrate when we cash the first check. Move on."

"All right," Bradshaw said, disappointed. "You've asked for a summary of the study, just the highlights. I think you will be delighted." He gestured toward Rosalind to begin.

Rosalind beat back a flutter of butterflies and clicked the remote control. Up came a beautiful color rendering of a DNA double helix that spun and morphed into a spinning globe.

"Our analysis of all the data is complete," Rosalind said. "We were able to analyze seven thousand DNA samples from populations all over the world. This gives our research an exceedingly high level of accuracy. We were looking for tiny variations in genetic code known as single nucleotide polymorphisms. We were able to identify hundreds of SNPs—snips—across all of the populations. These SNPs will guide your product team in developing new, targeted therapies based on a patient's unique genetic fingerprint." She pulled up the next slide.

"Alan, I know you don't want too much detail, so I'll just give you a small example of what my team and I found. This is actual translation code from the 2q13-2q14.1 region of the second chromosome."

"Better known as the CLAIRE gene," Dyer said.

"Precisely. This gene was originally named the DZPro1, until you kindly agreed to register it as CLAIRE, in honor of my daughter."

"It made sense from a marketing standpoint," Dyer said.

"Well, anyway, thank you. What makes the CLAIRE gene important is its location on the chromosome." Rosalind pulled up the next slide, a rendering of the second chromosome. "We know that the second chromosome was formed when two ancestral chromosomes, probably chimpanzee chromosomes, fused. This makes our second chromosome unique: it doesn't have a normal mid-section." She pointed at the narrow juncture in the center of the x-shaped chromosome. "This center region was previously thought to be non-coding or junk DNA. But now we know it contains two genes. On one side of the center line is DZPro1, or CLAIRE. On the other side is DZPro2. Another lab at Clearbrook is studying that gene. We know that both have markers for drug resistance."

Dyer nodded without taking his eyes off the screen.

"Everyone with leukemia has different genetic mutations, but there is one mutation that is shared by all of them." She pulled up another slide of the translation code. "Here we see a section of the gene, beginning with location 4651 of the base code, and location 1521 of the amino acid code."

```
4561   CACCCANCCNCCCTTCCTNCCCGGTGCGATTTCCTCCCACGCCCTGACCGCNTCCCCCAG
1521    T  H  X  X  L  P  X  R  C  D  F  S  H  A  L  T  R  X  P  Q
4621   AACNTCACCCACCCCTCGACTCCCCGGNCCTCCCTGCGGGCCCGANCGGAGGCCCGGGAG
1541    N  X  T  H  P  S  T  P  R  X  S  L  R  A  R  X  E  A  R  E
4681   GCGGCGGAGTTGNCGAGCTCCGGGNCGTTCGCCCTGTCCGAGAGCNCGAGTTTCNCGCCG
1561    X  A  E  L  X  S  S  G  X  F  A  L  S  E  S  X  S  F  X  P
4741   NCGTCTGGATACAGCNTCCCGCTTCGTCGCNCCNTCCTGGACCCCGGTAGCNCCGAGCCT
1581    X  S  G  Y  S  X  P  L  R  R  X  X  L  D  P  G  S  X  E  P
4801   GCCCGGNCGGCTNCCCTGCGCCGGCCTGGGGCGAAGGTCCAAGGGGCGCGGGGGGNCCGGA
1601    A  R  X  A  X  L  R  R  P  G  A  K  V  Q  G  A  R  G  X  G
4861   CGCGGGGCTGTGGCAACGNCTGGCCCTCTGCGAACGNCGGGGCCGGCGGGTCCGGGGCCA
1621    R  G  A  V  A  T  X  G  P  L  R  T  X  G  P  A  G  P  G  P
4921   CAGGCTGGGNCGGGAGCTGGCGGCCACTGGATCACCAACGAGTCCTCCAGGNCGAGGTGC
1641    Q  A  G  X  G  A  G  G  H  W  I  T  N  E  S  S  R  X  R  C
4981   ACCAGGGTCNCCGCGGCTGGGCCGAGGGTCGCAAGCAGAGGGGACCGGCGGCTGCCAGCA
1661    T  R  V  X  A  A  G  P  R  V  A  S  R  G  D  R  R  L  P  A
5041   AGTNCCAAGCAGATGCCTCTGGCGGGGCAGCCGCATTCTACAGCGCCCATTCCGCGTACA
1681    S  X  K  Q  M  P  L  A  G  Q  P  H  S  T  A  P  I  P  R  T
5101   TCGAGTATCCAAAATGAGNCCAATCGGTTTATACGTTGGAATGTAGCTTATGATTCCAAA
1701    S  S  I  Q  N  E  X  N  R  F  I  R  W  N  V  A  Y  D  S  K
5161   ATCTCANCGCCAGGCTGCCTAGATCACACGGCCCCGTTTCATTCANCGTTACTTAATAAC
1721    I  S  X  P  G  C  L  D  H  T  A  P  F  H  S  X  L  L  N  N
5221   GGTCGTTGGACAATTNCCNCCAGCAGCAGAGCCGGCGCCATCAACTCCACCGTCNCCCGG
1741    G  R  W  T  I  X  X  S  S  R  A  G  A  I  N  S  T  V  X  R
5281   CGGNCCGGACTGACAAGGCTGNCCGGGNCGTTGAGCAAACGGCGGCTTCTGAGTTGGCAC
1761    R  X  G  L  T  R  L  X  G  X  L  S  K  R  R  L  L  S  W  H
```

"For this project we used new beta software, the Deep X Sequencing Program. Only Clearbrook and Flemingham University in Palo Alto have it right now. It's brilliant. It allowed us to sequence and analyze 7000 DNA samples in a fraction of the time of other programs. The most distinguishing feature of Deep X is that it collates all the SNPs into a single, comprehensive document so that we can see them all at once. This is the holy grail—"

"Wait a minute." Dyer sat up, interrupting her. "What is this?" He pointed at a string of letters on the screen.

The intensity of his voice sent a chill down her spine. "It's translation code. The smaller letters at the top are base code and the larger ones are the amino acid sequence ..."

"I know that." Dyer walked up to the screen. He traced a circle around a group of letters with this finger and looked at Rosalind. The projected images played across his face. "What's this?"

```
4561   CACCCANCCNCCCTTCCTNCCCGGTGCGATTTCCTCCCACGCCCTGACCGCNTCCCCCAG
1521    T   H   X   X   L   P   X   R   C   D   F   S   H   A   L   T   R   X   P   Q
4621   AACNTCACCCACCCCTCGACTCCCCGGNCCTCCCTGCGGGCCCGANCGGAGGCCCGGGAG
1541    N   X   T   H   P   S   T   P   R   X   S   L   R   A   R   X   E   A   R   E
4681   GCGGCGGAGTTGNCGAGCTCCGGGNCGTTCGCCCTGTCCGAGAGCNCGAGTTTCNCGCCG
1561    X   A   E   L   X   S   S   G   X   **F   A   L   S   E**   S   X   S   F   X   P
4741   NCGTCTGGATACAGCNTCCCGCTTCGTCGCNCCNTCCTGGACCCCGGTAGCNCCGAGCCT
1581    X   S   G   Y   S   X   P   L   R   R   X   X   L   D   P   G   S   X   E   P
```

Rosalind stared at the translation code. For a long, tense moment, nobody said anything. Then Bradshaw chuckled. "Oh, that. It happens. With millions of combinations of letters in the genetic code, it makes sense that once in a while a word will pop out. We've seen it happen before. Don't give it a second thought."

Dyer faced Rosalind. "Is this some kind of a joke?"

"No, of course not, Alan," Rosalind said.

"Is this the real data from my project?"

"Yes," she said.

"Is it possible you made some kind of mistake?"

Rosalind felt her head beginning to pound.

"Don't worry about this," Bradshaw said. "Really, it happens sometimes. It's rare, but it does happen."

Dyer calmly circled another group of letters with his finger. It was the word 'WITNESS,' and then he circled another, 'AGAINST.'

```
4921  CAGGCTGGGNCGGGAGCTGGCGGCCACTGGATCACCAACGAGTCCTCCAGGNCGAGGTGC
1641   Q   A   G   X   G   A   G   G   H   W   I   T   N   E   S   S   R   X   R   C
4981  ACCAGGGTCNCCGCGGCTGGGCCGAGGGTCGCAAGCAGAGGGGACCGGCGGCTGCCAGCA
1661   T   R   V   X   A   A   G   P   R   V   A   S   R   G   D   R   R   L   P   A
5041  AGTNCCAAGCAGATGCCTCTGGCGGGGCAGCCGCATTCTACAGCGCCCATTCCGCGTACA
1681   S   X   K   Q   M   P   L   A   G   Q   P   H   S   T   A   P   I   P   R   T
5101  TCGAGTATCCAAAATGAGNCCAATCGGTTTATACGTTGGAATGTAGCTTATGATTCCAAA
1701   S   S   I   Q   N   E   X   N   R   F   I   R   W   N   V   A   Y   D   S   K
5161  ATCTCANCGCCAGGCTGCCTAGATCACACGGCCCCGTTTCATTCANCGTTACTTAATAAC
1721   I   S   X   P   G   C   L   D   H   T   A   P   F   H   S   X   L   L   N   N
5221  GGTCGTTGGACAATTNCCNCCAGCAGCAGAGCCGGCGCCATCAACTCCACCGTCNCCCGG
1741   G   R   W   T   I   X   X   S   S   R   A   G   A   I   N   S   T   V   X   R
```

"One word might be an accident," Dyer said. "But three?"

Bradshaw stepped in front of the screen. "No, no, no. It *happens*. Don't worry. We'll figure this out."

Mick the Tech was watching them through the crack in the door. See, he thought, I knew it was a word puzzle. He was squinting at the screen, looking for more words, when his cell phone buzzed in his pocket. He saw that it was the President's hottie calling, and he ducked quickly down the hall to take the call.

"Have you ever seen three distinct words on a page of code, Rosalind?" Dyer asked in measured tones.

"No, but we're not looking for—"

"Have you, Ben?"

"Look, Alan, don't worry about this. There is a rational explanation, I'm sure." Bradshaw said.

"Answer me. Have you ever seen three distinct words on a page of code?"

"No."

Dyer turned to his Director of Research, Peter Gleason. "Pete, have you ever seen anything like this?"

Gleason had a sinking feeling. He had no idea what was going on with these words, but he knew it couldn't be good. He, too, was a molecular biologist, and he was as mystified by the presence of words in the code as

Rosalind was. He suddenly felt as if he'd eaten a bad oyster. "Rosalind, is this a mock-up of some kind, or the real thing?"

"It's the real thing. It's a compendium of thousands of translated samples," she said. "It's the real thing."

Dyer looked at the three in turn, slowly. The good humor he'd walked in with was gone. "We've been hacked."

The words landed on them like lead.

"No way," Bradshaw said. "Because of words in the code? No. Don't be ridiculous."

Dyer stared at him with frozen eyes. "How else did they get there?"

The tension in the room was thick enough to stand a knife in. They all knew Alan Dyer was an expert in industrial espionage. As head of a pharmaceutical company, he had to be; pharma was the most cut-throat industry in the world. Espionage was *de rigueur*.

Bradshaw's ears were beginning to turn red. He didn't want to think about what would happen if Dyer was right. The ANSR 1000 vulnerable to cyber attack? Catastrophic.

"Someone has tampered with our data. It is the only possible explanation," Dyer said.

Rosalind stared at the screen, utterly perplexed. "Alan, genetic code isn't about words. These letters stand for chemicals. These aren't really words."

"Oh? Then what would you call them?" Dyer said. His Spock-like demeanor was chilling.

Bradshaw threw her a poison look. She kept her mouth shut.

"This facility is on lock down." Dyer said. He scanned the room as if looking for a place to spit. "I'm going to take apart the entire data management system and find out how this happened." He pointed at Rosalind. "I want you to go back over your data molecule by molecule and find out how far the corruption goes. Anything that looks like altered code, document it. I want a complete report from you by eight o'clock tomorrow morning. I want no more information extracted from or entered into any of these computers. Shut them down. I want all the pass codes invalidated."

"Alan, come on! It will take days to invalidate that many pass codes. There are thousands," Bradshaw said.

"Kill them all, starting with the ANSR 1000. We'll create two new pass codes, one for me and one for the best computer technician you've got."

"That would be Mick the Tech," Bradshaw said.

Rosalind glanced toward the back of the room and saw that the door was open, but Mick wasn't there.

"The entire sequencing facility is off limits until I find out how this happened and how bad the damage is," Dyer said.

"You can't shut down the sequencing facility!" Bradshaw yelled. "Everything stops if we can't sequence. We'll lose thousands in revenue every day!"

"Chump change compared to what I stand to lose," Dyer said. "Nobody gets in there except me and my men, and your technician."

"How long will this take?"

Dyer had seen plenty of incident responses in his career. It was easy for people to panic, but the only response that worked was a calm, methodical, patient investigation. There was no rushing it, and it wouldn't be over until it was over. "If we get lucky, a week, maybe two. If not, six months to a year."

Rosalind couldn't believe what she was hearing. Shut the sequencing facility down? Was he out of his mind? "Alan, wait. If I could re-sequence some samples, it would tell us whether there was an error," Rosalind said.

"The ANSR 1000 is off limits," Dyer said with the gravity of a priest at Mass. He stepped through the doorway, and then turned around.

"And don't forget, you have all signed non-disclosure agreements. That means everything we say and do is strictly confidential." His voice was calm, but nobody missed the fact that his eyes promised a fate worse than death for anyone who screwed up. He pointed at the stapled packets littering the table. "What is that?"

"Copies of the slides and the translation code for the CLAIRE gene," Rosalind said. "I thought you might like a copy—"

"Shred them." Dyer and Gleason left the room.

Bradshaw walked up close to Rosalind, glowered at her and whispered, "My office! Now!!" He turned and followed Dyer and Gleason out the door.

Rosalind forced a smile and tried to look casual as they walked out. Inside, she trembled. Hacked? Never had she considered the possibility that some unseen hand was guiding her research in the wrong direction. How deep did the data corruption go? How much of her work was now worthless and would have to be done over? Dyer might have no choice but to start again with another lab. That was something she couldn't even begin to think about. This project was the most important thing in her life. Finding out the reasons for Claire's death was the only thing that mattered. Instinctively, she reached into her lab coat pocket and took hold of the little glass marble she always carried. It was a silly thing to carry around, a little pink marble, but it was Claire's.

Mick the Tech walked in and tossed Rosalind a mischievous grin. "I hope you didn't need me. I had to take a phone call. Forgive me?" He held out his arms in supplication.

"Forget it," she said, scooping up the printouts scattered across the table.

He unhooked her laptop and handed it to her. He thought about asking if she wanted to go out for a drink later, maybe go back to his place. But she didn't seem to be the mood.

"Mind if I call you Rosalind? Roz, I saw more words in the code." He picked up a set of printouts, flipped the page and held it out to her.

"It says 'STEAL.' Pretty good, eh? I didn't even know genetic code was in English."

He flipped more pages and squinted at the letters, looking for more words.

"Hey! 'KILL'!"

"Give me that," she said, grabbing the papers out of his hand. She scooped up the rest of the papers from the table and was gone.

Jeez, he thought, what's got her panties in a bunch? And what about that private tour of the ANSR 1000 computer he promised her? Disappointed, he realized that he didn't have a date tonight. Rozzie wasn't in the mood, and the President's hottie told him to get lost for missing their rendezvous this morning. Oh well, he thought, I'll solve the rest of the genetic code tonight. That oughta impress Rozzie when she's in a better mood. He shouldered his backpack, grabbed the almost-full champagne bottle, and headed to his office.

* * *

Benton Bradshaw felt his fortunes slipping like a bad set of suspenders. The ANSR 1000 was the most powerful super-computing cluster in the world, the pride of Clearbrook and the envy of every sequencing facility on the planet. If it had been hacked, then he was dead. That kind of loss of confidence in the research marketplace would be fatal. He stared out his floor-to-ceiling windows at the broad expanse of Lake Michigan to the east. It was a Chicago lakefront view that mere mortals paid a fortune for, but he'd earned it by pure finesse. The view always pleased him, but not today. The city was cloaked in yellow haze and the lake was lifeless; there wasn't a hint of breeze, no swimmers yet, no sailboats, only a few joggers on the lakefront path. It depressed him. Who cares, he thought. The lakefront is for tourists and drunks. This is *my* world, right here.

Bradshaw's penthouse office on the 23rd floor of Clearbrook Hall was a place he had aspired to for as long as he could remember. It was his sanctuary; he spent more time here than at home. He designed the décor himself, everything from the plush carpet to the velvet-corniced draperies to the aircraft carrier-sized desk, above which hung a larger-than-life, gilt-framed portrait of his father. The whole 1200 square feet was a blatant mockery of feng shui, but he didn't know that. To him, it was perfect.

Rosalind stood across the room, looking like a lost child. The sight of her usually aroused in him a primal spark or two, a nice flutter at the sight of those long legs and the nonchalant way she tossed her head when she spoke to him. Even back when she was his student at Rutherford, he'd been attracted by a certain geeky sex appeal in her. He'd quickly seen that she was brilliant and unobstructed in her passion for science, but it was the way she moved her body that first caught his attention, graceful and fluid, like a ballerina. Bedding co-eds wasn't a problem for him back then; something about his diminutive stature drove them wild. The problem was that Rosalind stood 5'10". Out of an abundance of caution for his personal safety, he'd stayed away from her. She was still beautiful, but today he felt no spark, no flutter, only the primal urge to wring her neck. He poured himself a cup of coffee, offering her none, and leaned against one of the two six-foot ceramic Foo Dogs perched imperiously on either side of his desk.

"What did you do?"

"Me?"

"Yeah, you. What kind of a stunt is this?" He spat the words at her.

"Stunt? Are you out of your mind?"

"You've embarrassed Clearbrook and put both our jobs in jeopardy!"

"I don't think so, Ben. Somebody obviously hacked in and messed with the data."

"Impossible! We've got massive security. Dyer put most of it in place himself."

"Are you saying *I* put those words in the code?"

"Or you made a massive error. Roz, you're losing it! I know grief can get in the way of your work ..."

"I have *never* let my grief get in the way of my work! My grief *is* my work!" Rosalind glared at him, wishing she had a baseball bat. The man's utter lack of empathy still surprised her, even after all these years. She stopped herself from saying more. It was useless.

"I want you to do what Dyer said. Go over that data with a magnifying glass and find out what went wrong. Maybe a member of your staff thought this would be funny. Dammit! Until we give him a logical explanation for the words in the code, he'll keep looking for a breach in security. We could be shut down for weeks, maybe months. I can't let that happen."

"Why don't you just tell him to get out? It's our facility."

"The University has a contract with him for fifteen million dollars. He still owes us half. I can't just blow that off!"

"I will re-examine the data, but without the ANSR 1000, I can't rerun samples."

Bradshaw paced and chewed an unlit cigar. "And you can't go anywhere else to run them without compromising our security," he said.

She thought for a moment about the daunting task of going over all that data again and still only having half the picture. "Ben, I have to see the DZPro2 analysis."

"Not a chance," Bradshaw said. From the beginning, Dyer's strategy was to have two different labs working on the two different genes because of both time pressure and security. He wanted to be sure no one person had access to all the data. Like the recipe for Coke.

"Why not?"

"Don't be an idiot. You know why. Dyer wants the data segregated, period. It's in the contract."

Rosalind looked at Bradshaw standing there like Buster Brown with his two giant dogs. The fact that he was the boss didn't keep her from having a fully-formed vision of how satisfying it would be to kick his tail right though that window and watch him flail all the way to the pavement.

"Do you know how much faster I could resolve this if I had access to all the data instead of just part of it?"

"The DZPro2 has nothing to do with it," Bradshaw said.

"It might be corrupted, too. If it is, it proves this wasn't my mistake!"

"You better hope it's a mistake! If it's a security breach, Clearbrook is finished!"

"OK, just let me see the data. We don't have to tell Dyer."

"And risk losing seven and a half million dollars? He has his own mafia. He'd know. And, may I remind you that he's the client, and we do what *he* wants?"

"May I remind you that children are dying every day of leukemia while we play stupid games with proprietary data? Why don't you ask Dyer if he wants me to wear a blindfold while I'm at it?"

Her eyes flashed, and for the first time in over a year, he caught a glimpse of the brash, brilliant student of his from years ago. He had come to believe that the fiery old Roz had died with her daughter.

"Dyer owns this project and all the information it generates. Period. Forget the DZPro2. I need you to focus," Bradshaw said.

"If I were any more focused, my head would implode. I didn't make any mistakes in methodology."

"I think you did. It is impossible for anyone to have hacked in through our security."

Weariness descended on her, along with the utter futility of trying to reason with Bradshaw. "I've got work to do." She turned to leave.

Bradshaw followed her and put his arm around her shoulder. "Don't be glum. Remember, I'm on your side. Nice sweater, by the way."

He watched her walk out, wondering if she knew how close she was to losing her job. He couldn't fire her; she was tenured. But he could take her lab away, and might have to.

He looked up at the portrait of his father, hoping on some subconscious level that the old man's expression might have softened a bit. But it was the same as ever, a glowering look of disapproval that was burned into Bradshaw's soul. The youngest of four boys, the rest of whom were scholarly and good looking, little Benton was the runt of the litter, smart to be sure, but ... as Father put it ... not world class like his brothers. Over time, the deep longing for respect felt by an unloved little boy evolved into a raging thirst for dominance in the one thing he was good at—science. Benton Bradshaw sought to rule the Clearbrook empire not so much for the glory of science as to ratify his worth in the eyes of his father.

He walked to the sideboard and poured himself a scotch. He tossed it back and thought about what he would say to Dyer. Perhaps he would say that Rosalind had suffered a mental breakdown. After all, everyone knew she was never the same after her daughter died.

Chapter 2

IN THE HEART of Chicago's Magnificent Mile stood the studios of InfoNet News Channel, the rising star of twenty-four-hour cable news networks. Since its inception five years earlier, InfoNet had rapidly gained audience share. Banking on the world's insatiable appetite for the sensational, the founders aimed with every policy and hire to amp it up for the viewers. They wanted to be the habanero of cable news, numero uno in the daily purveyance of legend and lore. The battle was now at fever pitch. It was July of a Presidential election year, and the media dogs were foaming at the mouth, none more so than Ron Vaniere.

Ron Vaniere was InfoNet's stud dog in the political arena. He was instantly recognizable on the air and on the street because of his good looks, running-back physique, and edgy reporting style. He was a lot like InfoNet: brash, hungry, always spoiling for a fight. And ruthless. It was the ancestral anger in his DNA that accounted for the ruthlessness, the sense that life was a series of unpaid debts, and his job was to collect. InfoNet saw the fire in him early on. Now in his second Presidential election cycle, Vaniere was their undisputed star of political reporting.

He knew that solid reporting was important to ratings, but he also knew it was the easy part; stories about the candidates materialized out of thin air. The hard part was keeping the tension high. You had to constantly juice the airwaves with pithy pundits arguing endlessly about whose candidate was ahead in the polls, whose strategy resonated loudest with the American people, whose was the party of peace, prosperity, and justice for all. You had to pit candidates against each other, keep them off-guard. And most importantly, you had to know where to dig up the dirt. His success evolved from his conviction that dirt underpinned the actions of the privileged and powerful, and dirt would bring them down. Early in his career they called Ron Vaniere the best black political reporter in America. Then they called him the best political reporter, period. Now, they just called him "The Shovel."

He was beginning his day as he always did, perusing his usual web sites, digging for little details that could build into a big story. This he wouldn't relegate to his staff; this was the kind of research he enjoyed. The Presidential nominating conventions were six weeks away, and it was still anyone's race. All the major campaigns were scrambling to manipulate and manage the news cycle in order to bring all the factors into line at just the right time. Vaniere's job was to outwit them at every turn.

As always, he brought up the Starry Messenger blog first. It was the most-read blog in the world, and a terrific reporter's tool if you knew how to use it. To his mild surprise, the lead story was not about politics, but about Rev. Joseph Steele. The high-spirited Steele was holding one of his First Light Campaign rallies in Chicago that morning. Vaniere didn't know a lot about Steele except that he loved the spotlight and could really draw a crowd. He was going around the country holding rallies and frothing up the folks to join him in shutting down facilities that engaged in human cloning and embryonic stem cell research.

The religious part didn't interest Vaniere, and the genetics issues were passé for him. But there was something that caught his interest. At the rally in Chicago later this morning, Steele would announce his endorsement of the Governor of South Dakota, Willard 'Wild Bill' Hitchcock, for President. It said that Hitchcock had aligned himself with Steele, embracing his staunch fundamentalist views and vowing to steer American policy back in the 'right direction' if elected President. Well, well.

Vaniere had already dug into Hitchcock. He hadn't found any significant dirt yet, but he knew there had to be some. Every career politician had a dark secret or two in the closet, hidden bombshells that could blow at any moment and throw a campaign into chaos. Vaniere considered it his patriotic duty to find these bombshells and set them off before anyone else could. Just a month ago, he broke the story about Bruce

Randall, a rising presidential hopeful. He was adopted as an infant, and his biological father turned out to be none other than the notorious Leonard Monk, the investment banker who embezzled millions from his employer and then fled to Brazil with a blond and a Maserati. Thanks to Vaniere, the country was spared the burden of a President with a shady heritage. You can't be too careful, after all, about what genetic predispositions toward thievery might have been inherited by the son. Randall was quickly vilified in the press, and he dropped out of the race—another bombshell detonated by the Shovel. Reading the Starry Messenger blog, Vaniere knew instantly that this unlikely alliance between Joseph Steele and Willard Hitchcock had the smell of gunpowder all over it. Holy rocket's red glare.

Vaniere pulled up Steele's website. There he was, a few too many Moon Pies over the line, nevertheless tall and imposing with his perfectly tailored suit and flashing eyes. The picture of hellfire and brimstone. He reminded Vaniere of the blunderbuss of a preacher they had at the church he grew up in. His mother was a full-tilt churchie, and he had been in the pew every Sunday, hell or high water, feasting on the teachings of a man infused with virtuous rage that spilled out of the pulpit every Sunday. For as long as Vaniere could remember, the undercurrent of every message was anger at the oppressor. "When will our struggles be over?" the preacher asked, and then answered: "Never. Oppression is eternal. The injustices follow us to the ends of the earth." Journalism seemed to Vaniere the perfect vehicle for hunting down down those injustices and exposing them.

Vaniere clicked on a video of Steele at an earlier First Light Campaign rally, ranting in classic Steele style, railing about God's work and the devil's work. Vaniere watched it and smiled. God vs. Satan with a twist of presidential politics. He glanced at his watch. He had plenty of time to get to Clearbrook Hall where the rally was scheduled to start in an hour.

"I'm covering the Steele Rally," he told the assignment editor.

"Very funny. I've already got an intern on it," she droned.

"I want it."

"Why?"

"Because I need evangelizing."

"True. But why go out in this heat when you can stay inside and play stud reporter?" she said.

"Well, you know me. Ever the optimist, searching for authenticity in a hopelessly confused world."

"You're in the wrong business, my friend."

"Tell me about it," Vaniere said.

"Go. But you better bring me back the freakin' apocalypse. Blood, profanity, the whole nine."

* * *

Rosalind sat in her office, staring at the data on her computer screen. This was intentional, she thought; there was no lab mistake on earth that could yield what they saw on that screen today. If there was anything Rosalind Evans knew for certain, it was how genetic code behaved. To Dyer's untrained eye, this looked like a mess of letters. But to Rosalind, it was the genetic code, the secret of life, and it stirred her in ways she couldn't explain. It always had been that way, from her first exposure to it in junior high school. While the other kids were struggling to pronounce the names of the twenty amino acids, Rosalind had already memorized the three-letter codons for each one. To this day, whenever she looked at sequenced DNA, something mystical happened. Her mind took her beyond the empirical and obvious into a deeper place, where the DNA spoke to her in beautiful and elegant ways. It whispered its vast mysteries, gave hints about the grand orchestration of the human body, of disease, of life itself. In those special times when she was free of distraction and totally absorbed in her work, her mind would grow open and receptive to sudden flashes of intuition. The flashes would build into leaps of understanding, and each leap brought her closer to the mission that drove her—to decipher the vast secrets of the genetic code, to outwit it, unravel it, and extract from it the ultimate triumph—a cure for cancer.

Now someone had invaded her magical place and made a mockery of her work. Why? How much of the data was corrupted? How had she not noticed that something was wrong? Where would she find the strength to go back over all that data? She had no answers. It was going to be a long day. A long heartbreaking day.

The base code was the key. Deep X sequencing had determined the order of the bases in the DNA in the CLAIRE gene. If the base code was correct, then the amino acid code was also correct. So why was the amino acid code spelling out words? There was only one explanation: someone hacked in and changed the base code and/or the amino acid code. The only way to find out for sure would be to re-sequence the samples. But that was out of the question for now. In the meantime, she would have to go through the translation code, find any additional words, and study them to see whether the base code or amino acid code was tampered with.

All at once her computer screen went black.

"No! Don't do this to me!" She tried the power button and every other button, but nothing would make it come back to life. Dyer had actually done it. She opened her laptop. Dyer had taken control of every computer in the place, but he didn't have control of her laptop. It was now the only tool she had. Her report for Dyer was due in less than 24 hours, and the only access she had to the translation code was the Power Point presentation, and the power of her own brain.

She poured herself a cup of coffee and settled in. Fighting off exhaustion and a growing panic that she might lose her project, she trained her eyes on the letters, forcing herself to do something totally counterintuitive—look for words in the code. After only a few minutes of searching through the sea of letters on page one, she was disheartened. There were 28 pages in all; she was still on page one. Her iPhone rang.

"Evans Lab."

"Rosalind?"

She sat up straight. "David?"

"I want to see you," David said.

"I can't."

"I'll pick you up in five minutes. It's really important."

She looked at the computer, then at her watch. "There's no way. We have a major catastrophe brewing here. I can't possibly get away."

There was a brief pause before he spoke. His voice softened. "I really need to see you right now. No choice. It won't take long, I promise."

"You don't understand. I *have* to work. Please, let's do it another time."

"You always say that. There is no other time. I'll pick you up in the portico," David said. He hung up.

Rosalind listened to the silence for a long moment, then she threw the phone down. No! You can't just *summon* me. She closed her eyes and willed his image to go away. David. She closed her laptop and made her way to the ladies room, wondering what she would see when she looked in the mirror.

David hadn't been home in weeks. He was so busy that he needed to sleep in his office, or so he said. He came home once in a while to get clean clothes and if she was there, they would talk, but never about anything important. Lately, their home seemed to be just a stopping-off point in a journey he preferred to make alone. He never seemed to understand how important her work was, how finding the genetic reasons for Claire's death would free them both.

She looked in the mirror. She had never been one to focus on her looks. David always said she didn't need to, that she had all the natural beauty in the world. She looked at herself for a long moment, hoping for a clue about who she was supposed to be. All she saw was skin and hair and bones, and eyes that had nothing interesting to say. Wiping the back of her neck with a wet paper towel, she smirked at the notion that this stranger looking back at her was even remotely connected to the woman David had once thought beautiful. Nausea washed over her and she wished she could lie down right there on the tile floor, to feel the coolness and steady herself for a moment. David. You complete bastard.

Chapter 3

A NERVOUS, AGITATED crowd was gathering on the plaza outside Clearbrook Hall. TV satellite trucks lined the street as reporters and cameramen waited for the Steele rally to begin. These were not student protesters. They were men and women of all ages, some in jeans, some in suits, some scruffy, some well-groomed, all focused with nervous anticipation on the empty podium. They were not smiling, and their demeanor was tense, as if they were sacrificing their normal daily activities—work, shopping, lying on the beach—in order to stand up for something really important. Their aura of sacrifice was intensified by the oppressive heat. It was a notorious hazy, hot, and humid day in Chicago; the kind that drove even devoted outdoorsy types inside. But these folks seemed to have a higher calling today.

The crowd stretched from the street, across the courtyard, and up the broad front steps to the entrance of Clearbrook Hall. This was the University's "Free Speech Zone," a space set aside for anyone to stand on the concrete 'soapbox' and speak their mind. In summer, the venue went days or weeks with no one using it, but today it clearly was set up for something big. At the top of the steps stood a podium surrounded by banks of loudspeakers. From every direction, protesters were making their way toward Clearbrook Hall, even as passersby stopped to see what it was all about. The crowd began to surge toward the podium area, where children in choir robes were assembling.

The crowd was completely blocking the steps of Clearbrook Hall when Rosalind stepped outside. She saw that it would be nearly impossible to make her way to the portico on the far side of the building where David was to pick her up. She surveyed the landscape for a moment, debating whether she should fight her way through, or give up and try a different route. It was not the first time she had seen a crowd gather to express their disapproval of something going on at Clearbrook. It was the Galileo principle: Whenever science pushed the boundaries of human knowledge and understanding, somebody pushed back. Some people were scared of the power of genetics, angry about the privacy implications of someone looking inside their cells.

"Blessings to you brothers and sisters!" Cheers rolled through the crowd, and people raised their signs. Through the courtyard and for several blocks in every direction, there boomed the unmistakable voice of the Reverend Joseph Steele, televangelist, rabble-rouser, and arbiter of all things moral.

"Amen?"

The crowd cheered. "Amen!"

Steele pulled the microphone close until it touched his lips. "I said AMEN?"

"AMEN!!"

Curious, Rosalind shouldered her way forward a few dozen yards to get a closer view of him. He was dressed in a perfectly tailored grey suit, waving a Bible over his head. His eyes were intense, his face radiant; he was clearly infused with a passionate energy that radiated all around him. Rosalind had seen him on TV but never in person, and it was obvious right away that his legendary charisma came not so much from his appearance nor the content of what he had to say, as from the manner and authority with which he said it. He was known to beguile audiences with his rhetorical style. It was rhythmic; with each new phrase his voice rose, tremulous with anticipation, rolling up in pitch and volume to a crescendo, and then tumbling syllable by syllable down to the basso profundo. He would pause for effect, and then start the whole process over again. It didn't matter what he said; it was masterful.

He could be seen on television every day, holding the Bible over his head and rolling up and down on the balls of his feet, denouncing evil with courtly passion. This was the routine he repeated now in front of a frenzied crowd in downtown Chicago, and they were loving it. He gestured toward Clearbrook Hall behind him.

"Evil, brothers and sisters. There is EVIL going on in there! In the name of science, these people are playing God with our lives! They are doing unspeakable genetic experiments and they must be stopped!" The crowd stomped and whistled and hooted. Sweat trickled down Steele's temples and his short-cropped hair glistened.

"Make no mistake about it, there is grave risk at hand. There is a cabal of evil men and women in there who want to reduce all that is human and holy down to a string of DNA, a clump of chemicals. Is that all we are? Is THAT how God made us?"

"No! No!" the people yelled back.

"Will you help me stop this evil?"

"Yeeeeeesssss!" People cheered and waved their signs. This is no ordinary rally, Rosalind thought. What in the world are these people so worked up about? She felt like she was caught in the middle of a massive public delusion. If they believed Clearbrook was doing evil things, then this man clearly had them in some kind of trance. In her view, Clearbrook was doing the most noble work on the planet.

Steele paused for a moment, mopped his head with a handkerchief, and gazed heavenward. What a day this was turning out to be, he thought. It's hotter than Hades, but it takes more than that to keep my people away! It was a larger crowd than he had been led to expect, and more passionate than he could have hoped.

Steele's First Light Campaign had grown from a single television event six months ago to a massive national movement. He was opposed to embryonic stem cell research and human cloning on the grounds that they amounted to 'playing God.' He adhered to basic creationist beliefs and was fiercely anti-Darwinian on both scientific and religious grounds. Weekly, he railed from his pulpit, admonishing his flock to wake up and see how badly their hearts and minds had been manipulated by a 150-year socio-scientific conspiracy that centered power in the Darwinian movement. He was criticized by some for being ignorant and narrow minded in insisting that the Universe came into being at the hand of a Creator. By others, he was reviled as a dangerous threat to human rights and free thinking, a man who used superstition and fear-mongering to mesmerize the masses. But none of that mattered to his adoring flock of adherents. To them, he was bravely standing up to a bunch of atheists who were trying to undermine the Bible and ruin the country.

Steele scanned the crowd, and he was pleased. In his career as a pastor, author, and television personality, he had amassed a following of millions of people and a fortune to match. His book *Hand of the Creator* had been number one on the New York Times Bestseller list for six straight months and banned by school districts all over the nation. And now, the First Light Campaign was succeeding beyond his wildest dreams, taking his ministry to a whole new level. Everywhere he went, controversy followed. Even now, anti-Steele signs were appearing in the crowd calling him ignorant, dangerous and living in the Dark Ages. For his money, it didn't get any better than this.

He was especially pleased to see that there were dozens of TV cameras aimed his way. The media were his angels in this holy war. They loved him and he loved them. He loved Chicago. Too bad he had to fly out right after the rally; it would have been nice to get up to Gibson's for a steak. But all was not lost. He'd ordered steak dinners-to-go for everybody on his Cessna Citation, and enough bottles of Chateau Margeaux to get them safely back to Dallas.

"Brothers and Sisters, I want you to welcome the next President of the United States, a man of God, a man I heartily endorse and you should too—Governor Willard 'Wild Bill' Hitchcock!"

Governor Hitchcock stepped to the microphone and waved to the crowd, the silver Concho on his Stetson gleaming in the sunlight. He was tall and trim, with a smile as broad as the Cheyenne River. Dressed in crisp khakis and white cotton shirtsleeves, he was a picture of Great Plains independence and vitality.

"Mornin', friends!" Hitchcock shouted to a roar of approval. "I want you to know that this very afternoon I will be on the floor of the Senate introducing a bill to ban testing for the intelligence gene. Of all the evils of genetics, this is the worst. Science has found a gene that determines a person's level of intelligence. If we allow testing for this gene, it will open a Pandora's Box of discrimination, including unfair tracking in schools, blocked admission to colleges, employment discrimination, and the creation of designer babies who are genetically altered to be super-intelligent! God either made you smart or he didn't! We can't tamper with that!!!"

The crowd cheered.

"This has grave moral ramifications, and I aim to stop it with the Stop Intelligence Testing bill. Will you support me in this?"

More stomping and hooting and whistling in the crowd. Wild Bill was making his mark in the presidential race. Every candidate worked to create a mark, a linchpin that distinguished him from all the others. The Stop Intelligence Testing bill, or SIT, was his, and it gave him the lead in the polls in July. He would have to be very careful and play it smart: the trick was to play the advantage all the way to the convention.

Three blocks away from Clearbrook Hall, David Evans was stuck in traffic. The Steele rally had snarled everything from the river to Superior St. He inched along, hoping Rosalind would wait for him. He'd told her he would be there in five minutes, and it would be like her to call the whole thing off if he didn't appear right on time. She had systematically called off everything in her life since Claire died. Everything except her work. He clenched the wheel and willed the traffic to clear. He was determined to have this moment with his wife.

What should have been a five minute drive took twenty. When he finally pulled into the portico, Rosalind was nowhere to be seen. He texted her. It was a useless exercise, he knew. It would be easy for her to ignore it. But he had to try.

where r u?

To his surprise, she answered right away.

Lost in rally. u?

portico

Can't get there. Mob scene.

Keep trying. I'll wait. hurry

Steele took a pause while the children's chorus sang a rousing rendition of "Onward Christian Soldiers." Rosalind pressed forward, toward the portico. She wished she could stay a while and listen to Steele. She was curious about this man, a relatively unremarkable, 50-ish TV pastor among many a few years ago, and now leader of a passionate anti-science movement.

As the children finished singing, Steele stepped back to the microphone. His voice took on an ominous tone. "Inside this building behind me, innocent human embryos are being killed in the name of scientific research. Will you stand with me brothers and sisters against this evil called embryonic stem cell research?" The crowd roared, cheering and raising their fists.

Rosalind stopped in her tracks. She couldn't believe what she was hearing.

Embryonic stem cell research?

Clearbrook had never engaged in embryonic stem cell research. There was a persistent myth to the contrary. A fictitious story had emerged on the Internet about a mother who had an abortion, then brought the fetus to Clearbrook in the mistaken belief that the stem cells could be extracted and used to provide treatment for her son, who had been paralyzed in an accident. The grisly story went viral on the Internet. It was a complete urban myth, categorically debunked; yet it planted the idea that Clearbrook was engaged in deplorable, illegal experiments. For some conspiracy theorists, Clearbrook Hall—this soaring monument to the pursuit of scientific discovery—became a dark symbol of evil. Bradshaw lamented how hard it was to dispel even the most outrageous myths once they got a toehold on the Internet. Every few months the story surged again via chain e-mails and blogs, each time brainwashing a whole new generation of readers who had no way of knowing what was truth and what was myth. The President of Rutherford University had issued statements through the media and the blogosphere, but despite their efforts, the myth morphed into a maxim.

For Rosalind, it was unbelievable to hear this supposedly virtuous man using a myth as fuel for his campaign. Surely he knows it's not true, she thought. He's not stupid.

The crowd had grown and now stretched down the block in both directions. This whole thing is wrong, Rosalind thought. Bradshaw needs to know about this. She turned to go back into the building, but the crowd was now so thick that she couldn't go forward and couldn't go backward. The heat of the sun seemed to fuel the surging mass of people. The more energized the Rev. Steele became, the more frenzied the crowd became. Media helicopters buzzed overhead, echoing through the steamy canyons of downtown Chicago. Reverend Steele showed no signs of letting up.

Rosalind saw that her way back inside was blocked by angry, agitated protesters. So was the way to the portico, where David was waiting. She spotted a TV camera just a few yards away, and next to it a well-dressed man with a perfect haircut and a microphone in his hand. She shoved her way through and tapped him on the arm.

"Excuse me," she yelled over the noise. "This man doesn't know what he's talking about. We don't do embryonic stem cell research here at Clearbrook." She waited for his response, assuming he would be interested. The reporter ignored her and continued making his way closer to the podium. She watched him disappear into the crowd. She looked around and spotted another reporter. She elbowed her way to him.

"Excuse me. I work here and I need to set the record straight. This man is either misinformed or lying—there is no stem cell research going on at Clearbrook ..."

"You're in my shot."

"No, I'm telling you, what he is saying is not true ..."

"Get out of my shot, lady." The reporter took her by the arm and pushed her aside.

Rosalind heard sirens in the distance. There were several policemen making their way toward the podium. She pushed and shoved through throngs of people who by now were in no mood to be polite. They were filled with anger, shaking their fists, raising their signs like bludgeons. They chanted, "Shut it down! Shut it down!" She looked around for a way out. A man backed into her, nearly knocking her over. Instinctively, she grabbed his arm.

The man turned and reached out to her to keep her from falling. A flash of recognition crossed his face. "Dr. Evans? Rosalind Evans?" he said.

He saw by her expression that she didn't recognize him. "I'm Ron Vaniere. InfoNet News. We met at a reception for Yves Allard when he won the Nobel Prize for medicine."

Rosalind recognized Vaniere from TV, but she didn't remember meeting him. She did remember the Allard reception; she had been no more than an observer at the back of the room, a newly appointed member of the Clearbrook team who had felt fortunate just to be in the same room with the great Allard when he was honored for his groundbreaking genome research. "That was six years ago. We met?"

"Not officially. But I knew who you were." He remembered her standing next to her husband, the lawyer David Evans. Together they made the perfect picture of a Chicago power-couple—beautiful, rich, privileged and, he suspected, wholly lacking in empathy for the plight of the underclass. While he got along fine with them on a day-to-day basis, people like the Evanses melted together into a soft vanilla ooze that had absolutely no bearing on his life except as reminders of his own struggles. As she stood there in the heat, he couldn't help noticing that some of her earlier gloss was gone. She had on a straight skirt and stretchy top that clung to her contours, with a white lab coat thrown over the top of it all. She wore sandals, and her hair was pulled up in a loose poof on top of her head with tendrils hanging down. The effect was unremarkable, and a close look at her eyes told him that despite the money and success, she wasn't very happy.

Steele's voice was so loud that Vaniere had to lean in close to be heard. "I remember that Allard mentioned you by name from the podium. Said you were a superstar in genetic medicine. A 'disease slayer,' he called you. Have you slain any diseases yet?"

She tilted her head, unsure how to answer the question. Last night she would have said yes, but the events of this morning had her questioning the validity of the entire project. Vaniere's cameraman interrupted, tapping him on the arm. "Sixty seconds, Ron."

"I have to go. Live shot coming up."

"Wait! You have to tell everyone that we don't do stem cell research at Clearbrook. There is no truth in what this guy is saying."

"Really? Come on, I'll put you on camera. You can tell your side of the story."

Rosalind recoiled. The mere thought of standing in front of a camera made her queasy. She hated cameras, hated the limelight. "No! I don't have time. And it's not just 'my side' of the story. It's the truth. There is no other side of the story."

"Then tell it. If you don't, who will?"

"Can't you do it?"

"I don't know the truth."

"I just told you. Don't you trust me?" she said.

"I'm a reporter. I don't trust anyone." Straightening his tie, Vaniere turned and faced the camera.

Images from the Allard event flooded Rosalind's mind, and with them memories of that time in her life. She remembered what it was like to feel David standing next to her at the reception, the smell of him, the warmth of his body. She had been shocked and embarrassed when Allard spoke her name, but David had smiled as if he'd expected it. They had been married barely six months at the time, and the social set was still buzzing about what an unlikely pair they were. He was the flamboyant, handsome rising star of the Chicago legal and social scene, she the serious scientist toiling in the lab, hiding her beauty behind thick glasses and a perpetual pony tail. Yet somehow their energies melded. Rosalind had resisted him at first, unwilling to give thought or emotion to anything that might distract her from her work. Plus, she didn't like lawyers. They were smarmy and untrustworthy, and she'd sooner eat soap than kiss one. But David wasn't like other lawyers. He soon won her over with his insatiable appetite for life and his boundless determination to share it with her. She had never imagined being loved the way David loved her. He told her that she was beautiful and intelligent. He praised her strong sense of purpose as a scientist. "You talk about the genome with reverence and longing, the way some people talk about God," he said. He always encouraged her, and he didn't laugh when she told him that her dreams bore images of the base chemicals of DNA— Gs, Cs, Ts and As—twirling in glittering spirals, revealing their secrets to her as she slept. It was almost as if her deep intuitive connection with things unknown was an aphrodisiac to him. His persistence paid off; after several weeks of resisting his advances, she simply gave in. Six months later they were married, and by the time of the Allard reception, they were old souls together. It was a golden time. Rosalind had just received her appointment to the Clearbrook Institute, and David was finishing his first year as partner in a boutique law firm in downtown Chicago. Life was at its abundant best for the two of them. Everything was pure potential. And the great Yves Allard had singled her out in front of the whole world! She smiled at the memory of how happy she had been, how full of love and optimism and purpose.

Steele's voice brought her back to reality. What he said hit her like a thunderbolt.

"I have filed suit in federal court to shut down the Clearbrook Institute for using federal funds to play God. This institution took federal money to build a super-computer, and then used it to do research that is not only evil, it is against the law. Where is the money coming from? Who is behind this secret research? To what extent is the government involved? We WILL get to the bottom of this!"

His intense tone of voice sent a chill through her. Clearbrook shut down? It was absurd. Or was it? She felt a rush of anger. How can this man spread lies and make charges that aren't true? She pushed forward, propelled by an unseen energy. If no one else would do it, she would tell him herself. She shoved her way toward Steele, pushing at people with both hands.

"No!" she yelled at him. "It's a lie! We don't do stem cell research here. You don't know what you are talking about!" She was nearly touching the podium when a beefy body guard stepped in front of her.

Steele turned and looked at her. Well, well, he thought. Her tousled hair and flashing eyes sent a brief lascivious flutter through him. He pushed the body guard aside and put his heavy, damp arm around her shoulder. He drew her in toward the microphone and flashed a smile at his flock, seducing the cameras to catch the moment. "What's that you say? I'm lying??" he said, not looking at her, but smiling out at the audience. The crowd was quiet except for a few jeers and cat calls. "Why don't you give us the truth? Come on, speak up."

His sweat dripped on her as he squeezed her toward him. She was close enough to feel the heat of his body and see the mocking anger in his eyes. She twisted herself out of his grip. He thrust the microphone toward her. She wanted to shout the truth, but her voice came out like a child's.

"You are wrong. We have never done stem cell research at Clearbrook," she said. She heard the reverberation of her own voice in the PA system. Cameras flashed all around her. She had the urge to run but was finding it difficult to breathe. Steele shot a twisted grin at her, his eyes shining with malevolent charm.

"No? I have evidence to the contrary. The young woman who brought her fetus here. She knew. Betty Freud knew."

She jerked away from him, her eyes flashing. She fought to keep her voice in control. "That's a lie. There was no Betty Freud."

"You'd like us to think that wouldn't you?"

Rosalind's voice rose. "What gives you the right to come here and tell lies about us on our own front steps?!"

He smiled down at her and then at the audience.

"Why, this is the Free Speech Zone, ma'am. I believe I have the right to say whatever I like." She lunged away from him, wanting badly to get to the door of the building and disappear back into the safety of her lab.

"That's enough, lady, you're coming with us." She felt her arm being grabbed and twisted behind her. A pair of Chicago cops firmly led her away from Steele. The crowd hooted and cheered.

Steele pulled the microphone close to his mouth. "The enemy comes in many forms, brothers and sisters. We must stand our ground. Can I have an Amen?!"

"AMEN!!!"

"Let me go!" Rosalind yelled. She struggled to free herself from their grip but was powerless against them.

"Excuse me, Officer." It was a man's voice, loud and authoritative. The policemen stopped and turned around. "I'm David Evans. This is my wife." David brought out his ID and showed it to one of the officers. "I'm sure she meant no harm."

The officer took the ID and studied it. He recognized both the name and the face. This was the lawyer who had defended a police officer accused of excessive force a few months ago, and won. It was all over the Chicago media for several weeks. The officer smiled at him, and then at

Rosalind. "I'm pleased to meet you Mr. Evans. Thanks for what you did for Officer McBurnie. Now, I suggest the two of you go home and leave the Reverend to his preaching. You can't interfere with a peaceful assemblage like that."

"I wouldn't call it peaceful. These people are ready to tear this place apart," Rosalind said.

"Roz, why don't we go inside?" David said, leading her toward the door.

Steele's voice was at fever pitch; the crowd was more agitated than ever. "Shut it down! Shut it down! Shut it down!" they chanted.

"David, I can't just walk away!" Rosalind jerked away from David and again shoved her way toward Steele. "You can't do this!" she screamed. In one deft movement, the cop swung her around. Shielding his actions from the crowd with his large frame, he muscled her to the doorway of the building and let her go. "Get out of here. Now!" he said in her ear. He let her go and turned back toward the podium.

She reached for the door to enter the building, but several of the protesters surged forward and blocked her from going in.

"How can you live with yourself, working in a place like this!" a woman shouted.

"At least I tell the truth!" Rosalind yelled back at her. "Your Bible thumper over there is a liar!" She pulled on the door, but it was locked. She banged on it as hard as she could. The security man inside started to open it to let her in, but a protester grabbed her by the arm and pulled her back out. She whirled around and kicked him. David tried to push the man back, but he swung at David and hit him in the mouth. The scuffle attracted the attention of the surrounding protesters, who turned to watch. The cop yelled at them to back off, but no one paid attention to him. One wild-eyed protestor reached into her purse and pulled out a plastic bottle, unscrewed the top and flung sticky red liquid in Rosalind's face. "Remember Betty Freud! The blood of the innocents is on you! I hope you burn in hell!"

Rosalind wiped the sticky mess from her face. "Get in line for that, lady," she said under her breath. The blood matted her hair and smeared her face. Cameras flashed everywhere. Behind her the door swung open, and the security man pulled her inside the building with David close behind. The door closed. Suddenly it was quiet. And cool.

"Those people are crazy," the security man said. "I had to lock the doors. Are you OK?"

She nodded.

"I'll need to see your ID, please," the guard said.

"But you know me, Bud."

"I might *think* I know you, but you never know for sure."

Rosalind pulled her security tag out of her pocket. Bud looked at it closely, then studied her face for a moment. "Hmmm. How long ago did they take this picture?"

He led her to the biometric security check point. She wiped her hand on her sleeve and laid it on the glass. It left a smudge of dirt and blood, but she cleared. Bud studied his computer screen for a moment.

"Mother's maiden name?" he said.

"Oh come on, Bud. Are you serious?"

"This is what they're telling me I have to do, now. I'm not allowed to rely on what I think is right. I have to follow procedure. Mother's maiden name?"

"Margeson."

"Thank you, Dr. Evans. Have a nice day. Oh, Mr. Evans, I can't let you in. Security lockdown."

Rosalind turned toward the elevator. "I have to go back to work, David. I'm desperate. We've had a security breach and we could lose the whole project." She was breathless and sweaty and had blood on her face. She pushed the button on the elevator and fished through her pockets for a tissue. The elevator door opened and Bradshaw stepped out.

"Roz! What happened?!"

"This is insane, Ben. Joseph Steele is out there saying he's going to shut us down for doing stem cell research, which we don't, and then somebody I don't know threw blood at me and told me to burn in hell. Who are these people?"

"Idiots, Roz. Some people are so stupid they don't deserve to live. Somebody ought to test them for the smart gene!" Bradshaw chuckled at his own cleverness and handed her his handkerchief. "This is all about the

Great Myth. Don't worry, I'll handle this. How are you David?" He turned and headed for the door. He stopped briefly to check his image in the glass window of the security booth. He patted his pocket to make sure he had his cell phone, stood as tall as he could, and strode outside.

Only then did Rosalind notice that David had a cut on his lip. "What happened to you?" she asked.

"I was trying to help you. That's never an easy thing to do." He smiled at her in a way she hadn't seen in months. He was handsome standing there, and she felt a brief stirring of the passion they once shared. Standing there so calm and smiling, he unnerved her. Why was it that he didn't seem to have any of the emotional incapacitation that dominated her life?

"I have to get back to work. Goodbye, David." A weary sadness descended on her as she turned toward the elevator, but before she could step in, he reached out and firmly took her arm.

"I need you to do something for me. I'm not leaving without you."

Chapter 4

INFONET ANCHORWOMAN CLAUDIA Moray gave her satin pink lips a quick lick and leaned in toward the camera. She took a moment to clear her mind and focus her eyes through the lens, through the camera, all the way into the souls of her viewers. Her piercing look was her trademark. It was a skill she'd carefully cultivated and honed to a fine edge. In an increasingly cynical world where beautiful newswomen were a dime a dozen, you had to project sincerity any way you could.

"Our guest today is Senator P. Philip Bosch of Illinois, Chairman of the Senate Judiciary Committee and a candidate for his party's nomination for President of the United States. Welcome Senator."

Claudia flashed her gorgeous $40,000 smile at the Senator and leaned forward, revealing just a smidge of what he guessed to be a considerable amount of cleavage hiding beneath her v-neck sweater.

"The pleasure is all mine," Bosch said, returning the smile.

"Senator, you have said that the defining issue for your campaign is social fairness. Your fairness platform proposes middle class status for all. Lifting the poor out of poverty is a noble goal. But tell me, how do you convince the rich that they would be better off in the middle class?"

"They'll be convinced once they see how happy the middle class is. People only *think* money can buy them happiness. But we all know it's not true. It is a burden being rich, always looking over your shoulder, trying to protect your wealth. Ruthlessness is stressful, and there is a heavy burden of guilt to bear when one has too much while others have too little. The Middle Class is the happy class," the Senator said, the words flowing like sap in the spring. "Why do you think it is the biggest?"

"What happens if someone refuses to give up their upper class status?" Moray asked.

"That's what government is for. To make sure everyone does the right thing so everyone has a fair chance."

"A fair chance at what?" Moray said.

"A house, a car, food for the table. Would you deny someone food?"

"How will you convince successful people to tamp down the talent, ambition, and hard work that made them want to be rich in the first place?"

"I don't want to tamp down anything. I just want a fair outcome for everyone. There is too much wealth concentrated in the hands of too few. Doesn't it make sense to spread it around a little?"

"Your position is very compelling for workers, minorities, and the poor. But do you really believe it is possible for everyone to have the same economic status?"

"I believe it with every fiber of my being. There is a principle in physics known as equilibrium, where everything levels out. Why wouldn't that apply to the economy as well? I care about people. I want them to be happy. My opponents favor a policy that allows a few to succeed in life at the expense of the working people and the poor. They care more for money than for people."

"But isn't it in the nature of human beings to want to succeed?"

"It is in the nature of humans to want to succeed on the backs of others. For every rich person there are thousands who suffer."

"How do you define rich?"

"Anyone with more money than they need."

"How do you define need?"

Bosch looked directly at the camera with doe-eyed sincerity. He managed a slight smile. "Ask a single mother who works two jobs and is three months behind on her gas and electric bills. She'll tell you about need."

"Isn't your plan anti-capitalist?"

"Of course not! Capitalism is the American way."

"But capitalism means competition. When you have competition, there are winners and losers."

"Not necessarily. When I am President, I will level the playing field. That's government's job! That's why we have regulations and taxes—to make sure the rich don't take advantage of the system."

"Wouldn't that be *tilting* the playing field?"

"You sound like someone with a bias against equality, Claudia. I'd prefer to focus on what *can* be done for the needy in our country."

"I don't have a bias Senator. I'm just trying to understand your position. What was your profession before you went into politics?"

"I didn't have one."

"So you've never run a business or managed a staff?"

"I beg your pardon! I have almost two hundred people on my campaign staff, a hundred on my office staff and then there's the staff of the P.P. Bosch Fairness for America Foundation. I think I know a thing or two about managing a staff."

"You have a foundation? How is it funded?"

"Contributions from the good, solid working people of America. They've heard our appeal. It touches their hearts. They give what they can. You can't put a price on fairness, you know."

"What do you do with the money?" Claudia said.

"We give it to those in need."

"How do you decide who gets the money?"

"People apply. I have a staff of over a hundred people who decide."

"So the middle class donates money to benefit middle class—"

"Our web site is www.PP—"

"—wait, just a minute, Senator. We have breaking news. I'm being told that violence has broken out at the Joseph Steele rally here in Chicago. InfoNet reporter Ron Vaniere is live at the scene. Let's go to him now. Ron, what's going on over there?"

"Claudia, this huge rally became violent a few moments ago as a woman rushed at Rev. Steele and had to be subdued by police. The woman was Dr. Rosalind Evans, a scientific researcher who works at the Clearbrook Institute. In the ensuing scuffle, Dr. Evans was apparently injured and taken inside Clearbrook Hall bleeding profusely from the head.

A man was also injured. We believe the man was Dr. Evans's husband, noted Chicago attorney David Evans. I just spoke with one protester who said that any means is justified to—" Vaniere looked down at his notes. "Quote 'stop innocent unborn babies from being sacrificed on the soulless altar of genetics' unquote. We understand that Rev. Steele was uninjured. Ironically, I had just spoken with Dr. Evans a few minutes before the incident. She seemed angry and said that Steele was wrong and that they don't do embryonic stem cell research at Clearbrook."

"Ron," Claudia said, "There was a story a few years ago of a woman who came to the doorstep of Clearbrook Institute with her aborted fetus in a Tupperware bowl. Her name was Betty Freud, and she wanted scientists there to use stem cells from the fetus to help her son, who was paralyzed after being hit by a bus at State and Randolph. This would indicate that they *do* do embryonic stem cell research at Clearbrook. What's the truth, Ron?" Claudia asked.

"It's a good question—" Vaniere was interrupted by a man who walked up next to him and stepped into the shot. The man reached out to take the microphone, but Vaniere kept a vice grip on it.

"Excuse me," the man said. "I'm Benton Bradshaw, Director of the Clearbrook Institute. I can answer any questions you have about our work." He smiled stiffly at the camera.

"All right, Mr. Bradshaw. Rev. Steele is saying that there is secret embryonic stem cell research being done here and that it must be stopped. What do you say to that?" Ron asked.

Bradshaw stood up straight and tugged at his lapels.

"He's mistaken. Nothing of that kind has ever taken place at Clearbrook. It's a crazy urban myth on the Internet."

"Are you saying there is no Betty Freud?"

"Betty Freud is mythical. A mythical woman can't have a real name. Period. Our work here is focused on conquering disease and easing human suffering."

"He has called for your facility to be shut down in order to stop the slaughter of innocent embryos. What do you say about that?"

"He's confused. We don't slaughter anything here. Our goal is to save lives."

"Is Dr. Rosalind Evans all right? It appeared that she was injured."

"She's fine. Just spoke to her. Never better."

"Do you believe embryonic stem cell research is murder, as Rev. Steele believes?"

"Of course it's not murder. You can't murder a cluster of cells. But it doesn't matter; we don't do it here."

"Dr. Bradshaw, Reverend Steele says Clearbrook is engaged in secret research. Is that true?" Vaniere asked.

What a snake in the grass, thought Bradshaw. Of course it was true, but he couldn't say so. Alan Dyer had called him just minutes ago, and he was as emotive as Bradshaw had ever heard him. He evidently was watching all this on TV, and warned Bradshaw not to mention PharmaGen in any way, shape or form.

"Clearbrook has an unimpeachable record of scientific integrity," Bradshaw said. "We are very proud of the work we do here. Thank you." He spun on his toe and left.

Vaniere turned back to the camera. "Dr. Bradshaw denies that Clearbrook is involved in embryonic stem cell research, but Rev. Steele seems convinced otherwise. One more thing, Claudia. I've learned that Rev. Steele will assemble his top advisers for a meeting at his six million dollar estate outside Dallas to, quote, 'develop a battle plan for the holy war against the evil forces who seek to make DNA the new God.' Unquote. Back to you, Claudia."

"Thanks, Ron. By way of background for our viewers, Rev. Steele first gained national prominence when he hacked into the computers of the Dallas School District and changed the science grade of every student to Incomplete. He argued that because the students weren't allowed to learn about Creationism along with Darwinism, they only had half the story. In addition to landing him in jail, the stunt launched him to national prominence."

Claudia turned again to Senator Bosch. "Senator, I'd like to get your take on this situation. Is Rev. Steele justified in wanting Clearbrook Institute closed?"

"It's important to stay focused in the campaign. You know I have a five point lead in the polls. I believe this means ..."

"Senator, federal funding for embryonic stem cell research is a political football. It was illegal, then legal, and now it's illegal again. As Chairman of the Senate Judiciary Committee are you concerned about Steele's charge that Clearbrook Institute is using federal money to fund embryonic stem cell research and then lying about it? Is the federal government in cahoots with Clearbrook?"

"Absolutely not. I was in a private briefing this week where I learned that scientists can now genetically alter adult stem cells so that they act like embryonic stem cells. Nobody dies! Nobody's moral code is offended! As for cloning, it happens every day in labs all over the world. Cloning is as basic to genetic research as earmarks are to legislating. That's a little joke, but I'm just saying ..."

"—We'll have to leave it there, Senator. We're out of time."

Claudia Moray turned to the camera and smiled, pausing, centering, soul-to-soul. "Well, it's clear that we don't know yet what we are dealing with. We will keep a close eye on this story for you, to see whether Rev. Steele just might be on to something. I want to thank our guest, Senator P. Philip Bosch, for joining us."

As soon as the cameras were off, Claudia and the Senator rose and shook hands. She found his to be larger than she expected, and warm.

"Thanks for coming, Senator."

"It was a pleasure, Ms. Moray. I thought that went rather well."

"Call me Claudia, please."

"With pleasure. You can call me Philip. Or Paul." Bosch winked at her. "Just don't ever call me P.P."

Chapter 5

DAVID PULLED HIS car out of the side portico of Clearbrook
Hall, as he had hundreds of times over the years, and swung onto Lake
Shore Drive. Rosalind sat beside him, scrubbing off the last of the blood
with a wad of wet paper towels. In the past, when he pulled in to the
portico to pick her up from work, she would come bounding out of the
door and jump in next to him, eager to see him and to share the day's
events. He always loved that she took such joy in her work. He loved the
way it propelled her through life. It was the thing that had first attracted
him to her—her unbridled love of scientific discovery. But all that joy
disappeared with Claire's illness. Overnight it seemed, Rosalind withdrew.
The love of his life became a stranger.

"You OK?" he asked.

"I'm rushed. What's this about?" she asked.

"Well, so much for the idle chit chat." He began to weave his way
through downtown traffic. "I wanted to talk to you about us. I wanted to
see you without any distractions. You always seem so distracted."

"Oh really? I'm about to lose my leukemia project, this Steele character
wants to shut us down, and my husband hasn't been home in three months
except to change his clothes. Yeah, I'm a little distracted." She stared
straight ahead.

"I didn't think you'd notice I was gone. You certainly don't seem to
notice when I'm there."

Rosalind avoided looking at him. She stared out the window. Despite the heat, the city was alive with festive summer energy. It reminded her of past mid-summers in Chicago: Joggers and cyclists filling the lakefront path, and streets filled with shoppers and sightseers. From every streetlamp hung an American flag, dressing up the city for the big Fourth of July celebration. Grant Park was filled with tents for Taste of Chicago, where throngs of happy revelers roamed in search of culinary delights. It was the magical land of Chicago at the height of summer, the biggest little city in the world, with its breathtaking skyline and parks and boulevards dressed in flowers of every description and color, their rich fragrances mixing with the lusty smoke from dozens of barbeque fires. Rosalind used to love all this, loved seeing Claire enjoy new sights, tastes and smells. She knew there were thousands of people out there doing just that, but it was an abstraction that she had neither the time nor the heart for anymore.

"Where are we going?" Rosalind said.

"To the cemetery."

"No! Stop it!"

"I really need you to do this for me," he said. Without looking at her, he reached over and squeezed her hand.

"Let me out of the car now!"

She couldn't believe he was doing this. She hated the cemetery and he knew it. She'd gone there with him only a few times, always at his urging, and it was always the same awful routine. They wouldn't talk. She would watch from a distance as David placed a bouquet of flowers at the base of Claire's gravestone. The flowers laid there like lost souls in the wind, and it didn't really matter to her whether they blew away or stayed right there and rotted. David would stand over Claire's grave and talk to her and cry. "I miss you, Baby," he would say, looking up. "I can't stand that you're gone. But I know God is taking care of you ..." At the end, he would always get down on one knee. She would stay silent so as not to intrude, but inside she raged. She's dead! Who the hell are you talking to? She would scream inside until she was exhausted, then they would leave. The trip never seemed to get any easier. On the way home, David would smile, his tears all gone, and tell stories about Claire, as if he were lighter, cleansed somehow by communing with things he couldn't see. He went every few weeks; she vowed never to go again.

"I can't, David. You know what this does to me. I live it all over again. Please …"

He swung the car in and parked. An unbearable gloom swept over her as David opened her door and took her hand. There, up a rise to the north, was Claire's grave. Claire's grave. The words still would not compute. But there it was. The sight of it brought back the funeral in stark detail. Again she squeezed her eyes shut, but the images came back to her, the day of Claire's funeral, that awful, final day. She opened her eyes, but still it came, the memory of the funeral in stark, sickening detail.

It was November, and a bitter nor'easter was sweeping through Graceland Cemetery as dark-clad mourners snaked their way toward the gravesite. Except for an occasional sniffle or stifled moan from somewhere in the crowd, the only sound was the clatter of bare branches in the Alder trees overhead. David and Rosalind were seated in the front row of folding chairs, he with his hand on her arm, she staring down at her hands. The smell of the open pit was sickening enough; she couldn't bear to look at the little white casket poised above it.

"Friends, today we celebrate the life of Claire Evans, a child who brought so much joy to those around her. Who could ever forget that dimpled smile, so innocent and sweet …?" Mourners nodded soberly as the Pastor droned on about a little girl he hardly knew, trying for just the right mix of sincerity and optimism in his voice, and failing badly. Rosalind stared at her hands in a futile attempt to blot out the sickening reality of this place, but the tapes kept playing over and over in her head. Claire giggling, running across the lawn, eyes sparkling and mischievous, waving a wand with giant soap bubbles streaming from it in the sunlight. That little voice, so curious, so smart and full of promise. Another image, of the chemo making her sicker. At first better, then suddenly worse. Nothing working. A genetic defect, treatment not working. Another image, of Rosalind pouring over sequenced DNA, desperate for an answer. Letters, nothing but cursed letters, no answers. Claire in her hospital bed, a dreamy look about her, as if she's passed through some kind of portal. A kind of wisdom around her, calm acceptance, no fear. "Mommy, the stars are warm …"

In Rosalind's tortured mind that awful day, as in the awful months that preceded it, she knew she had failed. A life devoted to genetic research, and there was nothing she could do. The nightmare of desperation, her utter failure to find a way to save Claire, to understand what the genetic code was trying to tell her, hundreds and thousands of letters of genetic code swirling in her head, confusing her, mocking her ...

... "Our Father, who art in heaven, hallowed be thy name, thy kingdom come, thy will be done ..." Tiny snowflakes glistened in the sunlight and for a moment all was silent. This was it, the cold reality of burying her only child. The Pastor took a deep breath and looked out upon the crowd.

"... And now, friends, we celebrate Claire's brief life with us, and her new life in the arms of God."

Rosalind felt a bead of perspiration on her lip despite the freezing weather. She rose unsteadily from her chair and put her hand on the casket for support.

"What God?" The wind blew her auburn hair in a swirl around her face. "The one who just stood there and let my baby die?"

Tears filled her eyes for the first time in days. She whirled around and looked at the people, her friends and family, searching their faces for some sign that they understood. They just stared. A voice that Rosalind didn't recognize rose from somewhere deep inside her.

"I needed another day. God wouldn't even give me one more day!" She pounded on the casket again and again. David stood and gripped her arm. Her eyes flashed as she jerked away from him.

"No! Don't you people think he could have given me just one more goddam day?!" She looked at the Pastor. "You can have your God. I don't want anything to do with him!"

The Pastor reached out to her with robed arms. "Oh, Dr. Evans, you don't mean that, please ..."

"Go to hell!" With a choking sob, she turned and ran without looking back ...

The awful vision suddenly vanished, popped like a soap bubble in the sunlight. David reached over and took her hand. Her face was pale, her eyes wide and staring.

"You OK?" he asked.

"I just lived it all over again. That's what happens every time I come here. You know that, David."

His eyes softened and he took hold of her with both arms and tried to embrace her, but she did not respond. "I know. It's OK. You need to walk over there with me. Please ..."

She was impassive; not resistant really, just zombie-like, enveloped in a thick shroud of grief that seemed to incapacitate her. "I can't. Leave me alone."

David let go of her and walked over to the grave. He bent down on one knee and gently touched the gravestone, working his fingers over the letters of Claire's name. He set a bouquet of flowers wrapped in pink ribbon at the base of the stone and lingered for a moment, head bowed. After a moment he stood and reached for his handkerchief. He turned to Rosalind, but she was looking off in the opposite direction, as cold and lifeless as the gravestones.

He realized that it was hopeless to think she would engage with him, even for a moment, in grieving for Claire. He'd had to try one more time. He wanted to see if maybe this time she would open up and let him in so that they could share their grief together. But now he saw how foolish he'd been to think the gap could be closed after all these months. Long before Claire died, her illness had begun to drive a wedge between them. After the diagnosis, each day brought a new wave of uncertainty, the need to make decisions they had no strength for, and the chilling realization that they were losing her. The irony was that as the weeks of their little girl's decline wore on and their need for solace increased, he and Rosalind seemed less and less able to comfort each other. Something in them changed utterly, isolating them in their grief. Somehow Rosalind had convinced herself that Claire's death was her fault. So complete was her self-absorption that she had no idea of the depth of his need for her. Every once in a while she would seem to soften, to open up to his love and affection, but not for long. With time, she slipped ever more easily back into the dark place, where the only ones welcome were her and her damn work. She was so obsessed with the science of why Claire died that she'd stopped listening to her heart. And to him.

He thought he might somehow jar her out of it today by coming to the cemetery. The grieving process had begun to heal him, but she remained lost and isolated in her self-made prison. If she had only shown some small sign that she was willing to let him in ... Well, he thought bitterly, she can have her darkness. I want no part of it.

"I got an offer from Sanders and Fox in New York. It's huge. I wanted to tell you face to face," he said, staring at the ground.

She shivered slightly, despite the heat. She had never considered the possibility. What did he need with a new firm? He loved Chicago. They both loved Chicago.

"You're leaving me."

"No. You left me. I've made peace with Claire's death and I'm ready to move on. I only wish you could move on, too."

"Move on? To *what?*"

"Will you come with me?"

"I can't leave my work. You know that. How can you ask me to leave this project?"

"You know, Roz, it's not my business any more, but the stress is starting to show on you. You don't look well. Beautiful, but not well." he said, looking into her eyes.

The comment stung because she knew it was true, and because of the gentle way he said it.

"Are you taking her with you?"

David shoved his hands in his pockets. He weighed his words carefully. "Of course not. It meant nothing."

"Then why did you do it?"

"I was lonely. How could you expect me to sit by and let you have control of my loneliness?"

"If you were lonely, you could have come to me!"

"I did. You weren't there."

Rosalind turned away from him, stung by the ease with which he seemed to justify his infidelity. He had confessed it to her two months earlier, insisting that it had been just once, but she had no way of knowing whether he was lying. She couldn't understand how he could do that when she was grieving so deeply.

"Well, David, I hope you have a wonderful life in New York."

"I will Rosalind, because I am at peace. I miss Claire terribly, and sometimes the pain grabs me and twists so hard I can't breathe. But I get past it! And each time I do, I am stronger. I guess you don't want that freedom, do you? You would rather wallow in your self-pity and your twisted sense of guilt." His voice rose and his eyes glistened. He grabbed her hard by the shoulders and held her at arm's length. "I brought you here because I wanted to *feel* this with you. I wanted us to hold each other and cry for our daughter, *together.*"

Rosalind said nothing. She could see David, but his voice was faint, as if someone had turned down the volume. She had no clue what to say or do; she felt no anger, no sadness, no nothing. Her emotions had run dry.

David turned from her, no longer able to contain the bitterness and heartache he felt toward her. "Fine. You've shut me out for the last time."

They drove south toward campus in silence. The air in the car was clogged with tension, unexpressed feelings hanging between them like storm clouds. Outside, traffic was heavy on Lake Shore Drive. Two blocks from campus as they were stopped at a light, she opened the car door.

"I'll walk from here."

"Goodbye, Rosalind."

Sweat trickled down her back as she watched him drive away into the sunlit afternoon.

The mid-day heat lay heavy and damp over the city. The sidewalk was crowded with people engaged in conversations on their cell phones or deep into the music on their headphones, locked in their own little worlds, all passing through the same space and time, yet oblivious to one another. Ghosts, she thought. I am alone here, sweating through my clothes, waiting with a hundred ghosts for the light to change. And David has left me.

A CTA bus rumbled by, raising a grey cloud of diesel exhaust. She desperately wanted to escape reality like all these other people, just dial her iPhone and chat with someone who might convey some shred of empathy or say something noble or make her laugh. But she couldn't. She was starkly in the here and now, rooted in the moment by the rising fear in the pit of her stomach. Don't you ghosts know that my daughter is dead, my husband just left me, and I am about to lose my life's work? She forced herself to walk, to keep moving. The oppressive heat intensified her feeling that the world was tilted the wrong way.

Up ahead was the Starry Messenger ticker, shouting the question of the day. She squinted at it in the harsh sunlight. 'What's trying to happen here?' it said, 'What's trying to happen here?' Sometimes Starry's question changed every five minutes, sometimes every five hours, depending on whether the mysterious Starry Messenger was satisfied that he or she had gotten the answer. The ticker was twenty-feet tall, scrolling across the side of a building at the tenth-story level. Starry had the most popular blog in the world, and now the ticker. Nobody was sure how it got there; one day about a year ago it just suddenly appeared. Some people thought it was exceedingly thought-provoking, others found it irritating and pedestrian. But no one could ignore it. Similar to a news crawl in Times Square, it operated twenty four hours a day, scrolling Starry Messenger's question of the moment.

'What's trying to happen here?' Rosalind walked on. I'll have to get back to you on that, Mr. Messenger. She bought cold lemonade from a street vendor and walked across the street. On the corner there, in the glare of the midday sun, an elderly man was quoting scripture through a cheap portable PA system. Dressed in a shabby suit, he held a Bible that was tattered and torn by decades of use.

"... The LORD has anointed me to preach good news to the poor. He has sent me to bind up the brokenhearted, to proclaim the year of the LORD's favor and the day of vengeance of our God, to comfort all who mourn."

The tinny loudspeaker distorted his voice so that it was almost unintelligible, but there was no mistaking his conviction. Perched against the wall of the building behind him were weathered, hand printed signs with Biblical verses.

"Are you straight with your Creator?" he said to no one in particular. Throngs of people walked by him without a glance, but he didn't seem to mind. He had been at this corner for as long as anyone could remember, long enough to have evolved from a fiery, self-styled young evangelist into a frail old man. He had spent his life on the street in good weather and bad, shouting scripture, preaching love and forgiveness and redemption. Rosalind had walked by him a thousand times over the years and had never even made eye contact with him. But this time there was something that caught her eye, something about the relaxed honesty of his face, the leathery black skin and the earnest way he spoke of redemption. He was the antithesis of Joseph Steele. She walked up to him.

"Would you like a cold lemonade?" He stopped speaking and looked at her as if he hadn't quite heard her right.

"I thought maybe you could use a cold drink in this heat. Go ahead. I haven't touched it," she said.

The man wiped his brow with a dingy handkerchief. He smiled and took the drink from her. He placed his parched lips around the straw and took a long drink.

"My, that's good," he said. "I am grateful to you, ma'am." He took several more gulps. "Who are you?"

It was a fair question. She couldn't think of an answer. "I have seen you here for years, but never thought to stop. Do many people stop?" Rosalind said.

"There's lots of people looking for redemption. But not too many of them stop."

"If nobody pays attention, why do you do it?"

"It's not about me. There might be somebody pass by here one day who needs to hear the Word." He offered her his gnarled hand. "I'm Boone Wilkes. What's your name?"

"Rosalind."

"Are you right with the Lord, Rosalind?"

She laughed. "I seriously doubt it."

"Don't be so sure. Jesus' second great commandment was to love thy neighbor." He held up the cup of lemonade. "Thank you."

"What was the first?"

"Love the Lord your God with all your heart, mind and strength."

"Well, one out of two ain't bad."

"Not bad at all. You don't love God?" He raised his eyebrows slightly, as if he were asking 'you don't love ice cream?'

"I don't believe in God."

"Where do you think all this came from?" He pointed a crooked finger up at the gleaming buildings towering overhead, then at the throngs of happy people enjoying a summer day. His face was soft and kindly, like a teacher. He held up his Bible. "What about all this evidence?"

"Fairy tales."

"What *do* you believe in?"

She thought for a moment. "I don't know."

He smiled at her. "Sure you do. We all believe in something."

She shrugged.

He laughed and sucked the last of the lemonade from the cup. "In case you are wondering, I believe you are a very good girl. You are kind to strangers. God loves that. Bless you, Rosalind."

Chapter 6

BENTON BRADSHAW FELT a chill as he, Dyer, and Gleason
made their way through the basement labyrinth of the Department of
Information Services and Security. It was brightly lit with florescent bulbs,
but the lack of natural light gave the place a sickly green pallor. The
ramped-up air conditioning enhanced the feeling of having stepped into a
tomb. The people who worked there seemed not to care; they smiled and
nodded their greetings as the men passed by on their way to the office of
Information Security Director Sam Lockett.

Lockett smiled as they came in, but the smile was short-lived.

"Here's what's going to happen," Dyer said. "You're going to check
the computer logs, look for malware, run virus programs, track key strokes
and, if we have to, take the computer code apart to see whether it has been
tampered with. We have to find out where in the system this problem starts
and ends."

Lockett knew full well how to respond to an incident; this was his
profession. So who was this guy to tell him what to do? He looked over at
Bradshaw, whose expression was something between sheepish and flu-like.

"Ben, what kind of incident are we talking about?" Lockett said.

"I don't think it's anything, Sam. Mr. Dyer thinks there might have
been some tampering with data for the PharmaGen project."

Dyer jumped on his words. "As of right now we are in full incident
response mode. Full lock-down. There has been a potentially fatal attack on

my data and I need to know how and to what extent. My security men will be here within the hour," Dyer said.

Lockett gave Bradshaw a quizzical look, as if waiting for the punch line.

"Do whatever Mr. Dyer says to do," Bradshaw said. "I'll leave you to carry on." He walked out like a man needing badly to pee.

"What makes you think we have a security problem?" Lockett said to Dyer.

"Last night I learned that our competitor, Danka-Saba Pharmaceutical, recently had a surge in the pace of their research," Dyer said. "This morning I saw clear evidence that our data has been tampered with. None of this is coincidence."

"What?" Peter Gleason barked. "A surge? What does that mean?" Up until then, Gleason had been quietly observing the conversation. As Dyer's Director of Research, he had little interest in the computer side of things. But he had every reason to care what Danka-Saba was up to.

"It means they are further along than we thought," Dyer said.

"How far along? Oh man, don't tell me this!" Gleason said. Like Dyer, he had risked everything, personally and professionally, on the leukemia project. The two had eleven years of history together, beginning when both of them worked for Danka-Saba. Their early friendship grew around beer, basketball, and a shared annoyance with the leaden culture of big pharma. At that time, the mapping of the human genome was nearly finished, giving rise to the new field of pharmacogenomics. They saw the potential in it, both for human benefit and for profits. They were mavericks by nature and wanted to be a part of the coming revolution, but they had no patience for the cumbersome product development processes at Danka-Saba. Dyer's entrepreneurial talent and Gleason's love of the scientific hunt made them a perfect match for a new venture. They bolted.

They designed PharmaGen as a small, nimble, outrageously gutsy start-up company. Their strategy was simple: work fast and fly under the radar of the slower-moving big companies. They targeted their research toward finding the genetic variables that effect drug tolerance, and then engineering new drugs around them. The goal was to be the first to patent a new generation of targeted leukemia drugs. They mortgaged their homes, cleaned out their bank accounts and convinced several large investors to quietly come with them. They gambled everything on Clearbrook Institute's ability to do the basic research quickly and in complete secrecy. They knew leukemia would be on the docket of all the major pharma companies. There was no time to waste. They figured they had a six month jump on the competition. If their gamble paid off, they could make billions and revolutionize medicine. If not, they would be passing out drug samples in doctors' offices for the rest of their lives.

"How much are they surging?" Gleason said, feeling as if he'd suddenly lost his balance. "Are you sure?"

"Bag Man is sure," Dyer said.

Bag Man was a member of the PharmaGen intelligence team. Dyer and Gleason didn't have a vast covert intelligence network like Danka-Saba and other big pharmaceutical companies. What they had was a team of insanely good snoops who could divine meaning from mere scraps of paper and hack a database like nobody's business. Bag Man got his code name from the black garbage bags that held the collected contents of waste baskets inside rival companies. Planting a janitor at a rival company was one of the oldest tools in industrial espionage, and still one of the best. In a world increasingly focused on electronic transmission of information, people underestimated the importance of paper. They used it, then forgot they used it.

At the end of each work day at Danka-Saba, a janitor would collect the trash from labs and offices, put it in black plastic bags, take them out back and throw them toward the dumpster. Except that the 'janitor' would add a little extra arc to his lob and toss them into the alley just beyond the fence. It was absurdly low tech, which was probably why it worked. A waiting van would then quickly scoop up the bags from the alley and take them to a warehouse, where, under Bag Man's direction, the PharmaGen intel gang would pour through the contents for useful intelligence about what had gone on that day in the labs and offices of their rival. It was the small things that could change the game, anything from a phone number to a formula to a passcode hastily scribbled on a scrap of paper—these were the booty the Bag Man sought. As he was known to say, "You would think that in an electronic world there would be no need to write important things down on paper. But you would be wrong."

This was how they had learned that Danka-Saba was in the leukemia game. Now, Bag Man had uncovered solid evidence that Danka-Saba's scientists were nearly finished with their basic research. Just days ago, he laid out a series of communiqués that had been collected from Danka-Saba's office of Research and Development over a week's time. Dyer would not have believed it if he hadn't seen it. There was no hint of computer hacking or sabotage in the communiqués, but the message was clear: They were further along than Dyer had suspected. In Dyer's mind, the only way Danka-Saba could possibly have overcome PharmaGen's head start was to steal the data.

"No!" Gleason was exhibiting decompensation behaviors. "How could this have happened? I told you Evans was a whack job!"

"Evans is the strongest thing we've got. She's the reason we went with Clearbrook in the first place," Dyer said.

"Yah, but we didn't know then that she was a nut bag. Now she's a mole!"

"She's not a nut bag, Pete," Dyer said.

"She wigged out at her daughter's funeral and she's made life so miserable for her husband that he doesn't even go home any more except to get clean underpants!"

"Bag Man tell you that?"

"Yes. David Evans sleeps in his office. Has for several months now," Gleason said.

"No wonder she's upset. But she's not nuts, Peter. And I doubt she's a mole. That woman is a force of nature. Nobody else could possibly have analyzed that data as well and as quickly as she did."

"Then what happened? We have every computer protected. Every employee vetted. We've threatened everyone at Clearbrook with prison or torture if they break the confidentiality agreement. We've even segregated the data," Gleason said.

Dyer had put in place every security safeguard known to man. He knew from his experience at Danka-Saba that pharmaceutical companies will stop at nothing to penetrate a competitor's cloak of secrecy, anything from sophisticated electronic invasion devices to planting employees. Nothing was safe. No one could be trusted. Iron-clad nondisclosure agreements vetted by high-octane teams of lawyers were in place before details of a project were even seriously discussed. The stakes were simply too high to do otherwise. Big pharma's intelligence modus rivaled that of the CIA.

"What we saw on that screen was not a lab error or a typo, Pete. It was a message from Danka-Saba. It was their gotcha moment."

"How could they have broken through all this security?" Gleason said.

"That's what I intend to find out."

"You go ahead. I'm going home to tell my family we have to sell the house and go on food stamps. Once Danka-Saba goes into phase two, we'll never catch up. How could this have happened?"

"Stop it. We got in this to win and get rich. And we will."

Gleason looked at his friend, wondering why the guy never seemed to feel any emotion. Alan Dyer's logic was his mightiest tool in business. The man was an analytical monster. He could navigate his way in and out of the diciest business situations. The greater the danger, the more he liked it. But when it came to feelings, he was flat-lined. Gleason had never seen his friend express any emotion stronger than satisfaction at sinking a thirty-foot putt. "Funny, I thought we got in this to help sick people" Gleason said.

"People die, Pete. We can't change that," Dyer said. "All we can do is cure leukemia. And then we'll have more money than God. Lockett, let me see the floor plans for the sequencing facility."

Lockett fished through a file and brought out a thick roll of blue-prints for the newly remodeled ANSR 1000 space. He pulled out one and laid it on his desk. Dyer bent over it and studied it for a moment.

"This place is built like a sieve. What were you people thinking? There are four doors leading into the room with the ANSR 1000."

"This one is a closet that isn't used anymore. There are only three that lead to the hallway," Lockett said. He managed to keep his disgust to himself. He couldn't stand the thought of an outsider running his show, but his hands were tied; he had orders from Bradshaw to do whatever Dyer wanted.

"I want all three doors locked and an armed guard outside each, twenty four hours a day until I say otherwise." Dyer said, aiming a long, steely glare at Lockett.

"Armed? What are you afraid of?"

"Everything."

Chapter 7

IT WAS NEARLY one in the morning, and Rosalind was sitting head-in-hands at her kitchen table. She had made little progress in her analysis of the supposedly corrupted data. She could not push David out of her mind. She alternated between tears of anguish and tears of anger, all the while staring at translation code that just stared back. Her eyes, to say nothing of her nerves, were shot. David kept creeping into her head, standing there in the cemetery, telling her he was leaving.

Dyer's eight a.m. deadline was looming. The bad news was that even though she was only three pages into the translation code, she already had found more words—words that could not possibly have gotten there as a consequence of lab error. Bradshaw would be furious. Dyer would shut them down completely. The thought made her sick. But she had no time to be sick: she had 25 pages to go.

This whole snipe hunt went against her scientific sensibilities. These letters were symbols for amino acids. To try and attribute some other meaning to them was counterintuitive. Looking for words was like being lost in the desert; she could only wander and hope her eyes landed on something familiar. Through trial and error she found that what worked best was to train her eye on a letter and then scan forward to see if there was a pattern that formed a word. If not, she would look at the next letter and scan forward. It was mind-numbingly tedious, more so because she wasn't working with a full 'alphabet.' The amino acid code did not include the letters B,J,O,U,X and Z. The letter X, however, did appear in her translation code because it was the symbol chosen by the Deep X sequencing program to indicate SNPs. But far more problematic was the absence of the vowels O and U. This seriously limited the number of English words that could be formed by the code.

Another problem was that so far, the words appeared to be scattered. There was no rhyme or reason to the placement. Or was there? Logic was abandoning her. David, get out of my head, she thought. Her eyes were beginning to shut down when something caught her eye.

```
4321  GGGCCANTCCCCGGATTTCTTCCTCCCGGCCTCCTCCCACGCCCTGACGGTGCAGGACGC
1441   G   P   X   P   G   F   L   P   P   G   L   S   H   A   L   T   G   A   G   R
4381  GCTTTGCTCNCCCCGAGACCCAGACGCGCTGAAAGCNCGGCGCGGGCAGTTCCCCGCCCC
1461   A   L   L   X   P   R   P   R   R   A   E   S   X   A   R   A   V   P   R   P
4441  ACGCCCCNCGCTGCAANCCCACCCGCAAAGCCTCNCGCGAGTGCGCTCCACCGAGGCCCT
1481   T   P   X   A   N   X   T   P   A   K   P   X   P   S   A   S   T   E   A   L
4501  GGACTCCCCNCGACCGCGCTCCCGCGCACGNTCGACCGGAGCACCCCGCTTCACNCCGGC
1501   G   L   P   X   T   A   L   P   R   T   X   D   R   S   T   P   L   H   X   G
```

OK, so somebody's playing God. I get it. And it really isn't funny.

She shook her head and rubbed her eyes.

Based on the words she'd found so far, this was adding up to be a scheme perpetrated by someone with a Bible fetish. It made no sense, especially considering that they didn't have use of the letters O and U. She was far from a Bible expert, but she reckoned that O and U were pretty important in Biblical parlance. What was scripture without the word God? Or thou? Or Jesus?

Asshole. If I ever get my hands on whoever did this, I'll break his knees. She could understand why Danka-Saba would corrupt the data to lead the project down a blind alley. But it would have taken weeks to reverse-engineer that much genetic code, hack in, steal her data and replace it with the phony data. Why go to all that trouble? Especially when it would greatly increase the chance of detection? Random shuffling of the letters would be simple and take longer to detect. And why would they use passages from the Bible, of all things?

The image of Joseph Steele popped into her head. He wanted Clearbrook shut down. Maybe this was his way of getting it done. Could he have hired someone to concoct this elaborate hoax? Would he use the Bible to create havoc with their work?

She reached for her phone. She dialed and waited. After several rings, there was an answer.

"Hullo?" The voice was deep and gravelly, clearly not thrilled at being awakened.

"Stefan. It's Rosalind. I need your help."

"What time is it?"

"1:30."

"What's going on?" the man said.

"That's the problem. I'm not sure. I'm coming over," Rosalind said.

"Now?" He sounded reluctant.

"Yes, now! Get up. I'm on my way."

She tucked the translation code printouts in her bag and headed out into the darkness

Chapter 8

MICK THE TECH sat at his computer, cruising the Internet, looking for action. He had spent an hour or so with the genetic code printouts, looking for words, and he had found a lot of them. He couldn't figure out why people thought this was so hard. All you had to do was just look at the letters and the words were there. You didn't even really have to look that hard, they just sort of popped out at you. Like in a word jumble puzzle. He was good at those. Now, he'd been through the whole genetic code and was done with it. Next, he'd checked out his usual online techie chat rooms, but it was a pretty dry night there, too. He thought that before he went to porn, he would check out the Starry Messenger blog one more time. Like half the population, he had the page bookmarked.

How much can you eat?

Kittens, you know that the body of human knowledge grows exponentially every day, and that information is spewed continuously in every direction via the mass media, right? Did you know that information is as tangible as an apple or an egg, and that you ingest it like food? So, how much information can you take in without getting sick? How can you choose between junk information that tastes good but has no value, and nourishing information that feeds your mind and soul but doesn't always taste good?

And when is enough enough?

In the same way that we don't want to inadvertently eat a poison mushroom, we don't want to inadvertently eat the wrong kind of information, do we? It is tempting, when we are hungry, to eat the first thing that comes along and ask questions later, and who of us hasn't done that? So, Kittens, in a world rife with good and bad information, will you please tell me how you decide which to eat?

Mick sat up straight. Dude. I got one for you. He quickly entered his on-line name 'Bitman' and typed a post, hoping that this might be his chance to actually get a personal reply from Starry Messenger. Wouldn't Rosalind Evans be impressed if that happened? Starry was the most famous person in the universe.

From Bitman: There is a Bible verse in the genetic code. That ought to taste good.

He sat back and waited. He had spent many hours tracking the Starry Blog, and had posted hundreds of times. Even though other people had chatted back at him, Starry never had. C'mon man, write to me! He always thought it would be totally cool to actually chat with a superstar like Starry. But Starry was picky; he didn't chat with just anyone. Mick waited. There were twelve recent posts, none as cool as his. None even close to as cool as his. Come on, Starry. He trained his eyes on the screen and waited as one reply after another came from other readers. And then, there it was!

From Starry Messenger: Wouldn't that be nice, Bitman?
From Bitman: It is nice. I saw it today.
From Starry Messenger: Where, Kitten?
From Bitman: Dude, are you a girl? Cause guys don't call people kitten.
From Starry Messenger: Why? Does it matter?
From Bitman: If you are a chick, what do you look like?
From Starry Messenger: Are you a chick?
From Bitman: No, but I've fantasized about it.

From Starry Messenger: Who hasn't? **Where did you see this genetic code?**

From Bitman: At Clearbrook Institute. This scientist was doing a Power Point and there it was.

From Starry Messenger: What was the scientist's name?

From Bitman: Dr. Rosalind Evans. She's famous.

From Starry Messenger: A Power Point about what?

From Bitman: Genetic code, Dude. Duh.

From Starry Messenger: Got proof?

From Bitman: Yeah. A printout.

From Starry Messenger: What does it say?

From Bitman: Lots of things. 'bear false witness, kill, steal, wife.' I think they left some letters out. It's the Ten Commandments though Dude. For sure.

From Starry Messenger: Can I get a copy?

From Bitman: You don't believe me?

From Starry Messenger: How would I know unless I saw it for myself?

From Bitman: It says at the bottom, 'property of Clearbrook Institute and PharmaGen, Inc.'

From Starry Messenger: Will you send it to me?

From Bitman: Sure, dude. It's on its way. Hey, thanks for getting back to me.

From Starry Messenger: How could I not?

Mick popped open another beer. He scanned the printouts and e-mailed them. He felt pretty proud of himself about solving the genetic code, but to get the attention of none other than Starry Messenger? Dude! That's huge! I guess we're on a first name basis now, buddy. The only thing that would make this night better would be if foxy Rozzie would call. He turned his attention back to the Starry Messenger blog and waited for a reply. He tossed his beer in the sink. This deserved a real celebration. He lit up a joint and grabbed a bottle of Captain Morgan.

Chapter 9

DR. STEFAN GUNQUIST'S six foot, seven inch frame filled the front doorway of his townhouse. His Viking immensity was accentuated by the black wool robe and anvil-sized slippers he wore, and one easily could have imagined that he had a helmet and spear hidden behind the door. He yawned and motioned Rosalind in, not even attempting to tame his disheveled mass of grey hair. He hadn't seen the far side of midnight in years. It didn't suit him well. As Professor Emeritus of Theology, he'd earned the right to sleep whenever he wanted. There weren't many who could roust him at 1:30 in the morning. Rosalind Fanning Evans was one of them.

"Hello, Roz. I can't say much for your timing, but come on in."

"Hello, Stefan. Thank you for letting me come over."

"I had a choice?" he said, wiping sleep from his eyes. "Sit down. The coffee's on."

"I hope I didn't wake Ida," Rosalind said sheepishly.

"No. It takes an Act of Congress to wake my dear wife."

Rosalind pulled out a sheaf of papers and sat down at the kitchen table. "I'm here because I have to make a report in six hours or I could lose my project. I need help, and you're the only person who won't think I'm nuts. Someone has tampered with my data, made it look like a passage from the Bible. I need you to help me figure this out."

"Why don't you show me what you're talking about? And remember, I'm no scientist, so keep it simple." She smiled at the irony; of all of her professors from undergrad at Rutherford, and all of her elite colleagues at Clearbrook, Stefan Gunquist was the one she trusted most. His kindliness and lack of pretention had endeared him to her when she took his Pragmatism and Religion class her sophomore year. She was at the time an agnostic, and her scientific sensibilities contrasted nicely with his wise, spiritually evolved persona. They often engaged in intellectual sparring and had great fun doing it. She showed him the page with the words Dyer had found, and explained how the codons and amino acid code line up to spell words.

"So it is rare for the code to spell out actual words?" he said. She nodded. "And there are other words in this code? Show me."

She showed him everything she had found, taking time to explain how the absence of Os and Us made it harder to decipher the words. He scanned through the 28 pages, squinting at them, and then he sat back and thought for several moments.

```
721  NCGGACCCCGCCTCCCAGGACATGTTCNCCAATGGCAGCTTTCTCCGGCGTAGGAAGCGT
241    X   D   P   A   S   Q   D   M   F   X   N   G   S   F   L   R   R   R   K   R
781  TTCNTCCGCCACCAACTGACCCCGGGAGCCNCGCTGCCCCACCCCTTCCCTCTANCCGCT
261    F   X   R   H   Q   L   T   P   G   A   X   L   P   H   P   F   P   L   X   A
841  GCACACNCGGCCCTGCACAACCACNTCAACNCCCGGCTGCTTGGGGCCNCCGCCCTGCCG
281    A   H   X   A   L   H   N   H   X   N   X   R   L   L   G   A   X   A   L   P
901  CAGCCAGTCNCGGGGGCCTACNCCAACACCGCCCCCGGGAGANCCCCTTACGCTCTGCTG
301    Q   P   V   X   G   A   Y   X   N   T   A   P   G   R   X   P   Y   A   L   L
961  CACCCGNCGCCTACCCACTACCTACTGNCGTCGGCCCCCGCCTATNTCGGGGCACCGAAG
321    H   P   X   P   T   H   Y   L   L   X   S   A   P   A   Y   X   G   A   P   K
1021 NCGGCAGAAGGCGCGGACNCCGCGACCCCCGGCACCCTTCCCGTGCTGCAGNCGTCACTT
341    X   A   E   G   A   D   X   A   T   P   G   T   L   P   V   L   Q   X   S   L
1081 GGTCCTCAGNTCTGGGAGGAGGGCAAGNCCCTGGCGTCGCCACCGGGAGGCGGATGCATC
361    G   P   Q   X   W   E   E   G   K   X   L   A   S   P   P   G   G   G   C   I
1141 TCTTTCAGCATTGAGAGTATCATGCAAGGGGTCAGGGGAGCGGGTACAGGGNCCGCCACC
381    S   F   S   I   E   S   I   M   Q   G   V   R   G   A   G   T   G   X   A   T
1201 CACGAGCGGCCGACCGCGNCGAGCTACNTCCCCCTGNCGCAGCGACCGTCAAGCCTGNCC
401    H   E   R   P   T   A   X   S   Y   X   P   L   X   Q   R   P   S   S   L   X
1261 GACAATTTTGCAGCAACANCCNTCNCCTCAGGAGGAGCCAACGACCAACGGCTGCGCTCC
421    D   N   F   A   A   T   X   X   X   S   G   G   A   N   D   Q   R   L   R   S
1321 CACCAAGGGCGCGGTGCTGGGCGGGCACCTGTCGGCCGCGTCGGCGCTGCTGCGGTATCA
441    H   Q   G   R   G   A   G   R   A   P   V   G   R   V   G   A   A   A   V   S
1381 GGCGGTGGCAGAGGGCTCNCGGCTGACATCGCTGGCNCCCCCTTTGGGCGGAGAGGGGAC
461    G   G   G   R   G   L   X   A   D   I   A   G   X   P   F   G   R   R   G   D
1441 CTCNCGAGTTTTTTTTAGTATCGCCNCGACCCACTACCCTGGCCAAGTCCGCAGGGCCCTC
481    L   X   S   F   F   S   I   A   X   T   H   Y   P   G   Q   V   R   R   A   L
1501 CTAGAGNCGGGTGGGAGTGGGGAGCGATCCGCANCCGCTCACTCCACCTTGCGCGGCCCA
501    L   E   X   G   G   S   G   E   R   S   A   X   A   H   S   T   L   R   G   P
```

```
1561 TACTGGNTCTGTGCATCTGAATCCTGCTGGAGAGCANCCACGAACTTCTGTTCCCTGCAA
521   Y  W  X  C  A  S  E  S  C  W  R  A  X  T  N  F  C  S  L  Q
1621 AATGGTNCGAAAGAAACAGCTGGAATGNTCACCCACGAGCGGCACCTGAACGTAACCTTC
541   N  G  X  K  E  T  A  G  M  X  T  H  E  R  H  L  N  V  T  F
1681 GCAGGGNTCCAAGTCATCTTTTCTTGCCTTCGGCTGTGGNCCCTGTGGCTTTCCGGATTT
561   A  G  X  Q  V  I  F  S  C  L  R  L  W  X  L  W  L  S  G  F
1741 GCACATTTCCTGGGGTACTATGAACGTGAGTGGGGTATTTTGTTCTGGCATNCCAAGAAA
581   A  H  F  L  G  Y  Y  E  R  E  W  G  I  L  F  W  H  X  K  K
1801 AACAAGCAAGCANCCAAAAACACAGCCTCCGATGCCAAANTCGTTCCCCCTTCTTCACTT
601   N  K  Q  A  X  K  N  T  A  S  D  A  K  X  V  P  P  S  S  L
1861 CCTTGGAACTGGNTCTGTTATTCCNCCGTCNTCTGCAAAATGCTTCTACTCTCTGTGTCT
621   P  W  N  W  X  C  Y  S  X  V  X  C  K  M  L  L  L  S  V  S
1921 TCCNCCNCGGGATGTTTAATGNCGGTAGGATATNCGTTTCAGAACATTGATTTCTTATCT
641   S  X  X  G  C  L  M  X  V  G  Y  X  F  Q  N  I  D  F  L  S
1981 GTGTGTNCCACGTGCCATCTTNCGTGTNCGAATNCGGGTGTTAAAATTAAGCCTAGTTAT
661   V  C  X  T  C  H  L  X  C  X  N  X  G  V  K  I  K  P  S  Y
2041 ATAGACGAAATANCGTGCNCGGTCACTACACTACATCGTTATTTTCTANCGCGTCTCATT
681   I  D  E  I  X  C  X  V  T  T  L  H  R  Y  F  L  X  R  L  I
2101 CTTCCCTTTCTAAATGGAACTTTTNCGAACCTACATTATTTTCCCTCAAACMCGTTATTT
701   L  P  F  L  N  G  T  F  X  N  L  H  Y  F  P  S  N  X  L  F
2161 TCACAATTCATATTTATTATAGATAGCAGAAGTAATCCATTTNCGTATGGCNCGTAAAAA
721   S  Q  F  I  F  I  I  D  S  R  S  N  P  F  X  Y  G  L  X  K
2221 TTCCAAATATTTNTCGTTGAAAATGTCNTCGCTTTTAAAATAGGAAATTTACTATTTATG
741   F  Q  I  F  X  V  E  N  V  X  A  F  K  I  G  N  L  L  F  M
```

"Tell me what this code represents in biological terms."

"This is the code from a gene at the center of the second chromosome. The smaller letters, the Gs, As, Cs, and Ts, represent the four base chemicals that make up DNA. They line up in groups of three to form codons. Each codon codes for a specific amino acid."

"Amino acids are the building blocks of proteins, which carry out all the functions of life," Gunquist said with a smile. "You see what a renaissance man I am?"

"That's right. Genetic code is the recipe book for life. Each of the 20 amino acids is represented by a letter—these larger letters on the printout. In our study, we were looking for genetic variations, or SNPs, in the genetic code that cause bad reactions to certain drugs. It's the genetic variation that Claire had."

The mention of Claire's name saddened Gunquist. He had been with Rosalind and David often during Claire's illness and passing, and it grieved him to watch Rosalind's life force drain away. She had been a favorite student of his, a brash young woman with an unabashed, hubristic sense of destiny and willful disregard for the likes of the Almighty. When she returned to Rutherford as a Post Doctoral researcher, she was a bit tamed down, but no less cynical about theology. David, on the other hand, was very spiritual. He had always shown curiosity about things theological and was a faithful Christian. They made quite a pair. Gunquist had grown very fond of them as a couple, and he had great respect for Rosalind as a fellow faculty member and a woman of science.

"It looks to me as if the amino acid part of it is spelling out words that come straight from Exodus and Deuteronomy—The Ten Commandments. But I don't see more than bits of it," Gunquist said. "Is there more?"

"That's what I need you for. You know the Bible. I don't. I need you to study these pages and see if your eyes can pick out more text."

Gunquist looked at the stack of papers on the table and smiled at her. She looked like a woman whose resources were wearing thin. "OK, Roz. I'm game. Show me the way."

The two gulped coffee and began scanning the endless strings of letters. All at once, Gunquist stopped. "Wow, look at this."

```
2341  ACCCCCCAACAAACCCACNTCNTCTTTGAGATCAATTTGGAATGTNTCGGCCAACATGTA
 781   T  P  Q  Q  T  H  X  X  F  E  I  N  L  E  C  X  G  Q  H  V
2401  CTCAGGNCGAATAAAAGGCTANCGATGTACATATATATATATATATATNTCTACATTTTT
 801   L  R  X  N  K  R  L  X  M  Y  I  Y  I  Y  I  Y  X  Y  I  F

2461  CTAGCACTAGAATTTTCAAAACTTATTTCTNCCAAAAAAAAAAAACTCTGAAAAGACTTTG
 821   L  A  L  E  F  S  K  L  I  S  X  K  K  K  N  S  E  K  T  L
2521  CAACTANCCAGGTTTAAGTGTTACTCGGCGCCACACGAACTGACCGGGNTCAACCAGACA
 841   Q  L  X  R  F  K  C  Y  S  A  S  H  A  L  T  G  X  N  Q  T
2581  AGAACGAACNCGACCAATTGCTCCCCACAAAGANTCCATATTTCTAGGAACNCGGCCGTT
 861   R  T  N  X  T  N  C  S  P  Q  R  X  H  I  S  R  N  X  A  V
2641  TTCCCCNTCCCCGAGTGGGGTNCGCGATTCCGTGCCGCTTTGAGGGAAGCTGCTCTGNCG
 881   F  P  X  P  E  W  G  X  R  F  R  A  A  L  R  E  A  A  L  X
2701  ATGNTCGAAAGTTTTTCCCCCAAGATCCTGCTGCTGCCCACCCCCAGCTATGAANCCCTT
 901   M  X  E  S  F  S  P  K  I  L  L  L  P  T  P  S  Y  E  X  L
```

"The words 'shalt' and 'kill' are obvious. But look at 'thxx' and this 'nxt.' Could the Xs stand for o and u? If you make the substitutions, it reads, 'thou shalt not kill,'" he said.

It took Rosalind a moment to see what he was talking about. Her brain still struggled to make the leap from chemistry to language.

"Why would they use x instead of o and u?" Gunquist asked.

"X is the symbol that the new sequencing program, Deep X, uses to show a SNP."

Gunquist thought about it for a moment, then looked at her with an amused expression. "You know what else X is a symbol for, don't you?"

She shrugged.

"It's the symbol for Christ."

She shook her head as if to clear out any thought that this might be some kind of religious hocus-pocus. The whole idea gave her the creeps. "OK, enough already. Look Stefan, the use of Xs actually makes our job easier. Let's look for Xs."

They perused the pages for several minutes, each quietly engaged in the hunt for Xs.

"OK, here is another thxx!" Rosalind said. "Then several lines later, shalt. Then down here nxt. On the next page is steal. Thou shalt not steal." Rosalind threw Gunquist a self-satisfied smile. Even though it meant that the corruption went deep, there was something oddly satisfying about finding the words she suspected were imbedded in the code. More importantly, she was beginning to think she might actually have the report for Dyer done by eight a.m. They continued to pour over the pages. With time, their eyes became better able to discriminate between gibberish and word pattern, and they began to move more quickly. Every once in a while one of them would draw a circle around a grouping of letters. The phrases were broken up, but identifiable. They were on a roll. Less than an hour later, they had scoured all 28 pages.

"This is unquestionably the Ten Commandments," Gunquist said. "The only problem is there are only six of them here. These are commandments 5-10, the ethics. I wonder where the first four are."

Rosalind thought for a moment. DZPro2 and CLAIRE were right next to each other at the center of the chromosome. Might the other four commandments be on the DZPro2 gene? If so, it would prove conclusively that none of this was her doing because she had never had access to DZPro2.

"Whoever did this may have gained access to both CLAIRE and DZPro2. Maybe they stole the real data from both and left behind a corrupted version," Rosalind said.

"Could you repeat that in English, please?"

"Sorry," Rosalind said. "What you see here is the data from only one of two genes in that region of the chromosome. I don't have access to the data from the other gene, but it's possible that the other four commandments are there."

"That would be very important to know."

"Yes, in fact it is critical. It would tell us the true extent of the corruption, and it might get me off the hook."

"The big question is how did this get into the genetic code?"

"We think it is sabotage by a competitor. There is a lot of it these days, even in the vaunted halls of science. The company that is sponsoring this research has competitors who would love to compromise our efforts. But I shouldn't say any more. When they throw me in jail I want you to be able to deny knowing anything about this."

"Jail? For what?"

"I've signed dozens of non-disclosure agreements, non-competes, confidentiality agreements—you name it. PharmaGen owns my soul. But it might not matter, because I'm starting to think it might not be a competitor. The Biblical thing makes me think this whole thing might have been the work of Joseph Steele."

Gunquist laughed out loud. "I saw on the news tonight that you tangled with him," he said. "The video showed you bleeding. But another news show said it was blood that somebody threw on you. Then a story in the Journal said that you tried to attack Joseph Steele. And a story on Blog Chicago said you were arrested and taken off in handcuffs. That's a lot of versions of the same story. Sounds like somebody is confused. What's the truth?"

Rosalind had been so buried in her work that she hadn't seen a television or newspaper in over a week. The thought that she had been the subject of a news story made her nauseous. "I'm fine. Some crazy protester threw blood on me but I wasn't hurt. David had a cut lip, though. I didn't attack Steele; I just wanted him to stop lying. And no, I didn't get arrested."

"You weren't hurt, then?"

"Only my pride. But I think Steele would stop at nothing to shut us down. I think it is possible he messed with our data to intimidate us or make us look bad," she said.

"How would he be able to do that?"

"Hire someone like me to engineer the code and then hire a hacker to plant it."

"Rosalind, how sure are you that this data has been tampered with?"

It was her turn to laugh out loud. "There is no way, mathematically, that this could happen naturally. So either it's sabotage or it's a message from God."

"A message from God?" Gunquist raised one eyebrow.

"I'm kidding. There is no God, so it has to be sabotage."

"No God? Really? You're sure?"

Here we go, she thought. Ever the professor of theology. He'd challenged her thinking when she was his student, and by the look of things, he was going to challenge it now.

"Stefan, let's not waste time, here. Can we just agree that even if there were a God, he wouldn't write the Ten Commandments in genetic code?"

"No, we can't. It sounds exactly like something He would do. But I want to know what makes you so sure there is no God. Bad experience as a youngster? Academic brainwashing? Scientific desensitization? Everybody needs God."

"I don't," she snapped.

"Where's your sense of humor?"

"This isn't funny."

"The Ten Commandments written in our genes? You don't think that's funny?"

Rosalind sat up straight, her face flushed. "If you are trying to get me to talk religion with you, forget it!"

"I'm not talking religion. I'm talking God. Religion is a man-made construct, an attempt on the part of humans to connect with their creator. Sometimes it's very useful, sometimes incredibly harmful, but in the end, religion has more to do with the frailty of man than the majesty of God. I know. I grew up in a strict Methodist household. Wesley was a brave man, but he had no sense of humor. Neither do you. You used to."

"Fine then. Let's say there is a God. What does that have to do with this code?"

Dr. Gunquist sat quietly for a moment, staring at the pages in front of him.

"If someone went so far as to tamper with this data by inserting a passage from the Bible, then they obviously wanted you to find it. So, why did they spread out the message in such a fractured way over such a large stretch of DNA? Why not put it all in one long string where it would be easily detected?"

"Because genetic code naturally has gaps in it. Stretches of coding DNA are separated by stretches that don't code for anything that we know of," Rosalind said.

"So this mimics nature?"

"Yes."

"Maybe it *is* nature."

"The odds would be astronomical," she said.

"If you can put odds on it, then it is possible," Gunquist said. "It seems to me that there were much easier ways to mess up your work than to plant this incredibly complex message when a simple one would have worked just as well."

"Are you suggesting that this is something supernatural?"

Gunquist sat back and looked off into the blackness outside. The house was dark except for a single light in the kitchen above their heads. Gunquist sat in silence for several moments, his long, angular face looking ghostly and tired.

"Did you say this DNA comes from the middle of the second chromosome?" he said.

"Yes."

Gunquist got up and walked into his study and flipped on a light. He scanned the bookshelf for a moment, then pulled out two volumes. He brought them to the table and opened both.

"This is an abstract of an article presented to the National Academy of Sciences in 1991. I want you to read the abstract and tell me what it means."

Rosalind took a minute to read. "This article presents the evidence that there was a head-to-head fusion of two ancestral chromosomes that gave rise to the human second chromosome."

"Two chimp chromosomes fused to form what is now the second human chromosome?"

"Yes."

"Do you believe it?"

"Of course. The evidence is overwhelming: the fact that all primates have 24 chromosomes except humans, who have only 23, identical banding patterns—"

"Whoa. Banding patterns?"

"Yes, each chromosome has a unique pattern, like a bar code that distinguishes it from every other chromosome. If you lay the two chimp chromosomes over the human second chromosome, the banding patterns are nearly identical."

"OK. The evidence is overwhelming. There is a discrete place in the human genome where a monumental evolutionary change occurred. Isn't this the exact place you are studying? The place where the Ten Commandments are written?"

"Yes."

"Now I want to read you something else." He picked up the second volume.

"This is Pope John Paul II speaking to the *senatus scientificus*, the Pontifical Academy of Sciences, in 1996. Prior to this, evolution was accepted by the church merely as a theory. The Pope says, 'New knowledge has led to the recognition of the theory of evolution as more than a hypothesis. It is indeed remarkable that this theory has been progressively accepted by researchers, following a series of discoveries in various fields of knowledge.' The new knowledge he's referring to is the discovery of that chromosome fusion."

"Big deal," said Rosalind. "The Pope says the Bible and evolution aren't mutually exclusive. Tell me something I didn't already know."

"Here's the fun part. The Pope goes on to describe an 'ontological leap' that links material man and spiritual man. You see, all creatures on earth are defined as living matter. But we humans are different. Somewhere along the line, we made a leap beyond matter into the realm of soul. We are body *and* soul."

"My head is exploding," Rosalind said.

"My dear Rosalind, what I'm trying to tell you is that perhaps you have discovered precisely where that ontological leap took place. It is entirely conceivable that at the instant he created us, God sealed the deal by writing the Ten Commandments as an instruction manual for us and imprinted it where we would never lose it ... in our genes. And then he chose you, an atheistic molecular biologist from Chicago, to discover it. Now that's a sense of humor!"

Gunquist broke into rolling fits of laughter.

"This isn't funny."

"It's hysterical! Roz, you may have discovered the next clue in God's grand scheme. It started with the big bang, the emergence of human life, the Prophets, Jesus, Galileo, Mendel, Watson and Crick ... and now Rosalind Evans. Why not? Isn't that much more interesting than the reductionist scenario that casts us as nothing more than a bundle of chemicals that one day slithered out of the muck by accident?"

"You sound like Steele." This was not going the way Rosalind had hoped. "I'm a scientist, remember?"

"Ahhh," Gunquist said, leaning back. He was in his professorial glory. "So science is the only pathway to knowledge? Is that not the height of hubris? Might science be only one of many tools for solving the great mysteries? Like who lit the fuse on the Big Bang? After all, the universe didn't invent itself. Perhaps God remains unproven not because he is unprovable, but because we mere mortals haven't figured out a way to prove him yet. Think *big*, Rosalind!" Dr. Gunquist smiled at her and took her hand in his.

"Please, Stefan. I have bad history with God. I grew up going to Sunday school. Then I went to college and had my ideas about God challenged like everybody else did. Then science taught me that God is irrelevant. Then came David and I had to admit that sometimes our lives are so filled with grace that it couldn't possibly be coincidence. Then came Claire, and I knew with crystal clarity that God was embraceable. Nothing else could explain the miracle of that precious being in my life. For the first time, I was utterly humbled. I knew I had done nothing to deserve it, and I was so *grateful!*" Rosalind tossed the papers across the table. "And then she was gone." She sat back and looked at Gunquist intently. "At first, I hated

God, but that wore me out. Now, it's just easier to accept that we wander aimlessly and then we die. I am very happy with that."

"You don't seem happy to me."

"I'm as happy as I'm ever going to be. I have to finish this work because it will finally tell me why Claire had to die, and hopefully it will save other kids. So drop the God crap and let's get this done."

"We all want to discover the truth. But we had better have eyes to see it when we do," Gunquist said.

"I have the eyes of a scientist," Rosalind said.

He saw the weariness and sadness in her eyes and felt a stab of sympathy for the dear girl. "And beautiful eyes they are," he said. "But weary. Your spirit is weary, Rosalind." She gave him an annoyed look. "What happens when you stop feeding your body or your mind? It atrophies and begins to die. The same is true with your spirit."

"Maybe I don't have a spirit. I don't feel like I do."

"Of course you do. We all do. It is vital to our happiness and well-being. Dear Rosalind, you have a strong mind and body. But your spirit is failing. You must feed it."

"Feed it what?"

"Love, kindness, faith. Mostly it is hungry for God."

"First I have to find out what all this means," Rosalind said, holding up the papers. She rose to leave. He held her arm and walked her to the door.

"I've spent my life studying the personality of the Almighty," he said, "and this is right in character. He's planted clues to his existence all along. Why not place one in our genetic code? It's just as good a place as a stone tablet or the heart of a prophet. Rosalind, I don't know what you have found here, but I suspect it is more than meets the eye. I just wonder what the world will make of it. We humans are not very good at handling large truths. Tends to bring out the skeptic in us."

"The world will never know about this because I will never tell them. Neither will you, I hope. It's nothing more than a dirty trick. I just wish they'd done it to somebody else."

"Your secret is safe with me, Rosalind. The only thing that matters is that you find the truth. Keep your spirit open to the possibilities. Godspeed."

Rosalind hugged him goodbye, but she was already thinking about her next move. Her night was far from over.

Gunquist stumbled back to bed. But he did not sleep

Chapter 10

MICK THE TECH was nearly incoherent, lying on his back in bed, laptop on his chest, talking to his computer screen. He was willing the great Starry Messenger to reply to him about the genetic code sheets he'd sent him an hour ago. He stared at the glow of Starry's blog on the screen and was warmed by his brush with fame this evening, and warmed by the quart of Captain Morgan he was about to finish.

"Call me! I know you are reading the code I sent you right now. Call me, Dude!" Then, in a flash of insight available only to the profoundly drunk, he realized that no, wait, Starry Messenger is a *chick*. You're blonde, 5'7" with big boobs. Yah, oh yah, that's what you are. Starry, my baby. Everybody thinks you are a guy, but I know better! You're a girl. And you're hot for me even though you don't know it yet. Get to know me, baby. You wrote to me, now you need to call me! I want to hear your voice. I gave you my number, now call me. Mick the hunkin' Tech, that's me. Call me before I pass out! He laid there and fantasized about the goddess Starry Messenger. A screamer. A total screamer.

He was slurping the last shot of rum when the phone rang. He rolled up onto one elbow and fumbled with the phone, trying to find the right button to answer, but he couldn't see very well. It had to be Starry Messenger!

"'lo?"

"Mick? It's Rosalind."

It was Rozzie? Ha, I knew she would call. She can't stay away. I knew it. "Well, well … well. Hullo there. What can I do for yooo?" He was already thinking of several things he could do for her. She was a fooler that one. She didn't really dress sexy, but he could tell by the way she moved that she was a hot one. He loved the ones who were long and lean but had boobs, and he was pretty sure hers were real.

"I need your help with something."

"Betchya do."

Rosalind could tell by his voice that he was beyond smashed. She would have to work fast; this was her one and only chance to get what she needed.

"I love the way you handle computers. It's impressive," she said.

"That's not all I handle thas'impressive."

"I'll bet. Thanks for teaching me how to plug mine in. You're a good teacher."

"Any time," Mick said.

"Let's play pretend," she said.

"Oh yeeeah."

"Let's pretend that we are at work, and I ask you to show me the biggest computer you've got."

"Go ahead. Ask me."

"Show me the big one."

"Say it again."

"Show me the big one."

"Say it again."

"Show me the big one."

"OK, here, *look* at it." Mick laughed a throaty laugh.

"What if I want you to show me how to turn it on?"

"I'm turning it on right now." Mick laughed again.

"What do you do to get into the computer? What's the magic word?"

"My passcode?"

"Say it, Mick. I want to hear it."

"Uh uh, can't do that."

"I know, but just for pretend. Play along with me, Mick."

"Just for pretend?"

"Yes, just for now. Tell me."

"Wait, I got a new passcode. Uh ..." He went silent.

"Mick? Mick!"

"Huh? Oh yeah, Bitman7683."

"Then what?"

"Enter."

"Enter?"

"Ooh, you are one filthy bisch!" She heard his phone hit the floor.

"Mick? Mick?"

There was no answer.

Chapter 11

THE NIGHT WATCHMAN at Clearbrook Hall opened the door a crack. "May I help you?"

Rosalind held out her security tag. "Couldn't sleep, so I figured I'd get some work done."

The man smiled and let her in. "Be careful in the corridors. They're doing maintenance on the security cameras. It's dark and they leave their ladders all over the place. Makes for a pretty boring night for me," the man said. He pointed at his video console. Every monitor was dark. Rosalind breathed her first sigh of relief. Just as Mick said that morning, the cameras were down for maintenance. The Guard pointed at the biometric scanner. She laid her hand on it.

"Mother's maiden name?"

"Margeson."

"Thank you Dr. Evans. Have a nice night."

"Looks pretty quiet around here."

"They've got the computers shut down."

Rosalind pushed the 'up' button on the elevator so that the watchman would see her go up, in case he was ever asked. She stepped off on the fifth floor. Her office was quiet and uncharacteristically dark. The room was usually bathed in a grayish glow from the computer, but not tonight. Everything was shut down except the ANSR 1000. That monster never slept. Dyer could limit its use, but he couldn't shut it down completely. She left the light off, in case there was anyone else around who might see her.

She gave Claire's picture a quick kiss and reached into her pocket. She rolled Claire's marble between her fingers. She'd given away all of Claire's toys and clothes, the furniture and books—all of it. Except the marble. She had no clue why, but for some reason the smooth roundness of it gave her comfort.

In the dark, she opened another drawer and fished around for a thumb drive. I thought there was one here somewhere, she thought. She tried the next drawer. Then the next. No thumb drive. She found a box of DVDs. I guess I could use one of these.

She sat for a moment staring at Claire's photo. I'm scared, baby. If they catch me, it's the end. There is no lab on earth that would touch me. But I need to know. Dyer and Bradshaw don't understand how badly I need to *know*. I need to know what went wrong with your treatment. If the data is corrupted, I might have to start all over, baby. But I won't stop until I have the answer. She felt tears stinging her eyes. Not now, she thought. The weariness, the frustration, the fear in the pit of my stomach—it would be so easy to lose control. Don't. Not now. She stopped herself just short of falling into that dark place beyond tears where there is only a pain too heavy to bear. Sometimes the pain would paralyze her, but for reasons she didn't understand, sometimes it propelled her. She could never make it go away, but sometimes she could transform the heat of it into fuel for her work. She put the marble in her pocket and headed for the door.

She quickly negotiated the narrow enclosed staircase six stories down. At the bottom, she opened the stairwell door and peeked around it. There was no one there. She hurried down the darkened corridor toward the sequencing facility. The ANSR 1000 was located in a dedicated room in the building's central core, surrounded on all sides by corridors and offices. She knew that there were three main doors to the sequencing facility, one in each of three corridors. She guessed that Dyer would have them locked. She hoped Mick's bragging about having his own entrance to the ANSR 1000 would prove true. With the sequencing facility shut down, she reasoned that nobody would be in there. She passed down the corridor leading to the Tech Support Department. Up ahead she could see someone

in the hallway, a man in a uniform, standing with his back against the door
to the ANSR 1000. Using her most casual ballet gait, she walked by him and
gave a little wave.

"What are you doing here, Ma'am?"

Rosalind smiled at the man and held out her security tag. She couldn't
help noticing the gun in his holster. "Working. I thought I'd stretch my legs
and get myself a candy bar. There's a vending machine around here
somewhere."

"Have a good evening."

Rosalind turned the corner and quickly looked for Mick's office. His
name wasn't on any of the office doors. Then she noticed a door smaller
than the others with no window. Taped to it was a cut-out of the numeral 1
and a photo of none other than Mick himself. This guy never made it past
Junior High, she thought. The knob had no lock. She opened it and quickly
stepped in. She closed the door behind her and turned on her penlight. This
was Mick's office, alright. It was only big enough to hold a desk and file
cabinet, and on the wall behind the desk was a collection of photos of Mick
with a large variety of women. To the left of the desk was another door.
She quietly opened it. There in the cold dark room, visible only by its
twinkling indicator lights, was the ANSR 1000. The most powerful super-
computing cluster in the world. This massive piece of computational
achievement could sequence more DNA in 15 minutes than any other
computer could do in two weeks. It had data storage capacity a billion times
greater than any other sequencing cluster, and Rosalind was betting it
contained the one piece she needed: The DZPro2 analysis.

She stopped and cocked her ear again. It was all quiet. The three doors
leading to the corridors each had a window. Outside each she could see a
uniformed guard. She would have to keep her head down and work fast.
Right now they all had their back to the door, but that could change. She
moved quickly to the console and slid into the chair. She could hear her
heart pounding. Just type in Mick's passcode, she told herself, pull up the
file, put the DVD in the slot, hit copy, and you will have it made. Move, she
told herself. Do it! Her fingers were trembling. She typed BITMAN7683.
Nothing happened. Again she entered the code. Nothing. A shot of
adrenalin coursed through her. Had he given her the wrong passcode?

Again she pushed the keys, carefully, making sure her shaking fingers hit the right keys. BITMAN7683. The screen lit up. PLEASE ENTER USER NAME. User name! Mick hadn't given her one. She carefully typed MICK. She hoped a last name wasn't required because she couldn't remember Mick's. Everyone knew him as Mick the Tech. ERROR: USER NAME AND PASSCODE DO NOT MATCH. PLEASE REENTER USER NAME. She knew that the system would time out if she got it wrong. She could only imagine what he might have for a user name—studly, Greek god, youknowyouwantit—she typed MICK THE TECH and held her breath. It took a split second to process. Yes. She was in.

A menu of files flashed onto the screen. Masses of data, billions of bits of data. With gritty eyes she tried to focus on the endless list of files, grey letters on a white screen. The titles were not alphabetical. Listed by date? The DZPro2 had to have been sequenced and analyzed within the time period of the PharmaGen project. Squinting, she poured through the last six months worth of files. It has to be in here somewhere. She scrolled, slowly so she didn't miss anything. Every day new elements of the genome were identified and named. How in the world was she going to find the DZPro2 analysis in the midst of all that? Be patient, she told herself. Focus. Slowly, deliberately, she scrolled and searched. She looked at her watch. It would be dawn in a few minutes. People would start arriving for work. Was there a night security man who might walk in? She would have prayed if she thought there was a God out there to hear her. Slowly, she scrolled through the masses of lines of data. And then it caught her eye: DZPro2! Beads of sweat formed as she realized with a sense of wonderment that this was it. Her fingers hung over the mouse. She had it. She fumbled for the DVD in her bag, put it into the slot and hit copy. Her heart pounded. How long would it take to copy? Please don't let me get caught now that I'm so close.

She scrolled through the pages of the DZPro2 analysis on the screen. Her head swam. This analysis had become iconic to her. Clear proof that you value what you can't have. 'Analysis performed by J. Hazard.' There were hundreds of scientists at Clearbrook. She knew the name, but had never met J. Hazard, bless his or her heart. She stared at it, transfixed. It was like walking into the Forbidden City, page after page of translation code plus the scientist's analysis of what it all means. Months of work, hers for the taking. As much as she wanted to dive into it right then and there, she knew she needed to copy it and get out before she was discovered. What she was doing was not just illegal, it was punishable by death at the hands of Alan Dyer. It should only take a few minutes for the data to copy, she thought, and then I'm out of here.

Out of the darkness at the far end of the room came a noise. A shot of adrenaline brought her up straight. On cat's feet, she dove for a small alcove next to the ANSR 1000, where a tangle of wires was stowed. The door opened and a light came on. The alcove would provide cover for the moment, but it had no door. If someone walked in front of the opening, she would be in plain view. She held her breath. And then she heard singing. She peeked around and saw a young man sweeping the floor, headed her way. He was wearing headphones, singing and sweeping in time to the music. She ducked back into the alcove and stood stock still. He kept walking toward her until he was just a few feet from where she was standing. She held her breath. Out of the corner of her eye, she saw her bag sitting on the floor next to the console.

"Oh baby, oh baby, doot doot ..." He was way off key, bopping to the beat, blissfully unaware that he wasn't alone. He passed the opening to the alcove not more than a foot from her. He was so close that she could hear the music from his headphones. Just as he was about to turn her way, he stopped and looked down.

"Hmm." He picked up the bag and threw it over his shoulder. He continued sweeping in the other direction, forgetting about the alcove. "You and me, doot doot, wooo, oooh, doot doot ..."

My security tag is in there, my money, my work—all that matters is in there, she thought. Grab it. Grab it and run. No, you idiot, just chill. Abruptly, he stopped singing, put the bag down, and yanked the IPod from his pocket. She ducked her head back into the alcove before he had a chance to look up. He tapped on the IPod with his finger, then ripped the earphones out and put the whole thing in his pocket. "Piece of crap's outta juice." He continued to sweep in the silence. She hoped he couldn't hear her heart thumping.

At that moment, the DVD finished copying and the slot opened with a click. He turned and looked at it with a curious expression.

"Well hello there. Hmm. Didn't know anybody was down here." He reached over, pulled out the DVD, and looked around the room.

"Hello? Anybody here? Your DVD is done." He cocked his head, listening. "Hello?"

She stayed put. He shouldered the bag again, stuck the DVD in the bag, and went on sweeping. His cell phone rang.

"Hey, baybeee. Nothin'. Just workin' in the hole, you know ..." He set the broom against the wall, shoved open the door with his foot and walked out into the main hallway. She moved to the window and peeked out. The guard was standing near the door, looking at the janitor. The janitor nodded to him and held out his tag, then walked up to a vending machine and fished in his pocket for change. Finding none, he reached into her bag and pulled out her wallet. He pawed through it and pulled out a fold of bills. He took a single and stuffed the rest back into her wallet.

He bought a soda and set the bag down. She could see him talking animatedly on the phone as he popped open the can. She looked at her watch. It was almost 5 am. Employees could begin arriving any minute.

Holding his soda in one hand and his phone in the other, the young man leaned against the wall and carried on his conversation. He was in no hurry. Slowly he sipped his soda. He shifted from one foot to the other. He laughed. He listened. Then he looked at the guard and turned away, as if he didn't want anyone to hear what he was saying. He turned and took a few steps down the hall. He stepped into an office to continue his conversation, leaving the bag on the floor.

Rosalind made a beeline for Mick's door and into his closet-office. She peeked out the door into the corridor and saw that the guard was looking in the other direction. She quietly exited and calmly walked down the main hallway. "Oh, there it is," she said, and casually picked up her bag. She smiled at the guard and sauntered down the hall.

"Hold it, lady. Put that down."

She turned and faced the guard. "It's my bag."

"Let me see your tag."

She held it out to him. She felt lightheaded, as if she were standing on a very high cliff.

"Do you have identification in the bag?"

She pulled out her driver's license and held it out to him. He studied it for a moment.

"All right. Thank you."

Rosalind turned and calmly walked the length of the corridor to the stairwell. She flew up to the fifth floor, took the elevator down, gave the watchman a cheery wave, and walked out the main front door. It would be a real shame to get caught at this stage of the game, she thought, now that I'm a bona fide thief.

The cool dawn air greeted her like a song. The streets were deserted. The lights up and down Chicago Avenue twinkled gaily as day began to break. Things were normal, and for now at least, she was safe. She felt the lovely cool breeze blowing through her hair. She was so relieved that she giggled out loud. "I did it!" she said to no one. She had in her possession everything she needed to get down to the truth. Relieved and exhausted, she headed for home.

Dawn was emerging in creeping threads of silver across the still surface of Lake Michigan. Gulls squawked and swooped as the first joggers bobbed along the lakefront path. Within moments of first light, the sun burst over the horizon and turned the soaring Chicago skyline a lurid neon pink. It was a brief but spectacular moment, a fitting punctuation to the strangest night of her life. As exhausted as she was, she felt exhilarated enough to walk the two miles home. I can see why thieves get hooked, she thought. The high is amazing.

When she got home, she opened the refrigerator and grabbed a carton of orange juice and a loaf of bread. She thought about how good a hot shower was going to feel. While the bread was toasting, she put her head down on the table to rest. She was asleep in seconds.

Two hours later, the phone woke her up. "Dr. Evans? This is Naibu, Dr. Bradshaw's assistant. He asked me to call you. He would like to see you in his office as soon as possible. He is kicking one of the Foo Dogs, Scout I think."

"Scout?"

"Or maybe it's Ed. One of them. Anyway, the cognac bottle is empty, too. How soon can you get here?"

Chapter 12

BRADSHAW POUNCED ON Rosalind the minute she walked in. He was listing slightly to starboard and smelled of strong drink. She braced herself for the worst: *he knows I stole the data and he's going to fire me.* Her heart pounded, and she held on to the back of a fuchsia velvet chair to steady herself.

Bradshaw held a piece of paper in his outstretched hand. "This is an e-mail from a friend of mine, congratulating me for our earth-shattering discovery of a message from God in the genetic code while engaged in a top secret research project funded by PharmaGen," Bradshaw said, his face purple with rage. "He learned this fascinating bit of information on the Internet of all places!"

"How … who …" Rosalind was utterly perplexed. This was not what she expected.

Shaking, Bradshaw shoved the piece of paper into her hand. It was a copy of an article from the Starry Messenger blog. She scanned the first few sentences.

From Clearbrook Institute: God In Our Genes?

Have you ever noticed that just about the time you hit your stride in your gallop through the universe, somebody sticks their foot out and trips you? Just when we were feeling smug about the difference

between science and religion, what emerges but a message from God in our DNA?

What do you think is going on at the Clearbrook Institute in Chicago? What's trying to happen here? Scientists there ...

Bradshaw stood by the window and drummed his fingernails on the glass. "Starry Messenger, no less. Half the people on the planet have already read this and I haven't had my breakfast yet!" Bradshaw smelled the acrid smoke of his career going up in flames. "How did Starry Messenger find out about this?"

"I don't know." Rosalind said.

"Wrong! You told him."

"No."

"Who else could have done it?" Bradshaw was yelling at her and pulling his hair at the same time. "When Dyer finds out about this, we're toast," Bradshaw said. "If you leaked this, I'll have your job. If Dyer doesn't have mine first."

"Wait a minute," Rosalind said. "Mick Tech was in the hallway just outside the room."

"He was?"

"I asked him to stay in case something went wrong with the projection system. I saw him watching through the door."

"Why would he tell Starry Messenger? He knows that if he broke the confidentiality agreement he'd lose his job and probably go to jail."

"About the time Dyer decided to shut us down I looked out the door and didn't see Mick. He told me later that he took a phone call. Maybe he didn't hear Dyer warn us about the confid agreement. It had to have been Mick."

"Call him. Tell him to drop whatever he's doing and come to your office NOW."

"Me? Why?"

"You're a broad."

She dialed the Tech Support number and fumbled her phone to her ear.

"Hi Mick," she said, trying to sound calm and flippant. "This is Rosalind Evans. Could you come to my office? Now. Good."

Mick shuffled from his office across the hallway toward the elevator. His head felt like a lit cherry bomb. He had a dim memory of talking to her the night before, something about his big one. He couldn't remember if it had a happy ending.

He walked into Rosalind's office wearing his best 'I know what you want' smile. When he saw Bradshaw standing there, his face fell. What's that ugly creep doing here, he wondered.

"Mick," Bradshaw began, "I want to thank you for your help with the technical details yesterday. You did a fine job."

Mick nodded. "Thanks. It's what I do."

"I imagine you thought Dr. Evan's presentation was pretty interesting?"

Mick raised an eyebrow. "Yes. I did."

"In fact, there was something about her on Starry Messenger last night. I guess you put that out there, huh?"

Mick smiled. "Yeah, I did. Starry Messenger was totally impressed. She wrote me back!"

Mick gave Roz his best crooked smile, but she didn't smile back. He looked at Bradshaw. He wasn't smiling either. Mick suddenly felt like a frog at the bottom of a ten-gallon bucket. "What did you need my help for?"

"She called to get you here so that I could tell you that you're fired. You know full well that you are not allowed to talk about anything having to do with work on the outside."

"But …" Mick was stunned. He never used his real name on-line, for that very reason. "Wait a minute. You're not my boss. You can't fire me."

"Oh, yeah. I can."

"But …"

"Save it. Not only did you violate University policy, you also violated an iron-clad confidentiality agreement between the university and PharmaGen. I suggest you go quietly. And call a lawyer."

"You little rat!" Mick picked up Bradshaw by both lapels and lifted him to his eye level. "You're gonna be sorry for this, you miniature piece of shit!" He discarded Bradshaw like a dirty rag. He turned to Rosalind.

"You! You can forget about the big one!" He shook his hair back and stomped out.

Rosalind reached out a hand to help Bradshaw up. He waved her off. His cell phone rang. "Bradshaw!" he said. He pulled himself halfway to a sitting position and listened for a minute, his face a study in misery, until the call ended. "Let's go," he said, scrambling to his feet. "Dyer and Gleason are on their way."

Chapter 13

RON VANIERE WAS scanning the blogs to see what was hot this morning and found no fewer than a dozen accounts of the Steele rally, each telling a different story. One said that Rosalind Evans was taken to the hospital. Another said that she had a history of anti-religion activism. In another, Vaniere himself was quoted saying that Rosalind was taken away by police. He had never said it.

He shook his head. *Why do I work so hard to dig up the facts when nobody cares?* He turned to the Starry Messenger blog, looking for political pearls. To his surprise, the lead story again had a Chicago connection.

From Clearbrook Institute: God In Our Genes? ...

He quickly scanned the article. When the name Rosalind Evans emerged in this story, he got very interested. Rosalind Evans, the eminent genomic scientist, had discovered fragments of biblical text in the genetic code? Vaniere laughed out loud. *This is great,* he thought. *Finally, some comic relief.* But as he read on, he could see that Starry Messenger wasn't laughing. *Was he taking it seriously? What was going on?* He quickly checked several other related blogs and found that they had the story as well, again, each with its own unique spin. Some implied it was real. Others said it was a hoax. Others took a conspiratorial tone, saying it was some kind of supernatural event. A quick scan of the TV news networks showed that they did not have the story. He grabbed his iPhone and dialed.

"Evans Lab."

"May I please speak with Dr. Evans?"

"I saw her come in, but I think she's in a meeting."

"Is her meeting there at Clearbrook Hall?"

"Yeah, I think she went up to Dr. Bradshaw's office."

"Thanks." Vaniere hung up. His next call was to his cameraman. Sometimes a stake-out was the best way to get the story. Unguarded, people usually gave pretty straight answers. It was when they had time to think things over that the story could get fuzzy. At least that was true in politics. He and his cameraman scrambled into the van and headed for Clearbrook Hall.

* * *

Up in Bradshaw's office, there was no preamble, no pretense. Dyer leaned down close to Bradshaw's face and spoke in measured tones.

"There is a story on Starry Messenger that names us as sponsors of a top secret leukemia research project that has discovered a message from God written in the genetic code. That's four problems in one sentence, problems I didn't have eight hours ago." Dyer circled the coffee table. "The story speculates about whether this is a proof of the existence of God or a scientific mistake. That's two *more* problems, for a total of six things that are totally ruining my day. Now, I would be tempted to blow this off as a fluff piece except that it is going viral even as we speak. It's being picked up by blogs around the world."

Rosalind stood stock-still. Dyer was exhibiting the behaviors of a hungry predator, wide-eyed and circling.

"In less than 24 hours we have gone from a respected force in the pharmaceutical business to a laughingstock. Yesterday only four of us knew anything about a Bible verse, and now half the population of the planet knows. Somebody blabbed, and it wasn't me. Was it you, Ben? Did you tell Starry Messenger? Or perhaps it was you Rosalind?"

Dyer tossed a handful of printouts of web stories on Bradshaw's desk. "This isn't exactly the kind of corporate image we are trying to cultivate," Dyer said through clenched teeth. He walked slowly toward her. "Rosalind, did you talk to anyone about the so-called Bible verse we all saw yesterday?" His dead calm voice unnerved her.

"No, but I know who did. It was Mick the Tech. He wasn't in the room when you talked about the non-disclosure agreement."

"Mick the Tech? How did he know about it?"

"He was standing just outside the door. I asked him to stay in case I had a problem with the projector."

Bradshaw scurried over to Dyer. "I've already taken care of it," he said with exaggerated gravity.

"You fired him?" Dyer said.

Bradshaw nodded. "You bet I did."

"You don't suppose that might motivate him to do us more harm?" Dyer said.

Bradshaw froze. It had never crossed his mind.

"Sometimes danger will masquerade as a solution, Ben. You need to remember that," Dyer said. "And of course you cancelled his pass-code?"

Bradshaw looked like he'd been shot. He grabbed his cell phone and dialed Sam Lockett in Information Services.

Dyer calmly pulled a folded paper from his breast pocket and handed it to Rosalind. "I've prepared a response to Starry Messenger over your signature."

Rosalind read the typed statement. It denied categorically that anything unusual was found in the genetic code. It affirmed that the research was proceeding full speed ahead and that the lives of thousands of children depended on finding new therapies for leukemia. It concluded,

'I know how the parents of sick children feel, what they face every day watching their babies suffer. My own daughter died of leukemia a year and a half ago. PharmaGen has shown exceptional generosity with this project, which they had hoped to keep confidential until the results could be reported. However, now that it has been made public, they wish to reaffirm their deep commitment to sick children everywhere. I consider it my sacred responsibility to do everything I can to make sure that one day soon no child will ever suffer as my precious daughter Claire did. I know Claire would want us to continue. Thank you.'

Rosalind crumpled the paper in her fist. "You are using my daughter's death to try and salvage your reputation? How dare you."

Dyer calmly looked away from her and took a sip of coffee.

"I won't let you bring Claire into this!"

"It's too late. I've already sent the memo to Starry Messenger."

Rosalind felt like she'd been punched in the gut. This man is beneath contempt, she thought. She felt tears of frustration welling in her eyes. She turned and left.

* * *

Out in front of Clearbrook Hall, Ron Vaniere checked his watch. He was about to call Evans again, when she suddenly emerged from the building. She was moving quickly, lugging a shoulder bag. She looked as if she had been crying.

"Let's go!" Vaniere grabbed his wireless mic and Bert his camera, and they bounded out of the van. They rushed up the steps toward her before she realized they were there.

"Dr. Evans. Nice to see you again. Can I ask you some questions about the story on the Starry Messenger blog? How did you discover a Bible verse in the genetic code and what did it say?"

"I can't talk right now." She wiped her eyes with a tissue.

"The gene with the bible verse. According to the Starry Messenger blog, you claim to have found ancient scripture written in genetic code. Is that true?"

"No. I mean, sometimes the code spells out words. It is nothing unusual. It's not what it looks like!" Rosalind held her hand up to shield her face from the camera. She was still raging about the memo Dyer had sent to Starry, and now this jerk was badgering her.

"PharmaGen is funding your research. What do they have to say about all this? Do they think it is a message from God?"

"Who said anything about God?"

"Are they saying it is some kind of prank?"

"Not a prank exactly …"

"So you're saying it's true?"

"I'm saying it … no … I'm saying …" Her voice trembled and her reddened eyes flashed at Vaniere. He was confusing her. She wanted to tell him it was corporate espionage, but if she said that, Bradshaw would wring her neck. She just wanted to get out of there.

"Dr. Evans, how often does something like this …"

Her mascara was forming black rivulets down either side of her face. "I don't know what the odds are of the genetic code spelling out the Ten Commandments like that, but it …"

"Wait … the Ten Commandments? I thought it was just a few words. Are you saying it was the Ten Commandments?"

"Yes, I think … it looks like it is …"

"How did it get there?" Vaniere said.

"Stop it! I can't talk about this right now!" Rosalind pushed Vaniere hard, knocking him into Bert, and causing the camera to shake. Bert got it under control and kept the camera on her.

Vaniere watched her as she disappeared down the street. He'd hoped she would give him more detail, but he could see by her eyes that something deeper was going on than just a prank. He had seen that look in her eyes the day before, a look of underlying sadness tinged with fear, as if she were being chased. What demons are haunting that woman, he wondered. She is running, but from what?

* * *

Later in the editing suite at InfoNet, Vaniere, the editor, and the producer of the evening news stood looking at the raw footage of Rosalind on the steps at Clearbrook Hall.

"I admit it is good visually, but there's no story. Even if there were, I don't have room for this in prime time," the producer said. "There's breaking news. They found out that the boyfriend of Senator Rockwell's daughter might have cheated on his college entrance exams. This is big," the producer said.

"You gotta be kidding me!" Vaniere shot back. "The woman on this video is one of the top researchers at one of the most elite universities in the world. Don't you think the public has the right to know that she is claiming she found the Ten Commandments written in the genetic code?" Vaniere said.

"Don't lecture me about the public's right to know. They have a right to know everything, but I only have so much time. That's why *I* decide what the public will know and what they won't!"

"Look, you've got mystery, intrigue, God, science—you've even got a mad scientist. She's wild-eyed and she's hot. What more do you want?"

"No, *this* is what I've got—a crazy woman making a ridiculous claim. That's not a story. If you can figure out what the real story is, I'll give you two minutes at the end of the show." The Producer walked out, texting on his phone and swearing under his breath.

Vaniere turned back to the editing screen. "We only have two minutes for the whole story. But I don't see anything I want to cut. This is great footage," Vaniere said.

"I don't get it," the editor said. "This broad found the Ten Commandments written in the genetic code? How does that happen?"

"That's what she says. Starry Messenger posted the code on-line. I downloaded it. It's the Ten Commandments alright. Nobody seems to know how it got there, but it's there. It might all be a big joke, but she wasn't laughing, that's for sure."

"Doesn't seem like your kind of story, buddy. Seems a little soft in the middle."

"Ah ha. You see? That's why I'm a TV news icon and you're sitting here in the dark. You watch. By this time tomorrow, this story will have legs."

"What *is* the story?" The editor looked confused.

"This woman is a respected scientist," Vaniere explained. "Something happened that upset her and scared her. Why did she try to get close to Steele at the rally? How did she find the Bible verse in the genetic code? Why was she so afraid to talk to me? It's a clash of science and religion, with a brilliant, beautiful scientist in the middle of it. It'll probably turn out to be a hoax or a trick, but for now, we have issues everyone can relate to. What's scarier than God? OK, play it again, Sam."

The editor looked at him with a smirk. "What, you hot for her or something? You've watched it two dozen times. There's nothing more to see. C'mon, man, I gotta cut the priest. I don't have all day."

Vaniere couldn't take his eyes off of Rosalind Evans's face. There was something in her expression he couldn't describe, something vulnerable and frightened. No guile whatsoever. The fact that she was scared made it golden. Emotional appeal was the nut of any good story, and the king of all emotions was fear. The trick would be to dig through the layers, all the way down to the fear. What if this woman actually did find the Ten Commandments written in the genetic code? What if it isn't sabotage? Or a hoax? Or a lab mistake? What if this really is a God thing? Terrifying thought.

"Hey, Ron, wake up. How do you want me to cut this footage?" the editor said.

"Don't. Run it uncut. Freeze frame a close up of her face at the end. Zoom in on it until the fear jumps out at you. I want viewers to feel her fear."

"You are hot for her. You ever date white girls?"

"That's not what this is about. I'm not hot for her. I just think she makes good news."

"How do you want me to cut the priest?"

"When I ask him whether she's a heretic, he says maybe. Cut it there. His words say one thing, but his face says another. Use that. And get me the footage of the Steele rally, the part where she's grabbed by the cops and the protester throws blood on her. I'll voice-over it live on air."

Vaniere jumped up and headed for the door. The tyrant clock was bearing down on him. He had less than two hours to get the piece ready for air, and he still had copy to write. His calls to Bradshaw and Alan Dyer were still unanswered. It would have been good to get their story, but that would have to wait. He turned and yelled over his shoulder, "Remember: without conflict, there is no story. I want this piece to look like a Chicago version of *The Exorcist*."

"I'm lovin' this. Little Ronnie goes to church. I just hope you still have a job tomorrow, Dude."

Chapter 14

IN LIVING ROOMS, bars, health clubs, and hotel rooms all across America, 30 million TVs were tuned to the six o'clock news, four million of them to InfoNet. Grimly determined to stay informed, if not titillated or outright horrified, everyday Americans turned their attention to the nightly smorgasbord of election season delights. They patiently endured the stories of murder, terrorism, high crimes and misdemeanors in order to get to the meat of American politics—The Great Beratement known as the presidential campaign. It was a World Boxing Association heavyweight extravaganza with suits and ties. The coup de grâce was Vaniere's laser beam political analyses. That's what the viewers tuned in for, but tonight, it's not what they got.

In the studio, Vaniere checked his look one last time. As always, the white shirt was the centerpiece; the way it contrasted with his dark skin. Then there was the suit. He was particularly fond of this cut because it gave definition to his still-fit physique. Good-fitting clothes were difficult for former jocks, even those like him whose football career ended with college graduation. Hair was not a concern; his was shaved to a short stubble that accented the perfect shape of his cranium. At 39, he no longer had the chops to deal with hair-fight. When he did the shave a year ago, it gave him a five-point boost in viewer ratings. He'd never looked back. He cleared his throat, readied his white-toothed smile, and took his cue.

"Yesterday we told you about an incident in Chicago involving Rev. Joseph Steele and Clearbrook genetic researcher Rosalind Evans."

The scene cut to tape of Rosalind being hustled away from Steele by police and mixing it up with protestors, as Vaniere continued—

"Before her tussle with Steele and the demonstrators, Dr. Evans told me that contrary to what Rev. Steele said yesterday, they do not conduct embryonic stem cell research at Clearbrook Institute. Federal funding for embryonic stem cell research was outlawed, reinstated, and now is again illegal, but Evans asserts that it has never been a part of Clearbrook's work. This would seem to conflict with the story of Betty Freud, the distraught mother who came to Clearbrook to have stem cells extracted from her aborted fetus to save her injured child. Whether that story is true or not remains a mystery. Meanwhile, Steele has filed suit to have Clearbrook shut down. It appears that Evans was trying to set Steele straight when she approached him at the rally. But neither he nor members of his audience were buying it. They blocked her way and threw a bottle of blood on her."

The scene shifted back to Vaniere in the studio. He held up a copy of the DNA translation code.

"This morning, Dr. Evans told me that in the course of a research project she is working on, she made a startling discovery: The Ten Commandments written in the genetic code. What she didn't say was how it got there or what it means."

The scene cut to the tape of the interview with Rosalind on the steps of Clearbrook Hall. The camera gave viewers a true sense of her panicked, almost incoherent state. Vaniere smiled inwardly. This was good theater. It wasn't politics, but at least he was on the air, and that made it a very successful day. When the camera freeze-framed on Rosalind's face, the scene came back to Vaniere live.

"We tried to contact officials from the Clearbrook Institute, but they declined to speak with us. The sponsor of Dr. Evans' project, PharmaGen Pharmaceutical, also is not commenting. So what's going on here? I spoke with Father John Newsom of St. Joseph Catholic Church about Evans's claim."

The scene shifted to tape of Vaniere and Father Newsom standing in front of the church. The priest was smiling, looking very comfortable in front of the camera. A marble figure of the crucified Jesus loomed behind them. Church bells sounded in the distance.

"The notion of a message from God in our DNA is preposterous. I believe this must be some kind of hoax," the priest said. Then he chuckled. "It would be nice if it were true. Life would be a lot easier if God spoke to us in plain English, wouldn't it?"

"Is it possible that God is sending some kind of message through the genetic code? A modern version of Moses and the tablets?" Vaniere asked.

"No. It is not for us to fully understand the depth of God's mystery. That is why we must have faith. Any attempt to portray God in human terms, other than in the person of Jesus, is heretical."

"Are you saying Rosalind Evans is a heretic?"

"It's possible. But let's be charitable: Until we have proof otherwise, she is merely confused," the priest said.

The scene shifted back to Rosalind's face, freeze-framed in fear. Vaniere's voice-over continued. "Has Rosalind Evans uncovered the site of the soul? Found the missing link between religion and science? Or is it all a hoax? What is the connection, if any, with Joseph Steele? Who is the real Dr. Rosalind Evans? And most importantly, has she proved the existence of God?"

The scene shifted back to Vaniere live in the studio. "This story first came out in the middle of last night when Starry Messenger broke it on his blog. Check it out. Whatever you think of it, the story is stirring up deep emotion in many people, and scaring the bejeezus out of others. We'd like to know how you feel. Let us know at **www.InfoNet.com/Vaniere**."

Vaniere was back in his office collecting e-mails after the broadcast, when the producer stormed in.

"What's wrong with you?! You sent viewers to Starry Messenger? Are you out of your mind?!" The producer yanked on his hair and spun 360 degrees.

Vaniere sucked on a beer. "Slow down pal. I didn't send anyone anywhere. People go there whether I tell them to or not. We get four million viewers a night; Starry Messenger gets twenty times that. He's more popular than God. Have you ever had a meaningful conversation where Starry's name *didn't* come up?"

"I've never had a meaningful conversation." The producer shrugged and walked out.

Vaniere turned back to his computer. Already viewer e-mails were pouring in, verifying his hunch that this story would touch a nerve. Opinions were all over the map: Evans was nuts. Vaniere had reached a new low. InfoNet ought to be ashamed for airing a ridiculous story like that. One person claimed to know Evans as an honest, decent person dedicated to the "highest standards of scientific integrity," and shame on him for putting her in a bad light.

Vaniere put his feet up on the desk and smiled. This was a better story than he even thought at first. Chewy. Viewers were inflamed. Nice. Very nice. And how dare they accuse me of putting Rosalind Evans in a bad light? She did that all by herself.

Chapter 15

THE NEXT MORNING, every TV news network in America had the story. Each ran their own version, quoting Vaniere and Starry Messenger as their sources. Rosalind was hailed as the new Messiah, the antichrist, a candidate for sainthood, a charlatan, an infidel, a crazy, bereaved woman who ought to get help. Each news organization presented the story in nuanced language, subtly configured to convey a sense of mystery, import, and most of all, fear. Who is this mysterious Rosalind Evans? Is this really a massive hoax? The end of times? Over and over again, the telecasts featured the image of the translation code from Rosalind's presentation. And over and over again they stated that Rosalind Evans claimed that her discovery proves the existence of God.

The only person in America who didn't see any of it was Rosalind Evans herself. She had avoided contact with mass media all the previous evening precisely because she feared seeing her own face plastered all over TV and the Internet. Now, for the third morning in a row, she was standing in Benton Bradshaw's office under the unrelenting glare of a man beyond distraught.

"The phone hasn't stopped ringing," Bradshaw said. "Naibu has already taken messages from the Archdiocese of Chicago, the President of the University, Senator Bosch, Alan Dyer, and dozens of ordinary citizens demanding an explanation. I only wish I had one."

"Explanation for what?" Rosalind said.

"For why the world thinks we actually *believe* the Ten Commandments are written in the genetic code!"

"They are."

"Stop it! They are not, or wouldn't be if you hadn't said they are!" He paused and looked at her, believing he was making perfect sense.

"Since when is this *my* fault?" Rosalind asked. She overcame the urge to slap him silly.

"You opened your big fat mouth to a reporter. It's the worst thing you could have done. You can't trust those people!" Bradshaw's eyes were glassy, and he smelled strongly of liquor. She hoped he would pass out.

"He ambushed me. He shoved a camera in my face. What was I supposed to do?"

"This thing is past the tipping point! Forty-eight hours ago we were the most prestigious research institution in the world. Now, we're a three-ring circus!"

"Why am I the scapegoat here? If you want to blame somebody, blame whoever messed with my data."

"Nobody did it!! Dyer brought in a half dozen top security experts and so far they haven't found any evidence that the computers were hacked."

"Well somebody obviously tampered with the data. How else could that text be there, word for word?"

"Word for word? How do you know that?"

"I went through the entire 28 pages of translation code and found it. Somebody went to a lot of trouble to plant this," Rosalind said.

"Why didn't you tell me that before?"

"When was I going to do that? I couldn't get a word in edgewise with you and Dyer. And then I went home to bed. I've been there ever since."

Bradshaw took the last swig of booze from his coffee cup and fell heavily onto the leather sofa. "Dyer wants you out."

"No! Ben, please! Let me talk to him myself. I'll apologize. I'll grovel. I'll do whatever it takes!"

"Not only should you not talk to him, you should turn around right now and go home. You don't want to be here when the president of the University gets here, which will be any minute. I can protect you from him for now, but not if he gets to you directly. Don't forget; he's the one who signs our paychecks. Go home. Better yet, get out of town for a while and don't tell anybody where you are."

"I'm not going anywhere. There is a rational explanation for all of this, and I'm going to find it."

Bradshaw jumped up and charged at her like a deranged Chihuahua.

"Where have you been for the last 24 hours?! Don't you watch the news? You are Dr. Frankenstein and the Clearbrook Institute is your evil laboratory. PharmaGen is paying you to do the devil's work, and half the people in America think it's the end of the goddam world! Don't you think it's a little late for rational explanations?" He kicked one of the ceramic Foo Dogs.

"Is that Scout?" Rosalind said.

"No, dammit, it's Ed." He looked at his watch. "If you leave right now, you'll get out before the president gets here. If you wait, I can't guarantee he won't fire you the minute he sees you."

Chapter 16

THE STAFF AT Steele Ranch in Dallas, Texas was busy with final preparations for the summit meeting, which was to begin at noon. From all over the country, the luminaries of the First Light Campaign were gathering to make a strategic plan for the next phase of the campaign. Everyone on staff, from the cooks to the carvery masters to the candle-lighters, was on high alert as the moment approached for the serving of the opening meal. Reverend Joseph Steele was making a final pass-through inspection of the great hall. He stopped at the head of the twenty-foot long hand-hewn oak table and smiled.

"Ah, nice touch on those flowers; good strong colors. Bold. Sets a nice tone for the day. Why the blue dishes rather than the red?"

"We are serving beef, sir. Beef on red is no good. Red is for fish or chicken. I think you'll be pleased with the presentation on the blue," said the event director.

Steele laughed and patted him on the back. He couldn't care less what color the dishes were, only that the man could rationalize the decision. A good rationale is something a man should always have on the tip of his tongue.

Steele had just put the finishing touches on the agenda for the day, and he was quite pleased with it. His board of directors was composed of smart, passionate people who understood the urgency in keeping the spotlight on the social and moral issues surrounding genetic research. Each member had volunteered their time, expertise and influence because they believed in the cause. Today, there would be reports on budget and campaign rally statistics, with the balance of the day devoted to media strategies. During his recent time in the media spotlight, he had come to understand the complexities of trying to stay there. It wasn't easy. You had to keep topping yourself, because once the media looked away, it was very hard to get them to look back.

The First Light Campaign rallies were the cornerstone of the media strategy. Not only did they serve to recruit and fire up new adherents, they attracted media like a magnet.

Steele had just one hour before the start of the luncheon meeting. He sat down at the computer in his study and scanned his RSS notifications. He noticed several stories that were red flagged. Thinking with relish that the stories would be about him, he quickly clicked on the first one, the Starry Messenger blog. He had headlined the Starry several times lately, the surest sign that he was at the top of the media game. Yesterday, there had been a flurry of stories linking him with that crazy woman who had accosted him in Chicago, but with all the preparation he had to do for today's conference, he hadn't spent much time reading them.

What he saw now made his heart sink. This Rosalind Evans woman was all over the Starry Messenger blog. She owned it. His name was nowhere to be found.

Steele would have found it funny if he weren't so threatened by it. He clicked on links, one after another, and saw that the Internet was full of it. With growing anger, he read story after story about this woman, whoever she was, from the Clearbrook Institute. This must be some kind of rotten joke! Someone was trying to get back at him for trying to shut them down! Rosalind Evans had totally stolen the news cycle. She even elbowed out the Presidential campaign. He read one story after another, and with each one, his heart sank further. How did this woman get so famous so fast?

At the appointed hour, the twelve members of the First Light Campaign cabinet filed into the great hall. Among them was The Rev. Eddie Rapp of Cincinnati, noted expert on Biblical principles of physical life and death. He had been a member of the cabinet since it began just over a year ago, and he brought to the table a massive knowledge of Christian interpretations of how and when life begins and ends. He had eagerly accepted Steele's invitation to join the First Light Board because, as Rapp put it, "Life and death is the province of God. We need to set the people's collective mind straight about who carries their water!" The board also included Saul Runyon, a former Presidential media strategist, Barbara 'Babs' Babcock, senior researcher at Danka-Saba Pharmaceutical Company, Reverend Dan Markie of the California Seekers Union and Pastor Shabazz Dunready of the New Life Temple Stove (We Heat You Up!) of Chicago. It was a group carefully chosen by Steele for their diverse expertise in matters of science and religion, and for their willingness to tell him what they thought. They were all highly successful and Steele loved to hear them out—so long as they remembered in the end who the boss was.

The group was in high spirits. The recent series of rallies in seven cities across the country had been a smashing success. Each had garnered good media coverage, and the collective effect was that of a vigorous national movement that had gotten the attention of all the cable news channels, the major denominational offices, and even the White House. They had received word that the President of the United States would soon announce the appointment of Rev. Steele to a special task force on Ethics in Genetics. The First Light Campaign had succeeded in bringing the ethical questions surrounding genetic manipulation to the American agenda. As Steele had long suspected, his anti-genetics crusade touched a widely held fear that technology was run amok, and that unchecked, science would do unspeakable harm to the sanctity of life. People knew deep down that life and death were the province of God alone. The science of genetics was dangerously close to playing God. He believed the tide of public opinion was turning his way.

The mood at the table was celebratory as lunch began. It was not until the salads were served that they began to wonder about their leader, who had not yet made an appearance. His assistant was dispatched to find him.

The assistant knocked on his study door. "Rev. Steele, are you in there?"

"Not now!" Steele yelled through the closed door.

"Reverend, everyone is waiting. The salads have been served."

"Save me one! I'll be there as soon as I can!"

Just as dessert was served, Steele stumbled into the great hall. His collar was open, his hair disheveled. "I asked you all here to begin work on the next phase of our campaign, the political agenda, to figure out how we are going to keep the issue in the media spotlight and get laws passed to support our beliefs. But something urgent has come up. There's a woman out there claiming to have discovered a message from God in the genetic code, and she's all over the news. Everywhere you look, there she is. TV, newspapers, Internet, Starry Messenger. We can't afford that."

"I read about that," said Saul Runyon, the media strategist. "I thought it was all a joke."

"Of course you did, Saul, you are a practical man. Don't you realize that it doesn't matter whether it is a joke or not? It's the lead story. We have spent a year training the media to drink out of our bowl, and we are absolutely not gonna let this woman get in our way. Her name is Rosalind Evans. She's the one who attacked me at the Chicago rally. Now she's stolen the news cycle from us. I think she's doing this because we are trying to shut down the Clearbrook Institute where she works!"

Babs Babcock of Danka-Saba knew the name. As a genetic researcher herself, she was well aware of Rosalind Evans's work at Clearbrook Institute, including the fact that she was working on a project for that traitor Alan Dyer and his cult at PharmaGen. "It's a joke," she said.

"She says it's true," Steele said. "She sounds like a nut case. I looked at news clips of her at our Chicago rally and the next day when she was interviewed about this so-called discovery. She looks totally serious. This is some kind of stunt to take attention away from us. She's the one who called me a liar about embryonic stem cell research at Clearbrook."

"Why would she say they don't do stem cell research if they really do?" asked Dan Markie of the California Seekers Union.

"She's a liar." Steele said.

"That's not very charitable, Joseph. If nobody at Clearbrook will admit that they do embryonic stem cell research, then how can you be so sure they do?" Markie asked.

"I'll give you twenty web sites right now that describe what they do in that evil place, and tell it in detail. Just ask Betty Freud. They absolutely do embryonic stem cell research," Steele said.

"But there are other sites that say the opposite, aren't there?"

Steele looked tired and strung out. "Of course, Dan. These people are rich and powerful. They will say anything to keep the truth from getting out. They are protecting their fortunes. This ridiculous story is just a tactic to hurt us and steal the news cycle from us."

"But it would be easy to disprove what she is saying about the Ten Commandments. I wonder if anyone has done that," said Babs Babcock.

"How in the world would you fake something like that?" Steele asked.

Babcock wrote on a sheet of paper a crude approximation of translation code and showed it to Steele. "It would be easy to fake it."

"It doesn't matter! I don't care how or why she did it. All I want is to get her off the front page. If there is going to be a headline about God, I want it to be mine!"

Rev. Markie leaned forward. "I don't think we need to do anything. If it is so easy to disprove, then somebody will do it and the whole thing will be over with."

Pastor Shabazz Dunready had been listening intently to the entire discussion. He secretly believed his role on this board was the same as it was in life—provocateur. And when needed, skeptic. "What if it's real?" he asked in a slow drawl. He raised his eyebrows and tilted his head back. "What if the Ten Commandments really are in the genetic code?" Everyone looked at him like he'd turned orange.

"That's impossible," Babcock said.

"No it ain't," Dunready said.

"Don't talk crazy. It's impossible," Babcock said.

"Why?"

"Because it is, that's why. It can't happen. Genetic code doesn't spell out words," Babcock said. Her tone was impatient and she seemed distracted.

"Why?" Dunready asked again. "It's a bunch of letters. Letters spell out words don't they?"

"No!" Babcock yelled, a little too loudly for polite company.

"Of course it could happen," Dunready said, smiling at the group, enjoying her obvious discomfort with his line of argument.

"Nonsense!" Babcock said. "You're talking supernatural mumbo jumbo and I don't believe for one minute …" Babcock stopped. All eyes were on her, waiting for her to finish her sentence. She stopped herself from saying more. Everyone thought she was on the board as the expert in genetics. In truth she was there as part of Danka-Saba's intelligence force to make sure Steele didn't get too close to hindering their operations. The strategy mirrored the oft-repeated mantra of the company CEO: keep your friends close and your enemies closer. God was a foreign concept to her.

Dunready folded his arms and leaned back. "What don't you believe? In God? Or you don't believe that God would write the Ten Commandments in our DNA?" Dunready waited, but she didn't answer. "God can do anything he wants. That's why they call him God," he said with a broad smile.

"Knock it off!" Steele railed. "We have a problem here and you two are not helping."

"Excuse me." Babcock stood and quickly walked out of the great hall.

"Joseph, we don't have a problem," Saul Runyon, the media strategist, said quietly. He was leaning forward, tapping his pen slowly on the table. "This is freaking golden."

"What are you talking about?" Steele said.

"The way you get the news cycle back is to steal it," Runyon said, a smile slowly spreading across his face. "You take the story and make it your own."

"Go on," Steele said.

"You have a scientist who claims she found the Ten Commandments written in the genetic code, right? No one knows for sure whether she is nuts or a genius or a prophet. That's good. Now, we could start a disinformation campaign to discredit her, but I like this better: you take advantage of the mass confusion by rising up and shouting from the mountaintops that this is the most astounding discovery in the history of mankind. It is proof that God exists," Runyon said.

Steele's eyes grew wide. "You are a genius, Saul, it's why I brought you in!" He slowly looked at each person around the table. His hands began to tremble, and for a moment it seemed as if he might detonate.

"It's the end of times!!!!! Hallelujah and praise God!!!!" Steele shook his hands in the air and danced around the table, eyes rolling heavenward. "Praise God! Praise God!"

"Joseph!" Runyon yelled. Steele stopped and stared at him. "Let's get busy and write the talking points. This story probably has a day or two of life in it. We have to jump in now, and if we play it right, it will launch you so far into the spotlight you'll glow in the dark. You'll be there long after this crazy lady is gone and forgotten."

"Yes! You think we had great rallies before! This will make people foam at the mouth!" Steele said.

Runyon nodded in agreement. "There is a basic rule of media management: The camera loves an angry mob, the angrier the better. Primal anger is a lot like sex—raw, out of control, and fun to watch."

"What if you say she's right but they prove her wrong?" Rev. Dunready asked.

"Then she'll be wrong," Steele said. "But *we* won't be wrong. You can't be wrong when you are on God's side."

Babs Babcock walked out onto the flower-laden terrace and dialed the office of Paul Raymond, CEO of Danka-Saba Pharmaceutical.

"Hello Babs! How are things in God-land?"

"What have you done, Paul?"

"What are you talking about?"

"I'm talking about the Rosalind Evans thing. It's all over the Internet. Did we have anything to do with this?"

Raymond roared with laughter. "No. Did you honestly think we would pull a sophomore stunt like that? No, Babs, when we put the screws to a competitor, we do it with class. This is something else. Maybe Evans snapped."

"None of it makes any sense. Who did this?"

"Don't worry. We are going to beat them in the leukemia market. Dyer thinks he got away with prancing out of this company on his high horse, but we're going to fry him in the marketplace *and* in court. He can't compete with us."

"By the way," Babcock said, lighting a cigarette. "I gave Steele your memos denying that we do human cloning or embryonic stem cell research. He is convinced we do only the things he considers to be ethical and beneficial for mankind. We don't have to worry about him coming after us. He's focused on taking Clearbrook down, and Dyer with it."

"Way to go, Babs. You are one get-it-done babe!"

Chapter 17

ROSALIND HUSTLED DOWN the concourse looking for a bar. So intense was her fear of flying, her overwhelming dread of dying in a burst of flames and twisted metal that she couldn't think about boarding without at least one double gin and tonic down the hatch. With steely determination, she wove her way through the throngs of people at O'Hare, down the interminable concourse, searching for a cocktail lounge. She spied one and made a beeline for it. She had grudgingly taken Bradshaw's advice and called her best friend Edie Dawson to beg shelter and comfort at her place in New York, just for a few days until all this nonsense blew over. Edie was ecstatic about the idea. They had not seen each other since Claire's funeral.

She sipped her drink and glanced at the TV over the bar. It was tuned to a news station, and blaring across the screen was a banner announcing a breaking story. Then, to her horror, her own face filled the screen. She could not hear the announcer above the din in the bar, but clearly, it was a story about her. She watched, stunned, as the caption appeared beneath her photo "Scientist claims proof of God."

Her head spun, not from the gin, but from the utter incoherence of the moment. Claims proof of God? Where on earth did that come from? She gulped the rest of her drink and grabbed her bag, but before she could get away, a man at the next table spoke to her.

"Are you Rosalind Evans? The one who discovered the Ten Commandments in the genetic code?"

Rosalind said nothing. More gin, I need more gin.

The man leaned closer. "Ma'am, excuse me, but you look like the woman in all the papers. You're all over TV today."

Rosalind glanced over at him. She could see that he was not mocking her, not taunting, but his face bore an expression of intense curiosity, like a child who's pretty sure he's looking at the real live Easter Bunny.

"I ... I ..."

"Hey, it looks like we have a celebrity here," another man said. "This is the lady who says she found God. Or maybe she thinks she *is* God." He laughed out loud, a humorless, mocking laugh.

"Well I'll be ..." a woman said. This got the attention of several more people.

"Did you really find God?" another said.

Rosalind grabbed her bag and ran out onto the concourse without looking back. She wove her way through throngs of people, hoping that no one was following her. She looked around for a place where she might duck in and hide. There were lots of open-air shops and food stalls, but they offered her no shelter at all. She turned onto another concourse. Everything was open air. She spied a women's restroom. She headed toward it, but then saw next to it an inconspicuous door with a small sign: Chapel. Chapel? In an airport? How incongruous, she thought. And convenient. She ducked in and closed the door behind her.

It was quiet inside. The room was no larger than 30 feet square. There were chairs in rows facing a lectern and a non-denominational altar. There were no religious symbols, yet the room seemed church-like in its appointments: stained glass windows, candles, little envelopes for donations. The only person there was a slim, middle-aged woman who was dusting. She was not wearing the usual airport custodial uniform; she wore a tidy shirtwaist dress and low-heeled pumps.

"Come on in," she said. "You're the first person I've seen all day. Make yourself at home."

"No, I can't stay," Rosalind said, fishing in her purse for her boarding pass.

The woman laughed. "I'm not surprised. Most people who come in here made a wrong turn. Go on, catch your plane. I'll do your praying for you. What's your name?"

"Rosalind."

"OK, Rosalind. We'll see you around. God bless you." The woman smiled and continued her cleaning, carefully lifting each object and dusting underneath. The place was spotless. Rosalind watched as she filled a vase on the altar with fresh flowers.

"Excuse me, but it seems odd to have a chapel in the airport. Who comes here?"

The woman laughed again. "People used to stop by every day and pray before their flight, but nowadays everyone is too rushed to stop. It's kind of ironic that with all these security procedures, we think we're safer. We pat down grannies and kids, but don't take time to connect with God. Where is the wisdom in that?"

"I wish someone would give me some wisdom about how to get out of here without being spotted," Rosalind said.

"You're on the run?"

"Yes."

"From whom?"

"Everyone."

The woman smiled at her. "I'll be right back." She walked into an anteroom and returned a few seconds later. She handed Rosalind a pair of sunglasses.

"Will these help?"

"Yes. Thank you." Rosalind noticed her name tag: Sadie Luft, Pastor.

"You're the pastor? Who is your congregation?"

"Anyone who comes by. You."

The room was quiet and peaceful, wholly unlike the terminal just outside the door. A deep weariness penetrated Rosalind to her core, and she wished she could stay for a moment and rest. It seemed that all she did anymore was run, and all she felt anymore was a heavy, lifeless compulsion to keep on running. She looked at her watch. "I have to go."

"Rosalind, you look like you are running on empty. When you get on the plane, why not try closing your eyes and thinking about your creator? Sometimes the quiet alone will restore you. Brings wisdom."

"Thanks, you're nice." Rosalind pulled her scarf from around her neck and tied it into a turban around her head, tucking in her hair. She put on the sunglasses and cracked open the door. All right, Rozzie, she told herself, take a breath and go. She stepped out the door and melded into the crowd. She tried for a look of nonchalance and made every attempt at a casual saunter, as if she were anything but a marked woman. Just look nonchalant and saunter your way to gate B5, she told herself. She pulled her cell phone out and pretended to scroll through e-mails. Head down, saunter. Left foot, right foot, sauntering and sauntering. And then she was there. The good news was that she had made it to the gate without being spotted. The bad news was that they were closing the door to the jet way. She quickly waved her boarding pass at the agent. The agent took the pass, hardly making eye contact. "Enjoy your flight."

Not a snowball's chance in hell, Rosalind thought.

She tried to keep her head down as she sidled through the coach cabin, which was filled to capacity. To her relief, the passengers were preoccupied with settling in and took no notice of her. Many were reading newspapers with her picture plastered across the front page, the one of her tussling with protesters at the Steele rally, looking more than a little deranged.

When she at last got to her row, the aisle and the middle seats were not only occupied, but well settled-into. A couple was cozied up together talking, a skinny woman with frizzy blonde hair and pale skin, and a dark-haired man with long legs. Books, laptops, cell phones and granola bars were spread out on their tray tables; it looked like they were staying for a month. They're not going to like me, she thought.

"Excuse me," she said, bracing herself against their disapproval at having to get up to let her in. "That's my seat by the window." The blond-haired woman looked up.

"Oh, hi! Here, we'll get out of your way." She and the man quickly dismantled their little clubhouse, putting everything in its proper place, and stood up.

"Don't worry about it. We were going to stow everything in a minute anyway," the man said. Smiling, he took her blazer and laid it carefully in the overhead bin. His eyes were very blue, and Rosalind thought he looked entirely too ... serene. He smiled and stepped aside to let her pass. She muttered a thank you and took her seat by the window.

She swallowed hard as the engines revved and the plane taxied to the runway. She shut her eyes and clutched the armrests. Takeoff was always the worst. Her thoughts fixated on fire and panic and burning flesh. As the wheels left the ground, she counted. She'd heard somewhere that if there were going to be a catastrophic failure of some kind, it would be within the first minute after take-off. By the time she had counted to 60, they were banking to the right and seemed to have survived.

"Hi! I'm Summer Ellison," the woman next to her said brightly. She was smiling and holding out her hand.

"Hello," Rosalind said, wondering what strange impulse led the woman to want to socialize at a time like this.

"I used to be afraid to fly, too. But then I decided that when it's your time, it's your time." Summer said. She patted Rosalind's arm lightly. "Just relax and let God fly the plane."

"I'm Lex," the man said, turning toward her. "Are you from Chicago?"

Rosalind nodded, staring straight ahead. Are you from Mars, she thought.

"Where 'bouts in Chicago?" he asked.

"Streeterville." She reached under the seat in front of her and pulled out her briefcase. She fished inside and pulled out a journal to bury her head in and disappear.

"Are you a scientist?" Lex inquired.

Rosalind nodded.

"Wow. What kind of scientist?"

"Molecular biology."

"Wow ..."

"Yeah, wow," Rosalind said, looking past him at the flight attendant with the beverage cart. "Gin and tonic," she said. "Double."

The attendant reached across and handed her the drink. She took a swig and turned toward the window. She hated looking out at all that air beneath her, but it was preferable to further wowing with the couple from Mars. It was a clear afternoon. The plane banked out over the broad expanse of Lake Michigan, glistening in the sunlight several thousand feet below. She thought that from up here the world looked deceivingly tranquil, easy. She sat back and let the gin work its magic on her shattered disposition. There would be time on the flight to process the events of the last two days. But for now, she just wanted to close her eyes and rest …

"Look at that!" Summer Ellison was leaning forward, looking out the window.

Rosalind's heart stopped for an instant, until she saw the ecstatic look on the woman's face.

"Isn't it awesome?!" she trilled. The sunshine streaming through the window bathed her pale skin in rich warm light. "To think that God created all of this!"

Lex craned his neck to see out the window. "Whoa, head buzz! Don't you just love it up here?" He grinned at Rosalind. "Switches me on big time."

Rosalind regarded the two for a moment. Their faces radiated an awed contentment that struck her as exceedingly annoying.

"What kind of tea is that?" she asked.

Summer laughed. "We do sound crazy, don't we?"

"No. High."

"It's not the tea. Getting high on God is what we do," said Lex. "It's our job. Summer and I are pastors."

Oh great. Rosalind reached up and pushed the call button. She held her empty glass up to the flight attendant and mouthed the word 'More.' Then she turned to Lex and addressed him head on. "I don't do church."

"Neither do we," said Lex. "Our church isn't really a church. It's a spa for the soul."

"A spa for the soul? What's that?" Rosalind asked, and immediately regretted it. Lex reached into his satchel and handed her a brochure.

"Welcome to The Convocation of Manifest Souls."

Wondering how much gin they actually stock on an airplane this size, Rosalind leaned back and tried to focus on the brochure. The cover had a painting of a muted face in the clouds. He was looking down, his eyes pinpoints of light that emitted diaphanous rays of yellow light in all directions. He had no discernable body, but seemed to be made of swirling vapors that floated all around him. There were men, women and children dressed in bathrobes and looking up at him. Across the bottom of the brochure it said 'Convocation of Manifest Souls. Reconnecting with God.'

In another photo, there was a group dressed in robes sitting around a table eating pizza. At the head of the table was a holographic image of the Virgin Mary, with whom they seemed to be engaged in happy conversation.

"That's the Interactive Virtual God Experience," Summer said, pointing at the photo. "We have holograms of various figures from art, history, religion and science that talk and answer questions. It stimulates the hypothalamus and releases endorphins."

Seeing the look of skepticism on her face, Lex pointed at another photo, of a person who seemed to be floating in space.

"In this venue, you fly with God through the cosmos. You fly for as long as you want, and then you have a cup of tea, get a massage, hang out with friends in the God Consciousness Hot Tub, whatever you want," Lex said.

Rosalind barely stifled a laugh. "You're real pastors? I mean, ordained?"

Lex nodded. "We pastored a small church for several years. We loved the people, but we realized that religion can get in the way of knowing God. So we tried to peel away the traditional religion and get down to the essence," Lex said. "This is the pre-Christian experience. It emulates what the followers of Jesus did before the Church was formed."

Next to the Virgin Mary pizza party was a photo of a lone person sitting in an outdoor garden, surrounded by bright pink hibiscus flowers and a waterfall in the background. Her arms were outstretched, eyes closed, head tilted toward the sky. The caption read 'A Spa for Your Soul. Everyone Welcome. Open 24-7.'

"Who has time for this?" Rosalind asked.

"You'd be surprised. At first, our goal was just to juice up the church experience, which has gotten pretty dusty over the last 50 years. We decided to see if we could use technology to help create a God experience that would turn people on," he said.

"Sounds New Age," Rosalind said.

"Not really. We believe in one God, the God of Abraham, creator of all. There's a big difference between New Age and what we believe."

"People at CMS have shockwave experiences of God. They vibrate!" Summer's wide eyes made her look blitzed. "Their spiritual genes are expressing!"

"It's a hallucination," Rosalind said. "Gene expression might have something to do with it, but there is nothing supernatural about it."

Summer shoved a thick swatch of fuzzy blonde hair behind her ear. "When you get back to Chicago, come visit us at CMS and judge for yourself. We'll hang glide the Sistine Chapel. Or you can sing in the Choir of 10,000 Angels!"

"But hey, enough about us," Lex said. "Tell us about your work."

"Do I have to?" She was beginning to slur her words.

Lex nodded enthusiastically.

"I decipher genetic code, but lately the code is acting mighty strange." She took a big swig of gin for emphasis.

Lex regarded her for a moment. "Rosalind Evans. Wow! I knew you looked familiar!" he said.

"Oh great," she muttered. She held her finger to her lips. She looked furtively around, and was relieved to see that no one else had heard him.

"I am not surprised that we ended up sitting next to you on a plane," he whispered. "That's how God works. We heard about your discovery yesterday and have not stopped talking about it. It's awesome!"

"It's crap," Rosalind said. "It's ruining my life."

Summer squeezed Rosalind's arm. "THIS IS SO EXCITING!! You've found a message from God. Hebrews 8:10 says 'I will put my laws in their minds and write them on their hearts.' You found where He wrote them!"

"I don't know what I found. But it's not a message from God. I think it's a case of industrial sabotage. Forget about it."

"I don't think anyone is going to forget about it," Lex said.

Through a solid gin buzz, she realized that although the Ellisons were total screwballs, they were nice to her. Nicer than most of the people she had dealt with in the last 48 hours, that's for sure. God Consciousness Hot Tub. Pizza with the Virgin Mary. Ummm. Pizza sounded good … The gin finally won. Rosalind slept.

Chapter 18

THE NATIONAL CAMPAIGN headquarters for 'Bosch for President' were located in the Senator's home district an hour south of Chicago. He had headquarters in every state, but he was especially fond of the home office in Bourbonnais. It was the town he grew up in, a town confident in its small town identity but not confident in the ability of the average person to pronounce it. The sign at the edge of town welcomed visitors to 'BOUR-BO-**NAY**—home of Senator P.P. **Bosch**!'

The Bosch for President HQ was manned by his friends, the good people who had known and supported him throughout his political life: teachers, laborers, farmers, retirees, and church-goers. In his twelve years in the Senate, Paul Philip had brought home the bacon to Kankakee County. A new bridge over the Kankakee River, a regional airport, and an Olympic-class aquatic training facility were just some of the little niceties he had been able to insert into legislation without anyone noticing. You had to keep it subtle, he always said, so that the pork would be hard to find in case anyone decided to read the bill. He was a master at the fine points of creative legislating, so much so that even the folks at home were often surprised when a gift came their way that they weren't expecting. It was Bosch's way of leveling the playing field for his modest district, and saying thank you to the good people who kept him in office. When asked why he was so generous to his community, he would just smile and shrug his shoulders. "It's only fair."

The nominating convention was just six weeks away, and while Bosch had a five-point lead in the polls, nothing in politics is ever set in stone. There was no clear winner yet, and there was always the chance that someone in the still-crowded field could surge. He had to be on his game every minute of every day. One slip-up could be fatal. It was a tortuous, demanding business, running for President, exhausting, frustrating, and low-down dirty. He loved it with every fiber of his being.

Bosch's town hall meeting was underway and the Bourbonnais Village Hall was standing room only, with an overflow of more than a hundred people spilling out into the parking lot. Many were there to cheer their favorite son, others to challenge him on the defining issue of his campaign, societal fairness.

The event was in full swing. Dressed in shirtsleeves and khaki pants, he was working the crowd with a microphone, approaching questioners directly and answering them face-to-face. Most other candidates preferred the safety of the podium or the dais, but Bosch loved getting close to his people.

"Senator, you say you want middle class status for everyone. But, what if I don't want to be middle class?"

"You don't? Why?"

"Because I want to be upper class. I want two cars and a boat, and I am willing to work for them."

Bosch shook his head vigorously. "You never want to own a boat. A boat will eat you alive. Something is always breaking. The second happiest day of my life was when I sold my boat," Bosch said.

"But—"

Bosch pointed to another person in the crowd, a young woman with a baby in her arms.

"Senator, how will you make sure everyone is treated fairly? I have three children and no husband."

"No husband?"

"He was cheating on me." She looked up at Bosch as if pleading with him to lift her burdens.

Bosch put his arm around the young woman's shoulder and patted the baby on the head.

"Young lady, you have nothing to worry about. I will do everything in my power to make sure you and your children are properly cared for. I can't make a nice guy out of your husband, but I can sure find a way to take care of you and your family. What kind of a country would we be if we just let you starve?"

"Senator," another woman yelled. "How are you going to pay for all that?"

"We are the richest nation on earth. There is more than enough to go around. We just need to spread it out a little. In a fair society, the rich pay their fair share to help those less fortunate than themselves. Both ends of the economic spectrum are squeezed toward the center, and voila! Chicken on everybody's table!"

There was a roar of applause from the crowd. Bosch beamed.

"The previous administration did everything in its power to protect the selfish interests—big business, Wall Street, wealthy people. Look where that got us! The biggest recession we've ever seen. Millions out of work. Dried up credit. Bank failures. People starving. Under my plan for societal fairness, everyone shares. Close your eyes and imagine a world in which you never have to worry about money again. It is not this young lady's fault she married a jerk, so it's only fair that the rest of us reach out and help her. Isn't *that* the America you want to live in?"

There was a huge outburst of applause and cheering. The crowd began to chant the Bosch campaign slogan. "It's only fair! It's only fair! It's only fair!"

The next questioner was a college-age young man. "What about free enterprise? It's our way of life. I believe it is what makes us great. Under your plan, what happens to capitalism?"

"Capitalism is what got us in this pickle. We have a permanent underclass because the selfish rich are oppressing them. It's how people are wired. They take advantage of each other. It is the government's responsibility to protect the common people from those who would oppress them. Isn't that what the Constitution says? Provide for the common defense? I'm not saying we eliminate capitalism. It's just that we must make sure no one has the chance to oppress. Where are you from, young man?"

"Bonfield."

"What is the primary industry in Bonfield?"

"Agriculture."

"Right. And it still will be. Under my fairness plan, if the math doesn't work out, you will be subsidized to grow your corn and soybeans. The prices will be regulated so that you never lose money selling your crops. The world eats, you make money. Free enterprise."

Another citizen raised his hand. Bosch approached him.

"Senator, what about that scientist who says she discovered Bible verses in somebody's DNA? They're saying that she is part of a plot to overthrow freedom of religion. How fair is that?"

There was a burst of applause. Bosch had to think fast. Of course he had seen the story on Starry Messenger, but he thought it was a joke, a parable of some kind to prove a point. He hadn't taken time to learn more about it, and now he saw that he was behind on this one. He hated it when someone asked for his opinion before he actually had one.

"I have been looking into this. I certainly think there are issues of fairness involved. Is it fair for someone to try and force their religious views on others just because of what they call scientific evidence? I don't think it's fair at all. We all have our opinions, especially about God. I promise you that as President, I will make sure we have fundamental fairness in every aspect of American life, especially religion!"

The audience cheered. Bosch smiled, and began shaking hands with the people in the audience. That would be the end of that. He couldn't risk any more questions on this subject. He had his applause line; it was time to get out. The cameras were here to record his full support for saving Americans from the calamity of societal unfairness, not to show him floundering for answers. He made a quick, but suitably triumphant exit.

Bosch was one of those rare candidates whose charisma permeated a room and penetrated the TV barrier. In his humble opinion, nobody could top him for the smooth answer to the tough question. Tonight, though, he almost got caught with his pants down on the question about the genetics thing. He had work to do.

Once home, he opened his laptop and logged in. He was shocked to find the Internet blazing with stories about this woman, Rosalind Evans.

The name rang a bell. When he saw the photo of her with the protesters, he remembered that this was the woman who attacked Rev. Steele at the rally in Chicago. He'd seen the tape when he was sitting in the studio with Claudia Moray. He dialed his chief-of-staff.

"Why didn't I know about this?? Get busy and find out who this Rosalind Evans woman is. Find out everything you can about her; where she's from, who she associates with, who she's slept with. And why she has cooked up this ridiculous scheme about proving the existence of God. I don't like this one bit. I want to know what she's up to, whether she poses any kind of threat to my candidacy."

Bosch turned on the TV and began flipping through the channels to check on the 6:00 coverage of the Town Hall. The news was all about Evans. Only at the very end of the newscast was there a quick clip of him smiling and waving to the crowd. Who was this woman and how did she get so famous so fast? He realized that the important thing now was to dig in and find where the connecting points were between her and his campaign. You could always find a connecting point if you wanted one, he thought. In this case, it might be that she posed a threat to US security. Maybe she was doing something illegal or unconstitutional. Maybe she was nuts or a fraud who should be fired from the Clearbrook Institute. After all, it was one of the nation's most prestigious scientific institutions. On the other hand, she might be a genius who should be publicly lauded. Perhaps he could help her with funding for some new groundbreaking medical research. The woman must be good for something. I'll figure it out, he thought. But for now, I just wish she would quit being so stingy with the media coverage and share the limelight with me.

He settled back and began nosing through the Internet, starting with Starry Messenger.

Our genome: What else does it say?

My Kittens, if the Ten Commandments are written in the code for a gene on the second chromosome, then what might be written on our other genes? You, my bright readers, surely know that the God Gene is one out of more than 20,000 genes in the human genome, right?

And you know that each gene is made up of 3000 to 2.4 million bases, so isn't there plenty of room for more messages from the Almighty? Room for the entire Bible perhaps? The Torah? The Qur'an? The musings of a God looking to be found?

Wouldn't it be prudent to carefully search the rest of the genome?

Science has spent several decades studying the structure and function of genes, noble work indeed, but might there be information of another kind lurking in the chemical soup? Amid the revelations about the workings of the human body, might there also be revelations about the meaning and purpose of life?

The Global Genomic Access web site is the repository of every bit of genomic data known to man and it's free, so why not go in and have a look?

At the moment we are consumed with the Ten Commandments, asking questions like—what will happen to our behavior if we find out that God really *is* holding us up to high standards? What would the world look like if we stopped lying, stealing, and coveting each other's things? What if there was no more killing? How different would our lives be if we truly loved one another?

Sound anything like the Garden of Eden? Are we ready for that?

Bosch sat bolt upright. Other messages in the genetic code? He clicked on a related link and pulled up another story.

Biotech billionaire Booth Slattery has offered a one million dollar prize to the first person who finds the Twenty Third Psalm in the genetic code. "It's my favorite," Slattery said. "There are three billion base pairs in the genome. If we get enough people looking, I figure we can get through it in a matter of a few weeks. Rosalind Evans's discovery is amazing, and I figure there must be more, maybe the whole Bible. I want the best minds working on this, so I've decided to give a million dollar prize. Let's go get it done!"

Bosch dialed his cell phone as fast as he could. "This is Senator P.P. Bosch. I need to see the President first thing tomorrow."

Chapter 19

"ROZ!" EDIE DAWSON waved and ran towards Rosalind across the airport concourse and hugged her hard. "Let's get a taxi. I know where they keep the martinis in Manhattan!" Rosalind looked her best friend up and down. She looked fabulous in her casual chic turquoise dress and sandals. Good taste was something she had in spades, and it didn't hurt that she was an outrageously successful advertising executive who could afford, and always indulged in, the best clothes. Unlike me, Rosalind thought. She looked down at her wrinkled linen skirt and blouse and realized that she hadn't bought anything new in over a year and a half. They jumped into the cab and were off on what Edie saw as a long-delayed girlfriend adventure, but what Rosalind saw as exile.

Roz and Edie had a long history together. They were college roommates, Edie was Rosalind's maid of honor, and they were as close to sisters as you can get without sharing DNA. And a fine pair they made. Roz, 5'10" 135, auburn hair and violet eyes, ballet. Edie, 5'5" 120, blonde hair and blue eyes, cheerleader. To the casual observer, they were opposites. To the tune of their own hearts, they were one and the same. It had taken two, maybe three seconds for Edie to say yes when Rosalind called to ask if she could take refuge at her place.

Edie knew that the things they were saying about her on TV were beyond outrageous. She knew Roz well enough to know that rest was only one of the things she needed. She needed great soft shoulders to cry on, boxes of tissue, gallons of gin, and a sister to watch her back. She needed a competing voice that affirmed her, a voice that was truthful and grounded in reality. That's what the baby girl needed. That, and a bag of Oreos. Chocolate milk. And comfort food. Lots of comfort food.

Edie directed the cabby to drop them at her favorite little tavern in the financial district, Grammy White's. The Midwestern ambiance would be good for them both. "This is a good start," she said. "We'll have a martini, Grammy's meatloaf, a good gawk at the local hunkage, and then we'll go home and get down to business. I want to hear it all."

Rosalind had no argument with any of it.

Grammy's wasn't anything like the other bars in the neighborhood. It was more like something from Peoria: warm, gingham-curtained, full of good home cookin' smells, and a TV tucked into every corner. It couldn't have been cozier and safer-feeling. Rosalind leaned back and was about to put her feet up on the chair across from her when she noticed that at the moment, every one of the TVs featured her full-face visage on the steps of Clearbrook Hall, raving, waving her arms. She was mortified. She tried to disappear behind a menu, to hunch her way out of existence. Over and over they played the tape of her encounter with the reporter and, to her utter horror, of her skirmish with the demonstrator at the Steele rally. She couldn't hear what they were saying, but the images were unceasing. They also had a still photo of her, which seemed glued to a little box in the upper right corner of the screen no matter what else was going on. She recognized it as her faculty ID photo. Who in the world gave them her faculty ID photo?

"Two peach-tinis!" Edie said to the waitress.

Rosalind grabbed her arm and whispered in her ear. "Did you have to bring us to TV-o-rama?"

Edie looked up and gasped. "Holy moley, Roz, look at that. You *are* the woman!"

Rosalind gulped her peach-tini. It sucked, but she gulped it anyway. This was no time to be choosy. She chanced a look around the crowded room. So far, so good.

Edie stared at the TV screen, transfixed. There was her friend's face, peering out at her from the lofty air of InfoNet News. The commentators were mouthing her name, Rosalind Evans this and Rosalind Evans that. There didn't seem to be any other news, just Roz, over and over.

"This is beyond insane," Edie said.

"Way beyond. I don't understand any of this. Do these people really think I discovered a message from God? Really?"

"Evidently so."

"Then why aren't they talking about God? Why are they so obsessed with me? I'm all they're talking about."

"It's safer. If they say something you don't like, they get sued. But if they piss off God, it's game over."

Rosalind sat looking at the screen for a long moment, chewing her straw.

Edie knew the look. "Don't let them intimidate you."

"I'm not intimidated; I'm acutely, massively irritated."

"What's it like?" Edie said.

"What's it like to be ruined? Mocked? Made a fool of? Oh, it's not so bad, really. At least I still have my looks." Edie laughed out loud, then quickly put her hand over her mouth. The last thing she wanted to do was draw attention. She summoned the waitress and ordered two meatloaf dinners.

Rosalind dove right in when the food came. "Ummmm. My stomach thinks my throat's been cut," she said. She shoveled in a spoonful of mashed potatoes, buttery and hot, and savored the simple joy of comfort food. She couldn't remember the last time she sat down to a full, balanced, hot, gloriously caloric meal. She was buttering a hot roll when a jock-looking guy walked up to the table.

"Hey, are you her? That lady who found that God thing? We got a bet goin'."

"No, you've got me confused with someone else," Rosalind said, diving into her food.

"I don't think so. Hey, you guys. It's her. Dude, she *is* hot." Several guys moved toward the table.

Roz and Edie looked at each other and the old telepathy clicked in. Edie threw a hundred on the table and they made a clean get-away.

Chapter 20

TIMES SQUARE PULSATED with energy as the cab inched along on the way to Edie's place. The lights were dazzling, and Rosalind might have actually enjoyed it were it not for the frequent ringing of her cell phone. Most of it was Bradshaw calling, and that made her nervous. None of the calls was from David, and that made her sad. She decided to shut the ringer off and pretend it was 1980.

New York was always exciting, with lots to occupy the time and energy of two young women from the Midwest. From the moment she set foot in Manhattan for the first time years ago, Edie reveled in the grand scale of the Big Apple, the center of the universe. Rosalind always acknowledged that yeah, it was great, but nothing could compare to the biggest little city in America. Chicago was a big family of neighborhoods, each with its own rhythm and identity, that shared a downtown, a lakefront, and a Midwestern sense of independence and adventure. While she always loved coming to New York with Edie, she never once considered moving there. Besides, New York didn't have a clue how to make pizza.

Up ahead scrolled the Starry Messenger Ticker—"Are you asking the right questions? Are you asking the right questions?"

"What do you think that means," Rosalind said.

Edie thought for a minute. "I'm not sure. What questions are you asking?"

"I'm asking 'Why me?' 'How do I get out of this?'"

"Are those the right questions?"

"I doubt it. Nothing I do is right."

"Lordy, girl, I gotta get you home."

Home was a cozy, eclectic apartment on the East Side. Edie wasted no time making her best friend comfy. The place belied Edie's phenomenal success in advertising. She drove a Jag and dressed in designer clothes, yet her place had homey, hand-painted charm. The furniture was a mélange of styles, from Southwestern to mountain lodge, and the colors reflected a world view that was optimistic and joyful. The sofa was deep and soft, perfect for Sunday afternoon naps or late-night rendezvous. Edie was not married. For now, she was blissfully happy dating an endless array of beautiful men, and living alone in independent splendor.

"What's this?" Rosalind picked up a bright pink 60s-era princess phone. "You have a landline? Why?"

Edie laughed. "It's my safety line in case the wireless universe crashes. Besides, there isn't a cell phone on earth as cute as this baby, do you think?"

"If the wireless universe crashes, I don't want to be around to see it." She picked up her iPhone. "Speaking of, I need to charge my phone. It's dead."

Edie quickly grabbed the phone from her and plugged it into a kitchen outlet. "Never mind the phone for tonight. Right now, you need another pillow. And another drink," Edie said.

The two sat on the sofa in their jammies with a plate of Oreos between them. Rosalind took her contacts out and put on her trusty tortoise shell glasses. "This is one of life's underrated pleasures, taking out the contacts," Rosalind said. "One more minute with them in and my eyes would blow up."

This was just like old times, except that Rosalind felt that certain vulnerability that comes with having your mug plastered on every TV screen in America. The TV was turned on with the volume muted.

"Yikes, woman, you've really screwed things up for yourself, haven't you?" Edie laughed and flipped channels.

"Yeah, and you know how much I love the limelight."

Rosalind recounted the bizarre events of the last two days, and Edie listened with growing amazement.

"Your version of things doesn't bear any resemblance to what they are saying on TV. They said you claimed to have proven the existence of God. Did you say that?"

"Of course not. How stupid do you think I am? It's a hoax or some sort of industrial espionage. Even on the ridiculously small chance that it is a naturally occurring thing, it is certainly not proof that God exists because God doesn't exist."

"Really?"

"No."

"You sure? Because I was just talking to Him a little while ago."

"About what?"

"You."

"Don't bother. He hates me."

"Don't be so sure. He told me he misses you. He's worried that you haven't called."

Rosalind looked away for a moment. "When I needed God the most, he wasn't there."

"He sees it differently. Maybe you should ask Him. Hear Him out."

Rosalind squinted at the TV screen. "It's Bradshaw. Un-mute!"

Bradshaw was smiling indulgently at the horde of reporters with their microphones thrust at him. He's enjoying himself, she thought. The man is enjoying himself!

"I assure you that Rutherford University has the situation under control. Dr. Evans has been removed from the project and has been put on administrative leave until further notice. The research project with PharmaGen Pharmaceutical is continuing, and we are all very excited about the results so far."

The reporters yelled questions all at the same time.

"Where is she?"

"Why is she on leave?"

"Has she been hospitalized?"

"Have you verified her findings yet?"

Bradshaw ignored them and went on. "We feel that this project has the potential to revolutionize cancer treatment. In the meantime, the

University is investigating the situation and no stone will go unturned as we seek to determine how she could have perpetrated such a massive hoax on the American people. PharmaGen offers its sincerest apology to anyone who has been offended by this incident."

Rosalind felt a surge of adrenalin. Hoax? Administrative leave? She grabbed the landline. "Does this thing actually work?"

"Of course."

Rosalind dialed Bradshaw's cell number. A moment later, she heard his phone ringing over the TV. Bradshaw was the kind of guy who couldn't let a ringing phone go unanswered; he hated the thought that someone might know something he didn't. As she knew he would, he instinctively reached for the phone and brought it to his ear. The reporters moved in close and thrust their microphones into his face.

"Hello?"

"Hoax? You think I perpetrated a hoax?" Rosalind screamed.

"Rosalind?"

The reporters went wild and began yelling questions at him:

"Where is she?"

"Can we talk to her?"

They thrust their microphones toward his cell phone, trying to pick up her voice on the other end. He cut off the call and put the phone in his coat pocket. "It was a crank call, ladies and gentlemen. I'm sorry about that. As I was saying ..."

With reporters crushing in on him from all sides, Bradshaw pressed on with his talking points. He assured the reporters that he had everything under control. He smiled at them condescendingly, confident that he had the upper hand in every way. What he didn't know was that someone had picked his pocket.

Ron Vaniere elbowed his way out of the crowd as unobtrusively as possible and found an inconspicuous place where he could search Bradshaw's cell phone call list. The last call was from area code 212. New York City. He quickly noted the phone number, erased the call from the incoming calls folder, and shoved his way back into the jostling crowd. With the utmost discretion, dropped the phone back into Bradshaw's coat pocket, undetected by anyone.

"What a jerk!" Rosalind yelled, slamming down the phone.

"Forget him, sweetie. Come on, let's change the subject. How's David?"

Rosalind dipped an Oreo into her gin and tonic. "Well, starting next week, you are likely to see more of him than I am. He's moving to New York."

"No," Edie said softly.

"He's taking a job in a big law firm."

"Oh Roz. Oh man. I knew things were stressed but I didn't know you guys were anywhere close to splitting up. How bad is it?"

"He hates me."

"Bull. He adores you."

"A couple of months ago he called to say he was working late and might not be home at all. I didn't think anything about it, until he did it again the next week. Then it got to be a regular thing." Rosalind munched on her cookie and stared at the floor.

"Is there another woman?"

Rosalind felt the tears coming and reached for a tissue. "He claims it was only once. Who knows?" Rosalind felt a heavy despair descending on her, a feeling as hopeless and bleak as the days after Claire's death.

"I can't figure out how this happened. I've never known two people who loved each other more," Edie said.

It took a two-hour flight to New York, a gallon of gin, and the proximity of her best friend for Rosalind to finally let loose. The pit loomed; she gave up and let herself slide in. It was not a purgation she sought, nor one she welcomed, but nonetheless it came, great waves of sobbing interspersed with uncontrollable ramblings about David and Claire and life in general. Edie could only sit close, dispense tissues and encourage her to let it out.

"What kind of a man leaves his wife while she's still grieving for her daughter?" Rosalind wailed. "I hope his plane crashes and he rots in hell!" The words came out in a sloppy, boozy slur, and both knew they weren't true. Rosalind blew her nose, and blew it, and blew it, then took a deep breath and wept all over again. Edie was about to suggest beddy-bye, when Rosalind suddenly looked up and stared into the distance, her face blotchy and swollen. Edie wondered for a moment whether she'd had a small stroke.

"Did I ever tell you about when we first met?"

Edie smiled. Rosalind loved telling it, had told it often, reveling in the nuance of their unlikely romance, always with a sense of awe at how unbelievably lucky she had been to find David. They were the couple everyone admired—smart, beautiful, wildly successful in their chosen professions, yet wildly unlikely to have landed together.

"Tell me again, sweetie. I want to hear it," Edie said.

Rosalind sat back and stared at her for a moment. It tore at her to remember, but she needed to relive it, to spill their story out and look at it, examine every shred of it to see why it ended. How could it possibly have ended? She took a deep breath and began to tell the story. Her voice was thick and the words flowed like blood from an open vein.

It started almost eight years ago, when her new boss, Ben Bradshaw, invited her to the opening of the new genetics exhibit at the Museum of Science and Industry. Attending an affair with Bradshaw was not her idea of fun. Social events, even the thought of them, had always made her queasy. Her place was in the lab or the classroom, where the high, strong walls of academe protected her from small talk and stiff bearing, and where she always had the words to finish her sentences.

If it had been anyone else doing the asking, she would have begged off. The only consolation was the location; the Museum of Science and Industry was her favorite. And the new genetics exhibit was the hottest ticket in town.

The Museum glimmered in the late afternoon sun as Bradshaw and Rosalind drove up. Billowing between the marble columns of the grand entrance were seven huge vertical canvas banners announcing the opening of a new exhibit, "Wonderfully Made: The Human Genome Revealed." The banners featured silvery blue and gold double helixes against an amber background, with the letters A,C,T and G swirling among them. It was billed as the most elaborate educational exhibit ever built, a tour de force that combined the best of Hollywood production values with the latest in technology. The press kit promised an unforgettable journey through the majestic and mysterious world of chromosomes and genes to the very essence of life itself. Visitors would take a breathtaking, twisting roller coaster ride up and down a double helix, then venture deep inside the DNA to hunt for nucleotides and polymorphisms.

It was a beautiful spring evening. As the lights of the city twinkled to life against the deepening sky, satellite trucks were positioning themselves in the parking lot as reporters from local and national media prepared to interview the assembled luminaries of show business, science and high society. Inside the museum's great hall a large red ribbon hung across the entrance to the exhibit, to be cut later by the honorary chairperson of the opening gala, Dr. Benton Bradshaw.

At the same time, David Evans was in his 35th floor office downtown, wishing he were going sailing instead of going to the Museum of Science and Industry. Lake Michigan shone like gold satin in the late afternoon sun, and he could see his boat from his office, nestled in her slip on B dock in Du Sable Harbor. He grabbed his jacket and headed down.

He walked quickly across Illinois Street and headed for the lakefront, thinking that before he hailed a cab, he might at least walk along the lake for a moment—smell the water, listen to the gulls. There was no time for a sail; it was his turn to represent the firm, which had done pro bono legal work for the Museum of Science and Industry for years.

The museum's grand hall was already crowded when Rosalind and Bradshaw walked in. Guests, fluffed and buffed from head to toe, sipped champagne and nibbled hors d'oeuvres. Rosalind had put on the best outfit she had, a sleeveless white satin blouse and long black skirt, thinking she would get by with it. But as usual, she felt dowdy, disheveled, hopelessly un-chic.

An orchestral fanfare boomed in the hall, and there suddenly appeared a one hundred foot tall holographic representation of a double helix. Twirling and glittering, it soared from the marble floor of the great hall all the way to the domed ceiling. The audience gasped and applauded, awed by the technological amplitude and sheer beauty of the display. The hologram was amazingly detailed and gave viewers a sense of being on a microscopic par with the DNA, yet it also had an ethereal, fluid characteristic, almost like it wasn't there at all.

Rosalind was so absorbed in the exhibit that she did not notice the handsome young man who walked up to Bradshaw.

Bradshaw put his hand on her arm. "Roz, have you met David Evans? He is a hotshot attorney in Chicago. Defense lawyer. Wants to see our lab, learn about DNA. I told him you were just the girl to teach him."

David put his hand out. "A pleasure to meet you, Rosalind. Ben has said wonderful things about your work." He smiled broadly at her.

"Thank you, David," she said, taking his hand. He was by far the most handsome man in the room, and she felt her face flush when their eyes met. She was no good at social events, and even worse with men. She had never really needed men, and had never learned the rules on charm or allure. When she did date, it was fellow academics, most of whom were functional and nice, but rather geeky. This guy was James Bond. He was tall and lean and judging by the tan, an outdoorsman. She pulled her hand away with the fleeting thought that maybe she'd held his a little too tightly or a little too long. "What is it you want to know about DNA?" she asked.

"DNA is the star witness in criminal law these days, and the more I learn about it, the more I want to know. Would it be possible for me to visit your lab?"

"Any time you like."

"How about Friday at 6:00?"

The next Friday, David stuck his head in the door of Rosalind's lab at exactly 6:00. He had thought about little else all week than seeing her again. He couldn't stop thinking about her sculpted face and the graceful way she moved. There was a slight dimple in her left cheek that he found intriguing, and then there was that auburn hair. She was bent over a pile of papers when he walked in.

"What, no bubbling beakers? No wild-eyed scientists? You call this a laboratory?"

"David! Come in." She jumped up quickly and stuck her hand out. He had on a perfectly tailored dark gray suit, and she couldn't help noticing how his tanned face contrasted with his white shirt, and how his blue tie was the same color as his eyes. She took a deep breath, wondering why on earth she had butterflies. "Well, what do you want to know about genetics?"

"Everything."

"How long have you got?"

David enjoyed the earnest look on her face, and the soft pink of her lipstick. "As long as it takes."

They sat at her computer and she scrolled to a page of translation code. He noticed with a certain satisfaction that in the glow of the computer screen, she had very good, very fair skin. He was sitting close enough to her that he thought he caught a faint scent of roses. He wished he could take off her glasses so he could see her eyes. He tried to focus on the letters arrayed in front of him on the computer screen, but his mind kept drifting to the woman beside him. What was she made of? What was going on inside that incredibly intelligent and lovely head of hers?

"We each have our own, unique genetic fingerprint," she said.

"My code probably says 'nice enough guy, but scientifically challenged.' Yours probably says 'scientifically brilliant and very beautiful.'"

She paused for a moment, still looking at the screen. She was too flustered to respond to his remark, so she simply went on.

"When we talk about the language of DNA ..."

She went on explaining the science of DNA, but he was having trouble listening. After about ten minutes, he interrupted her.

"Do you know how to swim?"

Rosalind sat back and looked at him. "What?"

"Do you like the water?"

"Yes. Why do you ask?"

"Have dinner with me tonight. I know just the place."

After the briefest moment of indecision, she smiled and nodded. David could already feel the wind in his hair. And in hers.

Conditions for an evening sail were perfect. David performed the ritual of untying *Proteus* and easing her out of the slip with the grace of one born to it over many lifetimes. Rosalind watched as he hoisted sails, his strong hands and muscled arms manipulating the lines and winches with ease. She had never been sailing before. She thought it looked complicated, all those ropes and all that canvas. But he obviously knew exactly what he was doing. The sails flapped and the lines clanked and it was very noisy. There was a lot for him to do, but he did it with calm confidence until all of a sudden, it was quiet. They were sailing.

She stared at the lake for a long time. "How far to the other side?" she asked.

"Forty miles to the closest point in Michigan, 333 miles if you head north up to Mackinac Island."

"Have you ever just sailed off into the night?"

"What do you think we're doing right now?" David said.

"What? You can't be serious."

"Don't worry, I'll have you home before curfew," he laughed.

Rosalind found him every bit as attractive as the moment they first met, maybe even more. He poured wine for her, made sure she was comfortable, offered her food. He treated her with such innocent respect that she found it a bit unsettling; no man had ever treated her with such deference.

After they had sailed for about an hour and finished the sandwiches he'd made, David walked to the bow of the boat.

"Come up here for a minute," he said, motioning her to follow.

"Who's driving the boat?"

"Otto," David said with a smile.

"Otto?"

"The autopilot," he said. "With light winds like this, and flat seas, Otto can hold the course just fine."

He sat, half reclining against the coach roof, with an unobstructed view of the sky. He patted the fiberglass, and she sat down next to him. As dusk fell, the moon rose over the lake to the East.

"This is incredible!" she said.

"I love the mystery of it. Don't you wonder how it all started? How all of this came to be?"

"We have a pretty good idea how it all started. It's called the big bang," she said.

"Yes, but, what about before that?"

"You mean what started the process? That is something we can never know."

"What about God?"

"The beauty of the natural world is that it doesn't require God to make sense."

"Aw, c'mon. You're no fun! Where's the mystery?"

"Mystery is the enemy. My job is to eliminate mystery and replace it with truth."

"Didn't Einstein say that science without religion is lame?"

"And religion without science is blind. Yeah, he said that," Rosalind said.

"I suppose you don't believe in Santa Claus either?"

They laughed. It felt good being with a man who made her laugh. A beautiful man who made her laugh. She could barely remember what it felt like to be interested in a man. Men were a distraction from what was really important to her. She had recently received an appointment to the Clearbrook Institute, a dream come true. She needed to prove herself and get her own lab and establish herself in the serious realms of cancer research. There was so much work to be done before she could ever think of having a relationship. Yet, looking at this man, she had a sense that he might convince her to shift her priorities, if only enough to allow a small place for him in her life. She looked up at the sky. The evening air was cool. She shivered slightly.

"Here, put this on," he said, taking off his sailing jacket. He slipped it around her shoulders and helped her wrap up in it.

It smelled faintly of cologne, a good smell, and it felt odd, almost intimate, to be enveloped in his smells and his warmth. It disoriented her for a moment.

He resisted the urge to leave his arm around her shoulder, to put his hand through that incredible hair. They sat silently for several minutes, *Proteus* rocking gently on the waves, the water lapping at her bow.

"Ontogeny recapitulates phylogeny!" David suddenly said, triumphantly. "I learned that in biology class. I don't have a clue what it means, but aren't you impressed that I remember it?"

"It's an early twentieth Century idea from a German named Haeckel. He said that ontogeny, which is the development of a species from conception to birth, mimics phylogeny, which is the evolution of life forms over time. Remember in elementary school science class, looking at a picture of a human embryo? Remember what it looked like?"

"A tadpole."

"And when it was a few weeks more developed, it had gills, right?"

"I remember. The gills were a vestige of our evolution from sea creatures."

"That's what you learned in school. But we know now that these are not gills. They're the precursors of ribs. They only *look* like gills."

David turned to her with a look of mock innocence. "You mean ontogeny *doesn't* recapitulate phylogeny? I'm devastated."

"Sorry to ruin your day." Rosalind laughed, thinking how engaging it was to talk with someone so gleefully unburdened by scientific rigor. She admired his easy, cheerful nature. To say nothing of his amazingly blue eyes. No, admire wasn't the word. This guy was flat out distracting. Six feet, she guessed, and a smile that made her heart race. I need to get out more, she thought. This guy is making me sweat and I just met him. He moves like an athlete and looks like a god. What in the world is he doing here with me?

"I wonder what other lies they told me in school?" David said.

"Science evolves. Today's mysteries are tomorrow's truths. It's the hunt for truth I'm interested in. One day I'll have my own lab. That's the goal anyway. There is so much I want to do …"

Her voice trailed off, and in that moment David sensed that she had a very different take on the world from his. She was able to grasp things about the natural world that he couldn't even imagine. What was going on in that wonderful mind of hers?

"Oh, I switched the lights on for you. Turn around."

Rosalind turned around and looked back at the city. The sight took her breath away. The magnificent skyline was backlit in a burst of orange from the last rays of the setting sun, while millions of lights glittered against the evening sky. The lights spanned the horizon, curving to the south around the tip of Lake Michigan and to the north as far as she could see. On one side of the boat was this spectacular light show, and on the other, the deep, silent expanse of Lake Michigan stretching away to the north and east, with no land in sight.

"This is fabulous! I suppose it's old hat to you?"

"No. It gives me chills every time. The juxtaposition of man-made and natural is stunning, don't you think?"

David always said that it was she who made the first move toward him, she who lifted her lips toward his first. She remembered it the other way around. It really didn't matter. It was the first of many kisses that night.

Their courtship was fast-paced, a tug of war between her penchant for the empirical and his for the adventurous. She wanted to read books; he wanted to sail to Bermuda. She looked for the logic in things, he for the wonder. On weekends, he flew out of the office like a kid at recess, but it took all of his persuasive skill (which was legendary) to get her out of the lab. They were attracted to each other precisely because they were so different. They filled each other's gaps.

Pregnancy came as a shock to Rosalind, both because they had been married only four months, and because she had never imagined herself a mother at this stage of her career. David saw this child as a fulfillment of his deepest longings.

One evening soon after they brought Claire home from the hospital, Rosalind was awash in emotion. She held Claire in her arms and leaned against her husband. "And to think I wanted to be an old maid professor." They laughed at the image of a doddering old Roz, dressed in tweed, drinking tea by herself. "How could I have been so wrong?"

Rosalind finished telling Edie her story and sat quietly on the couch for a long time, lost in memory. That time with Claire and David had been the happiest of her life. She looked up at her friend with bloodshot eyes. "How could I have been so wrong, Edie?"

Edie gently took Rosalind's glass from her and set it on the table. "Maybe that's the right question. All of us should ask that now and then."

"I fell so completely in love with both of them ... I had such utter happiness ... David is gone and I don't know why. Claire is gone. All I've wanted for two years is to know why, but I failed at that, too. I don't know *why*. I want to know *why*." Rosalind sat staring at the floor, the corners of her mouth brown from Oreos. Then she suddenly looked up, like a little child with a bright idea. "I have the data. I'll look at the DZPro2 and then I'll know why." She got up and stood unsteadily for a moment, then sat back down with a heavy thud. She looked over at Edie with a fallen expression and began to weep all over again. "I forgot my laptop."

Edie held her, and they sat in each other's arms for a long time. Edie wished that she could, for just one moment, absorb her friend's pain for her. But all she could do was share it. She said a silent prayer that Rosalind would find peace and happiness again somehow.

Chapter 21

IT WAS SLAM-DOWN party-time in the blogosphere. From one end of the cyberverse to the other, bloggers pontificated and chat rooms bubbled over with conspiracy theories and rumors about Rosalind Evans and her startling claim. The person known as Starry Messenger surveyed the action with a mix of amusement and disgust, thinking that the Internet was nothing if not the perfect vehicle for hysteria, for people saying whatever they wanted and calling it truth. That's what made it so darkly appealing, Starry mused; you read, you respond, you get angry, you write things you wish you could take back, you question your values and curse your parents for telling you lies when you were young. Worst of all, you believe only what you want to believe. Sometimes you go out into cyber-space willingly, sometimes by accident. The simplest little word search could, if you were not careful, seduce you deeper and deeper into the nether reaches where truth turns murky and rational discourse mingles with the ranting of cyber-trolls who live under bridges.

With diligence and an almost mystical ability to persuade, Starry Messenger rose from that morass to become philosopher-king of the blogosphere. His (her?) almost humble way of asking questions catapulted him beyond the run-of-the-mill blogger into the realm of cyber-hero. Readers flocked to Starry's site to be challenged by its authenticity. Hanging with Starry provided glimmers of enlightenment in a world of vast uncertainty. He promised his readers that he would divert them from their central tendency to think small merely by asking them questions. His style was the opposite of didactic, and readers found it immensely refreshing. Certainly there were heated exchanges between readers, but Starry always somehow managed to stay above the fray, the calm voice of reason who never let anyone go away mad.

Starry Messenger's popularity was heightened by the fact that no one knew who he or she was. The anonymity of the Internet made it possible for Starry to be the perfect invisible man (woman?): fully conscious, brimming with ideas, yet untouchable. Protected by a cloak of perfect privacy, Starry Messenger quickly became the most prolific and fearless of the new media mavens and garnered the largest Internet audience by far.

To Starry, the Rosalind Evans saga was the best thing since broadband. Part apocalyptical mystery, part corporate intrigue, part science fiction, it had something for everyone. Other blogs lured readers with headlines like "Psychiatrist: Rosalind Evans Bipolar!" "Bible Foretold God Gene" "Husband of God Gene Discoverer Disappears!" "Bioterrorism at Clearbrook?" Starry Messenger went a different direction:

Is God Gene Hysteria Overshadowing the God Gene?

Kittens, don't you agree that it looks like we are on the brink of chaos? We broke the God Gene story less than 48 hours ago, and, what is it they say in the demolition business, the dust is still on the up? So, no matter what we *think* we know, until the dust settles, do we really know anything?

Isn't it a great story? What's not to love about a story that has God, science, big business, academia, religion, mad scientists, government conspiracies, and a cure for cancer? Are you as eager as I am to see what happens next?

So is there real danger in all of this?

Do you remember the last time we faced a disastrous information meltdown? You remember the first hours after the September 11 attacks, when the electronic media experienced a rapid, massive infusion of information and didn't take time to properly vet it before it went public? What happened? Did we have clarity, or did the lines between fact, opinion, and speculation blur? Bits of information

flying in all directions spawned more bits, and soon all bits took on equal importance, and then, instead of an orderly, linear dissemination of information, what did we have? Chaos? And what is chaos, Kittens? Can you say: the last step before anarchy?

Will we stand by and let it happen? Will you please call the media on it every time you see obfuscation, speculation, lying? When you see things presented as morally and ethically equivalent that aren't, will you yell like hell? With your fine discriminating minds, your high-speed Internet and your portable devices, can you deny that you, my Kittens, are the last great hope of mankind? Can we any longer ignore the reality that somebody out there thinks God wrote the Ten Commandments in our DNA? Can we all calm down and find out what's trying to happen here?

Does anything else matter?

* * *

Cardinal Christopher Duffy leaned back in his seat as the chartered Gulfstream nosed up and away from Ciampino Airport in Rome and arced around to its heading toward Chicago. His heart was heavy, and as he anticipated ten hours in the air alone except for one flight attendant and three pilots, it was with a sense of weary gratitude that he didn't have to make conversation with anyone but the Lord. Ten hours might not be enough time to come up with a plan for the distressing task the Holy Father had just given him. After a hastily-called meeting with Vatican officials, the Holy Father had concluded without reservation that whether she was insane or an instrument of Satan, Rosalind Evans posed an imminent threat to the Catholic Church. For reasons no one fully understood, belief that the Ten Commandments were written in the genetic code was growing exponentially. By what power, the Holy Father asked, was a heretical idea like that gaining strength? He insisted that every moment the God Gene went unchallenged was a moment of increasing danger to the Church. Something had to be done about it. Immediately.

The Papal Council believed it was unwise for the Pope to comment publicly on the matter at this time. Instead, they felt that as the Archbishop of Chicago, with offices a stone's throw from where Evans lived and worked, Duffy was in the best position to work behind the scenes to develop a plan to silence and/or discredit her and change the trajectory of public opinion.

As added incentive, Duffy was also in the upper echelon of the College of Cardinals, and a strong candidate (though such things were never officially discussed) to replace the ailing Pope. Doing a good job on the Rosalind Evans assignment would win him favor in the College.

It was obvious to him on this momentous night that failure to silence Rosalind Evans was not an option. Duffy declined an offered glass of wine. He would need the clearest head possible as he pondered how, in the name of God, he would accomplish such a thing. The Pope was in worsening health. Might his judgment be clouded by his illness, Duffy wondered? Of course not; he is the Pope. In any case, he is serious enough about the matter to put the fear of God into me. I only wish he had been more specific on how far I'm supposed to go to discredit the woman. Rosalind Evans might be insane, she might be an agent of Satan. But what if she's just a victim of circumstances? Does the end justify *any* means to silence her? Dear Lord, I hope not, Duffy thought. God forbid we hold the institution of the Church to be holier than the God we worship.

Right now Duffy had many more questions than answers, but one thing was clear: by the time he touched down in Chicago in the morning, he'd better have a plan. He looked out the window at the lights of the Eternal City receding in the distance and saw with crystal clarity the shape of his dilemma. He closed his eyes and prayed.

Chapter 22

EDIE WAS MAKING toast when Rosalind stumbled into the kitchen the next morning with a face that looked like it had been crumpled into a wad and put away wet. She shuffled over to the counter and picked up the remote control.

"If you even think of turning on that TV I'll break both your arms," Edie said. She gave Rosalind a stern look and handed her a cup of coffee.

"But I need to see what ..."

"Step away from the remote. Now."

"OK, OK. Give me five eggs scrambled in butter, three pieces of toast, and your laptop."

"Why not just relax and pamper yourself? I can get you an appointment for a massage at the club. It's just down the street."

"I'm not going anywhere. They're all out to get me, and it's giving me a real bad headache."

Edie laughed and held up the empty gin bottle. "*This* is giving you a real bad headache."

Rosalind munched on her eggs, put the DVD into Edie's laptop and dove into the DZPro2 data. She was desperate to analyze it but first she had to find out whether it had been corrupted. Even though Dyer had shut her down, she was not about to give up. She was desperate for this nonsense about the God Gene to blow over so that Dyer would rev up the project again.

Using the process she and Gunquist had used to find the Biblical phrases, she began looking for Xs in the DZPro2 code, hoping that the data was clean and would yield useful scientific information. A tiny part of her, though, hoped it was corrupted, which would prove the she had not made a mistake in her work and get her off the hook with Dyer and Bradshaw. And the media. Within moments, she had her answer.

I AM THE LXRD THY GXD THXX SHALT HAVE NX XTHER GXDS XEFXRE ME

"Edie, look at this. Help me find the rest." She explained to Edie how the code worked, and together they poured through the rest of DZPro2. In short order, they found all four of the missing commandments. CLAIRE and DZPro2 were both corrupted.

"Who did this?" Edie said.

"Maybe Danka-Saba. Maybe Joseph Steele. The problem is they are preventing me from finishing my work!" She grabbed the remote control.

Edie grabbed her hand. "Don't make me get the rolling pin."

"Back off. I have to see what is going on out there." She went to InfoNet and there was that pushy reporter, Vaniere. She watched as he recited details of her life from the time she was born. There were photos of her parents, of her at her first dance recital. Where did he get these pictures? And I didn't go to Red Bird Kindergarten, dammit, it was Red Feather! She switched channels and there she was again. It was her, David, and Claire by the Christmas tree. Claire was smiling and holding a doll. David was smiling that handsome, crooked smile of his, his blue eyes sparkling as he held Claire in one arm, and had the other around Rosalind's shoulder. She couldn't look. It was one of her most cherished photos.

She switched channels again, and this time it was a reporter telling about how when she and David married, the Chicago social elites were shocked and dismayed that sexy David Evans was paired with a geeky science professor. There was their wedding picture!

Rosalind sat with the remote in her hand, dazed. In addition to the assault on her privacy, these people were obsessed with the idea that she had discovered some kind of divine message in the genetic code. She sat in a stupor while they attacked her motives, her character, her scientific integrity. At one point Edie tried to take the remote from her, but she had a death grip on it. They referred to her in the past tense, the former star molecular biologist, former wife, former mother. Aside from a sense that life as she knew it was over, she was amazed at the lengths people would go to keep the focus on her. Why? Didn't they have anything else to talk about? What little they knew about her they repeated ad nauseum, and when some new bit of information became known, it was treated as breaking news. It was like watching herself getting raped, methodically, over and over again, with the whole world watching.

Three days ago, she was a research scientist looking for polymorphisms in her safe little lab at the Clearbrook Institute. Today, her face was plastered on every newspaper and television screen in the country, maybe even the world.

The doorbell pierced the mood. Edie looked at the intercom video screen. "Don't look now, but I think it's the reporter who just made mincemeat out of your reputation."

Rosalind jumped up and looked. It was him, that idiot Vaniere. She pushed the intercom button. "Get out of here!"

"Dr. Evans? Open the door, please. I just want to hear your side of the story. I feel like this is my fault. Please, just talk to me for a few minutes."

It had been ridiculously easy for Vaniere to get this address based on the phone number, and he could not believe his great luck at finding her there when he arrived. It was nine a.m. and here he was, standing outside the front door of an apartment building in New York, talking to Rosalind Evans in person. Through several locked doors, admittedly, but he was talking to her.

"I can't tell a fair story if you won't talk to me. Please. I flew out here to hear your side of the story. C'mon. I brought breakfast." He held up a sack of donuts.

"I'm not hungry. And you are an idiot. Get lost," Rosalind said.

"Who else has bothered to get your side? Anyone? You have to let me in. The public has a right to know your side of this. All they are getting right now is everyone else's side of it. Buzz me in, please."

Edie was standing next to her. "I think you should let him in," she whispered.

"Are you out of your mind? This is the guy who got me into this mess."

"Maybe he's right, though. Maybe you ought to get your side of the story out."

"But I don't know what my side of the story is," Rosalind said.

"I'm going to let him in."

"If you do that, then I'll have to talk to him. If I talk to him, I'll say things I'll regret. He'll pry things out of me. It's what they do. Don't open the door."

"But if you don't talk to him, he'll make things up. Which is also what they do. So which is better, the real truth, or his version of the truth?"

"But what if I say too much?"

"That's why you've got me."

"He's probably got a camera. I don't want any cameras. Don't open the door."

Edie pushed the intercom button. "Do you have a camera?"

"No. Just me."

"No!" Rosalind said in a hoarse whisper.

"Yes. You'll do fine. Look, there's a hot-looking TV star outside and you want me to tell him to go away? That dude is gorgeous! I think I need to meet him."

"Shut up."

"You shut up. It's my door."

She buzzed him in.

Ron Vaniere sat down on Edie's couch and put a small recorder down on the coffee table. "Do you mind if I record our conversation. It's for accuracy."

Rosalind looked at Edie, who gave her a nod. "OK."

"Good. I have a pretty good understanding of basic genetics. You found something in the amino acid code that appears to be Biblical text. Exactly what did you find?"

"It spells out The Ten Commandments, to be precise," Rosalind said.

"How did it get there?"

"It's industrial espionage. Or maybe Joseph Steele did it."

"What evidence do you have that it was a trick?"

"My brain. Try using yours. If you know about amino acid code, then you know that the odds against it spelling out something intelligible are incalculably large. What else could it be but a trick?"

"How about divine intervention?"

"Oh you think so? God Almighty decided to send a message through the genetic code? Nice of him to do it in English. I don't speak Hebrew."

"Point taken. So when do we get real here? There is a whole world of people out there who are scared that this is the end of the world or something."

"*They're* scared? At least they have their dignity, their jobs, their husbands and their children! Don't talk to me about scared, Mr. Vaniere!" A tear escaped from her eye. She quickly wiped it away.

"Look, call me Ron. Rosalind, let's go off the record here for a minute. The media is going nuts out there. People are in a frenzy. What do *you* want to happen?"

Rosalind was silent for a long time. "I want my daughter back."

Vaniere was surprised, not by what she said but by his reaction to it. She was suddenly very real and he almost felt a stab of sympathy for her. He quickly pushed it aside. "I mean about the God Gene."

"I'm telling you," she said. "This code nonsense is nothing more than a case of industrial espionage. Spread the word, friend. I need my life back."

"I'll be glad to spread the word," Vaniere said. He looked at the TV, where her face was plastered across the screen. "But God only knows how you get your life back."

"I have a question for *you*, Ron. How did this get to be about me? Why are you guys making me the bad guy?"

Edie gave her a 'be careful' look with her eyes.

"Us guys?"

"Yes, you, the media," Rosalind said.

Vaniere had come here to extract every shred of information he could from her, but this woman was no shrinking violet. Even out of her element, holed up in a friend's apartment, dressed in sweats, her hair pulled back under a baseball cap, there was an aura about her that he found potentially disarming. Be careful, he told himself. "If the story isn't about you, then what is it about?"

"Some criminal out there tampered with my data! Now people really think there's a message written in the genetic code. It's insane."

"I'm not making you out to be the bad guy."

"Then why did you tell everyone that I claimed that I proved the existence of God?"

"I didn't say that. I asked the question: *Did* Rosalind Evans prove the existence of God?"

"What's the difference?" Rosalind asked.

"One is a question and one is a statement. I *asked*."

"OK, you asked. But the effect of your question is that now everyone thinks I said that. I never said that. It would be absurd."

"I can't be responsible for what everyone else thinks. I just ask the questions."

Rosalind looked at him for a long moment. He was an imposing presence, tall and strong. And obviously very smart. Did he really not know the effect his words had on people, or was he fast-talking her? "Then be very careful that you ask the *right* questions," she said.

"OK, let's start from the beginning. Tell me the whole story from your point of view. People out there need to hear the truth as you see it."

"The truth is the truth, no matter how I see it," she said.

"What is the truth?" Vaniere asked.

"I don't know how this happened. I only know I didn't put it there."

"Why do you think everyone is so obsessed with this story?" Vaniere said.

"Clearly they don't understand. They actually think there is a God out there who put a message in their genes."

"You don't believe in God?"

"Of course not. Show me one shred of evidence that there is a God out there who cares about us."

"Have you ever believed in God?"

She paused. "I suppose. My parents took me to church as a child. I learned about a nice man named Jesus, the son of God, who said everything would be alright. Everything's not alright."

"What *do* you believe in?"

Rosalind held her cup in both hands and blew on the steaming coffee. She held the cup up. "I believe in this … what I can see and hear and touch and taste and smell."

"And that's enough for you?"

"The natural world is plenty for me. Why would I clutter my mind with delusions when I have the mysteries of the natural world to solve? Life is hard, so man invented God to help him cope. I don't need that."

"Turn up the sound!" Edie yelled.

The screen had a News Alert banner, and the anchor, Claudia Moray, was talking.

"We are just getting breaking news. Associated Press is reporting that scientists at Flemingham University in Palo Alto have completed DNA testing in an effort to replicate the work of Dr. Rosalind Evans, the woman who discovered the so-called God Gene. We take you now to a live news conference with Flemingham's Director of Research."

The scene cut to a man standing at a podium outside a campus building. He was surrounded by several lab-coated men and women. They faced two dozen reporters and a rasher of TV cameras.

"Ladies and Gentlemen, I know it is early here on the West coast, but we wanted to inform you the minute we finished our analysis. We have been conducting DNA analysis from the exact location on the second chromosome that Dr. Evans was analyzing, the 2q13-2q14.1 region, and specifically, the CLAIRE gene. We have tested 15 DNA samples, using the same beta Deep X sequencing program that Dr. Evans used. We are now ready to announce that the Ten Commandments definitely are not written in the genetic code."

The reporters all shouted questions at the same time.

The Director of Research put up his hand. "Please, please, let me continue. Here is a page-by-page comparison of our findings and hers. As you can see, our results show an amino acid code that spells out a few words, but certainly not the entire Ten Commandments. Clearly, what Dr. Evans found is impossible. Either someone has intentionally manipulated her data, or she made a mistake such as a frameshift error."

Rosalind came out of her seat. "No!" she said. She turned up the volume and stayed very close to the TV screen, watching intently.

Edie saw the concerned look on her face. "Roz, what does this mean?"

"Shhh!" Rosalind said, her eyes glued to the screen.

The Director of Research went on. "We found a few words, but we most definitely did not find the Ten Commandments spelled out."

"How many words did you find?" a reporter asked.

"It is not unusual to find short words such as had, hat, the, day. We found a predictable number of those."

"Is that all?"

"No. We found two longer words: shalt and graven. CLAIRE is a very large gene. While it is very rare, we think the occurrence of these longer words is well within the realm of possibility. It happened naturally."

"Are you saying that Evans is lying?"

"We are saying that she is wrong. This should put an end to all the fuss." The Director of Research smiled broadly. "Well, if there are no further questions, thank you very much for coming."

"Wait, if you saw some of the words but not all, maybe it was you who made the mistake."

"We have sequenced and analyzed our samples in replicate; we are confident in our data. We are Flemingham. We maintain the highest standards in the scientific community. Others may continue analyzing the data, but as far as we are concerned, this case is closed."

The Director again thanked everyone and made a quick retreat.

The screen came back to Claudia Moray in the InfoNet studio. She looked as if someone had just asked her the square root of 5739. She tried to center, soul-to-soul, but she was too confused to make it happen. "Well, folks, there you have it. Flemingham University has replicated the work of Rosalind Evans, the God Gene lady, except they haven't really. I guess. We will be back at noon with more."

Edie turned the sound down. There was silence in the room for several moments. Rosalind drew her feet up onto the couch and chewed on her thumbnail. Vaniere and Edie watched her in silence, not knowing what to say. She sat for more than a minute, staring, thinking. Then she looked up with a smile. "This is great."

"Why?" Vaniere asked.

"I studied 7000 samples, using the most advanced software and the fastest computer on the planet. I didn't make a mistake. There is no frameshift."

"What is a frameshift?" Edie asked.

"There are several possible ways to group base code into three-letter codons. Only one produces the correct amino acid sequence and thus the correct protein. When bases are incorrectly grouped, it is called a frameshift error."

"So why did they get only a few words and you got the whole Ten Commandments?" Vaniere said.

"My data was tampered with. It's the only explanation."

"Why don't you rerun your samples to make sure?"

"Because Alan Dyer has the ANSR 1000 under siege until he finds out how the security breach took place and who did it."

Rosalind's cell phone rang. She quickly answered it. "Ben."

"I told you so. You made a mistake in your work."

"No I didn't! Weren't you listening? This proves we were hacked."

"Nonsense. Flemingham said you were wrong. The world thinks you were wrong."

"Then let me rerun the samples. That will prove I'm right."

"That's not going to happen any time soon. Get packed. Dyer is sending a Learjet to bring you home. It'll be at Newark in an hour and a half. Be there."

"Why?"

"It's safer for you to be here where we can protect you."

"Wouldn't I be safer here, where nobody knows where I am? Come to think of it, how do you know where I am?"

Edie pointed out the window. An army of media trucks and vans filled the street in front of the apartment building.

"The whole world knows where you are," Bradshaw said.

"I'm not getting on any small jet. There is no way."

"You don't have a choice."

"Get lost, Ben." Already her stomach was churning. Going down in flames.

"Be there. Your career depends on it"

"Are you threatening me?"

"No, Rosalind, I'm trying to save you."

"What are you talking about?"

"There have been death threats. Probably hacks, but we can't take any chances. We want you safe."

Death threats? Who on earth? "I'll be there," Rosalind said, and hung up. She looked at Vaniere and Edie. "He said there are death threats. He's sending a plane to take me home."

"Death threats?" Edie said.

"Yes, evidently there are people out there who still believe what they read in the papers and see on TV news. Here, Ron, sit down and watch for a few minutes. It's Independence Day and I haven't heard one word about it on any station." She turned up the sound. A reporter was talking, with a large picture of Rosalind as background.

"So what would have prompted Dr. Rosalind Evans to lie?" the reporter said. "Why would she go to such lengths to perpetrate this kind of fraud ..."

Vaniere watched for several minutes, flipping from one news channel to another. At last he shook his head and looked at Rosalind. "This is incredible. How does anyone know what the truth is?"

"Welcome to my world. Do you think I lied, Ron?"

"I don't know. But it doesn't matter; people *think* you did."

"Ah, and that's how we process information these days? He said, she said, take your pick? Can you understand why I feel all alone out here? I have no one willing to dig in and find the truth. And I can't do it myself, because Bradshaw locked me out."

Her head began to ache, a pinching, nervous throbbing in her temples, just thinking about getting on a little plane. She jumped up and headed for Edie's liquor cabinet.

"Anyone else want a drink?"

Edie and Vaniere both declined.

Rosalind flew into action dressing and packing and gulping gin. "All I do is run. I ought to run the New York Marathon. Do they allow gin in the Marathon?"

Edie had the curtain pulled back and was peeking out the front window. "You're going to have to run faster. There are more satellite trucks coming down the street," she said. "We better go. I know how to get you out of here through the basement."

Forty-five minutes later, the three were at Newark Airport. They said goodbye on the tarmac.

"I just have one more question, Rosalind," Vaniere said. "Why did Flemingham get two obviously Biblical words, but not the rest?"

"Either it happened naturally, which I doubt, or they made some sort of error. They don't have the ANSR 1000 you know. No one does but me."

"I'm going to call you when we get back to Chicago. There is more to this story than meets the eye."

She shook his outstretched hand. "You said it. Now I have a question for you. Are you looking for ratings, or the truth?"

"Both," Vaniere said.

"Maybe that's your problem. I hope you dig in and find the truth. Just remember, this isn't about me."

"If it's not about you, what *is* it about?"

"You're The Shovel. If anybody can find the answer, you can."

Chapter 23

SENATOR BOSCH WAS ushered into the Oval Office the minute he walked into the West Wing.

"Mr. President, happy Independence Day. Thank you for seeing me on such short notice." Bosch knew he would have to choose his words very carefully; there were voice recorders in the President's office. He could never understand why a man would intentionally allow his words to be recorded day in and day out. A man can make a mistake, and he ought to be allowed to do it without the whole world listening.

"I'm making my Independence Day address in just a few minutes. What's on your mind?"

"This God Gene thing has me worried," Bosch said. He pulled a paper from his pocket. "I think we need to do something quickly to protect ourselves from any future abuses of genetic information. I want to introduce a bill in the Senate to protect the nation. Here is my position statement: 'The God Gene crisis has shown that genomic data in the wrong hands can wreak havoc on our society. We believe this God Gene incident highlights a weakness in the way we protect sensitive scientific information. Right now, anyone can go to the Global Genomic Access site, take whatever data they want, and use it any way they want. They could cause panic among the people like Rosalind Evans did, they could engage in inhumane genetic engineering experiments, or they could build deadly biological weapons to be used against us. Therefore, I am introducing a bill in the Senate to regulate access to the Global Genomic Access center so that this kind of thing never happens. I believe our national security is at risk until we pass this bill.'"

"You want to nationalize the GGA?" the President said.

"Oh well, no. No, I would never do that." Bosch paused to choose his words. Blasted recorders, he thought, why can't I just say what's on my mind? But then, I know why. The American people wouldn't like what's on my mind right now; I need to get the news cycle back. By highlighting the danger Evans poses and offering a high profile solution, I might boot her to page two. The trick is to convince the President without coming right out and saying it. "We run the GGA for the world now. We bought the data storage racks from Japan with federal funds, we installed them in San Jose, and we staff the facility. I think we have the duty to protect the facility and the data."

"How will you protect it?" the President asked.

"We will block access to anyone who isn't a subscriber."

"And what would someone do to be a subscriber?"

"Pass some sort of background check and pay a fee."

"But isn't the scientific world going to balk at our charging a fee for something that really belongs in the public domain?"

"The information will still belong to the public. It will just be ... controlled. Someone has to be the gatekeeper, and that costs money."

"Won't the free-speechers go nuts?"

"We're doing it for national security. We can't just let every kook and terrorist have access to this stuff," Bosch said.

"That's a tough sell, Philip. I don't like it."

Bosch put his finger to his lips and handed the President a copy of the Starry Messenger story suggesting people go to the GGA and search for more messages in the code. The President read silently.

"Will people really do this? Who has the time for this kind of nonsense?" The President shoved the paper back at Bosch.

"Look at this," Bosch said. He produced a copy of another news item from the Internet.

Students at Arizona State University have issued a nationwide challenge to other colleges and universities to scour the human genome in search of

additional text messages. Student spokeswoman Stefanie Smith said, "We
consider it our responsibility as scientists to find whether or not there are more
messages, even in other languages, in the genetic code. Rosalind Evans's
discovery might just be the tip of the iceberg. We encourage scientists the world
over to join us in this search."

Bosch handed the President the story about Booth Slattery's million
dollar prize offer. He read the first paragraph.

The two men looked at each other, their mental calculators whirring.

"Hmmm. National security. Of course. And it is incumbent on us to
act quickly, before something bad happens," the President said.

"Yes sir. We have the opportunity here to do something big and bold
for our country. Will you support me on this?"

"It would have to be a long, detailed bill. These are complicated issues
with lots of scientific and computer language. How fast can you get that
written?" the President said.

"I've already started. I will call it an emergency bill. I'll call it the
'American Freedom of Scientific Information Act.'"

"Excellent."

"National defense is job one, isn't it?"

"The people are going to love you for this, P.P. Especially the swing
voters. How many subscribers do you think we can get to the GGA?"

"Globally, every university, research institution, school, hospital—tens
of thousands."

"Are you kidding?" The President raised his eyebrows.

"We can have levels of licensing, $500 a year for an individual, $1000
per year for a school, up to $10,000 per year for large research institutions.
That's a nice chunk of change."

"You're not kidding. We can put it under the Department of Health
and Human Services."

"Not urgent enough. Why don't you appoint a scientific information
czar to manage it?"

"Brilliant. But we'll have to hurry."

"There is no time for public debate on this. The people won't understand it, anyway. I'll get with the Speaker and the Leader this afternoon."

"I'll have my staff draft a message in support."

Bosch pulled another paper from his briefcase and handed it to the President. "I've already done that for you, Sir."

The President smiled. He read aloud: "I have no greater responsibility than to protect the security of the people of the United States. I ask Congress to place this bill on my desk as soon as possible. Do not be sidetracked by partisan politics. You must act now."

"This is your legacy, Mr. President."

"Nice job, P.P. This *is* urgent. It might be the most important thing I'll do as President."

Chapter 24

REV. JOSEPH STEELE was on his tenth and last TV news
interview of the day. His body was tired, but his spirit was invigorated. He
smiled at Claudia Moray and said a quick prayer for strength as the floor
manager counted them down.

"Our guest is Rev. Joseph Steele, pastor and TV evangelist. Rev.
Steele, earlier today at a news conference, scientists from Flemingham
University announced that they have disproved Dr. Rosalind Evans's claim
that our DNA carries an imprint of the Ten Commandments. What is your
reaction?"

"They're wrong! Great God Almighty, this is the most stunning
discovery since Moses and the tablets!" Steele said, in classic Steele
oratorical style. "Hallelujah, brothers and sisters, this is the second coming
of Christ! Get your affairs in order, my friends, reconcile with your maker,
for this is the end of times!!!" Steele was standing, waving his fist as if he
were in front of a live audience. Claudia motioned for him to sit, but Steele
ignored her. His eyes glistened as he thrust one hand heavenward and the
other clutching his chest. "Jesus, God Almighty ..."

"Rev. Steele, I can see you are enthused about this. Please sit down.
Thank you. Now, some say Dr. Evans was wrong. What do you think of
that?"

"How could she be wrong? It is right there in black and white! It is the
word of the Almighty. It is the fulfillment of the promise. It is God telling us
in no uncertain terms that we had better behave! Could I have an AMEN?"

Claudia shifted in her chair. "OK, amen. But what about Jews and Muslims?"

"That's the best part! Like Christians, they too believe in the God of Abraham, the same God who gave us the Ten Commandments. We all believe in the Ten Commandments as a code for living."

"So it's not just a Christian thing?"

"Certainly not. It is for all of us."

"Atheists, too?"

"Atheists above all! To all you atheists out there, if you do not believe this is a wake-up call, then I challenge you to come forward and have your DNA tested to see whether you have the imprint, too. It is written on our hearts just like God said! Hebrews 8:10 says 'This is the covenant I will establish with the people of Israel after that time, declares the Lord. I will put my laws in their minds and WRITE THEM ON THEIR HEARTS. I will be their God, and they will be my people!'"

Steele stood and waved his arms in the air. "Come on brothers and sisters. Rejoice! Our time has come!" He began to sway and dance to a beat only he could hear. He sashayed over to a young woman, a member of the floor crew, and began to dance with her. The cameraman struggled to keep him in the shot.

The producer yelled to Moray through her earpiece, "Stay with it! This is great! Camera one, stay on him!"

"Amen! Amen! All God's people said, Amen!" Steele grabbed a female camera operator and twirled her around. The young woman tried to pull away from him, but Steele grabbed her and pulled her back. She struggled as he danced her around, swung her and dipped her. He was oblivious to her wails of protest.

"AAAAWWWLLLLL God's children said AMEN!" Steele fell back into his chair, out of breath, smiling broadly. He had been at the top of his TV game for 24 hours now, making the rounds and shouting the good news: The God Gene is in us!! The God Gene is here! Our almighty God has revealed himself! For the first few hours after learning about the God Gene, he'd resisted, cynical as a heathen. But when his board urged him to embrace the God Gene, he saw clearly that it was the light of God shining down on him. You can't pretend something this big doesn't exist, he told himself. Get out there and spread the happy news!

"Rev. Steele, just two days ago, you vowed to shut Clearbrook Institute down. Is that still your plan?"

"Hellfire NO! That'd be like pourin' Roundup on the burnin' bush! Clearbrook is the holiest of holy places. I have dropped the charges and shut off the investigation. It is clear now that God WANTED them to be doing that genetic research. He wanted to be found! I have begun efforts now to have Clearbrook Hall placed on the National Historic Register. We are going to rent space inside for our First Light Campaign International Headquarters, so that we can conduct daily tours. I'm looking to have Rosalind Evans's lab declared a holy site by Christians, Jews and Muslims alike. It is a shrine that must be preserved!"

Claudia was having one of those misty moments. Not the crying kind, but the 'I don't know where to go from here' kind. "Rev. Steele, you're scaring me. What's happening here? The end of times? I mean, for real?"

"Of course you're scared, dear girl. This is a whoop stompin', gut wrenchin' get-down-on-your-knees-and-pray-for-mercy moment! I mean it! Get down on your knees!" Steele got out of his chair and knelt down on one knee next to Claudia. "Here, get down on your knees with me! Do it now! Can I have an AMEN?!"

Part II
Epiphany

Chapter 25

THOMAS O'ROARKE, U.S. Attorney for the Northern District of Illinois, held his hand out to his old friend. "Come in Duff! I am glad to see you."

"Blessings to you, Thomas. I have just come from the Holy Father."

O'Roarke gave his friend a bear hug and motioned for him to sit on the sofa by the window looking out on the Federal Center plaza five stories below. He poured coffee and handed a cup to the Cardinal.

"You look exhausted. Please sit down," O'Roarke said.

"Thank you, Tommy. What are you doing working on the 4th of July?"

"I'm knee deep in a Grand Jury investigation right now. We're investigating home-grown terrorism. Ugly. What about you?"

"Over the last 22 hours I flew to Rome, met with the Holy Father and his highest circle of advisors, including the *senatus scientificus*, and flew home. The first thing I did after we landed was call you." The Cardinal's face was serious and his hand trembled slightly as he raised the cup to his lips.

"No wonder you're wiped out," O'Roarke said. "How do you fly to Rome and back in 22 hours with meetings in between?"

"Well I didn't fly commercial, if that's what you mean," Duffy said.

"Ah, a charter. So my tithe is being put to good use? I'm so relieved."

"Tommy, you surely know about this God Gene thing? I'm afraid it's causing a crisis for the Church."

"Are you kidding me, Duff? This God Gene thing is a flash in the pan. I thought it was a joke."

"Sadly, no it isn't."

"What are you talking about?"

"This woman Rosalind Evans is claiming to have proof that God exists. The blogs have blasted it all over the globe. It's out of control. There isn't anyone who hasn't heard about it. The problem is, people *believe* her!"

"People believe the Ten Commandments are actually written in the genetic code? Come on."

"Yes. They do." The Cardinal stared out the window. His eyes showed weariness tinged with fear. "This thing has the potential to destroy the Church."

O'Roarke had grown up in Catholic schools from first grade, alongside his buddy Duff. While his attendance record at Mass these days wouldn't win any awards, O'Roarke still considered himself a man of faith. This God Gene thing is causing a media frenzy, but destroy the church? It made no sense. "How could she possibly do that? She's an obscure scientist who most people think is loony. Who would ever take her seriously?"

"*We* take her seriously. She is trying to turn the majesty and magnitude of God into something unholy! It doesn't matter whether she is crazy or not. She's evil."

"Evil? You mean *really* evil, as in an agent of Satan? That's crazy."

Cardinal Duffy's face twisted into a snarl that sent a chill down O'Roarke's spine. "That's how the enemy works. Subtle at first, disguised as something harmless, until it rears up and bites your head off."

"Wait a minute, Duff. Do you believe that the Ten Commandments are *actually* in the genetic code, put there by God?"

"Of course not."

"So where's the threat?"

"The Holy Father saw it right away. It took me ten hours alone on a plane to get it: From the moment the story broke, people have been profoundly affected by the idea that God is in our genes. The problem is, if enough people buy into this false theology, it could reach a point where we can't undo it. The momentum gets to be overwhelming and the Church goes into a death spiral."

O'Roarke felt a cold lump in the pit of his stomach. He had never heard Duff talk with such gravity about Satan or, God forbid, the death of the Church. What had happened in Rome that scared him this way?

Duffy looked at his watch. "Can you do better than coffee, Tommy? I have a conference call with the Vatican in half an hour."

O'Roarke opened a drawer. "Red Bull or Scotch?"

"Both," Duffy said.

O'Roarke was concerned about him. He looked as if he had fought a 12-round boxing match and lost. "Come on, Duff. This will all blow over. Nobody really believes any of it."

"You don't know what I saw. As I left for the airport, I saw people marching in the streets of Rome with signs that said, 'End of Days.' I saw people kneeling on the sidewalk, praying. There were throngs of people in St. Peter's, some of them crying, others radiating peace, as if they'd seen the face of God. The media in Europe are talking about little else. They think God put the Ten Commandments in our genetic code! What is happening to our world, Tommy?"

"But this whole story came out on Wednesday morning. This is Friday afternoon. How can it have spread so quickly?"

"We live in the age of instant communication. A decade ago, it took a week to get as much information as we now get thrown at us in one day," Duffy said.

"But why would so many people accept the concept of a message from God in the DNA when there is no proof?"

"Evans is an elite scientist. They think her discovery *is* proof. They desperately *want* God to be real. They *want* to believe."

"OK, but how can belief in God be bad for the Church?"

"You have forgotten one basic truth, Tommy! Faith is the church's only commodity; it's the only thing we have to sell. The essence of faith is doubt. You and I and billions of people around the world have faith in God because we don't really *know* whether he is out there or not! We have *faith* that he is, we believe that he is, but until we meet him face to face, we don't really *know*. So we struggle. We doubt. We pray. And most importantly, we turn to the *Church* to help us navigate all that mystery. The God Gene is destroying the mystery!"

Duffy held his glass out, and O'Roarke poured him another shot. There was no humor in Duff's expression, no warmth. His face was lacking color, as if he were deeply wounded and bleeding from the inside.

"Flemingham said it might be a frameshift. Doesn't that mean she was wrong?" O'Roarke didn't know for sure what a frameshift was, but everybody was talking about it in the media.

"You're not getting it, Tommy. A frameshift changes nothing. The truth changes nothing." Duffy ran his hand over his face and took a swig. "All that counts is what people *believe*."

O'Roarke, like most of the world's population, was clueless about the science of the God Gene. He was focused on the part of the story where the beautiful and mysterious mad scientist is publicly drawn and quartered. It was fun. But proof of God?

Duffy set his cup down and looked at O'Roarke intently. "We have to silence her."

"Whoa, buddy," O'Roarke said.

"We cannot allow her to destroy the Church."

O'Roarke leaned in close to his friend and spoke in a hoarse whisper. "You want her *killed*?"

"Jesus Mary and Joseph no, Tommy!"

"How can you stop her?" O'Roarke said.

"I don't know. That's why I came to see you. In the United States of America there has to be a way for the legal system to deal with people like Rosalind Evans."

"Only if she has committed a crime. To my knowledge, she hasn't."

"Isn't she perpetrating a fraud? She claims she proved there really is a God!"

"I'd call that a delusion or maybe a miracle. But not a crime."

"Then call it a conspiracy. Perjury. Heresy. I don't know, you're the lawyer. Think of something."

"What about evidence? All she has done is to find something strange in the genetic code, true or not."

Duffy ran his hand over his face in frustration. The Vatican was waiting to hear his plan, and so far there wasn't one. "She's terrorizing the faithful!"

"From what you say, it sounds like she's given the faithful something to rejoice in."

"Yes, well ... no. Tommy, listen to me. People don't know what to do. They're praying in the *streets*."

"Are you saying the churches are empty?"

"No. But they *will* be when people figure out that they don't need us anymore! Rosalind Evans is no better than a fanatical jihadist."

"Don't you think that's a little extreme?"

"No!"

"I have a special Grand Jury sitting right now that is investigating homegrown terrorism in Chicago. They have found things that would make your hair curl. You would be shocked if you knew how sick some of these jihadists are. And they are living right here among us! Rosalind Evans is nothing like them, Duff!"

Cardinal Duffy slowly drank down the rest of his scotch. "Clearbrook has federal contracts. Might she be violating the First Amendment by trying to establish a religion with federal funds?"

"It's what some are suggesting. I don't buy it. Besides, a constitutional case would take years."

"But that doesn't mean you couldn't launch an investigation."

O'Roarke thought for a moment. "It isn't enough to go on. Although, if we press her hard enough, ask enough questions, she's bound to say something under oath that isn't correct. Then we would have enough for a charge of perjury."

"All we need to do is marginalize her. Discredit her." Duffy said. The color was beginning to return to his face. "Then people will come to their senses."

"Hmmm," O'Roarke said, chewing the tip of his pen. He stared out into space for a moment, considering the possibilities. Then he abruptly stood up and shook his head.

"No, I don't want anything to do with this. I think you are out of your mind. I'm not going to risk my good name by trumping up some case that doesn't exist, especially when this is all a hoax to begin with. Besides, this Satan stuff scares the crap out of me."

The Cardinal stood and walked slowly to the window. In the Federal Center Plaza below, there were several hundred people taking part in a peaceful dance-like demonstration around the Flamingo sculpture, floating among the fifty-three foot vermillion arches as if enfolding themselves in the arms of God. Several were playing recorders and stringed instruments, others carrying flowers and singing. He couldn't hear them through the closed window, but he had the impression that they were holding some kind of vigil. What are they waiting for, he wondered. What will they do without the Church to guide them? The image of the Church of Rome under assault brought a deep sadness over his heart. The Holy Father has trusted me to do what is necessary. He is ill and knows that I will act in the Church's best interests, but by what means? How far do I go? After a long pause, Duffy spoke to his friend without turning around.

"Tommy, if Senator Bosch wins the election, he'll nominate you for Attorney General, right? Isn't that what you want?"

"More than anything."

"The Holy Father is going to make a Presidential endorsement. He will seek my council on that. If he endorses Bosch, it could put him over the top, don't you think?"

O'Roarke looked at his boyhood friend standing there with his back to him, dressed in black from head to toe, tall and imposing, silhouetted against the sunlit window. That's my Duff, he thought, never timid about playing the trump card. A little rattling of Evans's cage in exchange for a Cabinet post? He reached for the Scotch bottle. "Duff, the Pope's endorsement would be a game changer."

* * *

The God Gene: Who wins—science or religion?

My kittens, on this third day of the God Gene Era, who is winning— science or religion? If we are all carrying around a message from God in our genes, for whom is it a greater triumph—believers whose faith is justified, or scientists, whose methods revealed the truth? Are both equally victorious?

Science and religion have been at odds for hundreds of years, and the question of their reconciliation has been debated by the great

philosophers, so now, when it appears they may reconcile, what lessons have we learned?

How has your behavior changed in the last three days? Your mind? Your heart? How has the mere possibility of a message from God transformed you? Are you hopeful? Skeptical? Lightheaded? Nauseated? Is indifferent even a possibility?

If it all turns out to be a hoax and the Ten Commandments are *not* written in our genes, who wins then? Religion? Science? The perpetrators? Might the biggest losers be each and every one of us?

Chapter 26

TWO HOURS AFTER Cardinal Duffy's chartered Gulfstream
landed at O'Hare, Rosalind Evans's chartered Learjet touched down at
Midway. But time had no meaning for Rosalind Evans. She was deep
asleep, as she had been the entire flight. The pilot had to shake her several
times before she opened her eyes. The smell of gin permeated the cabin.

"Welcome to Chicago, Ma'am," he said. "We had a beautiful flight. Too
bad you missed it. There's a car waiting to take you home. I'll get your bag."

Rosalind slowly burbled into consciousness and realized where she
was. She mumbled a thank you to the pilot and climbed into the back seat
of the PharmaGen limo. She found an ice-cold bottle of water in the cooler.
She drank it all in one gulp and went for a second. Refreshed, she put the
window down and let the fresh air wash over her as the driver navigated the
busy streets of Chicago.

She was relieved to be back in Chicago where she felt in control of her
destiny. Now that I am home, she thought, I will be able to change the
course of events. Home. How wonderful it sounded. She would sleep in her
own bed, eat her own food, take a long, hot shower. She would be safe. She
reflected on the turn her life had taken. Dyer had first seen the Biblical
words in the code just four days ago. Since then, she'd been assaulted by
fanatics, called The Enemy by Joseph Steele, abandoned by her husband,
humiliated in front of her boss, put on administrative leave, attacked by the
media, and made a scapegoat in some kind of ridiculous public hysteria. No
wonder I'm exhausted, she thought.

There was not a breath of wind, and restless grey clouds roiled in the sky to the southwest. The oppressive heat wave was growing restless; Chicago was due for a change in the weather. The limo inched its way north on Lake Shore Drive. Gauging by the pace of holiday traffic, Rosalind guessed it would take 20-30 minutes to travel the three miles to her house. The limo suddenly lurched into the left turn lane at Balbo. Rosalind leaned up and tapped on the Plexiglas that separated her from the driver. He slid the window open a bit.

"Driver, I live in Streeterville. Why are you turning here?"

"You're not going home. Mr. Dyer is waiting for you. He instructed me to bring you to him. Your house is surrounded by media and tourists, so he arranged a safe place for you to stay."

"Where?" she asked, suddenly apprehensive.

"It's an apartment he keeps for out-of-town guests. He is waiting for you there now."

This sent up an instant red flag. She thought about the way Dyer had used Claire's memory to serve his selfish purposes; the cold, calculating way he had used her. *If he doesn't want me on the project anymore, so be it, but this has an ominous sound to it. I don't trust this guy. He clearly has no problem using people to suit his own needs.*

"I prefer to go home," she said to the driver.

"Sorry. I have orders."

"Let me out," she said.

"No can do, lady." He pushed a button and she heard the door locks click.

"Let me out, *now!*"

The driver said nothing.

They were in the thick of the traffic congestion around Grant Park. Taste of Chicago was in full swing, and a massive crowd was gathering for the fireworks later in the evening. The traffic light was red, and there were throngs of pedestrians in the crosswalk. The limo was stopped, waiting for the left-turn arrow. She made a split-second decision: She grabbed her shoulder bag and threw it out the window. She stuck a leg through and was about to launch herself out when the light turned green. Unaware that she was hanging out the window, the driver stepped on the gas. The limo lurched forward and Rosalind was thrown out the window like a sack of garbage. She landed flat on her backside on the pavement, next to her bag. The skirt of her sundress blew up in a flurry around her face. Unaware that he had lost his passenger, the driver sped West on Balbo.

Several men from the crowd of pedestrians rushed over and pulled her up. Cars screeched to a halt to avoid hitting them as they guided her to the curb. "You OK, ma'am?"

"I'm fine."

"Are you sure? Come on over and sit down for a minute …"

"No really. I'm fine," she said. "A little loss of dignity, but other than that, I'm fine, thanks."

The man laughed. "That was quite a stunt. There must have been something in there you really wanted to get away from."

"Yeah. The past." She turned and began to weave her way into the crowd in Grant Park. She suddenly realized that she had left her suitcase in the limo. It didn't matter. There wasn't anything in there she needed now. She was going home.

She took a deep breath and felt the same kind of rush she'd felt after stealing the data. She tucked her hair under her hat, put on her sunglasses and did the only thing she could: she hid in plain sight.

There were American flags everywhere, and the air was festive. No one seemed to have any inclination to look at her or to be concerned with anything beyond the reach of their own arms. She stood for a moment and watched the people, the city, the heat, the merriment, the firecrackers and sparklers. The scene was stunning: the streets were lined with vendors in tents selling food and drink, and people were celebrating amid a profusion of flowers and fountains, with Lake Michigan sparkling on one side and the Chicago skyline soaring on the other. She passed Buckingham Fountain and made her way to Columbus Drive. She heard the symphony orchestra playing patriotic music while children played games on the huge expanse of grass in Butler Field. This was Chicago's annual summer block party; there wasn't another like it in the world.

Famished, Rosalind walked along Columbus Drive, looking at the food offerings. There were tents on both sides of the blocked-off street selling all manner of food—Chinese, Indian, Vietnamese, African, hot dogs, pizza, barbeque—the smells were marvelous. The portions were small; the whole idea was to eat small portions so you could sample as many different foods as possible. She decided right then and there to set herself a new record for the number of foods sampled. The crowd was dense, but polite. Rosalind stopped and listened for a moment; strains of 'Stars and Stripes Forever' could be heard from the band shell. Nostalgia washed over her, and her heart ached to feel again the joy of just being, just taking in all this beauty with David and Claire and letting the summer air fill her with contentment.

She bought herself a slice of deep-dish pizza and carried it to a grassy spot under a tree. The smell of the sausage and gooey cheese brought back memories of the last time the three of them had been to Taste, exactly two years ago. She sat down on the grass and arranged the skirt of her sundress, just as she and Claire had done that day, and tried to connect to the lighthearted festivity of the moment. She munched the pizza and closed her eyes, listening to the music and the sounds of children playing tag in the park. She lay back on the cool grass and stretched her weary body. She badly needed the comfort of home. Maybe the limo driver was wrong about her house being surrounded. Maybe the media had grown tired of her by now and gone on to other things. A shower was going to feel so good. She felt herself beginning to relax. The breeze was picking up. The music …

She awoke with the feeling she wasn't alone. She opened one eye and saw a perfect circle of a dozen people looking down at her with curious expressions, their heads tilted, brows furrowed. A young lady gave her a sheepish little wave. "Hi-ya Roz." She turned to her friends. "Yeah. That's her." Several other people joined the group, craning their necks to see what was going on. Their slack-jawed stares were more unsettling than the frenzied reporters with their cameras had been. She scrambled to her feet and began to walk away.

A woman with a child reached out and pushed at her. "You're sick, you know that? You are messing with my little boy's mind. He was fine with God the way I taught him. And then you came along and now he's having nightmares. He thinks there's a ghost in his body!" The little boy, about seven years old, looked up at Rosalind with big frightened eyes.

A man spoke sharply to the woman. "Leave her alone. Are you crazy?" He reached out to pull her away from Rosalind.

The woman shoved him away. "Get your hands off me ..."

"Stop it!" Rosalind said. She turned to the mother. "I know what it feels like when your child is afraid. They need you to tell them everything is OK. This is one of those times when everything *is* OK." She leaned down to the little boy. At first he recoiled, but when she looked into his eyes he relaxed. She gently took hold of his shoulders. "What's your name?"

"Johnny."

"My name is Rosalind. Johnny, I want you to know that there is nothing to be afraid of. You are a fine, strong boy. Don't let anyone tell you that there is something wrong with you, OK?"

The boy looked at her with big eyes. "How do you know?" he asked.

"I am a scientist. The God Gene is nothing to be afraid of. You are fine, son. You are beautiful. Don't you worry about anything, OK?" The little boy nodded. The earnest innocence of his face reminded her of Claire. It tore at her to think that a little child was frightened of her. How could this be? She wanted so badly to hug him, to feel that connection again between mother and child: that precious, protective connection that you hope will never end. Even more, she wished that she could really believe this God Gene was something holy. It would be so nice to be able to let go of intellect and reason and believe it, like a child. But her empirical armor was too thick. She simply did not have the strength to chip away at it.

She smiled at the little boy. He smiled back. His mother took his hand and led him away. Before anyone could say another word, Rosalind Evans turned and ran like it was the end of the world.

She didn't care if she attracted attention; she had to get out of there. She had to go home. She ran north across Butler field, dodging folks on picnic blankets, all the way to Monroe Street. She stuck her hand out and within seconds a cab stopped. She jumped in and slammed the door behind her.

"Go!" she yelled.

The cabbie turned around and looked at her. He was about 30 years old, with dark eyes and a warm smile. "You are God Gene lady. Are you all right? You look frightened." He spoke with a Middle-Eastern accent.

"No, I'm not—well, yes I guess I am frightened. I want to go home." She gave him her address.

"Yes, of course," the young man said.

If my house is surrounded by media, she thought, I'll just have to face them head on. I'll just walk up my front steps, open my door, and walk in. They can't stop me.

The taxi turned onto her street. What she saw dissolved her courage. The street in front of her house was clogged with media trucks. Dozens of people were milling about on the sidewalk, in her yard, and even on her front porch. Camera lights blinked as reporters talked into their microphones. They were expecting her!

"Looks like you have company, mum."

"Don't stop. Turn! Quickly!"

"Don't worry, Mum. I will keep you safe." He swerved to the left and sped down a side street away from her place. "Where you want to go?"

Good question, she thought. I can't go to Clearbrook. She racked her brain, trying to think whom she might be safe with. Stefan Gunquist would take her in, but she felt she'd imposed on him enough. Taking in the great pariah Rosalind Evans would be like taking in a leper; no good could possibly come of it.

"I'll just get out here." It was a familiar neighborhood where there were plenty of cafes and shops. If she kept her head down, she could take a moment to gather her thoughts. She opened her purse and reached for her wallet. Her hand landed on the brochure that the couple on the plane had given her. She pulled it out and opened it. That crazy-sounding church of theirs, the Convocation of Manifest Souls. A Spa for Your Soul. Open 24-7. Weren't churches supposed to be places of sanctuary in times of trouble? Well, let's find out, she thought. "I want to go here," she said, handing the brochure with the address to the cabbie.

"Ah yes, I will take you there," he said.

Ten minutes later, the taxi pulled up in front of CMS. The cabbie reached over and turned off the meter.

"How much do I owe you?" she asked.

"You owe me nothing. It is I who owe you. We all owe you a great debt of gratitude. Thank you for this momentous discovery. I am in hopes it will help."

"Help?"

"Help stop the pain. There is too much pain in our land. Maybe now they will believe that Allah wants us to be kind."

Rosalind didn't know what to say. The young man reached his hand through the window. She reached up and they briefly shook hands. His dark eyes were smiling.

"Thank you." she said.

The CMS building was not a church; it was a twelve-story limestone mansion tucked into a side street off of State Street on the North Side. Inside the wrought iron fence was a lush, manicured lawn and garden filled with flowers. Outside the red front door was a beautiful, hand-painted sign: "A Spa for Your Soul. Come in." She walked in.

A woman at the desk looked up and smiled. She was fortyish, dressed in a white bathrobe with her hair pulled back in a loose ponytail.

"Hello there," she said. "Welcome to CMS. God bless you!" She smiled sweetly.

The lobby was high-ceilinged and spacious, painted in shades of blue and white. There were twinkling lights hanging from the ceiling, and people walking around in robes and slippers. Orchestral music played softly in the background, and the sounds of laughter floated from a room down the hall. There was a faint scent of incense in the air.

"I'm here to see Mr. and Mrs. Ellison, please."

"Well, sweetheart, you are in luck. They just got back. I'll get them for you."

She rang them up and handed the phone to Rosalind.

"Hello Lex. It's Rosalind Evans. From the plane? Can I come in?"

"Rosalind! Of course you can come in! Just jump on the elevator and push 12."

The elevator door opened on the twelfth floor, and there stood Lex, his arms open wide.

"I am so glad to see you. We have been watching the coverage almost non-stop and thinking you might not be taking this well. Are you OK?"

"Far from it. I'm sorry to impose, but my house is under siege. It seems I'm a hunted woman."

"I'm not surprised to hear it. We were just about to sit down to lunch. Come join us. Summer, we have a guest!"

Summer appeared from the kitchen clad in apron and oven mitts. "Rosalind! Gracious, how wonderful to see you, you poor thing. You are the woman of the week, I dare say!"

Summer gave her a big hug, which Rosalind did not resist, and led her to the kitchen, where she was greeted by the smell of garlic bread and spaghetti sauce. The few bites of pizza at Taste of Chicago had only whetted her appetite. She was famished. Summer poured her a glass of ice tea and handed it to her with a piece of freshly grilled garlic bread. "Take and eat!"

"Thanks," Roz said, taking a huge bite of the crispy, buttery bread and washing it down with sweet tea.

Summer motioned for her to sit down. "Take a load off. The spaghetti is almost ready."

"I hate to impose. It's just that I can't go home, I can't go to Clearbrook, and I just escaped a kidnapping attempt. I guess I'm throwing myself on your mercy …"

"Shhhh," Lex said. "Follow me." He led her down a hallway that was painted cobalt blue and lined with photos of smiling people. He pointed to a room on the left. "This is yours for as long as you need it. The bath is across the hall. We don't have any other guests at the moment, so it's all yours. Why don't you take a few minutes to yourself, settle in, and join us in the kitchen when you're ready?"

Rosalind walked slowly into the room and sat on the bed. She shook her head. She felt like she had just walked through the door to Oz.

"I don't know what to say. This is amazing. Thank you."

"You are more than welcome," Lex said. "Take your time."

The room was small, but full of lovely paintings and brightly colored, velvet-upholstered antique furniture. There were three white porcelain doves on the dresser, and a vase of fresh cut yellow tulips, almost as if they knew she was coming. The bed was an old-fashioned four-poster piled high with pillows and a down comforter. The reading lamp beside the bed was turned on, and there was a stack of books on the nightstand. On the wall above the bed hung a golden cross lighted from above. The Bose Wave radio on the dresser was playing 'String of Pearls' and the whole room smelled faintly of lavender. It was the most inviting place she'd ever been.

She took a deep breath and lay back on the covers. A profound peace settled over her and for a moment she forgot all about the turmoil and ugliness, and just let herself relax. Tears began to flow, but they were not the tears of anguish that had flowed last night at Edie's. They were tears of gratitude that these strangers had so willingly taken her in. No questions asked, they just opened their arms and took her in. Who does something like that? After several minutes, she sat up and stretched. Her headache was gone.

Lunch was all ready when she came back into the kitchen. A platter full of pillar candles burned in the center of the table, and as they sat down, Lex reached for her right hand, and Summer her left. "Would you like to say grace, Rosalind?" Summer asked brightly.

"I'll pass. I wouldn't have a clue what to say."

"Oh that's OK," Summer said with a solemn nod of the head. "Why don't we just do a silent blessing? That way you can let your heart talk instead of your mouth."

They sat silently, heads bowed for 20 seconds. "Amen! Amen! And Amen!" Lex said with a smile.

"I haven't done that in ages," Rosalind said, reaching for another piece of bread. "Thank you for taking me in. I feel like a refugee. I hope it will only be for a day or two."

"What are you a refugee from?" Lex said.

"An angry and confused world. People think something terrible has happened and they are blaming me."

"What is the world angry and confused about?"

Rosalind chewed her spaghetti and thought about the question.

"People are confused because they don't know what's true, and they are angry because the stakes are so high—God is important to them.

They're looking for someone to blame, and I'm it. All because of a misunderstanding of the facts."

"What are the facts?" Summer said.

"I found the Ten Commandments written in the genetic code. That is a fact. We don't know who put them there or why, but they are there. Flemingham found some of the same words, but not the entire Ten Commandments. And now, some people think a supernatural force is in their DNA. That really would be scary if it were true," Rosalind said.

"Scary? We think it would be awesome," Lex said.

"I don't want to be disrespectful," Rosalind said. "But this isn't about God. The God part is distracting us from finding out who is really to blame here. I only know it's not me."

Summer wiped the corners of her mouth with a lime-colored napkin. "Who is it then?"

"It might have been Danka-Saba Pharmaceutical Company. They are a rival of PharmaGen's. Billions of dollars are at stake in this pharmaceutical race. Or, it might have been Joseph Steele. He hates Clearbrook and wants us shut down. He might have done this to hurt us."

"I doubt it," Summer said. "I just saw him on TV praising you and the God Gene and saying he wants to turn your lab into a national shrine!"

"Shrine? To what, my pitiful excuse for a life?"

"What did the Flemingham findings mean?" Lex said.

Rosalind's fork stopped midway to her mouth. "Their base code is the same as mine. Their amino acid code is different from mine because mine was tampered with."

"But they got some of the words. Is it possible that someone hacked into both Clearbrook and Flemingham to plant data?"

"It's possible, of course."

"Is it possible that they hacked into Indiana University, Cold Harbor, Human Genome Research Institute and Edger-Fox Genomics, too?"

"I suppose so. But it's highly unlikely unless there is some kind of super cyber genetics plot we don't know about. Why?"

"Because all of the above found biblical words in the code today."

Rosalind dropped her fork. "Did they get the same base code?"

"Yes." Lex smiled at her across the candlelit table. He leaned forward and folded his hands. "Rosalind, this is a moment of discovery. You found a message from the Creator, a guidebook for living that he imprinted in our DNA so that one day, when science had advanced far enough, it would be found!"

It might have been exhaustion. It might have been the insanity of it all. Or maybe she was losing her mind. But Rosalind had no comeback for that. She just stared at him. He really was from Mars.

Summer shook her finger playfully in Rosalind's face. "Are you afraid of God, young lady?"

Rosalind cleared her throat, but her voice sounded raspy and tentative. "I am not afraid of God. What Lex just said is irrational. I can't accept it as a scientist."

"What about as a woman?" Lex said.

"You sound just like Stefan Gunquist. What is this, a conspiracy?"

"No. I'm just trying to look at this from another angle. When you are exploring something as a scientist, don't you have to set aside your prejudices and look at it from all angles?"

"Yes, but I do so within the laws of the natural world. You are talking voodoo."

"But the laws of the natural world change. Ancient man thought lightning, eclipses, and volcanoes were gods on the rampage," Lex said.

"Yes, we keep finding that things we thought were supernatural are not. In the end, I suspect we will find that there is no God at all and that there is a rational explanation for everything," Rosalind said.

"I see a lot of evidence to the contrary," Lex said.

Rosalind tossed her napkin down on the table. Her anger flared; she hated having to defend her lack of faith in God. It was easier to just live with it. "Well, if there is a God, why is the world such an unholy mess? Why doesn't he come down here and *do* something?"

Lex leaned in toward her. "You mean, why doesn't he come down here and do something for *me*?"

"I'm just saying, what good is a God who plays hard to get?"

"God isn't hard to get. He's *here*!" Summer said. "Why don't we go downstairs, and you can see for yourself."

Chapter 27

THE BOARDROOM AT corporate headquarters of Danka-Saba was peopled by twelve very agitated men and women. For three days now, they had been enjoying the madness; PharmaGen's leukemia research was in shambles, their lead scientist had gone completely off her rocker, and now they were the laughingstock of the industry. How lovely to watch a competitor self-destruct right before your very eyes. But Danka-Saba's merriment came to a screeching halt earlier in the day when their own good name was brought into the mess. The blogs and cable news had picked up on the accusation that Danka-Saba was responsible for altering Evans's code. The ripple of an accusation was rapidly becoming a tsunami. The Chairman of the Board had called an emergency meeting of the board to deal with the situation.

"The question is not why they accused us of compromising their data. That was predictable. They had to blame somebody for their incompetence. The question is—what we do about it now? This is a tricky situation that is spiraling out of control in the media," said Paul Raymond, the President and CEO of Danka-Saba.

"Don't you think the first thing we should do is deny it?" said the eighty-year-old Chairman.

"Why bother? Nobody will believe us," Raymond said.

"Because our reputation is at stake!" The Chairman pounded on the table with his fist. "We can't let them tell lies about us!"

"OK, let's think about this a minute," Raymond said. "At the rate they were going, they would have beaten us to clinical trials. However, thanks to Rosalind Evans, they are now dead in the water. I think we should lay low. As the saying goes, when your competitor is in the process of destroying himself, stay out of the way."

"How could it hurt to issue a simple statement saying we had nothing to do with it?" the Chairman said.

"Don't say a word." It was a voice in the back of the room.

"You always say that, Robert. You're a lawyer. If you had your way, none of us would ever get out of bed in the morning."

The Chairman stood. "Friends, I've heard enough. In my view, we cannot let our reputation be torn asunder with PharmaGen's. I am ready to vote to issue a statement saying that while we acknowledge the difficulty our esteemed competitor is going through, we categorically deny any involvement in it. We did not cause their data, or anyone else's, to be corrupted in any way. Period, the end."

"Don't say a word," the lawyer said again.

"Dammit Robert, the burden of proof is on them! If we don't deny it, we look guilty. The longer we stay silent, the guiltier we look. Show of hands, all in favor of issuing a statement? Eleven. Opposed? One. Paul, draft a statement and get it to me for approval. I want it released within the hour! Meeting adjourned."

As the board members rose to leave, one of them spoke up.

"Did we?" she asked.

"Did we what?" Paul Raymond said.

"Compromise their data."

"Well, there's the funny part. No. We didn't."

The President of Danka-Saba went back to his office and picked up the phone. This was a call he never imagined he would make.

Chapter 28

"YOU LOST HER?"

The limo driver stood in the entry foyer of Dyer's guest condo, fidgeting nervously with his cap and wishing he had the power to wind the clock back an hour. He didn't know Dyer well, just enough to be extremely nervous about delivering the news that somehow, the Evans woman had escaped.

"How do you lose a passenger from a moving limo with the doors and windows locked?" Dyer's demeanor was calm but the look on his face was stone cold.

"I have no clue."

"Where did she go?"

"I don't know. She must've got out on Balbo, somewhere between Lake Shore Drive and here. She probably disappeared into the crowd."

Without taking his steely eyes off the driver, Dyer drummed the coffee table with his fingertips and hummed slightly under his breath, a sinister, nameless dirge.

"Do you suppose our Little Miss God Gene performed a miracle? Did she just 'poof!' disappear like Jesus?" Dyer stared intently at the driver, who looked as nervous as a jackrabbit stuck in a wire fence. "Give me the keys," Dyer said. The driver handed over the limo keys. Dyer put them in his pocket, calmly took a sip of espresso, and looked over at Bradshaw, who sat silently on the other side of the room. There was no sound except the shushing of air through the ducts. Dyer stared at the driver for a full minute and then said in a disgusted growl, "Get out."

The driver took two steps backward, turned and made for the door.

Bradshaw stood and paced, his little footprints peppering the plush carpet. He looked out the window. "There are a million people in that crowd. We'll never find her," he said.

"We have no choice. We have to find her. We have to keep her from talking to the media."

Bradshaw agreed. Rosalind Evans was now the biggest threat to his job security. She had already brought Clearbrook a world of bad publicity, undoing a fortune in public relations just by talking to one stupid reporter for 30 seconds. Clearbrook's reputation was on perilous ground, and it was up to him to do everything necessary to protect it. He hated to think about what could happen if she really decided to flap her tongue about computer hacking and industrial sabotage.

"I want you to go find that computer guy," Dyer said.

"Mick the Tech? Why?"

"He has a score to settle with us and plenty of time on his hands. My guys discovered that data was copied from the ANSR 1000 the night he was fired. He has every reason to want to hurt us. The guy is a loose cannon."

"What did he copy?"

"The DZPro2 gene analysis. Now, listen carefully. With Evans on the loose, we are out of time. I want you to go find him and meet me in Millennium Park at the Bean in an hour. We have to get him on our side before she does. Go!"

Bradshaw looked at his watch. "I can't do it right now. I have plans."

"Plans? What, a midget convention?"

"No, I have to go see——."

"Do it later. This can't wait. The Bean. One hour." Bradshaw skittered out the door.

Dyer's phone rang and he quickly answered. "This is Alan Dyer."

"Hello, Alan. Paul Raymond from Danka-Saba."

There was a brief silence. "Why are you calling?" Dyer said.

"I think it is very important for you to know something, Alan. We did not corrupt your data. We didn't touch it."

"You're full of shit, Raymond. Don't waste my time."

"I wouldn't dream of it. But when my company's good name is in the game, I feel compelled to speak up. I can't explain what's going on with that data. You can blow me off and blame us if you want to. But you would be making a big mistake."

"Why are you telling me this? You know I have no reason to believe you."

"I know, and vice versa. But it's the truth. That's all I can say. We will be issuing a statement to that effect this afternoon."

There was a long silence on the other end of the phone. At last Dyer spoke, but the energy was gone from his voice. "If you didn't tamper with our data, then who did?"

"Even if I knew I wouldn't tell you."

Chapter 29

BRADSHAW STOOD IN his father's study and thought about what would happen if he ever actually did decide to skip one of these visits. But it was a useless exercise. These weekly visits were like taking cod liver oil: you had no choice, so you just held your nose until it was over.

"What kind of suit do you call that?" The old man sat in his recliner surrounded by books and papers. On the table beside him were an empty teacup and a single rose in a bud vase, slightly wilted, but still exhibiting signs of life. The study was dark and cool, as it had been for as long as Benton could remember. Father always kept the blinds half-louvered to keep the light out of his eyes. The room smelled of leather-bound law books and dust.

"What do you mean?"

"The pants are too long. You look homeless."

"It's the fashion. Women like it," Bradshaw said quietly.

"It's shameful. Take those off and I'll have Consuelo shorten them. Go on, it's OK. She won't mind."

"I'm not taking my pants off, Father."

"Consuelo! Come here please." A few seconds later the housekeeper appeared in the doorway.

"Stand up, Ben. Consuelo, shorten these pants the way they're supposed to be. Take them off, Bennie."

Consuelo eyed the cuffs of the pants, judging how much would need to come off.

Bradshaw slowly unbuckled his belt, unbuttoned and unzipped his pants. He let them fall to the floor, stepped out of them, bent over, picked them up, and handed them to the woman. She left. He sat back down.

"How are you feeling, Father?"

"Rather well. I won't bore you with my medical stories like an old man. Suffice it to say, I'm still kicking. Have you been nominated for the Nobel Prize yet? Isn't that why you do all that?"

"I'm working on a very important project, very profitable. I told you about it, remember?"

"Your brother Tom phoned yesterday to say he is now Senior Partner at Erickson and Blanke. He's moving the family to Los Angeles to run the office there. Great news."

Bradshaw felt even smaller than usual, sitting in the chair cross from his father. He felt that way not because the old man was so very tall, just six feet, and not because he was wearing no pants; Bradshaw's feeling of smallness came from Father's utter indifference when they conversed. For reasons Benton couldn't understand, nothing he said or did ever registered with the man. It wasn't that he disapproved; he simply didn't care. The reality was deeply etched in Bradshaw's soul, but it didn't keep him from trying.

"I have a classy office, too. It's at the top of the south tower at Clearbrook Hall. The penthouse."

"The penthouse? They have those in places like yours? I thought everything was stuffy laboratories and classrooms."

"Not everything. I'd like to have you come and see it. I have quite a view of the lake," Bradshaw said, searching the man's face for some sign of acknowledgement.

"You know I don't go out any more." He took a sip of tea and picked up the front section of the Trib. "This God Gene is making people crazy. It says here they are holding hands and singing on the CTA trains. Crime is down 80% in the city in the last three days. Fourth Presbyterian Church is holding worship services around the clock to handle the crowds. What the hell is going on around here?"

There was a momentary silence as his Father continued to read. Bradshaw hoped he was on to some other story-anything but the damn God Gene.

"What's all this about Joseph Steele wants to make Clearbrook a holy shrine? I thought he wanted to shut you down?" Father said, looking over the top of the paper at Bradshaw.

"We don't do anything at Clearbrook that warrants shutting us down."

"There is a lot of legal and moral controversy about genetic manipulation. Are you doing something illegal?"

"No, nothing like that. This project I mentioned is going to revolutionize leukemia treatment. I signed a deal with a pharmaceutical company for 15 million dollars."

The father snorted. "No wonder the cost of medicine is so high. Pour me some tea, will you?" He folded the paper and held out his cup. "What do you hear from your children?"

Bradshaw knew the question was coming. It always did. He imagined the sadistic pleasure his father felt asking it. The old man knew that Edward and Maggie lived on the East Coast, where they had moved years ago with their mother, and that they seldom, if ever, called their father.

"They're busy. I don't hear from them. I check their Facebook pages every day. As you know, Maggie teaches kindergarten, has a son three years old, and is divorced. Edward is single, a musician, and by the look of it, into dope."

"How can they make any money teaching and playing guitar?"

"I don't know."

"Edward should have been a lawyer. He's a smart boy. Can't you get them to do something better with their lives? They're poor."

Bradshaw tried to envision himself criticizing his son and daughter about their chosen lifestyles. It was the very image of futility.

"They're your children. Don't you owe them that?"

It might have been his state of exhaustion or his desperation about the PharmaGen project, but something about the question knocked open a new portal in him. Benton had lived a lifetime searching for a pathway to his father's soul, to the real man behind the façade. Now, sitting in the darkened study, he felt only a smoldering resentment toward the man. He suddenly had the urge to ask a question of his own, one he had always been afraid to ask. He leaned forward and looked directly into his father's eyes.

"Have you ever loved anyone?"

"I loved your mother very much." He said it without the slightest emotion, though Bradshaw didn't doubt it was true.

"Did you love us boys?"

The old man screwed up his face, clearly irritated. "You boys were born extensions of me. I had expectations about what you would do with your lives, how you would glorify the Bradshaw name. Your brothers understood that. But you never seemed to understand that you were brought into this world to conquer it. Nobody's ever heard of Benton Bradshaw the *scientist*. Nobody's ever seen you stand up and defend liberty in a court of law! You sit in a stuffy room and make deals with greedy businessmen to do what? Study chemicals? Raise the price of medicine? This is a profession?"

"Do you love us now?"

The striated light filtered through the blinds and cut across the old man's face like ripped cotton. "Where I come from, you don't ask a man a question like that. Be a man, Ben." He looked away.

Benton felt as if a taut line in his chest suddenly snapped. He stood and made his way toward the door.

"Where are you going? You've only been here five minutes," the old man said.

"Good bye, Father."

The father picked up a book and opened it to a marked page. He looked at Benton over the tops of his glasses. "I'll tell the boys you came by. They'll be pleased."

Bradshaw walked out into the sultry afternoon, his mind so consumed with bitterness that he forgot he was wearing only boxers. He walked to the corner and hailed a cab.

He jumped into the back seat and pulled out his cell phone to call Mick the Tech. "Millennium Park," he told the cabbie.

As the cab pulled away from the curb, the cabbie looked at him in the rear view mirror. "Did you forget something, sir?"

Bradshaw looked down with a start. The sight of his little twig legs sans pants snapped rubber bands in his head.

"Stop!" Bradshaw yelled. The cab slammed to a halt. For a split second, he considered running back into the house to retrieve his pants.

"No, never mind, go!" The cab lurched forward. It would have been the normal thing to do, to grovel in front of his father and beg for his pants back. But today wasn't normal. Sitting in the back of a taxi in his boxer shorts, he saw with laser clarity that the servitude was now over. All the self-loathing he'd endured at the hands of his father burst out in a hot plume of anger. He opened the window and shook his fist at the house. "I'll show you, you sack of sludge! I am NOT the sniveling failure you think I am! I am Benton Bradshaw the MAN!"

Chapter 30

LEX LED SUMMER and Rosalind down a quiet hallway at CMS and opened a door. When Rosalind stepped into the room, her first sensation was of having no senses at all. It was perfectly quiet, the air was filled with white mist, and there were no discernible edges that separated floors from walls and walls from ceilings. She could see no other people besides Lex and Summer.

"I feel like I've stepped off into another dimension," Rosalind said.

"You have," Summer said with a lilt in her voice as if she had a juicy, scandalous secret she was dying to tell.

The room got darker and darker, until they could barely see each other. Lex led Rosalind to what looked like a gossamer hammock, suspended from an unseen ceiling by an invisible mechanism. He motioned for her to lie down on it. She shook her head.

"It's easy," Summer said. "Try it. You'll like it," she said.

"Why? What's going to happen if I do?"

"You're going to fly with God! It's thrilling. The wind blows, the orchestra plays, and you fly through the stars. Everybody loves it!"

Rosalind shook her head and headed for the door. "I'll pass. I hate to fly. You mentioned holograms. What's that about?"

Lex smiled and ushered them out into the hallway. "We have a volunteer think tank that constantly comes up with new ways to enhance God-connectedness. The hologram team is a group of social scientists, theologians, and computer scientists who came up with a computer program that merges scripture, social science, and psychology to create a problem-solving model for modern day. Kind of a 'what would Jesus do' for the digital generation. The algorithm makes it possible to voice your concerns or questions directly to 'Jesus.' It's one thing to hear your pastor or your friend give you advice, but another thing to hear it right from the mouth of 'Jesus.'" Lex made quotation marks with his fingers each time he said Jesus. "It creates a power surge in your soul. They're working on the Spanish version right now." Lex swung open a door and they peeked inside a smallish room with chairs and mats on the floor. There, seated in front of a small group of people, was the holographic 'Jesus.' He looked real as life. He was speaking in a low tone, and she couldn't quite hear what he was saying, but the sight of him made her gasp. She backed away and closed the door.

"Holy realism! Way too much for me."

Lex and Summer laughed. "Nothing to be afraid of. Science keeps offering up new ways to behold the enormity of God's creation," Summer said.

"Did you say something about a hot tub? That I could get into."

"Yes, the God Consciousness Hot Tub," Summer said. "Follow me."

On the fourth floor was a large natatorium with a glassed-off area in the middle that contained a round pool, 40 feet in diameter, with steam rising from it and a number of oscillating underwater lights. Bubbles emanated from the bottom and outer perimeter of the pool. From a high ceiling shone a single spotlight that created a cross-shaped light in the center of the pool, where the water was still. People sat on an underwater bench in water chest-high, relaxing and talking. Some, wrapped in robes and towels, sat in lounge chairs scattered around the deck.

"The locker room is over there," Summer said. "You'll find swimsuits, robes and towels in there. Just grab what you need and jump in."

"Oh, I don't want to intrude on these people. They seem to be having some sort of gathering in there."

"No problem. This is an ongoing thing. No beginning, no end. Everyone is welcome. Just jump in when the spirit moves you and stay as long as you like. We'll be at the juice bar," Lex said, pointing to a gaily-lit café on the far end of the room.

Rosalind went into the locker room and changed into a conservative one-piece swimsuit. Suitably covered, she ventured into the pool area. She stuck a toe in and found it delightfully warm. Sliding into the bubbling water, she marveled at how relaxed she was. She'd felt that way from the minute she walked into CMS. There was something about the place. She rarely experienced true relaxation, had almost forgotten what it felt like, but a warm tranquility pervaded this place. The people seemed to have an air of anticipation, and their body language conveyed reverence and playfulness all at the same time. This was not like any church experience she had ever had. As the cleansing waters swirled around her, she felt for a moment that things might not be as bad as she'd thought just a few hours ago. Surely Bradshaw would reinstate her so that she could resolve the PharmaGen issues and get on to the next project. She needed to find out how this hoax or anomaly or whatever it was had happened. Flemingham found some words but not all. Why? She would call Bradshaw as soon as she got back to her room and persuade him to let her come back to work. There was so much work to do.

She closed her eyes and laid her head back against the side of the pool. The water felt light and rejuvenating and smelled minty. The bubbles and water jets played over her body, washing away the detritus of the past week. She felt like she could sleep, right there, for days.

"Don't want to stay in too long or you'll melt." A woman smiled and sat down next to her in the pool. She appeared to be about 60 years old, although it was hard to tell in the undulating light. She had a sweet smile and a warm countenance about her, and her curly blondish hair formed a halo around her face.

Rosalind opened her eyes and smiled. "I think I could stay a lifetime," she said.

"Your first time here?" the woman asked.

Rosalind nodded.

"I come as often as I can. I wish I had more time for it."

"What occupies your time when you're not here?"

"I'm a neurosurgeon at Rush Medical Center. You?"

Rosalind thought before she spoke. She was just beginning to feel safe and she didn't want to draw attention to herself.

"Never mind. I know who you are." The woman smiled. "Don't worry, no one will harass you here. If you've come for shelter from the storm, then you've come to the right place. You must be exhausted."

Rosalind nodded, looking around at the others in the pool and on the deck. They all seemed to be engaged in conversation or simply relaxing in solitude. Unlike at the airport, no one here recognized her, or if they did, they weren't concerned about it.

"You must be a devout believer to have been chosen for this," the woman said.

"I'm not a believer at all," Rosalind said, splashing water over her face and head.

The woman laughed. "Figures," she said. "The rest of us labor and strain to get closer to God, and you, a non-believer, get the golden ticket."

Ticket to hell, Rosalind thought. "You are a scientist. How do you justify your belief in God?"

"On a temporal level, I can't prove it. On a spiritual level, I can't deny it."

Rosalind looked around at the others. "Do all these people feel the same way?"

"I can't say for sure. Maybe some of them are here because it's the best spa in town and it's free."

"Who are all these people?"

"Humankind. Like people in every civilization since the dawn of recorded time, they seek God. It's a universal longing."

"I don't have it," Rosalind said.

"I suppose it's possible, but it's more likely you've forgotten you have it. A lot of things can make us forget. Like the secular media, for instance. Or science. Maybe that's what happened to you. But you have to understand that the God Gene is a life-altering discovery for most of us," the woman said.

"Then why is everyone making me out to be the bad guy?"

"They can only make you the bad guy if you let them."

"I don't think I can stop them. If I walk out there, they'll kill me," Rosalind said.

"How long do you think you can hide?"

"Lex says I can stay as long as I want. At the rate things are going, I might die here."

"It's quite possible. Many have."

"What?"

"Spiritually. Letting the old self die and a new self be reborn," the woman said.

"It makes no sense. All this sensory stuff—lights, smoke, mirrors—it just makes it *feel* like there's a ghost in the room."

"Not exactly. We westerners don't get it. We're all in our heads. Our minds are saturated with food, drugs, booze, sex, money, instant gratification—all the things that can stultify the spirit if you let them. CMS is about finding new ways to reconnect."

"Isn't it all just neurobiology? The lights and music cause changes in brain chemistry, which causes feelings of religious fervor. There's nothing supernatural about that," Rosalind said.

"You missed a step. When the lights flash and the music soars, it ignites chemical reactions in the brain that enlarge consciousness, and *that* opens spiritual pathways to God. God was there all along. This is just a way for us to connect with him on a deeper, more intuitive level. The way the pre-Christians did."

"Before Christ?"

"No. After Christ, but before the Christian Church."

"How did they do it?"

"They invoked him. Pure and simple. No rules, no liturgy, no fuss."

"Why don't you just do that today? Why do you need all this?"

The woman looked around the room, at the lights, the water, and the pilgrims seeking God. "Remediation. Just pick up a newspaper or watch TV news; we are a people gone missing from our Creator. We need drastic measures to get back in the groove."

"And are there fairies in your garden that dance at night?" Rosalind said.

The woman laughed. "Sorry, I'm over-articulating. Let's quit talking about it and just do it," she said.

People were leaving their chairs and getting into the water and arranging themselves around the perimeter of the pool. Some of them were holding hands.

"What's going on?" Rosalind asked.

"Intuitive prayer circle. Here, take my hand."

Rosalind did as the woman asked, feeling awkward and a bit wary. As a child she was taught that religion was a personal thing. You didn't talk about it or show it in public. But something about the warm water and the tension-reducing qualities of the jets and bubbles made her go along with it. Soon the entire perimeter of the pool was filled with people standing in chest-high water, holding hands. A man stepped out of the circle and waded into the center of the pool and stood in the cross-shaped light shining down from above. A voice from across the circle spoke out.

"John has asked us to pray for him and his wife, who has cancer. We pray, God, for the light of your love and wisdom upon them in this hour."

The man raised his arms and looked up into the light.

There was music in the background, an instrumental rock-orchestra that rose in volume. The people were silent, some looking up at the light with their arms outstretched, others with their heads bowed and their eyes closed. After a minute or two, the man lowered his arms and waded back to the circle. A woman took his place in the center of the pool. She asked that they pray for her as she struggled to support her family. Again, the music soared and the people prayed silently. Then another person came to the center of the pool and asked that they pray for the President of the United States and all who advise him. Again there came the music and the silent prayers.

The process went on for several minutes. Rosalind noticed that they seemed very focused, even intense, as they prayed. Without a word, they seemed to invoke some kind of collective power, and it changed the energy in the room. The whole place went from casual, with people splashing and talking, to highly energized. The people who were praying seemed to be concentrating, like they were sending out some kind of energy. The people who were being prayed for appeared to be absorbing the energy, and it seemed to change their countenance, to relax them. The receivers' faces took on a look of innocence and receptivity, like children hearing a story. She was reminded of a study she once read about how patients who were prayed for—even if they didn't know it—recovered better than those who weren't. She thought there must be some mechanism we don't know about yet that transfers energy via thought waves. These people seem to be transformed by the experience of being prayed for, even before any outcome could be realized. What was happening to them? Rosalind didn't know, but she did know that the focused spiritual energy of this group was having a calming effect on her. She wondered what it would feel like to walk into the center and ask for them to pray for her.

The woman leaned over. "Do you want to go to the center and ask for prayer?"

"No, please. I can't."

"Would you like me to do it for you? It's just as good," the woman said.

"Well ..."

The woman dropped her hand and waded to the center.

"God I lift up Rosalind to you. Please calm her and open the pathways of truth and peace." She raised her hands heavenward and the music again rose.

Rosalind looked around at the others in the pool. All appeared to be very focused and calm. What are they thinking, she wondered. They don't even know me. She closed her eyes. Something in her seemed to let loose and she felt a tingling sensation in her hands that spread up and across her chest. She began to feel light-headed. Under other circumstances she might have thought she was having a heart attack, but some higher place in her mind told her it wasn't. She breathed and waited. It was like being high; it felt good. The feelings intensified and she felt like a feather in the wind, weightless and drifting. There was no fear, only a mild curiosity. Where am I, she wondered. She slowly opened her eyes. The woman turned to her and smiled.

"What just happened?" Rosalind said.

"You tell me."

"Can't explain it. Don't know."

Rosalind leaned back into the warm water. The tingling was subsiding, and she felt a kind of headiness that wasn't dizziness and wasn't high. It was more like hyper-awareness; the lights were brighter, the colors deeper, the rush of water over her skin more stimulating.

"Rosalind?" Lex said in a gentle voice. He and Summer reached for her, but she didn't want to move. They each took an arm and helped her out of the pool and onto a chair on the pool deck.

"Here, drink this," Summer said. "Carrot mango delight."

Rosalind took a sip. To her surprise, she liked it. It refreshed her. "What just happened in there? I was watching these people praying and then the whole room changed. Are these people on something? Is that what you do here?"

Lex and Summer laughed. They had been accused of many things since starting their 21st century, pre-Christian congregation, but never of being drug dealers.

"No. Your God Gene is expressing."

"My God Gene." She glanced up at one of several TVs in the café. To her relief, her picture wasn't on it, but there was a scene of a throng of people in Jerusalem, singing and holding banners that featured a cross, a star of David and a star and crescent.

"Look at that! Everyone's God Gene seems to be expressing!" Summer said. "What you were feeling in the water was the Holy Spirit. You were totally opened to it. That's unusual for a first-timer."

"I'd rather have gin. At least I know what it will and won't do to me."

"It takes some getting used to," Summer said. "I suggest at this point that you rest and let your soul settle a bit. You're like a spiritual athlete on the first day of training." She handed Rosalind a towel.

As she toweled off, Rosalind found her thoughts returning to earth. "I'd love to go back in there and get high again, but I have a lot of work to do. There were only six commandments in the CLAIRE gene. This morning I found the other four. If you want to pray, ask God to give me a sign about what I'm supposed to do about it."

"I'd be honored," Lex said.

"I'm afraid I need to ask another favor. I need to go home and get my laptop and my notes. I have to study the data and see how Flemingham came up with their results. Could you drive me?" Rosalind asked.

"I'll go get the car while you change," Lex said.

Rosalind wondered what she would find when she got home. Would the TV trucks still be there? Would there be people milling outside the front door? How would she get in? Should she even try? She felt she had no choice; if she were going to spend several days at CMS, she would need her laptop and some fresh clothes. I think I can sneak in the back and avoid the cameras, she thought. The calmness of the last hour was rapidly dissipating. The thought of all those strangers and cameras gave her a chill.

Chapter 31

SINCE IT'S UNVEILING several years earlier, the popular sculpture Cloud Gate, AKA The Bean, had become one of the most popular attractions in Chicago. From all directions, the mirrored finish of the kidney bean-shaped arch reflected the sky and the surrounding buildings. Walking under the 25-foot arch and gazing up at the 'navel' of the bean provided visitors a sense of other-worldliness. For some, it was like floating, for others it was like spiraling downward into another dimension. For Mick the Tech, it evoked mirrored ceilings and very large female body parts. He was standing under the Bean, watching Fourth of July revelers make their way through Millennium Park and thinking how happy, carefree, half-drunk and hooked up they were. Like he had been just a half hour ago, until his nice day at the beach was rudely and needlessly interrupted by a phone call from the midget from hell. With lots of time on his hands and a sunny, hot Fourth of July stretching out in front of him, he could not have been more irritated at the call. He'd been just about to make a hit on a red-lipped redhead when the phone rang. Bradshaw said they needed to meet right away, but wouldn't say what it was about. He only said it would be worth it. Well it better be, Mick thought. I don't trust that guy any further than I could throw him.

Millennium Park was massively crowded. There were kids playing in the fountains, families picnicking on the grass, revelers dining in the café— Mick felt like the only unhappy person in the place. Bradshaw waved as he rushed toward him. Mick nodded at him and noticed with some curiosity that he was dressed in a coat and tie, black wing tips, black socks, and white shorts that almost looked like ... boxers?

"Nice outfit, Bradshaw."

"Thank you."

"Who's your tailor? This is hot."

"I forgot to put my pants back on."

"Ooh. My Man Bradshaw, shootin' off firecrackers on the Fourth of July! What's the chick wearin'?"

"I need your help," Bradshaw said.

"Help? I should beat the crap out of you."

"For what?"

"For getting me fired."

"I didn't get you fired. Rosalind Evans did."

"What do you want? I got better things to do than sit on a park bench with a dwarf in underpants."

"Dyer knows you stole some data from the ANSR 1000 the night before you were fired."

"What?! That's a crock. I didn't steal anything."

"Dyer thinks you did. You were the only one besides him who had a passcode."

"I was home all night that night. I was on my computer. You can check it out for yourself."

"Was anyone with you?"

Mick thought for a moment. For once in his life when he needed an alibi, he didn't have anyone to vouch for him. The fact was, that night was a blur to him. There certainly had been a load of booze and there might have been some weed. He was celebrating the fact that Starry Messenger wrote to him. He had a dim memory of Rosalind calling him.

"I was alone, but Rozzie called me at home. It was late. I was wasted."

"Rosalind called you? Why?"

Mick laughed. "Why do you think? She's hot for me. She wanted to have a little fun over the phone."

"What did she say?"

"I'm not the kind to kiss and tell," Mick said with a lascivious grin. "But she is naughty, if you know what I mean."

Bradshaw laughed out loud. Rosalind Evans naughty? He was amazed at the lengths this guy would go to impress the world with his manhood. He tried to imagine Rosalind talking dirty to Mick the Tech over the phone, but his mind refused to cobble together that vision.

Dyer appeared, walking quickly toward them through the arch of the Bean. He wasn't smiling.

"Mick, I have a proposition for you," Dyer said.

"Oh yeah? It better involve a woman. You're interrupting my 4th of July."

"I know you stole some of my data. That wasn't very nice of you."

"I did not—"

"Bag it, Morrison. I know you did it. But I'm willing to let it go if you will do me a favor."

"What kind of favor?" Mick looked skeptical.

"I want you to work with Ben. Snoop through Evans's computer and see if you can find something we could use against her, make her look bad."

"I'm not working with this guy. He got me fired."

"No," Dyer said. "Rosalind Evans got you fired. If you want to get back at somebody, get back at her."

"What would I be looking for?"

"You know, porn sites, nasty photos, something illegal. A smoking gun."

"Why me? You have your own computer spies."

"They're busy trying to figure out if we were hacked," Dyer said.

"This sounds risky to me. Forget it."

"So I should go ahead and press charges against you for stealing my data?" Dyer said with the slightest smirk.

"Go ahead. I didn't do it."

"Come on, Morrison," Dyer said, putting an arm around Mick's shoulder. "I want you to help me save my project. Our leukemia work is too important to let a nutcase like Rosalind Evans ruin it. We are in this to help children. You want to help children, don't you?"

"I'll do it on one condition; I want my job back."

"You find me a smoking gun I can use against Evans and you'll have your job back," Dyer said.

Bradshaw looked like he'd been shot. "What?! You don't have the authority to give him his job back. You can't do that!"

Dyer stared down at Bradshaw, his eyebrows raised and his head cocked to one side. "Really?"

Bradshaw slumped.

"I'm in," Mick said. "When do I start?"

"Right now," Dyer said.

"But it's the Fourth of July, Dude."

"How very patriotic of you," Bradshaw said.

"It's not about patriotism. It's about scenery. Have you been to the beach today? I'm not sitting in some stinking lab when I can be at the beach!"

"So you don't want your job back?" Dyer said, his voice dead calm.

Bradshaw turned and marched purposefully up Michigan Avenue oblivious to the people pointing at his boxers. Deflated, Mick followed. This dirt ball is too stupid to know that I am already way ahead of him, he fumed.

What no one knew was that he'd hacked remotely into Evans's laptop the day he was fired and found some very interesting stuff. The photos had already made him good money.

Chapter 32

RON VANIERE SAT on the plane from New York to Chicago, his laptop open in front of him and his brain running wild. *Just a few hours ago, Rosalind Evans told me this God Gene thing wasn't about her,* he thought, *but I've got news: it's all about her.* After spending several hours together, hearing her describe the God Gene, watching that dramatic moment at Flemingham with her, seeing her cry, he was more convinced than ever that the God Gene alone was a story, but the God Gene with the brilliant, beautiful, wounded, frightened Rosalind Evans smack in the middle of it was a blockbuster. *The God Gene lady wants her dead daughter back. The God Gene lady is an atheist. The God Gene lady thinks it's all a hoax. The God Gene lady insists she didn't make a mistake. And the whole world thinks she performed a miracle.* He wrote like a mad man, typing, deleting, typing, deleting—working to find the lead.

He couldn't pat himself on the back enough. *You are The Shovel, Man. You just scored the hottest interview on the planet. Now, since nobody knows what to think about the God Gene, you're going to tell them. Is it a hoax? A case of sabotage? Or a message from God?*

"You're the shovel, aren't you?" The boy next to him must have been about ten. He had a round, freckled face, a crew cut, and glasses. "My dad watches you all the time." The boy looked back down at the game he was playing on his iPhone. His thumbs continuously plied the keyboard as he kept talking. "I want to be a TV reporter when I grow up."

"Why?"

"Because you get to be famous and rich and you get girls."

"If you're good at it, yes. But that's not the point. You want to be a reporter so you can tell the truth."

"Well, it doesn't matter anyhow, because my Dad won't let me."

"Why not?"

"He says I have to do something important." The boy looked up at him with an expression of nonchalant acceptance, then looked back down at his game.

"He doesn't think reporting news is important?"

"No. He says they call you The Shovel because you're a big tool."

"Why?"

"You never say anything good about anybody."

"That's not my job. My job is to report the news. There is no good news. Not that anybody wants to hear, anyway."

"That's lame."

"It's true. If I went on TV and said 'The President beat up his wife today,' people would find that interesting. If I said 'The President and his wife got along fine today,' people would be bored and change the channel, and I'd get fired."

"You're lame *and* a tool," the kid said, sounding like someone who had just contributed greatly to the knowledge of mankind. He went on with his game.

"Have a little respect, buddy. Where are your parents, anyway?"

"My mom lives in New York, and my dad lives in Chicago."

"So you're flying alone?"

The kid nodded. "I do it every other weekend."

Vaniere wondered how a kid's life gets so deconstructed. "Hey, if your dad thinks I'm such a tool, why does he keep watching me?"

The kid shrugged. "Beats me. Maybe he's an idiot like my mom says."

Vaniere couldn't decide which was sadder: that the kid was a divorce victim or that he thought his dad was an idiot for watching the Shovel on TV. He went back to his typing.

The one thing he thought strange about the interview was Rosalind's lack of guile and pretense. He was so used to dealing with politicians who lied and dodged and evaded that he didn't know what to do with someone who seemed to be—how to describe it—real. She is cynical about the whole God Gene affair, he thought, yet she is frightened and bereft. She is an atheist, yet millions of people actually think she discovered a message from God. But she is real. No wonder she's cynical. Rosalind Evans, the cynical messiah. A chill ran down Vaniere's back. There it is. He typed as fast as he could.

A few minutes later, the kid reached over and poked him in the arm. "Hey Tool," he said without looking up from his phone. "You said all news is bad. What about that lady everybody's talking about who proved there really is a God? Isn't that good news?"

"Yes, it is," Vaniere said.

"So you're not reporting on it?"

"Yes, I am."

"Man, you really are lame."

* * *

When Vaniere walked into the InfoNet offices a couple of hours later, the place was like a morgue. No one was smiling. Not that the place was ever relaxed, but it was usually congenial. Not today. No one noticed him walk in, and when he greeted people on the way to his office, they barely nodded.

"Vaniere! Where on earth have you been? Look at this." The Assignment Editor gestured toward the assignment board. "Can you believe this?" His hair was disheveled and his eyes bugged out like he'd gulped a fifth of Jack. The board was overloaded. There were felt tip pen scribbles and sticky notes all over it.

"I've been in New York. What on earth happened?" Vaniere said.

"The freakin' God Gene, that's what. I have vetted the list and I've still got more interviews and press conferences than I could handle in a month. Take your pick. Oh, you can cross Steele off. He's been here and gone. Hysterical. It's leading at five. What were you doing in New York?"

"Interviewing Rosalind Evans."

The assignment editor's jaw dropped. He stared at Vaniere, awestruck.

"You ... are ... shitting ... me! No *way!*"

"I just spent two hours with her. I have to get the story ready."

"Video?"

"No."

"Audio?"

"Of course." Vaniere held up his recorder.

"Are you serious? Rosalind Evans? You're gonna make me cry."

"It's an exclusive."

The assignment editor threw his arms around Vaniere and gave him a bear hug.

"Don't you kiss me, man," Vaniere said.

The editor whooped and wiped a tear. Vaniere looked at the board. "I've only got a couple of hours to get my story together. Let's talk about this tomorrow."

"At the rate my blood pressure is rising, there won't be a tomorrow. I'll take the Mayor and ACLU press conferences, those are easy. I'll give the priest to Blake, she's Catholic. I'll put interns on the churches. We've got Washington covered by the bureau guys. Can you interview Bradshaw, O'Roarke, Bosch and Duffy?"

"OK."

"You'll lead at six with Rosalind Evans. You are the man!!!!"

"You need to take a break, buddy. You're going to blow up."

"No can do. Pass the Red Bull."

Vaniere poured himself a cup of coffee and went to his office. He needed to scan the news networks to see what they had on the story. He knew he had the only interview with Evans. This meant that everybody else was scrambling. But nothing could have prepared him for the chaos he saw as he channel surfed. The God Gene story was out of control.

"The ACLU announced today that it will file suit against Dr. Rosalind Evans for violation of the First Amendment. They have concluded that her research, which was partially funded by the federal government, claims to have proved that God exists as a physical certainty rather than as a matter of personal choice. This is a violation of the First Amendment, they say. PharmaGen, the corporate sponsor of Dr. Evans' research, and Dr. Benton Bradshaw, Director of the Clearbrook Institute, will be named as co-defendants."

"At a dozen university campuses across the country today, students staged loud and noisy demonstrations protesting the God Gene and demanding that Dr. Rosalind Evans renounce the findings. They say they will protest every day until she makes a public recantation. One of the protests was at Rutherford University, the home of the Clearbrook Institute where Dr. Evans made her discovery." The scene cut to film of a young man surrounded by other angry-looking students holding protest signs. *"We are outraged that this woman, working right here in our own backyard, is trying to subvert the free expression of religious belief. By shoving the God Gene down our throats, she is committing a government-supported act of terrorism against those who want nothing to do with her God. We are demanding that she appear here on the steps of the Student Center and publicly recant her ridiculous claim that she has found proof of the existence of the public delusion known as god."* The scene cut to a close-up of a girl, who was sobbing. *"I didn't come to college to be like terrorized. I want to believe what I want to believe. I don't want someone telling me what to believe. I look all around me and I'm like scared or whatever. Is there anybody I can trust?"*

"Senator P. Philip Bosch, Chairman of the Senate Judiciary Committee, said today in a press conference that he will call for an emergency Senate investigation into the God Gene affair. He said, quote, I feel it is my duty as Chairman to quickly find out whether this woman poses a threat to our national security. Her claim that she has proved the existence of God is a direct assault on the First Amendment. Freedom of religion is one of our dearest liberties in America, and we will not stand idle and let anyone, not even an esteemed scientist like Dr. Evans, trample on that freedom. We know that she is working in the very sensitive area of genetic engineering. We intend to find out what that's all about, too. Hearings on this matter will commence at 9 a.m. this coming Wednesday. I urge the public not to panic. I can personally promise you that I will find out what this lady has up her sleeve, unquote."

"In a clash of presidential contenders, Governor Willard Hitchcock today lashed out at Senator P. Philip Bosch for, quote, 'politicizing the God Gene.' He spoke with reporters this morning. The scene cut to Hitchcock in

front of the cameras. '*I question Senator Bosch's motives here. Dr. Rosalind Evans has discovered something that appears to be a message from the almighty. But he has ascribed motives to her that are anything but holy. He is attacking her as un-American! Really, Senator Bosch? A woman who has done nothing more than analyze bits of DNA is assaulting the First Amendment? And now, Senator Bosch, you are calling for an investigation? Hmmm. He gives all new meaning to the word opportunist!*"

This is chaos, Vaniere thought. Everybody on the planet is talking about the God Gene, but nobody has a clue what the story is. He smiled. All the more reason why they need me to tell them.

He sat down at his computer and began to type. Only a few hours ago, I saw this woman's tears and vulnerability, he thought. I felt raw fear radiating from her, like an animal that senses predators closing in. I know who she is. I might be a tool, but I'm the only tool who has looked Rosalind Evans in the eye and heard her tell her story. Now it's my story. too.

Chapter 33

ROSALIND AND LEX made their way to Dearborn and swung south toward her house. She opened the car window and let the summer air blow through her still-damp hair. She heard the sounds of firecrackers and children laughing and thought sadly that this was not the way she would spend the Fourth of July if she had a choice. But having choices was a thing of the past.

As they approached her house, she could see that the street in front was full of cars and media vans. They were stalking her like wild animals. "Drive around back," Rosalind told Lex.

She was relieved to see that there were no vehicles in the narrow, rutted alleyway. "Keep the car running." She jumped out, ducked into a gangway on the right side of the house, and waited. When she was sure there was no one watching her, she climbed the stairs to the back entrance, stuck the key in and opened the door.

The house was dim in the early evening light. She decided not to turn on any lamps, so as not to alert the hungry lions out front that somebody was here. Feeling like an intruder in her own home, she tiptoed toward the front window to peek out. How unfair, she thought; those people are trampling the flowers and will never in a million years pay for the damage. They only care that they get their story. She breathed in the familiar smells of home and thought about how good it would be to curl up in her own bed and go to sleep. Suddenly she heard a noise behind her. She whirled around and saw the silhouette of a man in the bedroom doorway. She froze.

"I've been waiting for you, Roz."

It took a moment to realize who it was. "What are you doing here?"

"I wanted to make sure you were safe."

"How did you get in?"

"I live here."

"You *used* to live here!"

"You look great," David said. "Where have you been?"

"You wouldn't believe me if I told you." She grabbed a bag and began stuffing it with papers from her desk.

"Have you heard the latest news?"

"What news?"

"The ACLU announced they're going to file suit against you."

She stopped and looked at him. "For what?"

"Oh, something about a First Amendment violation, infringing on people's right to free exercise of religion, that sort of thing."

"That's nuts!"

"Yes, but that's not going to stop them."

"But I haven't done anything wrong."

"Rosalind, you are in a heap of legal trouble. I want to help you."

"Ha. If you wanted to help me, you wouldn't have left me. I can find a lawyer by myself." She jammed a stack of papers into her bag, dropping half of them on the floor.

"Of course you could. Is that what you want?"

"David, you are so annoying. You think you can just have a fling with your secretary, skip off and abandon me, and then expect me to be glad you want to be my lawyer?"

"Abandon?"

"What would *you* call it?" she yelled.

"Survival. You were killing me. I didn't like being last on your priority list."

"You were *never* last."

"How was I supposed to know that? You hardly talk to me. We haven't made love in months."

"I needed time! You couldn't have had a little faith in me?"

"Why do you think I'm here?"

She hated it when he wore that expression he always used when he was trying to soften her up: a little vulnerable, a little wide-eyed, a lot sexy.

"I don't need a lawyer." She picked up her bag and headed for the door.

"Where are you going?"

"Back to CMS. It's a church. I am staying there until all this blows over."

"Roz, I hate to tell you this, but this isn't going to blow over. You are in deep trouble."

"I have to go." She looked out the back window. Two TV vans had pulled up behind Lex's car and a third was on the way.

"They'll follow you," David said.

"They can't follow me into the church."

"Oh yes they can. This isn't the Middle Ages. You should come to the boat with me. They can't follow you out there."

"No! I'm not going anywhere with you."

David put his hands on her shoulders and lifted her chin. "I will walk out the door right now if you want me to."

She looked out the window at the TV trucks. Cameras on tripods were pointed directly at her back door, ready for the kill. She looked up at him with wide eyes. "Just walk me to Lex's car, then you can go. You know I hate cameras."

"You can hide behind me, or you can walk out with your head high and get in the car. Either way they'll take your picture and smear it all over the front pages. It just depends on what you want the world to see."

"You really annoy me when you're right."

David took her arm and opened the back door. Immediately, the doors on the TV trucks opened and people rushed toward the landing. Spotlights shone in their faces as David held her arm and steered her toward Lex's car. She wanted to run and hide. The reporters shoved microphones in her face and shouted questions.

"How did you find the God Gene?"

"Do you think it is a message from the almighty?"

"Is it true that you are having an affair with Mick the Tech?"

"Why are you staying at CMS? What are you hiding?"

How could they have known where I'm staying, she wondered. She started to put her hand up to shield her eyes from the light and from the terrifying reality of all those cameras focused on her. Then she remembered what David said. She stopped and looked out at the knot of reporters.

"This isn't about me. I am looking for the same thing you are—the truth." They all started shouting again. She turned to get in Lex's car when a man walked up next to her.

"Rosalind Fanning Evans?" he said softly. The tone of his voice was friendly, so different from the frenetic reporters, and it made her think he might be someone she knew. He smiled warmly at her.

"Yes."

"You are served." He slapped an envelope into her hand. Seeing this, the reporters surged toward Rosalind. David quickly pushed her into the back of Lex's car and jumped in after her.

"Let's go!" he said. Lex peeled out, leaving the reporters standing in the alley.

"Where are we going?" Lex said.

"CMS," Rosalind said.

"Are you sure?" David said. "They know you are staying there. They will be relentless."

Lex drove as fast as he dared, dodging through side streets in an effort to evade the media trucks.

"Lex, this is my, uh, husband, David. He's a lawyer and a jerk."

"Looks like you'll need one. A lawyer, that is."

Despite the jostling in the back seat, David managed to open the envelope. He read quietly for a moment.

"Well, my dear, it seems that Senator P. Philip Bosch requests, or rather demands, the pleasure of your company at a special Senate Judiciary Committee hearing on national security, and the potential threat thereto posed by none other than your very self."

Rosalind saw by his expression that he was not kidding.

"Threat?! What are they talking about?"

"I don't know."

"Forget it. I'm not going into that lion's den."

"I don't think you have a choice. It's that, or a Contempt of Congress citation."

"Oh I have contempt for Congress alright."

"Sorry, Roz. You've been subpoenaed. If you ignore it, they can, and will, hold you in contempt. You don't want that, trust me."

"I have to go to Washington D.C. and testify at a Senate hearing?"

"Precisely."

"They allow cameras in there?"

"Afraid so."

"When?"

"Wednesday. This is Friday. You need a lawyer."

Lex slowed in front of CMS. It was surrounded by media. They were staked out, waiting for her.

"We better keep going." David said.

"No! Lex, isn't there another way we can get in?"

"Yes, but you need to know that CMS is an open door. We say 'everyone welcome' because we mean it. We don't screen people at the door. In God's house, everyone is welcome, even a reporter."

"Great. I'm a fugitive in my own town. Now where do I go?"

"Lex, turn right and head for Lake Shore Drive," David said. "And drive like you're in the movies. We need to lose these yahoos behind us." There were three media trucks still following them.

Lex squealed the tires as he made a hard right and zoomed east.

"Where are we going?" Lex said.

"Du Sable Harbor," David said.

"No!" Rosalind protested.

"You'll be safe on the boat. Let's go there and make a new plan," David said. "Lex, exit at Randolph."

"I will not go to the boat with you, dammit! You left me!" Rosalind was jostled around the back seat as the car swerved, accelerated, braked, and swerved again.

Lex drove as fast as he dared, dodging heavy Fourth of July traffic. He could see in the rear view mirror that several TV trucks were still there, though he was pulling ahead of them. He waited until the last minute, then swerved into the right lane and made a quick exit at Randolph Street.

"Pull into the parking lot and drop us there," David said.

"I'm not going with you, David. I'm going with Lex."

"Rosalind, let's not argue about this. I can help you. We'll be safe on the boat."

"Uh, I think you better make a decision," Lex said, eyeing the rear view mirror. "The paparazzi have arrived."

The dock was wall-to-water full of people waiting for the fireworks to begin. David grabbed Rosalind's hand and pulled her out of the car. He wove them through the crowd toward the gate to B Dock. David punched in the security code, pulled open the heavy steel gate, and they dashed through. The gate closed with a solid clank behind them. They were safe. They ran down the dock to *Proteus'* slip. Without a word, David started the engine and they untied her.

Outside the locked gate, a group of reporters and photographers watched helplessly as *Proteus* pulled out of its slip. They had put on a good chase, but their quarry was now on the other side of a locked gate, heading out of the harbor.

"Dammit! She's a slippery one. It's like she can beam herself from one place to another," one reporter said.

"Hey, who knows somebody with a speed boat?" another asked.

"Maybe we could rent one."

They ran to the Harbor Master's office at the end of the pier. It was late, but the office was open for the holiday.

Inside, the Harbor Master sat on a metal stool, reading a newspaper behind the counter. The place smelled of stale coffee and diesel fuel.

"We need to charter a power boat," one of the reporters said to him.

"Nope," the Harbor Master said without looking up from his newspaper.

"Why not? I know how to drive a boat. C'mon, man, we're in a hurry!"

"Nope."

"Why not?"

"Small craft warning. Big storm comin' our way. Trust me, boys, you do not want to be on the water when this bitch hits."

Chapter 34

ONCE *PROTEUS* WAS past the harbor entrance and out into the open water, Rosalind took the helm and swung her into the southerly breeze as she had done hundreds of times before. With a mighty effort, David cranked the winch and raised the mainsail up the sixty-foot mast. He instructed Rosalind to turn the boat a little left, off the breeze, and then he unfurled the jib.

"Take her on a beam reach heading east," David said. He shut off the engine and tweaked the sail trim until he was satisfied they were getting the most out of her. They were barely making three knots on a calm sea, but it didn't matter; they weren't in a hurry now. After clearing through a cluster of boats close to shore, David turned on the autopilot and stood in the companionway looking up at the sails. They had always enjoyed watching the huge white sails fill with air and feeling the boat surge along on the power of the wind alone. But not this evening. Rosalind was confused and angry about David's sudden reappearance and David was wondering whether he had made a mistake in offering to help her; it would be the challenge of a lifetime for a host of reasons. Neither of them noticed the beauty of the setting sun nor the gentle breeze that propelled *Proteus* eastward away from the city.

"Why did you come, David?"

"Because you need a lawyer. I'm a lawyer."

"How do you expect me to act like there's nothing wrong? How am I supposed to feel when every time I turn around, there you are, the man who cheated on me? The man who can't stand living with me?"

"I can't sit back and let them crucify you."

Rosalind sat silently for a moment, contemplating the idea of being humiliated by a bunch of politicians in front of the entire world.

"Why do I need a lawyer? I'll just answer the Senators's questions and leave. How bad could it be?" she said.

"They will tear you apart. It's what they do."

"But why? I haven't done anything wrong."

"That's not the point. They think you pose a threat. Whether you do or not is irrelevant."

"But they don't have any evidence against me!"

"Public uproar is all the evidence they need. The press is comparing you to Galileo."

"Except that in Galileo's day, the Church had all the power. Now it's the politicians and the media who run the show," Rosalind said.

"Remember that when the Church called Galileo a heretic for saying the earth revolved around the sun, he did the smart thing: he recanted. They let him live. Now the politicians are calling you a threat to national security. Recantation might be a smart option for you, too."

"You're kidding, right? Galileo recanted so they wouldn't kill him. But he didn't mean it. During his house arrest he wrote a treatise *proving* what he had just denied, that the earth revolves around the sun."

"You are proving my point. It doesn't matter what you believe; say you were wrong and everybody goes home," David said with a shrug.

"Wrong about what?"

"About the God Gene."

Rosalind stared out at the black water. It would be so easy to just say 'I'm sorry. I was wrong.' And let it go at that. I so badly want all of this to go away, she thought. I want to wake up in my own bed and go to work in my lab and forget this all happened.

"But I'm not wrong. The God Gene is not a mistake. The words are there. Flemingham found a few of the same words. So did several other labs."

"OK, so maybe you were right. Galileo was right, too. That's not the point. When the powers that be want to burn you at the stake, the smart thing to do is blow out the match. Say it was all a mistake," David said.

"I did not make a mistake! I will not lie, and you are NOT my lawyer!" Rosalind turned around and grabbed hold of the backstay. The breeze blew her hair in a flurry around her face. It was chilly and the wind was beginning to stir up waves, but she didn't care. There was a burning anger in her, at the reporters, the politicians, the religious maniacs, and at David for suggesting she lie to get herself out of this. She whirled around and faced him.

"I will not stop until I get to the bottom of this, whatever it is. I am a scientist! My life depends on the truth."

"What *is* the truth, Rosalind?"

"I don't know what the God Gene means or how it got there. All I know is it's there. It exists. Someone planted it there, but it's *there*. My work stands on its merits! Why should I apologize for that?"

"Can you tell me you didn't make a mistake in your analysis?"

"Yes!"

"Can you tell me you believe the Ten Commandments are written in the genetic code at the center of the second chromosome?"

"Yes!"

"Can you tell me it's a message from God and therefore proof that He exists?"

"No!"

"Then that is what you will say on Wednesday. And it wouldn't hurt to show a little humility in front of the Senators."

"I'll say what I want and I don't need you getting in the way!"

Silhouetted against the moonlit sky, she was the most beautiful thing he had ever seen. The life force flowed through her like a torrent, and he realized in that moment that she was more alive now than she had been since before Claire died. This was his Roz, full of passion, always looking for the truth; this was the love of his life. He took hold of her arm and spun her around. He pulled her towards him and kissed her hard. Before she could protest, he kissed her again. He ran his hands through her hair and breathed in her scent, the intoxicating smell of this woman he had loved so completely. He pulled her in close and felt the contours of her body against his. Not caring that she resisted, he held her tighter, reaching down her back and across the curve of her buttocks.

"I don't give a damn about being your lawyer," he whispered. He kissed her hard, again and again.

"Get away from me!" She pushed at him with all her might, but the harder she struggled, the harder he held on to her. She was no match for the strength of his sailor's arms, and no match for the determination in his grip. He pushed her down on the cockpit seat. He embraced her as she struggled, and the darkness closed in around them.

The suddenness and intensity of his passion took her by surprise. She had forgotten what it was like. She stopped struggling and looked into his eyes. What she saw surprised her. Instead of anger or desire, she saw vulnerability. His glistening eyes were pleading with her. His lips were inches from hers.

"Forgive me, Rosalind." His voice was deep and rough. "I'm sorry. Come back to me. Come back."

His eyes bore into her and he kissed her again and again. The realization flooded over her that he was not forcing himself on her; he was engulfing her. She pulled him close and closed her eyes. This was David, the only man she had ever loved. He was back. He was *here*. Some inner force let loose and she tore at him, devouring him with her hands and her mouth, pulling him close, closer than he had been in more than a year. *Proteus* swayed up and down in cadence with the building wind and waves, and with the rhythm of their union.

Afterward, they lay silently for several minutes as the night air cooled, and David wrapped his arms around her to keep her warm. A huge starburst lit up the sky over the city. They looked at each other and laughed.

"Fireworks," David said. "How fitting." They lay together and watched the massive display booming and soaring overhead. David looked around and saw that they were nearly alone out on the lake. That was odd for the Fourth of July when the lakefront was usually clogged with boats for the fireworks. Where was everybody?

When the show was over, Rosalind turned to him and buried her face in his chest. "I'm glad you're here," she whispered.

He ran his hand through her hair and kissed the top of her head.

"I am, too. You'd never be able to handle the sails by yourself."

"I'm serious."

"I know you are. I'm just using humor to cover up my massive fear that this isn't for real."

Rosalind leaned up. "This? You mean us?"

David nodded. "Maybe if you tell me you love me and we prick our fingers and mingle our blood, I'd feel better."

"I've always loved you."

"OK, then. Here's the new rule. You have to *show* me you love me, not just tell me, OK?" He laughed; she didn't.

Tears stung her eyes. "I stopped showing you, didn't I? That was as unfaithful to you as your infidelity was to me. I must have hurt you so badly …"

"The pain couldn't end the love. The pain only ended the relationship."

She hugged him. "I'm so sorry, David."

He sat up and took a deep breath. "You should be. You'll have to swim five laps around the boat for penance."

She smiled, and then her face grew serious again. "I was so preoccupied with Claire. And then she was gone."

"Claire is not gone. She has moved on to something better. She's with God. I believe that. People find it hard to hold deep spiritual beliefs these days. I don't."

"I wish I could believe it."

"Listen to you. People think you discovered proof of God and you don't even believe in God. How funny."

"Stefan Gunquist thinks God has a sense of humor, too. Maybe the two of you are right and I'm wrong."

He gave her a bear hug. "Did you hear that? You know what that was? A flash of humility! There's hope for you yet, love!" David smiled, but he could see that she wasn't in the mood for levity.

"I lost everything that was important to me, David." She looked up at him. "Claire, you, and now my life's work. The ground keeps shifting under my feet. Thank you for coming back to help me. You're right, I need you."

He wrapped his arms around her and held her tight. "I'm not going anywhere."

"I wonder whether it's possible to be happy again?"

"It's up to you. How happy are you willing to be?"

She lay there silently for a long moment thinking about the question, trying to visualize what happiness might look like now. For the first time in a year and a half, she had a glimmer of hope that it might be possible. She smiled.

David cocked one ear. "The wind's kicked up. I better check the instruments."

"Never mind the wind." She hugged him closer.

"You can't ignore mother nature. She always wins." He got up and pulled his pants on. He helped her up, and as she stood in the moonlight her skin looked like white silk, soft and luminescent. Her auburn hair fell across her shoulders, and her violet eyes glistened.

"You are a work of art, Rosalind." She smiled at him, and he saw something renewed in her. There was an openness in her expression that reminded him of the woman he'd first met at the Museum of Science and Industry those many years ago.

He stepped behind the wheel and checked the weather instruments. "Wind's up to 15 knots," he said. He pressed a series of buttons on the navigation system and pulled up the satellite weather map. "Uh oh. Not good." David pointed toward the west. Lightning flashed in the distance.

"It's almost on us," he said.

The radar weather map showed the entire Chicago area covered in red and yellow, indicating severe thunderstorms. The whole mess was now over the western suburbs and headed straight for downtown and the lake. The roiling waves and strong winds that precede a heavy storm would soon be upon them. They would have to work fast to secure *Proteus* for the brunt of the storm.

David dashed below and grabbed their foul-weather gear, two inflatable life jackets, and two tethers. Rosalind quickly threw her clothes on. She could see by his expression that the fun and games were over. Without a word, they each donned their rain suits and safety gear. He quickly checked their position on the GPS.

"We're five miles off shore. There's no way we can make it in before this storm hits. We're going to have to deal with it." Fingers of lightning flicked across the western sky, and the rumbling of thunder echoed through the buildings in the distance.

"Can't we motor in?" Rosalind said.

"No. We're 45 minutes from the harbor, at best. We don't have that much time."

"OK, Captain, whatever you say," Rosalind said, trying to sound a good deal calmer than she really was.

"Take the wheel. Fix your safety line to the binnacle. Turn 30 degrees left."

Rosalind took hold of the huge wheel and began to make the turn. She had a lot of experience helming *Proteus*, but never in a thunderstorm. She focused on the wind indicator and slowly began to ease the boat to the left.

"OK, hold this course while I reef the jib."

Reefing meant reducing the amount of sail area exposed to the wind. With too much sail out in a storm, there would be too much stress on the rigging. The sails could be ripped to shreds, the boat could be knocked on its side, or worse, the 60 foot mast could be torn loose and come crashing down. On the other hand, with no sail out, they would have no control over the direction of the boat, and they could be placed in the dangerous position of taking huge waves on the beam, which could capsize her. David knew he had to reef the sails down to the minimum amount needed to keep control.

Reefing the jib was relatively easy; he could do it from the cockpit. But reefing the main required that he go up onto the pitching deck and work the lines in wet, slippery conditions. There was no time to waste.

From the cockpit, David cranked hard on the winch, using both hands. Slowly, steadily, the roller furler did its job, winding the jib around the forestay until there was just a small triangle exposed. He set the locks on the lines. That part was done.

"Turn right and close haul her!" David had to yell to be heard over the building wind. The rain began as Rosalind threw her full weight into the big wheel and shoved it to the right. The vessel was slow to respond, wallowing heavily in the confused seas.

"Turn, baby, c'mon," Rosalind whispered.

Proteus finally responded, slowly swinging to the right. Rosalind eased the wheel and kept her eyes on the wind direction indicator until the boat reached the proper heading. "OK!" she yelled. The wind was gusting to 25 knots. The rain came harder, making the deck extremely slippery.

Lightning flashed all around them amid deafening thunder cracks. *Proteus* heeled sharply. The rain stung Rosalind's face and made it hard to see as she concentrated to keep the boat on course. She kept her eyes glued to the wind indicator, and used her ears to confirm where the wind was coming from. She fought back her rising fear. Don't think about it, she told herself. Just concentrate.

"Hold the boat steady, and whatever you do, don't let the wind fill this sail until I tie her off!" Rosalind understood. If the wind filled the sail as he was reefing it, the boat would be uncontrollable. David tightened the main sheet so that the boom would hold steady over the cockpit and not swing around while he reefed the mainsail to half its size. He loosened the main halyard and lowered the mainsail halfway down. He pulled in the reef line to secure the bottom of the sail, and then tightened the main halyard again. The reef was set. But he wasn't finished. In order to secure the reef, he had to tie three sail ties around the boom, one near the mast, one in the middle, and one at the end of the boom. This required that he leave the safety of the cockpit and go up on deck. There was no time to waste. A sudden wind shift could blow out the reef and leave them with an out-of-control mainsail. David quickly climbed up onto the pitching, slippery deck and made his way to the mast. The only thing he had to hold onto was the boom.

Rosalind tried not to think about what would happen if he lost his footing. What would I do with David in the water, possibly injured, in a storm, in the dark, and me alone on board—it was too terrifying to think about. They had done man-overboard drills, but never in conditions like this. Rosalind put all her weight into the wheel to hold the course, trying not to think about how fast things could go to hell. If she lost control of the boat, it could veer suddenly, knocking David into the water. "No. I will not let him go in the water," she said through clenched teeth. She tightened her grip on the wheel.

He tied the first tie, the one closest to the mast, then the second, halfway down the boom. She could see that he was fighting to keep his footing. A huge wave broke over the side and hit her full force, nearly knocking her over. She hung on to the wheel with all her might. David reached for the last sail tie, but the wind caught it and it flew away into the void. The sail was flapping violently. It was essential that he get it tied before it tore itself to pieces. He reached into his pants pocket and pulled out another tie.

That's my boy, Rosalind thought, always prepared. With a mighty effort, he horsed the last of the sail around the boom and secured it. The storm descended with full force.

A violent wind shift caused *Proteus* to heel over hard to the left. David was thrown off balance. He grabbed hold of the boom to steady himself.

"David, watch the jam-cleat!" Rosalind yelled. But it was too late; she could only watch as David's foot caught the main sheet and pulled it out of the cleat. In an instant, the line ran loose, and the boom swung wide to the left and out over the inky water. Instinctively, David hung on to it with all his might. The boat heeled sharply again, and the white-topped waves rose up and slapped at his feet. Rosalind gasped, sure that he would be swept under, but he kicked wildly and managed somehow to hold onto the boom.

I might be the world's biggest loser, she thought, but I'm NOT going to lose you a second time. "Hang on!" she yelled. She knew she had to bring the boom back over the center of the boat before David was washed away by the waves. She turned the wheel hard to the right. The boom swung back the other direction, and just as it was centered over the cockpit, she yelled at the top of her voice, "Now!" David let go and fell onto the cockpit floor in a heap, right next to her. The boom kept going, swinging wide out over the water on the right side. Tears of relief stung Rosalind's eyes. David was safe in the boat, drenched but unhurt. He scrambled to his feet and rushed to trim both sails for a new course in the worsening conditions.

Proteus pitched and rolled in the white-topped waves, rising up, then crashing down with a shudder. Lightning flashed all around them and the deafening thunder made talking impossible. Now in the brunt of the storm, it seemed as if the wind might tear the rigging to shreds. Rosalind closed her eyes and leaned into the wheel with all her weight, trying to get steerage, but her strength was waning.

David stepped behind her. He tethered himself to the binnacle and grabbed the wheel. Together, they held the helm in position until at last, the boat began to turn. The tiny handkerchiefs of sail caught the wind and snapped tight. They were in control again!

"OK, baby, hold her right there," David yelled. He knew that *Proteus* was a strong, seaworthy vessel, even in a thunderstorm. But these were the perfect conditions for sudden violent downdrafts that might demand more than the vessel could deliver.

"Now we pray," David said.

The rain fell in drenching grey sheets so dense that the lights of the city were obscured. The wind meter showed 45 knots. David kept his eyes fixed on the sails and fought to keep steerage. Holding a course was critical. His sailor's instincts told him the storm was not yet at its peak, that the wind and waves were still intensifying.

A sudden violent gust caught *Proteus* broadside and heeled her until the right gunwale was completely underwater. A huge wave crashed over the side of the boat, drenching Rosalind and knocking her off her feet. She screamed as she slid toward the stern rail. She closed her eyes. I'm going over. Oh God. Just as she reached the edge, her safety line caught, stopping her. David pulled her up and she grabbed the wheel again, but the boat was now completely at the mercy of the wind.

"It's a microburst! Hang on!" David yelled.

Rosalind shivered uncontrollably as the boat shook from side to side and the sixty-foot mast whipped in arcing circles over their heads. This was no ordinary storm; this was hell unleashed. She looked at David; there was fear in his eyes.

The incredible wind tossed *Proteus* around like a toy. Rosalind felt powerless against the forces around her, out of control. The dark, primal anger rose in her again, as it had at Claire's funeral. She threw her head back and yelled into the explosive sky. "What do you *want* from me?!" Wave after wave crashed over the rail, drenching her in black water up to her knees as she struggled to hang on to the wheel, and the cold tore through her foul weather jacket like it wasn't there.

"What *more* do you *want* from me!" Suddenly infused with preternatural energy, Rosalind screamed it over and over again. The lightning blinded her, but she couldn't take her eyes off the maelstrom with raindrops as big as quarters slashing through the furious air. She felt like an extension of the raw forces of nature exploding all around her, afraid of nothing—not death, not life—the two were one.

Proteus gave a ferocious shudder as the storm reached its peak, and then, as suddenly as it began, the wind dropped and the rain eased. The lake began to lie down, and the boat wallowed in a rocking motion. The whole thing lasted less than fifteen minutes.

His arms still around her, David felt Rosalind slump against the wheel. He caught her and held her up. "Roz. What is it?"

She turned and looked at him. Her eyes grew wide, and he knew instantly what was about to happen. He quickly stepped out of her way as she grabbed the stern rail and leaned over just in time.

She wretched violently, over and over again, until there was nothing left in her to expel. She hung on the stern rail for a moment, expecting to feel weak and depleted. Instead, a feeling swept over her that was more like relief, a wave of energy and weightlessness, as if a long-held burden had lifted. She stared out at the inky water as lightning flashed in the distance.

She slowly looked over at David. "Something happened just now."

"Yeah. Thor came for dinner." David started the engine, doused the sails and motored west. He'd had enough of sailing for tonight.

She looked at him with eyes as big as saucers. "Oh my God."

He looked into her eyes. They were as luminous as the sparkling city lights behind her. The muscles of her face were relaxed, and her voice seemed to have dropped into a lower register. "What?"

"I've been wrong."

"About what?"

"About Claire. I was terrified we were going to die, and then it hit me in an instant: it's not my fault Claire died. Is that possible?"

"Of course. It sounds like an epiphany," David said.

"An epiphany from God? Me?"

"Why not?"

"I mean, if God was looking for someone to help in a storm, it sure as hell wouldn't be me."

"Lots of people have epiphanies. I had one myself. Museum of Science and Industry. Seven years ago."

"God told you to marry me?" Rosalind asked.

"Yup."

"I didn't know He cared."

"Yup." David smiled.

"I kind of felt the same thing in the hot tub earlier, only this was much stronger."

"Hot tub?" David asked.

"At CMS. People were praying for me, and I felt the same kind of change in ... I don't know ... I've never had that happen before. Maybe it's some kind of energy field we haven't discovered yet." Rosalind shook her head. "Or adrenaline. Or maybe I just lost touch with reality for a minute."

"Or none of the above. Maybe your creator is trying to tell you something."

She sat back and took several deep breaths of the sweet, freshly ozonated air. "I'm utterly exhausted, but somehow energized."

"A near-death experience will do that to you," David said. She sat quietly, staring at the skyline. He could see that she was deep in thought, and after a long moment he reached out and touched her cheek.

"Let's go home," she said.

David laughed. "Our house is under siege by reporters. The only home we have is this boat."

Rosalind was completely drenched, her hair hanging in wet stringy clumps. "Well, I guess that's not so bad. *Proteus* does have food, water, satellite TV, and a nice cozy berth."

"And a locked gate to keep the press out."

Her cell phone rang. "It's Bradshaw."

"Don't answer it."

"Maybe he's calling to say I can come back to work." She answered it. "Hello Ben."

David pulled her over next to him as he steered Proteus toward the harbor. He put his ear close to the phone. He didn't want to miss a single word. She tried to brush him off, but he pulled her even closer and gave her a 'don't mess with me' look.

"Where are you?" Bradshaw said.

David gave her a cautionary wave of the finger.

"Never mind where I am."

"I think you ought to know that Danka-Saba says they didn't corrupt the data. They swear this wasn't an act of sabotage on their part."

"You believed them?"

"Dyer believes them. He has no proof we were hacked. I think we have a mole. Someone broke into the ANSR 1000 and downloaded the DZPro2 analysis," Bradshaw said.

Her heart skipped a beat.

"You told me straight out that you were desperate to see that data. A piece of advice: If you want a career as a jewel thief, don't go blabbing how much you love diamonds."

"But ..."

"Don't worry. Dyer thinks Mick Morrison did it. He's the only one with a passcode. I'll try to make sure he keeps thinking that, but you have to help me."

David shook his head and mouthed the words 'don't say anything.'

"Dyer wants you to stay in his guest condo until things calm down. He thinks you'd be safer that way. It would protect you from the media. It would also keep him on your side. I'll take you there. Where are you?"

Rosalind looked at David, who was still shaking his head. She hung up the phone and smiled sheepishly. "Well, counselor, chalk up one for your side. I won't make that mistake again."

"Did you do it?"

Rosalind smiled a sheepish little grin.

"You stole data?! What other crimes have you committed?"

"None that I know of."

"Darlin', there is no end to the challenges you present," David said, shaking his head. "We have work to do. You have to be in Washington Wednesday to testify. That gives us four days to decide what you're going to say."

"I'll tell them the truth. They can't put me in jail for that."

David laughed out loud. "They'll tear you apart. If they can do it to Supreme Court nominees, they can do it to you."

"Why would they do that?"

"They're politicians. Don't take it personally."

"But if I tell them the truth, won't that put an end to this whole thing?"

David took her hand and looked into her eyes. "Rosalind, listen very carefully to what I am about to say. When you walk into that hearing, they are going to take everything you say and twist it around to suit their agenda. They will ask you trick questions and try to get you to say things you don't mean. Look at me, Roz. You MUST prepare. If you don't think this thing through to the tenth decimal place, they will destroy you."

"The truth is, I don't know how the Ten Commandments got there. Dyer can't find any evidence of hacking."

"How else could it get there?"

"That's what I want to know."

Once the boat was docked and securely tied in the slip, David went below to find food. Grateful to be sitting still, Rosalind leaned back in the cockpit and stared at the city. The lights were brilliant in the clear air. She wondered whether the people inside all those high-rise buildings had any idea how violent the storm had been. She imagined them all cozy in their condos, watching TV. She looked at her watch. Oh no, she thought, they are probably watching me on the late news right now.

"Come and get it!" David put two cups of clam chowder and two glasses of red wine on the table in the main salon below. Rosalind flew down the steps and dove into both. "Turn on the TV. I want to see what the vultures are saying about me."

The two of them ate and flipped channels on the satellite TV. The late news was filled with stories about Rosalind and the God Gene. There was speculation about her motives for perpetrating such a grand hoax, about her scientific credibility, and about her mental fitness. When the third reporter in as many stations said that she was claiming to have proven the existence of God, she threw her spoon down.

"I never said that, David! People *assume* I said it because Ron Vaniere posed the question!"

"This is incredible. Speculation becomes truth in people's minds. Misinformation begets more misinformation, and there's no way to shut off the spigot," David said.

Rosalind shook her head. "It's scary. The media are God-like: omnipotent, omniscient, omnipresent. How do I defend myself against *that*?"

"You don't. You absolutely can't say anything publicly until after that hearing. It's too risky."

"You're right. But it won't be easy."

The sound of Ron Vaniere's voice brought their attention back to the TV.

"In an InfoNet exclusive, I spoke with Rosalind Evans today at the home of her friend Edie Dawson in New York City. Evans refused to allow me to bring a camera, but did agree to have the interview tape-recorded. Rosalind Evans is a brilliant scientist who professes only one goal in life: To help find a cure for leukemia. Why then, is there a growing perception all over the world that either she is a messiah or a heretic, a liar or a kook?"

Here came the familiar footage again, this time accompanied by personal photos of her at family gatherings, photos she had not seen on screen before. Vaniere continued.

"She told me she stands by her work and says there was no frameshift. She believes the so-called God Gene is nothing more than an act of industrial sabotage. Nonetheless, millions the world over believe she has proven the existence of God. But Evans is an avowed atheist who believes only in the natural world. Here is Rosalind Evans in her own words."

Vaniere played from the recording he'd made at Edie's apartment:

"Why do you think everyone is so obsessed with this story?"

"Clearly they don't understand. They actually think there is a God out there who put a message in their genes."

"You don't believe in God?"

"Of course not. Show me one shred of evidence that there is a God out there who cares about us."

Rosalind cringed. Did I say that? Vaniere continued. "Many in the media paint her as an arrogant, self-serving elitist with questionable motives. That was not my observation. I found her to be vulnerable, a private woman who seems sad and frightened. She asked me why the media is obsessed with blaming her for something she says she had nothing to do with. Is she a victim? She lost her daughter to leukemia a year and a half ago. Now she has been put on administrative leave from the Clearbrook Institute. And her husband, noted defense lawyer David Evans, is filing for divorce after seven years of marriage."

Rosalind turned to David. "Are you filing for divorce?"

"Not if you don't want me to," David said.

"I never wanted you to. Did you think I wanted you to?"

"Yes."

Rosalind grabbed David's hand and squeezed it. "I'm so sorry, David. Please ... can you ever forgive me?"

"I already have. I love you."

"I love you, too." She wiped her eyes. They turned back to the TV.

On screen came a montage of photos of Rosalind, Clearbrook, churches, priests, and people marching in the major capitals of the world.

Vaniere continued: "The message is clear: The God Gene isn't going away any time soon. For now, Rosalind Evans, The Cynical Messiah, is the lead character in an escalating drama that is causing all of us to wonder what is going on in our DNA. Is the world being duped by a cruel joke? Or is a vengeful God sending us a message that we better obey the Ten Commandments, or else? People are demanding the truth: what is the God Gene? The Cynical Messiah is the only one who really knows. When will she tell us? For InfoNet News, this is Ron Vaniere."

Rosalind switched off the TV and climbed the steps into the cockpit. She walked to the stern of the boat and looked out at the water shimmering across the harbor. The docks were quiet, which was unheard of on the Fourth of July. The storm must have chased everyone away. Strains of rock music drifted over from Navy Pier, and the lights of the giant Ferris wheel lent a festive air. David stood behind her and put his arms around her.

"Vaniere says I'm the only one who knows the truth. I'm the one who hasn't got a clue."

"To hell with Vaniere. He says whatever he thinks will keep people watching. He's not human."

"This morning, I woke up in Edie's apartment in New York thinking that if I just kept my head down, they would figure out the fraud, it would all blow over, and I could go back to my job. Here I am tonight—I can't go home, I can't go to work, they're blaming me for something nobody understands, I'm now the cynical messiah, and my own government is forcing me to submit to public humiliation or go to prison. Storms, epiphanies—if this is God speaking to me, I want earplugs."

"What do you think is trying to happen here?" David said.

"I saw that question on the Starry Messenger ticker. 'What's trying to happen here?' I didn't think about it at the time, but that really is the question, isn't it?" She stared out into the night sky. The moon was peeking through the receding clouds. "The Starry Messenger. That was the name of Galileo's first treatise on phases of the moon."

"An appropriate name for the mysterious blogger who prods us by asking us questions," David said.

"It's not questions I need; it's answers."

"That's why we need to focus on the hearing. We have to anticipate what the Senators will ask and formulate answers. We need to establish your position and write talking points. We need to craft your opening statement. We need to practice asking and answering the questions. We need to decide what clothes you'll wear, what color lipstick. We need to find key words and refine the language to support your position."

"What position? I'm more confused now than ever. I don't know what to do!"

"I'm telling you what to do. Our only goal is to get you in and out of that hearing without incriminating yourself. You need to be as sympathetic and believable as possible."

"That's the problem. I can't be believable when I don't know what I believe." She reached for her iPhone.

"Who are you calling, young lady. You are my client, and you don't talk to anyone unless I say so."

She kept dialing. "Sorry, Counselor. The Cynical Messiah needs help. I'm calling a summit meeting."

* * *

Every voice but one?

Well, kittens, do you think there is a pundit, politician or pastor we haven't heard from yet? Even in the face of all that opinionizing, do we know anything at all about the God Gene? Who is the one person who can tell us the truth and satisfy our earnest longings for meaningful information?

Where is Rosalind Evans? Why hasn't she spoken out? It looks as if Senator Bosch and the Judiciary Committee will give her that chance on Wednesday, but will she show? If so, what will she say? Will she tell us that she believes she has discovered a message from God in our genes? Will she deny it? What plausible explanation will she come up with to explain the assemblage of letters in the amino acid code? Given the orderliness of the amino acid code, how will she explain this incomprehensively unlikely deviation from the norm?

How likely is it that she poses a threat to national security? What is the Judiciary Committee's real motive for hauling her into their inquisition in front of the whole world? How are the American people served by this?

Is it even possible to know these answers until we hear from Rosalind Evans herself?

As for the folks at PharmaGen, do they have anything to add? Alan Dyer hasn't been heard from, except through Benton Bradshaw, and then only in vague terms; so what does this clever entrepreneur have to say? If he believes the God Gene is an act of sabotage, then why hasn't he said so directly? Is there perhaps a deeper agenda here? Something going on behind the scenes?

What's trying to happen here?

Chapter 35

"HEY BABY, WAKE up!" David knocked on the fiberglass, sending a reverberation through the cabin below. The noise woke her from a deep sleep, the best she'd had in months. It was nearly noon.

"Shut up. I won't and you can't make me."

"Maybe I can't. But they can."

Rosalind rolled over and opened one eye. "They?"

"Put your clothes on."

She quickly rolled out of the forward berth of *Proteus* and threw on the clothes she had thrown off helter-skelter the night before. She poked her head up through the main hatch. It was a glorious day. The storm the night before cleared out the mugginess. The air was clear, the sunshine brilliant. She took a deep breath and stretched. She felt an unaccustomed calmness, a feeling that first descended on her in the pool at CMS and again after the storm last night. And then she saw the army of reporters marching down the dock. "How did they get in here?" she said to David, who was standing in the cockpit, peering down the dock.

"They're like mice; they can squeeze themselves into places you wouldn't believe. You untie the stern, I'll get the bow. Let's get out of here."

The reporters were bearing down on them, all looking grim-faced and determined. What do they want from me, she wondered. What could I possibly say that would satisfy them? When will they decide they've had enough of me?

She stepped up into the cockpit and locked the main hatch behind her. "I'm not running anymore."

"Honey, these people want only one thing—to make you say something sensational. They don't care what you think or how you feel unless it sells. Don't say a word to them," he said.

The ten-foot-wide dock was now jammed with reporters and cameramen jockeying for position. If someone made a wrong move or lost their balance, a whole lot of expensive equipment would go into the drink. Experienced boaters knew that the idea was to keep your feet on the wood, because the water was 25 feet deep and cold, even in the height of summer; if something went in, it was gone for good. But this bunch appeared not to know that. They dodged and ducked and jumped, vying for her attention.

Rosalind walked out to *Proteus*'s bow pulpit. It provided a nice barrier between her and the vultures, and put her three feet above them. They surged toward her and all started yelling at once.

"Dr. Evans! Have you found more evidence of the God Gene?"

"Are you claiming you found God?"

"It has been reported that you are having visions. What do you see?"

"Have you spoken with the Pope?"

"Who put you up to this?"

She faced them with a smile. She simply waited and said nothing, with the idea that if they really wanted information from her, they would shut up. They didn't. Their shouting got louder.

"What is your strategy for the hearing?"

"Are you and David back together?"

"Shut up!" one of the reporters yelled. "Let her talk." Nobody listened to him. They kept right on shouting.

She folded her arms. I've been intimidated by these people all week, she thought. How stupid. They're just a bunch of people jumping up and down like monkeys in a cage. All at once she heard a loud splash, followed by a string of epithets.

A woman reporter was floundering in the water, her eyes as big as moons. Rosalind's sailor's reaction was immediate. "David, life ring!" In one deft motion, she jumped over the pulpit and kneeled on the dock. The woman grabbed the life ring and held on for dear life. Rosalind reached down and grabbed her hand. Several others reached down to help, but Rosalind yelled for them to back off before they all went in the water. She and David then helped the woman into the little inflatable dinghy that was tied next to Proteus, and then up onto the dock. She stood there dripping and looking as if she didn't know whether to laugh or cry.

"Takes the wind right out of you, doesn't it?" Rosalind said to the poor shivering woman.

"Oh no! Where's my bag? My computer's in there! My wallet. My iPhone. Everything." The woman was peering down into the water. "I've got to go get it!" She made a move to jump in.

Rosalind grabbed her by the arm. "Not a good idea. It's 25 feet deep, and there's a pretty good current."

"But it has to be right down there." The woman was shivering and looking at Rosalind with wide child's eyes. "My whole world is in that bag."

"Sometimes it's best to just accept what's gone and move on." Rosalind looked at her watch. "Sorry folks, but I have a meeting to go to. Careful on your way out."

Again they started yelling questions at her. Rosalind walked to the edge of the dock, untied the dinghy and jumped in with a deftness that comes from years of experience. David jumped in with her. With one quick pull, she started the outboard, and they surged away from the dock. As the babbling voices of the reporters faded into the distance, Rosalind threw them a hearty wave and laughed at the confused looks on their faces. Revving the engine, she navigated the dinghy out of the harbor and out into the lake. The waters were calm, and she felt like a young girl again, the wind in her hair, gloriously free, zooming around in a little boat with a great looking guy. She cut across toward Navy Pier a half mile away.

"Why was I ever afraid of those people? They're no better than the rest of us."

"Funny how the God-like media come disguised as two-year olds. But they have cameras and microphones. Don't ever underestimate them," David said.

Rosalind eased up to the dinghy dock at Navy Pier, and they jumped ashore.

"Where are we going?" David said.

"We're there." Towering above them was a giant Ferris wheel. Rosalind craned her neck and looked up at the 150-foot superstructure. Her pathological fear of flying extended to elevators, balconies, bridges—anything built to defy the natural force of gravity. Airplanes were by far the worst, but she'd always thought of the Navy Pier Ferris wheel as a particularly overt example of hubris. It was a prominent part of the landscape on the lakefront, and every time she looked at it she had a flash of vertigo, followed by a sense of relief that she would never have to go up in it. On visits to the Pier, friends used to try and cajole her into going up, but she had no trouble resisting. "I've got a better idea," she'd say to them, "I'll wait in the bar, and when you get back—*if* you get back—I'll buy you a drink with the money I don't have to spend on that thing."

She stared up at the gondolas in their slow rotation and tried to imagine how it would feel to be in one. They were enclosed, so she thought they looked fairly secure, assuming the bolts held and there wasn't an earthquake. She walked as close as she could and examined the connecting points where the steel supports of the wheel met the concrete foundation. It looked solid enough, but you never knew. As she was considering the amount of torque it would take to topple the whole thing, she heard the Darth Vaderesque voice of Stefan Gunquist.

"Rosalind and David! So good to see you both!" He smiled and waved as he lumbered toward them across the promenade. A moment later, Lex and Summer arrived. Everyone was right on time. Rosalind made the introductions.

"Stefan Gunquist, meet Lex and Summer Ellison, pastors at the Convocation of Manifest Souls. Stefan is Professor Emeritus of Theology at Rutherford."

"I've heard about your church," Stefan said. "You are shaking it up over there. I'd like to visit sometime."

"You are welcome any time. We are open 24-7," Summer said with a giggle.

"Hold on to your hat when you do, Stefan. Hanging around CMS for a few hours will give you a new chapter for your memoirs," Rosalind said.

"So I've heard. Did I read that the entire building is expected to levitate sometime this summer?"

They all laughed. "No," Summer said. "At least not *this* summer. Hey, we've both read your book, *Faces of God*. It's wonderful! Maybe you could autograph it when you come?"

"Happy to."

"Well, friends," Rosalind said, looking up at the Ferris wheel. "I thought this would be an appropriate place to for you to enlighten me about God. Shall we go up?"

"You want to go up *there*?" David said. "Are you nuts?"

"What's so nuts about that?" Lex asked.

"Rosalind is terrified of heights," David said.

"And just about everything else in life until last night," Rosalind said. "Last night some things changed for me. I think God's trying to tell me something."

Lex cocked his head and looked at her with a smile. "I thought you didn't believe in God."

"So did I. Let's go up before I lose my nerve," she said.

David put his arm around Rosalind's shoulder. Simple as it seemed, he knew that going up in this contraption was a huge step for her. Admitting her fear was even bigger. He quickly bought five tickets, and the attendant motioned for them to step into the slowly moving gondola.

They arranged themselves on either side of the gondola facing each other, Lex and Summer on one side, Rosalind, David, and Stefan on the other. As they began to ascend, Rosalind took hold of David's hand. Slowly, the distance increased between them and the ground. She held her breath and waited. She wondered whether she would feel the way she always felt in a plane—spinning out of control, panicky and helpless. Stay calm, she told herself. Calm. No fear. The panic didn't come, and a second later it still didn't come, and after half a minute, she began to think it wouldn't come at all. She wondered whether she could possibly enjoy this like thousands of people did day in and day out. She looked out the side of the gondola. She was no more than fifty feet off the ground, but the sight of all that air beneath her caused her to put an involuntary vice grip on David's hand. The view widened. Nobody spoke.

"It's a great day to get high!" Summer blurted out. Her childlike glee broke the tension and they all laughed.

Rosalind squeezed David's hand, leaned over, and looked out the window again. "Look at that. You can see all of Grant Park. Look how it's laid out, the paths and gardens and statues. You can't tell that from the ground. It's gorgeous." She looked at David. He was smiling, looking out at Lake Michigan.

"Look, there's a regatta going on, way off shore, probably ten miles. You can't see that standing on the shore," David said.

"You can see the curve of the southern shore of Lake Michigan, all the way to Indiana. David, is that the Michigan City smoke stack over there?"

David nodded. Rosalind threw her head back and laughed out loud.

"What's so funny?" Gunquist asked.

"David and I have sailed to Michigan City many times. It takes all day. You don't even see a sign of it until you have been on the water for hours. I always felt like such a brave adventurer sailing 35 miles all the way to Michigan City. But you go 150 feet in the air, and you realize it's right next door. I've been standing on the ground all these years thinking I knew how things worked," she said. She stuck her head out the side window of the gondola and let out a whoop. "I'm 150 feet in the air and I'm not hurtling toward the earth. There is order in the universe!"

They completed one seven-minute revolution and were approaching the exit platform. An attendant reached to open the gondola door for them to exit. Rosalind thrust a $100 bill at him. "We're going again!" The man smiled and put the bill in his pocket.

Rosalind turned her attention to the three guests. "On Wednesday, I have to testify before a bunch of Senators who think I'm the antichrist. They want to know where the God Gene came from. I don't know what to tell them."

"The truth!" Summer blurted out as if she were on a TV game show.

"The truth is, I don't know how the code got there," Rosalind said.

"Then say that!" Summer said.

"I can't justify any of this scientifically."

"Then say *that!*"

"I think they are disingenuous, self-serving bastards for putting me through this."

"Amen!" Summer said triumphantly, and then added quietly behind her hand, "But don't say that."

"They're going to ask me if I believe in God."

Stefan spoke first. "From what you've told me, you were a believer as a child, a non-believer as a student and young scientist, a believer when Claire was born, and a non-believer when she died. What does that tell you?"

"That I'm hopelessly confused."

"It tells me you're like most people—your faith wavers. Your belief in God is predicated on your situation in life. But you're not an atheist. You are a believer who quit doing the hard work it takes to have faith."

"My faith died with Claire."

"No it didn't. God promises to be with us in our suffering, even if we don't think He is. You just forgot that," Stefan said.

A small plane flew past Navy Pier towing a banner. The banner was a bright orange color with a simple message printed in large black letters. 'Celebrate! www.godgeners.org.'

"What is a godgener?" David asked.

"Ah," Stefan said, pulling his iPhone out of his pocket. "Allow me to find that out for you." He put in the web address, and ten seconds later had the answer. "Godgeners are a coalition of Muslims, Jews and Christians that started in India three days ago. They believe the God Gene is a gift from God. Since they put up their web page, they have collected— unbelievable—over five million members worldwide. Welcome to the electronic global village."

"No way. Are you kidding me?" Rosalind grabbed Stefan's phone and began scrolling the site. "How does something like this happen so fast? This is impossible."

"There it is right in front of you. Faith exploding all over the planet," Lex said. "The people are ready. Reminds me of what happened to you in the pool the other day, Rosalind. I have never seen anyone react so quickly to the prayer circle."

Rosalind thought back to the otherworldly feeling of strangers praying for her in the pool. "Those people didn't know me from Joe Bufulshnick, yet there they were, pouring their spiritual energy out so that I would feel better."

"And do you?"

"I feel better than I have in months. Did you put something in that water?"

Lex laughed. "It wasn't the water. You had a very intense God experience. It usually happens slowly. You went right to the heart of it in one session."

"That's not all that happened yesterday. David and I were out on the boat last night when that terrible storm came up. It was dark and cold, and I thought we both were going to die. I was shivering and crying, out of control. The boat was pitching in the waves and I looked up into the storm and I yelled at God. I was so angry. I asked Him what He wanted from me."

"Then what happened?" Stefan said.

"There was a tremendous crack of lightning and all of a sudden I was calm. Totally calm. When it was over, I threw up."

Stefan smiled at Lex and Summer, who were smiling, too. "A direct answer," he said.

"I wasn't thinking about Claire, but I suddenly had a deep realization that I'm not to blame for her death."

"God is doing some big-time work through you right now. You are blessed," Stefan said.

Rosalind shook her head. "That's a riot. I've thought for two years that I was cursed." The memory flooded back to when it all started, that awful moment when her life changed forever. She and Claire had been standing outside Rutherford Chapel, as they frequently did for the noon carillons. From the time she was a baby, Claire loved the sound of the chimes echoing through campus. As a healthy, beautiful five-year-old, she still loved them. She was an enthusiastic budding pianist and a lusty singer who needed no prodding to belt her latest arrangement of 'You Are My Sunshine.' The carillons were part of her musical awakening, and they never failed to evoke a smile. As they rang out that day, Rosalind looked down at her, but instead of smiling, Claire was staring up at the sky, not hearing the music any more, her face slack and pale as if she had glimpsed a reality no one else could see. Rosalind touched her shoulder, but there was no response. Only when she took Claire's hand and said her name did she turn slowly and look at her, as if emerging from a trance. It was just a few weeks later that the diagnosis came.

The memory opened the wound and tore at her heart. Tears stung her eyes. "If I was going to be blessed, why couldn't it have happened a year and a half ago, when I needed it?"

"You've been blessed the whole time," Summer said softly.

"Bull shit!" Rosalind's eyes flashed.

Lex suddenly grabbed both her hands and stared into her eyes. "You're retreating, Rosalind. You were talking about an intense spiritual experience, believing it, and now you're retreating. You're clinging to spider webs. If you do that, you won't learn anything from this."

His intensity startled her. She felt fear again, about Ferris wheels, storms, her grief, and mostly about the unknown. "Why *now*?"

"Because it's time," Lex said.

"No it's not!" Her eyes were wide and brimming with tears.

Stefan took her other hand. "This may be the first time in your life that you have a problem you can't solve with your brain."

"Second," Rosalind said, the bitterness spilling out. "I still don't know why Claire died."

Stefan's voice softened. "Yes you do. She died because that's how God made the world. We all die. This is temporary. One day your brain will figure out the medical reasons why she died, but your brain will never figure out what is happening between you and God right now. He's too grand for your understanding. He doesn't want to engage you in an intellectual discussion. He wants your heart."

Rosalind shook her head and stared out the side window of the gondola. "It's much easier being an atheist."

"Of course it is. Except that you aren't an atheist. You never were. Stop trying to outwit your creator!" Stefan's face had gone from kindly to stern.

They were at the top of the Ferris wheel. Oak Street Beach and the Gold Coast were laid out in front of them in the pristine golden sunlight. For a moment all was quiet in the gondola. Rosalind realized that Lex, Summer and Stefan had a silent bond of wisdom between them. She trusted them and sensed they had deep concern for her. She wiped her nose with a tissue. "OK, I give up. Tell me what to do."

"Stop thinking," Stefan said. He looked her squarely in the eye. "When God is working through you in this way, it is an intensely intuitive event. For now, you have to let the right side of your brain do the work, and tell the left side to be still."

"I don't know how to do that."

"Here's an idea," David said. "Let's see if you can go all the way around once without talking or even thinking. Just be. See what happens."

"But ..."

David put his arm around her and gently pulled her head down onto his shoulder. "Shhhh," he said.

The Ferris wheel started back up. Thirty seconds went by. Rosalind said nothing. Seven minutes, she thought, no way. I've never gone even one minute without talking or trying to analyze something. My brain might freeze up. Shhhh.

The fresh breeze was wonderful. She looked up at David. He put his finger to his lips. Maybe if I just close my eyes. OK, God, so speak. What does God sound like? George Burns? Joseph Steele? God forbid. I smell hot dogs. I'm starved. She opened her eyes. Traffic. I need to get the car serviced. Bradshaw, that moron. When all this is over, I'm going to let him have it. Sleepy. David smells good. Claire. Senator Bosch. Oh God, what do I say to the Senators? Shhhhh. I left a hatch open on the boat. Doesn't look like rain. Good. Lex is a great-looking guy. Good shoulders. Be quiet? Might as well ask me to walk up the side of a skyscraper. Throngs of people on Navy Pier. A group standing near the base of the Ferris wheel. Reporters. How do they know I'm here? There's a group of people in a circle—are they praying? Signs with my picture on them. My picture? Who are those people? Celebrate! www.godgeners.com. Popcorn smells good. Mmmmm. Hot buttered popcorn. Claire loved popcorn. Close your eyes. That feels good. Oh yeah, I forgot ... God. OK, so speak to me ... Hmmmmm. So peaceful ...

"Great job, Roz," Lex said.

"Huh?" She opened her eyes. It seemed impossible that seven minutes had passed.

"You did it. You went seven minutes without talking. How do you feel?" David asked.

"I don't know … I'm …"

"They have a word for it," David said. "Relaxed."

"I was going to say hungry. But you're right, I'm not worried about anything right this minute, and that is a strange feeling for me."

"God's most often repeated sentiment in the Bible is 'fear not.' So you're off to a good start," Lex said.

"What do you mean *start?*"

"I can't help feeling that this is just the beginning of what God has in store for you."

"The beginning? After the last five days, what more could He possibly want from me?"

Summer laughed. "Don't ask!"

"So when the Senators ask me if I believe in God, I can say yes, but that gives credence to their cockamamie idea that I'm trying to mess with people's freedom of religion. If I say no, they don't have a leg to stand on. The smart thing is to say no."

"You're right," David said.

Lex put up his hand. "You're both wrong. The smart thing—the only thing—is to tell the truth."

"But I'm afraid if I tell the truth, they'll put me in jail."

Summer burst out laughing "And what will God do if you lie?"

"I just want all this to go away," Rosalind moaned.

"Not likely," Stefan said. "On Tuesday this week you found the Ten Commandments written in the genetic code. Wednesday the whole world found out about it. By Thursday you were a household name. Friday you had an epiphany during a storm at sea. Today, God is the hot topic all over the planet. Muslims, Jews and Christians are celebrating their common heritage *together*. It took God six days to create the world. It took you five to transform it."

"I transformed the world? Ha! That's really ironic, Stefan. I put a slide up on a screen. Since that moment, I've done absolutely *nothing* to transform the world."

The Ferris wheel began its descent. Stefan took Rosalind's hands as the ground rose up to meet them. The sun shone in her eyes and he saw in them a new depth of wisdom, a liveliness that was far different from the weary eyes he'd seen that night in his kitchen. He smiled and squeezed her hands. "Maybe it's time to get started."

Chapter 36

"I GOT YOUR smoking gun, asshole."

Mick the Tech stretched his long legs out over the top of the coffee table in Bradshaw's office. He chewed on a Gurkah Black Dragon he'd lifted from Bradshaw's humidor. "Seems our friend Rozzie made a trip to Syria last year. There's this tribe of people there who have a high rate of blindness. Rozzie volunteered to go over there with some doctors to interview them and collect DNA samples." Mick had a wide grin on his face.

Bradshaw remembered when she went. It was right after her daughter died. She was only gone two weeks, and he really didn't think much about it at the time. He thought it was grief therapy for her.

"So?" Bradshaw said.

"There are photos from the trip. One of them gets me my job back. Check it out." He tossed Bradshaw a photo. It showed Rosalind with an Arab woman and two Arab men, standing next to a bombed out car. Rosalind was dressed in khaki pants and shirt, with a scarf on her head, holding a dirty little Arab kid. There were two young men in the background holding AK47s.

"So?" Bradshaw said. "What's the smoking gun?"

Mick pulled the cigar out of his mouth and tossed his hair back with a shake of his head. He smiled slowly and paused for effect.

"Suppose I was to tell you that the guy next to her is al-Qaeda?"

Bradshaw looked at Mick with a mixture of disgust and amusement. "Are you high?"

"I wish."

"Al-Qaida? How would you know that?"

"I'm Mick the Tech, remember? I'm lookin' at this broad standing next to a towel head, with AK47s in the background. I read in her journal that his name is Hassan Hussein. I'm thinking he looks a little seedy, so I Google the guy. There are tons of Husseins out there, so I narrow it down and what do you think I found?" He handed Bradshaw another photo. "This guy's name is Hussein Nomynatu. It's the same guy!"

Bradshaw studied the photos carefully. "They look alike, but I don't know if it's the same guy. So what if it is?"

"Hussein Nomynatu is a known al-Qaida operative working out of Syria. Badda bing!"

"If it's the same guy, why two different names?"

"Who knows? Maybe it's an alias. It's the same guy for sure," Mick said.

"Those guys all look the same. We can't be sure."

"Close enough for what we need. We don't have to prove it in a court of law, do we?"

"No. Just in the court of public opinion. This is actually pretty good, Mick."

"Good? It's a smoking gun, Dude!"

Bradshaw went to the sideboard and poured himself a scotch. "If we want to make her look bad, this ought to do it. It's not like anyone is going to do a DNA test to make sure. The question is, why would she hang around with a terrorist? She's goofy, but she isn't dangerous."

"You gotta get creative, short stuff. Suppose she was cooking up some kind of plot with this guy for a terrorist attack? Maybe she was making bio-weapons in her lab."

Bradshaw's glass stopped halfway to his lips. "You are way smarter than you look. Bio-weapons? Like anthrax, maybe?"

"Yeah."

Bradshaw thought for a minute. "She could have been making some kind of new strain of anthrax. She wouldn't have actually cultured the anthrax here, but she could have been designing the mechanism for the gene transfer."

"Hey, who was that Arab dude who used to work in the lab next to hers? Maybe he was helping her!"

"The guy from Jordan. Samir Okar. Holy shit, Mick, I think we could make her look very, very bad."

"I could cook a few files to create a paper trail between her and this guy Hussein and the guy from Jordan to make it look like they were in cahoots."

Bradshaw was up now, pacing like a miniature race-horse. "And maybe she cooks up the God Gene in order to scare people into thinking God really did put a message in our DNA. People panic and take to the streets, and this Hussein guy sets off some kind of device and sends vaccine-resistant anthrax all over New York City, Chicago and LA. Millions dead, just like that."

"Yeah, just like that."

"Wait a minute. Who's going to believe Rosalind Evans would do something like this?"

"When they get a load of my paper trail, they'll believe it. People will believe anything if it's juicy enough."

Bradshaw threw his head back and laughed. "Can you fake files that show she created the God Gene?"

"No problem."

Bradshaw laughed even louder. He picked up a copy of the Tribune from the coffee table and held it up to Mick. "If we play this right, we won't just discredit her, we'll incriminate her!"

Chicago Grand Jury Indicts 3 on Terrorism Charges
Chicago—U.S. Attorney Thomas O'Roarke today announced that the Special Grand Jury investigating Chicago-based terrorism has indicted three men ...

"Home grown terrorism. It will take our friend Roz months to dig out from under that accusation. By the time they figure out she didn't do it, people will have forgotten all about the God Gene. Clearbrook will be in the clear!"

"And we'll be heroes," Mick said.

"How do I know this photo isn't fake?"

"I copied it directly from her computer. Why would she fake a photo that would get her in hot water?"

"She wouldn't, but maybe you would. To get your job back."

"I didn't. There are ways to test a photo for that. Do it if you want."

"What else did you find?"

"Nothing except emails between her and Hussien. The rest of the files are boring. I thought a hottie like her would have a lot of racy stuff. Her browser history doesn't even have any porn sites. What does she do for fun?"

Bradshaw raised a conspiratorial eyebrow. "I guess now we know." He let go a bellow of laughter.

"What about my job?"

"You can start right now. Your office is just as you left it. You keep your mouth shut about all of this and get busy on that paper trail."

As Mick left, Bradshaw pulled out his cell phone. It was Saturday, but he had a hunch he might get lucky. It was well known that the U.S. Attorney was a workaholic.

"Hello, Mr. O'Roarke. This is Benton Bradshaw. I have a matter of some urgency to speak with you about, regarding my employee, Rosalind Evans. How soon can I see you?"

* * *

Mick sauntered down the hall to his office and opened the door. Danny Wu and Sammy Kew, his graduate assistants, were sitting across from each other at his desk. They looked up at him, startled. Kew quickly closed the screen on the computer.

"What the hell are you two doing here?"

"Nothing," Kew said.

"I guess we could ask you the same thing," Wu said.

"This is my office," Mick said.

Wu stood and faced Mick. "That's where you are mistaken, my friend."

"No, you're the ones who are mistaken. I'm back."

"Bull," Wu said.

"I said I'm back. So unless you're here to tidy the place up, you need to get out. What are you doing here, anyway? Are you spying on me?"

Wu and Kew looked at each other.

"Why would we do that?" Kew said.

"Because I lead a very interesting life."

"Hey, you're the one who left. This is ours now. Squatters rights."

"Wrong. I got my job back. So get your hands off my computer and get out." He plunked his backpack down on the desk, flexed his bicep and stared down at them.

The two quickly collected their papers and left.

Chapter 37

LATER THAT AFTERNOON, Cardinal Duffy opened his office door and an agitated Thomas O'Roarke burst in.

"I just talked to Evans's boss. Jesus, Duff, she really *is* a terrorist!" O'Roarke paused to catch his breath. "We might actually have a case here!"

Duffy cringed. "Tommy, you are brilliant, but you seem to have forgotten the Third Commandment, 'Thou shalt not take the name of the Lord thy God in vain.' Work on it. Now what's this about a terrorist?"

"I just talked to her boss, Benton Bradshaw. She met with an al-Qaida agent in Syria. There is a photo. *And* she knows how to make bio-weapons. I have means and opportunity. We can charge her with conspiracy to commit terrorism." O'Roarke was talking like a man set on fast-forward. "All I need now is a motive!"

"Slow down, Tommy. You don't need a motive. You don't need a case. You don't *want* a case. Our goal here is to discredit her and dispel any belief that the God Gene is some kind of message from God. All we are doing is shifting the momentum."

"I'm beginning to think she's not so crazy after all."

Duffy laughed. "Tommy, the woman claims she proved the existence of God. How else do you define crazy?"

"But if she really is a terrorist, we could all die!"

The Cardinal spoke slowly and softly. "Tommy, we *will* all die. In the meantime, don't lose sight of the fact that you are on a sacred mission here. You need to show the world that Rosalind Evans is wrong—the God Gene is *not* a message from God. That's our only goal here. The Holy Father is counting on us. Why don't you just leak the photo to Starry Messenger and be done with it?"

O'Roarke paced nervously. "No, this is great! I have a sitting grand jury right now investigating homegrown terror plots in Chicago. They've already indicted three men and they are on a blood hunt. The timing couldn't be better. I'll bet I can get an indictment inside of a week!"

"Indictment?! Do you have to go that far?"

"Of course I do; the woman is a terrorist!"

"Do you really believe that? That photo could be a computer-generated hoax. It could be mistaken identity. You don't know."

"Don't worry, Duff. We don't have to convince a jury: this won't ever come to trial. But an indictment makes people *think* she did it: her credibility is gone, we please the Pope, and *I'm* the hero who saved America from a terrorist plot!"

"Tommy, you don't have to trump up charges to achieve our goal."

"Who's trumping up charges? Bradshaw has evidence. Lots of it. He's pulling together the files for me now. It'll be enough to indict her for conspiracy to commit a terrorist act, arrest her, and throw her in jail. Bam, my stock soars. Then I'll go to Washington, and if the case ever does come to trial, it will be somebody else's problem."

"What happens to her in the meantime?"

"She probably bonds out on house arrest. Unless they think she is in imminent threat, in which case they hold her without bail."

Duffy felt a stab of regret. "Tommy, we can't do that to her."

"Why not? She wants us all dead!" O'Roarke stopped in his tracks. His eyes widened. "Wait a minute. What if she concocted the God Gene in order to foment a constitutional crisis? Our government could be thrown into chaos, which would give al-Qaida an opening to launch an attack. Aiding and abetting ..." O'Roarke slowly turned to Duffy. "Jesus, Duff. She committed treason! I never dreamed ... *treason*! I'll be immortal."

"Treason? Don't be ridiculous. No, Tommy. Don't do this. Just release the photo and let it go at that. It will cast doubt on her, and that's all we want."

"Duff, why mess around? The Holy Father wants her discredited. That's *guaranteed* if we indict her and arrest her for treason! Then Bosch gets his endorsement, I get appointed Attorney General, and who knows, Duff, you might get to be Pope some day!" O'Roarke let out a hearty, self-satisfied laugh.

"Are you sure about this?"

"Positive! It's the only sure way to shut her up."

Duffy slowly nodded. "You're right. The Holy Father's days are numbered, and I want him secure in knowing the God Gene will be laid to rest before he is."

Part III
Redemption

Chapter 38

RON VANIERE'S INBOX and social media pages were on fire with viewer feedback. By every indication, Rosalind Evans was still the top story, and he owned it lock, stock, and barrel. Opinions fell roughly into three camps: Rosalind Evans supporters, Rosalind Evans deniers, and the-world-is-ending ranters—all of whom looked to The Shovel as the ultimate source for information. He was feeling exceptionally smug as he read the latest spate of viewer emails, when the door to the office banged open and the news director flew in.

"Ron, the political situation is exploding! Have you heard? Willard Hitchcock has been accused of operating an illegal human genetic engineering scheme. It's going viral."

"You're kidding, right? You're trying to make an overworked, underpaid rock-star laugh, right?" Vaniere said.

"Go ahead and laugh," the news director said. "But this is your kind of story. You know that Smart Gene he's always railing about?"

"The gene that determines intelligence? The gene you don't have?"

"Hardy har. Hitchcock is always saying there needs to be a law against testing for it because it could lead to discrimination against people who aren't smart. But get this. The blogs are saying he is part of a black market scheme to use that very gene to engineer designer super-babies."

"Designer super-babies?"

"Yes. He's heading up a consortium of scientists who are making genetically modified, super smart embryos and selling them on the black market."

"Who buys an embryo on the black market?" Vaniere said.

"People who want kids who are geniuses, that's who," the news director said.

"What kind of weird science, pseudo-eugenic, Darwinian exploitation is that?" Vaniere tried to imagine what kind of parent would genetically engineer their offspring. "Do they get a refund if the kid turns out like you?"

"This is serious, Ron. Get on it. Here are the first postings from Starry Messenger and AP."

Vaniere read silently. This did have the earmarks of a juicy political scandal. But he was up to his eyebrows in God Gene at the moment. "I'm working the Evans story."

"Forget it, my friend. The frontrunner for the presidential nomination is in a nasty fix and our viewers expect The Shovel to have the inside story by six o'clock tonight."

"Have you been under your desk all morning?" Vaniere said. "Rosalind Evans is burning up the airwaves and the Internet."

"I'll put somebody else on the Evans story. A God story goes against type for you, Ron. You're The Shovel. You dig dirt."

Vaniere couldn't argue. An exploding political story like this was like crack to him. It had everything: Lies, innuendo, dark science, political ambition, and most importantly, a continuous, toxic blast of uncensored information on the Internet. It was chaos, and it was where he thrived. The truth about Hitchcock would come out eventually, but first there would be a bloody, violent war of words in the media that no one, not even the most sophisticated campaign apparatus, could control. Hitchcock might be guilty, he might be innocent, but Vaniere had a hunch that either way, the poor bastard was doomed. Evans, on the other hand, was far from over.

"The Evans story is still building; I think it's going to be historic," Vaniere said.

"Nah, stories like that come and go. Political malfeasance is eternal. It's what we live for!"

It was undeniably, nauseatingly true, and Vaniere knew it. The downfall of another rich, smug, self-interested politician had universal appeal.

"Come on, buddy," the producer said. "This is the biggest political blockbuster of the year! Get excited!"

Vaniere gazed out at the steady stream of people making their way up and down Michigan Avenue, moving with purpose, focused on getting from one place to another with as little hassle as possible, thousands of people every hour getting on with life. How many will put their head on the pillow tonight thinking about Wild Bill Hitchcock, he wondered. How many about God? I guess that depends on me.

"I'll do the Hitchcock story, but I also want Evans. I want both."

"You obsessed with her or what?"

"I'm obsessed with what her story is doing for my ratings. It's a mystery/science-fiction/doomsday thriller. And it's all mine."

"Just get me the story on Hitchcock by six. You don't have any other priorities."

"I can do Hitchcock with my hands tied behind my back," Vaniere said. "But just so you know, my top priority is to stay on the Evans story until I find the truth about what happened."

The News Director curled his lip. "Grow up, Ron. I care about accuracy. Truth is for dreamers."

Chapter 39

THOMAS O'ROARKE ACCEPTED a cup of coffee from
Benton Bradshaw. "This is quite an office, Ben."

"Thanks. I decorated it myself. Every square inch. They tell me I have
a knack for color."

"I'll say. You've managed to use most of them."

Mick the Tech handed a folder to Thomas O'Roarke. "Here are the
files, going back to before Rozzie went to Syria."

"Rozzie? You know her well?" O'Roarke said.

"I know her well enough, and I'm warning you; she's hot, but she's
wicked. She'll kidney-punch you just for fun."

O'Roarke studied the files for a moment. "So she was working with a
Jordanian?"

"Yup." Mick smiled to himself. This was work he was particularly
proud of. He and Bradshaw had spent hours making up a scenario whereby
Rosalind and the Jordanian were creating a bio-weapon. Bradshaw provided
the technical information, and Mick created back-dated files. It was a very
good job, if he did say so himself. He was becoming an expert at smoking
guns.

"Amazing," O'Roarke said. "They worked in the middle of the night
to create a vaccine-resistant strain of anthrax? Who would have thought a
meek little woman working in a lab could be conspiring to commit a
terrorist act against the United States?"

"I could have told you," Mick said. "I can read chicks' minds, especially when they're up to no good."

"I'll bet you can," O'Roarke said. "Tell me what you think about her motives. Why would she have conspired with al-Qaida?"

"It's obvious: sex. She goes over there, and let's say this guy Hussein is a stud. I've heard these Arabs are hung. She falls for the guy, he convinces her to help him, she comes back and gets the Jordanian to do the dirty work. And there it is—your basic terrorist manage a trios."

"That's dot-connecting on a whole new level, Mick. But tell me, did she ever say anything bad about America, or the President, or the war on terrorism?"

Mick and Bradshaw looked at each other. "Like what?" Bradshaw said.

"Like that she disagreed with the way we were handling the war, or that she sympathized with the plight of Muslims?" O'Roarke said. "Surely she must have indicated in some way that she hated America. Why else would she do something this drastic and dangerous? She must have had a motive. Think hard."

Mick and Bradshaw were silent.

"A traitor doesn't have to have a long history of anti-American sentiment," O'Roarke continued. "Sometimes people do treasonous things out of fear or stress. Was she stressed or fearful?"

"Oh yes. Her daughter was sick and died around that time. She was very stressed," Bradshaw said.

"Good! What about marital problems? Were she and her husband getting along?"

"Now that you mention it, no. In fact, I think he left her," Bradshaw said.

"Excellent! Now you're catching on. I want you to think long and hard about things she might have said or done that contributed to this contemptable plot to overthrow the government of the United States. The more evidence you come up with, the better case we have. Understand?"

"Can you indict her based on what we've given you?" Bradshaw said.

"I could indict a ham sandwich based on what you've given me." O'Roarke stood to leave. "You gentlemen have been a big help. There hasn't been a treason trial in America in over 60 years. It's going to be the trial of the century, and if you keep up the good work, you two are going to be the star witnesses for the prosecution. You're going to be famous. You're names and faces will be all over the news. You'll have TV appearances; maybe you'll write a book and make a lot of money. Are you ready for that?"

Bradshaw felt a rush of adrenalin. Star witness. Standing up for justice in a court of law. He turned to the portrait above his desk and flipped the old man the bird.

Chapter 40

JOSEPH STEELE KNOCKED hard on the door of room 813 at the Ragmoor Motel in Deadwood, South Dakota. It was overcast, and the sky was muddy brown. Water stood in puddles in the rutted driveway outside the motel where he knew Wild Bill Hitchcock was holed up. There were five locals sitting in metal chairs on the sidewalk outside the office, smoking and drinking out of bottles wrapped in plastic bags. They eyed the blue-suited Steele as if they weren't sure whether to rough him up right then, or wait until after he finished his business.

"Open up Bill! Come on, Man. It's me." There was no sound from behind the grimy metal door. "I know you're in there. Knock it off now." Steele waited. There was no sound. He glanced over his shoulder at the locals. Their overt attentiveness to his every move unnerved him a bit, but he couldn't let it worry him, not when he was on a sacred mission. He nodded to them. "God bless you, fellows." He turned back to the door and spoke again, this time louder. "What you don't know, Bill, is that I've got all the time in the world. I'm not going anywhere."

Fifteen seconds went by, and then slowly, the door opened. Steele walked in and shut it behind him. Standing there in the dim light was Wild Bill Hitchcock, Governor of the great state of South Dakota and current frontrunner for his party's nomination for president of the United States. He was slumped and pallid, wearing rumpled jeans and a t-shirt and looking nothing like his usual robust, trim, six-foot, sandy-haired self. Gone were the charisma and bubbling life force that made him so wildly attractive to voters.

"Sit down, Bill. You look like the backside end of hell."

"It's over, Joseph. Over." Hitchcock sank down on the bed and put his head in his hands.

"No. You can't let them do this. We're going to fight this thing. You're Wild Bill! Come on, buddy."

Steele sat down next to his newly minted friend. In the two weeks since he announced his support for Hitchcock, the two had made dozens of appearances together. They had flown together in Steele's jet, sat up late in hotel rooms discussing the future and all the things they would do to make the world a better place after Bill became president. He had watched Hitchcock work rope lines and rallies from dawn until late at night, tirelessly, often without eating or resting. He could see that Hitchcock received sustenance from being with the people, just like he did. Steele felt as if he had found a true friend, something he never expected to find in a politician. He'd always viewed politicians as TV personality wannabes; people who picked politics as a vehicle for fame because they didn't have what he had: talent.

"I brought you a sandwich and some coffee."

Hitchcock took the coffee, pried the lid off, and blew on it. His hand shook as he took a sip. "They got me, Joseph. They wanted me and they finally got me. Just one month till the convention and they got off the kill shot."

"Stop it! Right now! We will get over this and go on. Now get dressed and let's get out of here. I'll take you home."

Hitchcock said nothing, just sat on the bed staring at the floor.

"Bill, this country needs you. More importantly, *I* need you. Come on, I *endorsed* you."

"Is that why you came? This is about you?" Hitchcock looked Steele in the eye.

"No. Look. We have things in this country that need mending, and Bosch can't do it. You can. Look what you've done in South Dakota. You have no unemployment and a balanced budget. I know 49 Governors who would kill to trade places with you. You are a genius. And a good man. You can make us whole again. Don't give up."

The room was silent for a moment, except for the whining of cicadas outside the mottled screened window. Hitchcock sniffed and wiped his nose. "Nice words, Joseph. But wrong."

"OK, so what are you going to do, stay here? I admit it is a lovely place. You must have paid at least thirty bucks a night," Steele said.

"Twenty."

"Bill, you called me for a reason. You wanted me to come here. Why?"

"To say good bye."

"I won't listen to that." He took hold of Hitchcock's arm and pulled him to a standing position. "*Look* at me. Is it true what they are saying about you?" Hitchcock hung his head. Steele grabbed him by the shoulders. "Bill, for God's sake. You are not telling me it's true?"

Hitchcock sank back down on the bed and sobbed into his handkerchief. After a moment he caught his breath. "No, it's not true. It's absurd. Things that they are accusing me of aren't even possible. It's just that—there is so much I *have* done wrong. There have been drugs and booze and women ..." Hitchcock's voice trailed off. He was remembering those early years when he was invincible, when the accumulation of sins seemed utterly without consequence. "Joseph, you'll know soon enough— there is a child by another woman. When they find out ... I can't do that to my family. The election campaign hasn't even started yet. I can't put them through this. My only hope is that if I drop out of the primary race, maybe they'll stop digging for dirt and they won't find out." Hitchcock sat for a moment, lost in thought. "Who am I kidding? This sets a guy like Ron Vaniere on fire. I'm surprised he hasn't found it already."

"Bill, I want to read you something from the Bible that may help." Steele walked over to the cheap nightstand and opened the drawer. It was empty. He looked around the shabby room for other drawers, but there weren't any.

"Didn't you hear? Somebody's been stealing all the Gideon Bibles from hotel rooms."

Steele laughed. "What do you suppose they'll do, burn them? The Bible is one book you can't burn out of existence. Anyhow, the passage I want you to hear is this." Steele recited from memory:

"*'For the time will come when men will not put up with sound doctrine. Instead, to suit their own desires, they will gather around them a great number of teachers to say what their itching ears want to hear. Second Timothy, Chapter four, Verse three.'*"

"Bill, we live in a world of itching ears and an overabundance of people willing to say whatever they want to hear. You need to stand up to these ridiculous allegations about black-market babies. If you didn't do it, then deny it. Don't let them get away with it!"

"But what about the rest of it? They'll keep digging and find out the things I did. I don't know why I ever thought I could run for president and *not* have these things discovered. I thought I could keep it quiet. That's what ego will do to you." Hitchcock blew his nose loudly. "When they find out about the child, it will kill Annie and the kids."

Hitchcock's face was a study in anguish. Steele reached over and touched his arm. "Then you tell them first."

Hitchcock leaned back. "Are you serious? Confess to Annie? Forget it!"

"Confession is painful, but it will reconcile everything and make you stronger than ever. If the God Gene is teaching us anything, it is that we need to follow the rules in order to be happy. Living a lie is killing you. Your secrets imprison you, Bill, but nobody will be able to hurt you once you are reconciled."

"Reconciled? She'll leave me!"

"Maybe. But what is your alternative? She can find out from the media or she can find out from you. One way is betrayal, the other reconciliation. Which one sounds better to you?"

The two sat in silence for several long minutes, neither looking at the other. Tears ran down Hitchcock's face. Finally, he looked over at Steele. "You're a fake, Joseph." Hitchcock said the words quietly. "An articulate, charismatic, Bible-waving fake."

"Yeah, so?"

"I had you pegged as one of those opportunistic televangelists who only care about money and fame and don't give a thought to the little people who put them there. But I don't know … no rational man would ever suggest I confess to my wife. Only a real man of God would do that. Behind all that ranting and rabble-rousing, do you actually *care?*"

Steele smiled slowly. "It's my God Gene, Hitch. It's all fired up. The other day it hit me in a flash: God wants us all to know that He loves us and wants us to be happy. And He wants *me* to tell the world. Can I have an AMEN?!"

"You think the God Gene is real?"

"I know it is. I can feel it. I've spent the last three days shouting it from the rooftops! And if you stop feeling sorry for yourself for a minute, you'll feel it, too."

"I can't tell Annie. If I drop out of the race, there's a chance she'll never find out."

"Knock it off. Dropping out in disgrace would be a P.R. disaster for both of us, and there's no guarantee she won't find out anyway. Why take the chance?"

"I never should have called you, Joseph. You are making this very difficult." Hitchcock stared at the floor, his shoulders hunched, his face the picture of dejection. He felt his last bit of life force draining out. "I don't have the courage to tell Annie. I'm a dead man."

"No you're not! You have to do this."

Hitchcock sat silently for a moment, trying to process the idea of confessing his sins to his wife and kids. All his life, the goal had been to hide his sins, to stuff them into a locked box and throw away the key. Now he realized that there never really was a key. He mentally rehearsed telling Annie. It felt like standing on the edge of a cliff and leaning forward. But seeing his name in scandalous black headlines felt even worse.

"Your secrets are your prison, Bill. Confess. It'll set you free."

"Easy for you to say."

"A guy like Ron Vaniere will flay you alive. But if you tell Annie before he finds out, you trump his ace. Do it right now."

Hitchcock looked deeply into Steele's eyes. "Will you help me?"

"Of course I will," Steele said. "But it's not my help you need."

"God? Help *me*? Why would He?"

"Ask Him. Do it with your heart. He knows when you're jivin' Him."

Hitchcock walked slowly around the room, eyes cast upward at the dingy ceiling. After a moment he looked at Steele. "If reconciling with Annie could save my family, then could reconciling with the American people save my candidacy? Maybe it's my God Gene firing, but I think I need to confess my sins publicly after I tell Annie and the kids. Joseph, what if I hold a press conference and confess everything? What if I make a list of everything I've ever done that could possibly be used against me and post it on my web site? I'd put Vaniere out of business! I'd be free, washed clean like a newborn baby!"

"Hang on, there, Hitch. There's reconciliation, and then there's self-immolation."

A broad smile spread across Hitchcock's tear-stained face. "Cleansing by fire. Why not?"

"Hitch, you're either the bravest man I know, or the stupidest."

"This could get ugly."

Steele clamped his arm around Hitchcock's shoulder. "Reconciliation is messy, difficult, heart-wrenching—but it's never ugly. It's the most beautiful thing in the world." He turned toward the window and yelled loudly enough for the whiskey-drinking men outside to hear him, "Can I have an AMEN!"

* * *

Is it the media's job to wear a white hat?

Kittens have you seen these headlines?

    "Statehouses debate putting prayer back in school"

    "Godgener rallies in 10 cities—more planned!"

    "Churches, Mosques, Synagogues overflowing!"

No, you say? Might that be because nobody has picked up the stories except my blog and a few obscure cable news shows? How about this one:

"Hitchcock black market scheme!"

It's all you're hearing about? Why am I not surprised?

Would you believe that the first three are absolutely, unequivocally, quantifiably true? Further, would you believe that there is not one shred of evidence that Hitchcock has done anything remotely close to selling designer embryos on the black market?

So, what's trying to happen here?

Why, with God Genes lighting up all over the world, does the media focus on all the darkness? Darkness that serves no purpose other than to titillate? Why, in a world filled with negativity and fear, are messages of hope and reconciliation *ignored* by the media? I'm not suggesting that the media ignore their duty to keep a sharp eye on the behavior of the rich and powerful, but is that the only service they might perform in today's world? Where are those visionary media decision-makers who would also be healers and givers of hope?

Kittens, these are the questions I hear you asking; this is a common thread of frustration among all of us, but is our frustration valid?

Is the media's job to wear a white hat? Or to stir up controversy and debate? Or, as the founding fathers articulated, is it the job of a free press to shine light on the workings of government?

Or in the end, is the media's sole responsibility to attract and keep an audience?

But there is an even deeper question: is it the media's responsibility to be truthful and accurate? Perhaps we the people should take up arms, (arms as in fingers typing on keys) and let those in the media know that we don't want *unsubstantiated* attacks on our leaders, whatever their political stripe? Might Willard Hitchcock be the shining symbol of our demand for media honesty?

As the media proceeds to try, convict and execute Willard Hitchcock for fostering an unsavory genetic engineering scheme, in the name of God can we *please* have some evidence?

Chapter 41

"YOU ARE SPEAKING to the Right Reverend Shabazz Dunready of the New Life Temple Stove of Hyde Park!!! We heat you up!!!" It was Dunready's classic phone greeting. Sunlight splayed in thin shafts through his study window, highlighting the bright greens, yellows and reds of his pastoral cloak.

"Pastor, how are you? This is Ron Vaniere."

"Ron! My friend! I am entirely blessed. And you?"

"I'm confused. I've heard these stories about Willard Hitchcock, and frankly, I can't believe any of it. Designer super-babies?"

Dunready leaned back and let go a wail of laughter, rolling fits of it, until he could hardly breathe. "Super babies! I want one of those! My kids are only smart, beautiful, and blessed. I want me one of those super-babies!"

Vaniere couldn't resist the Pastor's infectious laughter. The man had a unique take on life; it was all good—fine, dandy, blessed, and heated up! Must be nice, Vaniere thought.

"I figured that since you are on the First Light board, you would have the inside scoop. What does Rev. Steele say about all this?"

"Well, we were supposed to have dinner tonight and talk about the shrine he's wantin' to put in over at Clearbrook Hall, but he called and said he can't make it. Said he was in South Dakota. So I guess he's with Willard just now."

"Do you think it's possible that Hitchcock is involved in something illegal?"

"No sir! That don't sound like him at all. They made it all up."

"Who made it up?"

"His political enemies, I guess. Who else?"

"Have you ever talked with Hitchcock about the Smart Gene?"

"Sure. He talks about it all the time. He is very concerned about what would happen if they let people test for the Smart Gene. Children would be discriminated against. I know what *that's* like."

"I'm with you on that, brother. Say, would you give me Steele's cell phone number?"

"You know better than that, Ron."

"Pastor, you know I would never ask if it weren't an emergency."

"What emergency?"

"I can't get a call back from Governor Hitchcock. His office won't tell me where he is. I go on the air at six o'clock and I need the true story. I know Rev. Steele will give it to me. I know he is a man of honor." Vaniere said it convincingly, even though Steele was all show as far as he could tell.

"You speak the truth, my brother, the absolute truth. I will have him call you."

"Well, the thing is, I can't wait for him to call me. I have to call him. I'm in a jam, running out of time."

"Hummmmm."

"Pastor Dunready, have I ever abused a favor from you? Have I ever done anything but tell the truth?"

"Well, no ..."

"Isn't it about time for a follow-up story about your unique, fiery brand of preaching? And your fired-up congregation? Our viewers loved it the last time we did a story on your church."

"Yes! You come right on down! Did you know that the New Life Temple Stove Street Fair and Tent Revival is next weekend?"

"No I did not. It's good to know."

"It's our major fundraiser of the year. Some publicity would be nice, get some folks on down here to Hyde Park, buy some raffle tickets, eat some pie, drop a dollar or two into the plate."

"E-mail me the details, Pastor, and consider it done. I'll get you on in prime time."

"687-555-8761. And you never got it from me."

* * *

Joseph Steele was helping Willard Hitchcock throw things into his suitcase at the Ragmoor Inn when his cell phone rang. He looked at the caller ID and hesitated. "It's Ron Vaniere."

"Oh no," Hitchcock wailed. "He's on it already. Oh, Dear God, no. Don't answer."

"I think I should. If I don't, he'll call someone else, and I don't have control over what someone else says."

Hitchcock closed his eyes and said a silent prayer.

Steele answered his phone. "I can guess why you're calling, Mr. Vaniere."

"I have to go on the air in just a few hours. The blogs are saying that Governor Hitchcock is involved in a black-market scheme. I just want to know if it's true."

"No!"

"How do you know?"

"Bill told me himself. It is a ridiculous charge. Even if he knew how, he would never do a thing like this."

"Is he dropping out of the Presidential race?"

"No. Never. He's determined to fight this thing."

"Pastor Dunready said you were in South Dakota. Are you with Governor Hitchcock now?" There was a pause on the other end of the phone. "Rev. Steele?"

"I am with him, yes."

"May I speak to him?"

Vaniere could hear muffled talking in the background. After a moment a voice came on the line.

"Hello Mr. Vaniere."

"Gov. Hitchcock, what do you say about these charges that you are involved in a black-market baby scheme?" Vaniere switched on his bull-o-meter. This was where the Shovel had the advantage: He could listen with both sides of his brain and hear things nobody else could.

"It's nonsense, of course."

"How do you plan to refute the charge?"

"You can't prove a negative. It's up to them to provide evidence. They will not be able to do that."

"Why not?"

"Because there isn't any."

"How will this affect your campaign?"

"I will keep fighting for the things I believe in."

"Will you still work for a ban on genetic testing for the Smart Gene?"

"Yes. A lie will not deter me."

"How is your family handling all of this?"

"We are all just fine. Please leave them out of it. Something devious is going on here; someone is lying to hurt me politically. If you want to report on something, report on that. I don't know who it is, but maybe you can find out. Good bye, Mr. Vaniere."

"Governor ..." The call ended. Here we go, Vaniere thought wearily. He said, she said, they said. Where is the truth? He wished they would put a litmus strip on the forehead of every politician in America that turned red when they were lying. It would save so much time. Vaniere sensed that Hitchcock was telling the truth. There was a lot more digging to do, and he didn't relish it, but his goal was to get it over with as quickly as possible. He remembered that there were allegations that Hitchcock was a womanizer and had an affair with an intern a decade ago. It was time to dig in and see what that was all about. Meanwhile, he would put his staff on the black market-thing. The Shovel put on his mental hip boots and deployed the heavy excavation protocol.

* * *

This is why I'm a legend, Vaniere said three hours later as he waited for the photo to download. He glanced at his watch: he would be ready for air with time to spare.

His staff had done a thorough job of researching the black-market allegations. They looked into the science of genetic engineering, what it would take to conduct the kind of operation that was alleged, and the costs associated with it. Their conclusion: highly implausible if not entirely impossible. It was likely pure fiction. But even if he said so on the air tonight, it would take days, maybe weeks, for the blogs to let go of the story. It would stay true for as long as anyone cared to believe it.

While the staff was busy doing their research, Vaniere did what he did best: he intuited, Googled, doodled, phoned, and intuited some more. He began from the point at which rumors of an affair with a staffer a decade ago began to get legs. Using his formidable tenacity, following one lead after another, pausing to reason it through, Vaniere found the woman in less than an hour. Not only did he get her to admit that she had borne Hitchcock's child, he persuaded her to email him a photo of herself and the boy.

The photo downloaded onto the screen. It looked as if someone had Photo Shopped Wild Bill's head onto a nine-year-old body; there could be no doubt it was Hitchcock's son.

The story was clear in Vaniere's mind: Despite the blog hysteria, Hitchcock had done nothing illegal, but he had made an error that was about to cost him his career. There is no way he survives this, Vaniere thought. I've seen it happen too many times: the tearful apology, the repentant attitude, and always, the trickle of leaks from other women he'd been involved with. There was never just one. Wild Bill was cooked.

Vaniere had everything he needed to break the story right now except a response from Hitchcock. He knew it was useless to call his office. He wouldn't be there, and even if he were, he wouldn't talk. So he did another end-around: He dialed Steele's cell phone number.

Steele's voice was ebullient. "Rev. Steele here. Can I have an AMEN!"

"Amen. This is Ron Vaniere from InfoNet. Are you by any chance with Governor Hitchcock right now?"

There was a pause. "Yes I am. But now would not be a good time to talk. He's with his family."

"I'm calling to get his reaction to something I just found out about him."

"Is it about the black market embryo thing?"

"No, it's not. It is about the child. I have a photo of Governor Hitchcock's alleged love child he fathered with an intern, May Mathews. I'm airing the story in a few minutes and want to give him a chance to respond."

There was a long pause. Vaniere could hear Steele breathing into the phone, deep breaths, almost sighs.

"Just a moment." There was a long silence, and then Hitchcock answered.

"Mr. Vaniere, I implore you not to run that story. Please. Wait until tomorrow. *Please.*"

"Tomorrow? Are you kidding? Why on earth would I give up an exclusive?"

"Because it is the right thing to do, Mr. Vaniere. I'm going to take a leap of faith here. Can I speak off the record? Way off?"

"Yes."

"I have gathered my family together to tell them about the child and all of my other transgressions. If you allow me time to do this, I may have a chance to reconcile with my family. If you run the story now, you'll ruin any chance I have. My fate is in your hands, Mr. Vaniere."

"I can't wait until tomorrow. It won't be a scoop tomorrow."

"Then at least wait a couple of hours. Please." Hitchcock's voice cracked.

"Why a couple of hours?"

Again, silence.

"Can you tell me anything else?" Vaniere asked.

"I will be holding a press conference in an hour. I'm going public with the whole thing. I'm begging you, Mr. Vaniere." The call ended.

Vaniere hung up and looked at his watch. It was 6:30 p.m.—the perfect time for a breaking news flash. He looked at the picture on the computer screen. This kid's life was about to go ballistic. Poor kid; he didn't ask for this. Neither did Hitchcock's wife and kids. No doubt about it, when you break news like this, you break hearts.

He walked into the news director's office.

"Did you get it?" the director asked.

"I got it," he said, handing the photo to the director.

"Dynamite! Go with it!"

"Hang on. I talked to Hitchcock just now, and he told me that he is with his family right now telling them everything. He's holding a press conference in an hour to go public with it. Shouldn't we wait to run this until afterward? I mean, doesn't the guy deserve a chance to explain this to his family?"

"Are you flaming nuts? You have an exclusive on the political story of the year and you want to *sit* on it?"

"Just for an hour."

"But then it won't be an exclusive, will it?" The news director ran his hand through his hair in exasperation. "*Will it?*"

"No."

"It's what we are in business for, Ron. Exclusives! Run the damn story now, or I'll find someone who will. *Now!*"

Vaniere threw his suit jacket on and headed for the studio.

* * *

After the news flash aired, the news director slapped Vaniere on the back. "You nailed it! That photo! Pure gold, Ronnie! You are a god! Our ratings are off the chart!"

Vaniere popped two beers and handed one to the news director. "You owe me big. Get off my case about the Evans story, OK?"

"Sure. Whatever you say."

"I'm headed for Washington tomorrow to cover the Senate hearing on Wednesday. But I'll stay on Hitchcock, too," Vaniere said, holding up his iPhone, iPad and laptop. "They used to get a whole day's work out of us each day. Now they get a whole day's work each hour."

"Those were the good old days. Before I was born," the news director said.

"What time is it? Hitchcock's news conference should be on any minute."

"Oh no. After you broke the story, we got word over the wires that Hitchcock cancelled his news conference." He clinked his beer bottle against Vaniere's and downed the contents in one gulp.

Chapter 42

"READY WHEN YOU are, Miss Moray." The InfoNet camera operator was focused, white-balanced, sound-checked and ready for what he and his crew felt was going to be one of the weirdest shoots of their lives. Ron Vaniere should have been here, but he was in D.C. , so here they were in this funky north side spa that was a mix of Disneyland and the Sistine Chapel with Claudia Moray, who had for some unknown reason decided to venture out of the studio and play reporter.

Claudia faced the camera and connected, soul-to-soul, with her audience.

"This is the place where Rosalind Evans hid out from reporters last week while they were trying to find her and question her about the God Gene. This is Chicago's hottest new spa, the Convocation of Manifest Souls. I put on this robe and slippers because that's what they do. I'm really comfortable, as you can imagine, and I think I am actually starting to feel something here, kind of relaxed and excited all at the same time. It's weird. Here with me are the owners of the spa, Lex and Summer Ellison."

While the robe made most people look like they needed to lose fifteen pounds, on Claudia Moray it was smashing. There is just no way to hide a perfect body, something she knew full well when she pulled the tie in tight around her waist and opened the collar just the right amount.

"We don't actually own CMS," Summer said.

"Who does?"

"God owns it. Like everything else in this life, we are just borrowing it for a while."

"Well, I think God needs to rent you a bigger place! Look at this crowd! There is a line around the block to get in," Claudia said. The room was shoulder to shoulder with visitors. Some were gathered around watching the TV shoot, but most were taking part in the various CMS venues.

"You call this a spa for the soul. What, exactly, does that mean?"

"It is a place where you can leave your worries behind and connect with God," Lex said.

"And, it's a place where you do things that soothe and pamper your spiritual side. What a facial does for your skin, our venues do for your soul! It's renewing," Summer said.

"Woo, can't wait. What's our first venue?"

"This is Images of God. The purpose is to strengthen our sense of God's presence in our lives. Here, put this on." Lex handed Claudia a large helmet that looked like a welder's helmet, but bigger, with large pads that rested on the shoulders. "This is our enhanced virtual reality machine. It has virtual reality capabilities like an arcade game, and it also has brainwave sensing technology that allows you to control the environment with your thoughts."

Claudia took the helmet from Lex. "Wow, it's lighter than it looks." She wasn't crazy about the idea of putting it on. I came here to look good, she thought, and these people want me to completely cover my head with this contraption. What about my hair? "What does it do, read my mind?"

"Not exactly." Lex helped her put the helmet on and adjust it on her head and shoulders. "OK, what do you see?"

"Uh, nothing?"

"OK, now, I want you to think about what God means to you. Keep your thoughts focused. What do you see?"

"I see a bright light in the clouds. Very far away. Wow, look at that. I swear to God, this is just like flying!" Claudia's head turned left and right and up and down. "It's like God is right here in the room with me!"

"Oh, He is," Summer said with a breezy smile.

"Yeah, no, but I mean, really, really here. This is incredible."

"Your thoughts are actually determining what you see. Wonderful new technology," Summer said.

Claudia was quiet, seemingly lost in the moment. "Woo. I guess you have to be careful what you think about! Don't want your mind to stray into forbidden territory, right? Oh my. Look at that." Claudia was silent for a moment. "I'm the only one who can see this, right?"

Lex and Summer laughed. "Right," Lex said.

"Good. Wow! Oh my ... Where can I get one of these?"

Lex touched Claudia's arm. "It is helpful to stay focused on your God experience."

"Oh, OK. So what does it do for my spirit?"

"Strengthen it. This is not an end unto itself. It is something you do in conjunction with your other activities here, things like worship, intuitive prayer, Bible study, music, community service. Each time you do this your connection with God will evolve and expand. This helps us strengthen our God-consciousness," Lex said.

Claudia took off the helmet and fluffed her hair. "Whew. OK, that's freaky. Let's move on. I see lots of young people here. What's the story?"

"They're looking for an authentic experience with God. These are the Children of the Microchip. We can't expose them to smart phones, TV, movies, music and the Internet, and then on Sunday expect them to pretend they live in the 1950s," Lex said.

"But I thought today's kids were all tech and no touch," Claudia said.

"They are all tech, but they also love touch. What do kids today do when they greet each other? They hug. Spiritually, their needs are the same as everyone who came before them. Only the pathways change."

"Huh. I thought they just wanted to drink, smoke dope and make out," Claudia said.

Cameras rolling, Claudia, Lex and Summer walked into the natatorium. It was filled to overflowing with people.

"Well, here we are at the God Consciousness Hot Tub," Summer said. "Want to get in?"

Claudia recoiled. "Put on a swimsuit? On camera? Heyell no!"

Out of the corner of her eye, Claudia saw a man walking across the pool deck dressed in board shorts and no shirt. In the soft glow of the cross light overhead, he looked like a Greek god. Claudia couldn't take her eyes off him. His upper body was ripped and tan and he had long blond hair that was pulled back in a pony tail. His wide, white-toothed smile lit up the room. He was clearly enjoying the company of the two beautiful, bikini-clad girls with him, one on each arm.

"Excuse me," Claudia said, walking away from Lex and Summer. Never one to be deterred by competition, she ignored the girls and walked right up to him. At the very least he would make a visually engaging interview, she thought. With any luck, he would make more than that.

"Hello there. I'm Claudia Moray from InfoNet News. We are here doing a story on the spa. What's your name??"

The man smiled and gave her a slow once-over. "Mick Morrison."

"Is this your first time here?"

"Yeah. It's awesome."

"How did you hear about this place?" Claudia asked.

"Same way everybody else did. Starry Messenger."

"So why did you come?"

"I heard people get high here," Mick said.

"High on God, right?"

"On God?"

"This is a church," Claudia said.

"A church? With a pool?" Mick looked at the two girls and laughed out loud. "I musta read it wrong."

"They call it a spa for your soul," Claudia said. "Have you done any of the venues?"

"No, we're just hanging out at the pool," Mick said. "Isn't there a bar here somewhere?"

"A smoothie bar, right over there," Claudia answered.

"I'm definitely in the wrong place," Mick said, shaking his head.

"Say, I was hoping you would do a few quick comments on camera for me?" She gave him flirty smile number 11. The two girls squealed with excitement. "No, just the gentleman. I'm going to suggest that you two ladies go and try the 'Images of God' venue. Awesome. It's right over there," Claudia said.

They looked at Mick for approval, and he nodded. "Come back soon," he said, blowing them a kiss. They scampered off.

With the competition properly disposed of, Claudia turned her mic off. She glanced coyly at Mick. "I need to get back to the studio, but I was wondering if you might be up for a late dinner tonight?"

"With you? Absolutely."

"Shall we meet at Miller's at ten?"

"You bet your booty, pretty lady. I'll be there. You're gonna change clothes, right?"

* * *

Miller's Pub was crowded, as usual. Claudia loved the place because the cheery stained-glass ambiance and the sound of clinking glasses and laughter made for an easy entry into a come-on. It was welcoming and non-threatening, not like those ultra-metro, trendy-menu places on the north side. At Miller's you just eased into it and waited for your moment. It was her absolute favorite. She was well-known there and always got the kind of celebrity welcome that was sure to impress a date. As always, she arrived first.

Mick got there precisely at ten, sporting a white open-collar shirt and black slacks with no back pockets. He smiled broadly when he saw her standing on the sidewalk outside the restaurant.

"Woo, sister. I like it. I had a hunch that robe you had on at church was hiding a multitude of delirious pleasures." Mick put his right arm around Claudia's shoulder and pulled her close. The pink cocktail dress was perhaps the best he'd ever seen, the way it wrapped her tight and squeezed her out in all the right places.

They were ushered to a table for two in the corner. Heads turned as they walked through the restaurant. Claudia Moray was instantly recognizable, and Mick, with his tanned face, golden hair and sizzling blue eyes, made a stunning companion. There was sure to be talk tomorrow about who this hunky guy was with Claudia Moray. She smiled her best 'eat your heart out' smile at the folks.

After drinks were ordered, Claudia leaned in. "You already know who I am, so tell me who you are."

"I am the magical mystical wizard of tech at Rutherford." Mick flexed a bicep as punctuation.

"Really? That's where Rosalind Evans works, right?"

Mick had a minor regurgitation at the mention of her name. "Yeah."

"Do you know her?"

"Yeah, unfortunately."

"Why unfortunately?"

"She got me fired."

"Why?"

"Because I ... wait, I'm not supposed to talk about it."

Claudia didn't have a nose for news, but even an anchor can sniff one out once in a while. She fought off the urge to rip his clothes off right then and there. Instead, she tilted her head and pursed her lips. "Come on. You can tell me."

"I don't want to talk about her. She is up to some very nasty stuff."

Claudia leaned in with an intimate little smile. "Ooh, tell me all about it."

Mick was imagining the long, slow process of separating her from her pink dress later on. She was warming up nicely. "Sure you want to know?"

"I'm ravenous to know."

Mick cracked his neck and flared his shoulders. Tossing a handful of hair over his shoulder he leaned in and spoke in a stage whisper. "I was there when she found the God Gene. I saw the whole thing. First hand."

"No. Really?"

"Oh yeah. And catch this; *I'm* the one who gave it to Starry Messenger." He sat back and smiled.

"Why did you give it to Starry?"

"Because I knew Starry would like it. And I was right. She wrote me right back. She relies on me now to tell her everything about it."

"Starry's a woman? How do you know that?"

"I'm Mick. I know."

"Are you two ... you know ...?"

Mick actually blushed. It wasn't something he did very often, but just thinking about Starry sent a flush through him. Starry. The Starry goddess. "Not yet. It's just a matter of time."

Claudia found his ardent attraction to Starry Messenger exceedingly sexy in a deviant sort of way. Maybe they should skip dinner and head to her place. "What about the nasty stuff Evans is up to?"

Mick smiled and leaned across the table. She did the same, until they were close enough to rub noses.

"She's the one who rearranged the code to spell the Ten Commandments."

"No! *She* did it? Why?"

"I can't tell you."

"Oh, Mick, you devil. Don't torture me!"

"OK. One hint: she's in with al-Qaida."

Claudia sat back with a jerk. "What? How do you know that?"

"I'm Mick the Tech."

Claudia took a slow sip of Galliano and tried to get a fix on this guy. This was the moment in a hook-up when you had to be very careful. Did you have a nut case on your hands? A pathological liar? Some kind of pervert? You never knew, but when they started talking like they invented fire, you had to wonder.

"Did she tell you that?"

"I really can't talk about this anymore. Bradshaw would kill me."

"Benton Bradshaw?"

"Yeah, you know him?"

"I've seen him. Kind of a pompous ass, right?"

Mick laughed. "I'll tell him you said so."

"Are you friends?"

"Hardly. He's the one who fired me. But then he hired me back."

"He hired you back after all that? Why?"

"Let's just say I provide services he can't live without. Now, I can't say any more. Let's have dinner."

Claudia was dying for more information, and she knew how to get it. If Vaniere was going to be off covering the Senate hearing tomorrow, then it was up to her to cover the story on the home front. It was the least she could do. She gave Mick her most sensual soul-to-soul connection look. "Hey, Mick, the food's great here, but I know a place that's even better. Why don't we go to my place and see if we can rustle up some grub?"

Chapter 43

STARTING AT STREET level of the Dirksen Office Building in
Washington D.C., there were a total of four security checkpoints on the
way to the Senate Judiciary Committee hearing room. Several thousand
people filled the sidewalks and streets: they were Christians, Jews, Muslims,
atheists and others, some carrying signs praising Rosalind Evans, some
carrying signs attacking her, some radiating religious ecstasy, and most
simply observing history in the making. There was a group of a hundred or
so standing in concentric circles with their heads bowed, holding hands,
praying without pause.

Upstairs, Room 224 was jammed full of media and spectators, all
waiting for the empty witness chair in front to be occupied. Ron Vaniere
scanned his notes and nervously checked his watch. He checked the
Internet for the umpteenth time that morning. The calls for God Gene
rallies were growing all over the world. There were also calls for Rosalind to
be arrested, lynched, stoned, deified, elected President, and everything in
between. People young and old, religious and secular, were calling for
demonstrations and rallies to make their views known. The godgeners had
managed to fire up huge rallies in seven cities across the country. Another
group, The Frameshift Coalition, vowed to be in those same cities
mounting anti-godgeners rallies. One video showed an angry Frameshifter
shouting at the camera. "This is settled science! There are no Ten
Commandments in the DNA. Period! The end! Anyone who says otherwise
is deluded or lying. Or just plain evil. LOOK AT THE EVIDENCE!!!!

Why don't you people all just go home?" Behind him were demonstrators carrying large posters of Rosalind Evans with devil ears.

Vaniere shut off his iPad. He was jittery. He knew these politicians; they were licking their chops at the chance to demonstrate superhuman levels of outrage and protectionism to an international audience. How would Evans handle it? The room was smaller than Vaniere had imagined. On TV, these hearings always looked larger than life, but in reality, Room 224 was intimate. The marble and oak-paneled walls were bathed in soft light from ornate brass wall sconces. In the front of the room was a raised dais with long curved tables and stuffed leather chairs for the committee members. Below the dais, on the main floor was a plain, long table covered in green, and a single wooden chair. The open area between the dais and the witness table was filled with photographers scurrying around on their knees. There were TV cameras in the front and back of the room. Every spectator seat was filled.

All at once a door in the right front of the room opened and the members of the committee filed in and soberly took their seats. It was rare for all nineteen members to be there at the same time, but this was no ordinary hearing. They shuffled their papers, leaned over and spoke to one another behind closed hands, surveyed their surroundings, sipped water and exuded an air of weighty importance, none more so than Chairman P. Philip Bosch.

Bosch was pleased. He and his staff had spent hours attending to every detail of the hearing, including his dress for the day. He had chosen his most telegenic power suit, a navy wool with wide lapels, a white shirt and red silk ombre tie. His silver hair was newly trimmed, and the facial tanning gel provided the perfect mid-summer hint of color. He fully expected a five-point bump in the polls by this time tomorrow.

Bosch nodded to the doorman at the back of the room.

A hush fell over the crowd. The few spectators lucky enough to get a seat had been there for hours waiting to catch their first glimpse of the elusive Rosalind Evans. Until now, they had seen little more of her than the now-infamous footage with Vaniere on the steps of Clearbrook Hall, at the Steele rally, and the photos that had been paraded endlessly on TV and across the Internet for the last week. They would have recognized her anywhere. But they certainly did not expect the well-dressed, self-assured woman who strode down the aisle leaving a scent of roses trailing behind. The fitted navy Armani suit and white satin blouse accentuated her height and her curves, and the skirt length left plenty of muscled calf for viewers to admire. Her auburn hair was pulled back from her face and tossed into a lustrous cascade down her back. She was a perfect vision of professional chic: glowing, gorgeous, supremely confident. The clicking and whirring of cameras was the only sound as she walked up the aisle with David at her side. Her glossy red lips parted in a warm smile at the Senators. There was absolute silence as she sat down at the witness table.

Man, she cleans up good, Bosch thought. That is one sexy handful of woman. He raised his gavel, smiled back at her and banged the proceedings to order.

"I want to thank my colleagues on the Judiciary Committee for their cooperation in preparing for this hearing in a timely and professional manner. Our only witness today is Dr. Rosalind Evans. The First Amendment to the Constitution of the United States says, and I quote, 'Congress shall make no law respecting an establishment of religion, or prohibiting the free exercise thereof.' Dr. Evans claims to have decoded a gene that spells out the Ten Commandments, word for word from the Holy Bible, a tacit if not overt confirmation by her that there is, indeed, a God. Furthermore, she made this discovery while using a computer that was paid for by a grant from the National Institutes of Health, a division of the federal government. And most disturbingly of all, she has set off a massive public uproar that threatens to destabilize relations among believers and non-believers all across the country. Accordingly, it is the duty of this committee to discover whether Dr. Evans, the Clearbrook Institute, PharmaGen, or anyone else has denied the rights of the American people by infringing on their First Amendment right to freedom of religion."

Bosch paused and smiled at Rosalind, a big, toothy, 'I'm in charge here' smile. "Thank you for coming, Dr. Evans. We will begin with your opening statement and follow with questions from the members of the committee."

Rosalind had been required to e-mail her statement to the committee ahead of time, so for them, there would be no surprises. But the masses of people watching in person and on TV were collectively holding their breath. She cleared her throat and surveyed the line of Senators before her. Fourteen men and five women, all in suits, already knowing what she would say, just waiting for her to say it out loud so they could scrap over it like junkyard dogs.

"Chairman Bosch, ranking member Fetters and members of the committee. I am glad to be here to discuss what has come to be called the God Gene. There has been much speculation about how it got there, what it means, and whether it really exists. I have anticipated some of your questions and will answer them quickly so that we can put an end to this and get back to doing something important with our lives.

"I am a molecular biologist engaged in cancer research. Yes, I did find the Ten Commandments written in the amino acid code of two genes at the center of the second chromosome while working on a leukemia research project funded by PharmaGen, Inc. I verified with Stefan Gunquist, Professor Emeritus of Theology at Rutherford University, that the wording was authentic.

"Yes, my research included DNA sequencing and analysis using the ANSR 1000 computer at the Clearbrook Research Institute, a computer that was built with grant funds from the National Institutes of Health, a federal agency.

"Yes, I think it is virtually impossible for the God Gene to have happened naturally. In fact, the odds are estimated by the Chairman of the Mathematics Department at Rutherford to be one in ten to the 28th power.

"Yes, I believed at the time that the so-called God Gene was an act of industrial sabotage by Danka-Saba, a competitor of PharmaGen's, in order to gain an advantage in the race to develop new leukemia drugs.

"Yes, I changed my thinking in light of several studies, using different DNA samples from the ones I had used, that replicated my base code. Flemingham claims to have found several words from the Ten Commandments in their translation code, but not all. We don't yet know why. But the fact remains: My base code was correct."

David did not allow himself to smile, though he was smiling broadly on the inside. Over the weekend, he had expected the two of them to spend hours working on the opening statement. But after the Ferris wheel summit meeting and a two-hour phone conversation with her best friend Edie Dawson, Rosalind sat down and wrote it in fifteen minutes. He tried to tweak it, but in the end they both agreed that it was perfect.

"No, I have never claimed that I discovered proof of the existence of God nor Creator nor Intelligent Designer nor the tooth fairy. All I have said from the beginning is that I discovered the Ten Commandments written in the genetic code at the center of the second chromosome. Now, many reputable labs all over the world have since confirmed my base code, and have found a few words from the Ten Commandments. The base code is correct, and the base code contains the Ten Commandments. I have been assured by Dr. Gunquist that it is perfectly in keeping with God's personality to have written an instruction book for life in our genes. Hebrews 8:10 says 'I will put my laws in their minds and write them on their hearts. I will be their God and they will be my people.'

"The Bible said it would happen. A leading authority on God says it could happen. I saw it with my own two eyes."

Rosalind paused for a moment. The only sound was audience members shifting in their seats and cameras clicking and whirring.

"The amino acid sequence for the CLAIRE and DZPro2 genes does, without the shadow of a doubt, spell out the Ten Commandments. Thank you, Senator, that concludes my statement."

"I will begin the questioning," Bosch said. "Dr. Evans, do you believe in God?"

Rosalind smiled to herself. They were wasting no time. She was glad now that she and David had rehearsed over the weekend. He asked her questions, then critiqued her answers. Her conversation with Edie had put the finishing touches on her strategy.

"Just tell the truth," Edie said. "Say what you believe and believe what you say. It wouldn't hurt to say a little prayer while you're at it."

"What do you think they would do if I told them it's a message from God?" Rosalind asked.

Edie burst out laughing. "Wet their pants. But they can't arrest you for that. It's not against the law to believe, baby girl. This is America."

"Well, Senator Bosch, I believed in God as a child. It's what my parents taught me. Then I spent years ignoring Him. Then I flat out denied Him; God didn't fit my scientific paradigm. Then my daughter died and that confirmed what I already knew: There couldn't possibly be a God. Then, a week ago, I discovered that in two genes, the amino acid sequence spells out the Ten Commandments. And here I am at the center of the biggest God kerfuffle in modern times. Senator, if I applied every bit of scientific knowledge I possess, every bit of energy and determination, I couldn't have cooked up a scenario like this. People are demonstrating in the streets, I've had three epiphanous moments in the last week, the media are obsessed with me, I'm here testifying before the Senate Judiciary Committee, and there isn't a person on Earth who isn't thinking about their relationship with the almighty today. Yes, Senator Bosch, I believe in God."

"But you've been quoted numerous times saying you are an atheist."

"I thought I was."

"So you lied?"

"No, but I knew you'd say that."

"You changed your mind?"

"No. My heart."

"Are you trying to foist your beliefs on the American people?"

"No. But I knew you'd say that, too."

"Are you trying to prove God exists?"

"No. I take it on faith that he exists. I don't need proof."

"Do you practice any religion?"

"I'm a Christian, but I'm way out of practice."

"What are your beliefs?"

"Senator, I believe in the laws of nature. I believe in truth. I believe in love. I believe in justice. And I believe God made all of the above. How about you? I'd be interested to know what all of you Senators believe in. It's hard to tell sometimes." There was a ripple of laughter in the audience.

"Dr. Evans, I suggest you take this seriously," Bosch said.

"Oh, believe me, I do. The whole world is watching you try to ascribe evil intent to a woman who is trying to help cure cancer so she can get a little peace after her only child died, a woman who has no history of subversive activity, no rap sheet, not so much as a speeding ticket, a woman who happened to be on duty when the strange code was detected, a woman who supposedly proved God exists, but who wasn't sure at the time that God existed, a woman whose life, job, safety and security have been ripped to shreds. This is pretty damn serious if you ask me."

"I'm glad you think so. Senator Ablom, do you have any questions," Bosch said.

Senator Ablom leaned forward and slowly removed his glasses from his shiny, misshapen nose. He coughed and cleared his throat with a raspy growl. "I am afraid. Vaarrry afraid." The words oozed out like sticky dough. "Never in my forty-five years in the Senate have I been *more* afraid. What we are dealing with here is a potential plot to overthrow the government of the United States by undermining the Constitution. What is more basic than freedom of religion? It is the very foundation upon which our great nation was built. What would those brave souls who fled England in search of the freedom to worship as they please—what would they think if they could see us now? My fear is that we have become victims of a cruel and dangerous plot to weaken that sacred foundation, to topple the greatest republic in the history of the world, and to do it by convincing Americans that they don't have the right to believe and worship as they see fit. This is the first step in dismantling our republic! Have you even *read* the First Amendment, Dr. Evans? What does it say? Does it say 'Congress shall make no law respecting an establishment of religion, or prohibiting the free exercise thereof, *except* for the God in your genes? For cry-eye woman, what gives you the right to singlehandedly change the Constitution? Don't you know that there are jihadists out there who want to take over our country and establish Sharia law? You are giving them the red carpet!" Senator Ablom paused for a moment, as if he had lost his train of thought. He mopped his brow and surveyed the room with lathery blue eyes.

"Do you have a question, Senator Ablom?" Bosch said.

"What? Oh. Yes. I do. Dr. Evans, is it true that you flunked biology in high school? Twice?"

"No."

"I have in my hands a transcript that says you did!" He held out a paper in his shaky gnarled hand. A Senate page handed it to Rosalind.

"That must be another Rosalind Fanning. It's not me. But I have a question for you, Senator? So what if I did?"

Senator Ablom squinted at her, then leaned over and had a word with his colleague, Senator Walker. "Have you been fired from the Clearbrook Institute?"

"No, I am on administrative leave."

"It has been alleged that you were carrying on an illicit affair with Mick Morrison, also known as Mick the Tech, a member of the technical support staff who had access to all the data in the ANSR 1000."

"Not true."

"I beg to differ, Dr. Evans. It was on Starry Messenger!"

"It's not true."

"But if you were his illicit lover, you would have had access to all that data as well, and you might have been able to tamper with it and create the God Gene yourself, wouldn't you?"

"I am not his illicit lover, Senator."

"Mr. Morrison said in a sworn affidavit that you stole his passcode in order to break into the computer."

David leaned up and whispered in Rosalind's ear. "Here we go. He is scenario-building in order to prejudice people and confuse you. Just tell the truth and don't editorialize."

"No, I never had an affair with Mick Morrison. And I didn't have an affair with the computer guy at Flemingham either, even though their base code was the same as mine."

The audience tittered. Bosch glared at them and banged his gavel. "I'm warning you all. I will maintain the dignity of these proceedings. One more sound and my boys back there will throw your sorry asses out of here. Now be quiet!"

"Mick Morrison has been on staff at Clearbrook for almost a decade; clearly he is an employee who is in a high position of trust. Are you calling him a liar?" the Senator asked.

"Yes."

"Why would he lie about this?"

"Because he blames me for his being fired."

"He says he quit because he didn't want to be part of your nefarious activities."

"He's lying."

"He gave his testimony in a sworn affidavit. Are you suggesting he perjured himself?"

"Not suggesting, Senator," Rosalind said calmly. "He lied."

The Senator looked around with big surprised eyes. He shook his head. "No further questions."

Rosalind wondered how far into the Twilight Zone this was headed. She glanced at David but did not dare smile.

"Senator Farthing?" Bosch said.

Senator Eleanor Farthing of Minnesota sat up straight, ran her hand through her short silver hair and looked intently at Rosalind.

"Dr. Evans, science is a very competitive, cut-throat business. At the elite level, the pressure to be first is incredibly intense. The pressure sometimes causes people to cheat. Hwang from South Korea is just one example. He altered data to make it look like he had created a dozen new stem cell lines. In truth, he perpetrated a hoax by altering the data to look like something it wasn't. He fooled everyone for a while. He made a mockery of peer review. He proved how easy it is to use science to create myth. When his paper was published, he was hailed as the new messiah. But the truth always comes out. They nailed him. Pure science isn't always as pure as we think, is it Dr. Evans?" The Senator folded her hands and waited.

"That's true."

"Scientific immortality is a much sought-after prize. Who wouldn't want to be an Einstein or a Watson or a Crick? Who wouldn't want to win a Nobel Prize? A coveted research position like yours at the Clearbrook Institute is the perfect platform for making notable discoveries, for publishing papers, for winning a Nobel Prize. A position like yours must be protected at all costs. It's very stressful, so one could understand how a person might be tempted to change a bit of data here or there to get headlines. One could understand that, couldn't one?"

"You might. I don't," Rosalind said.

Farthing leaned in and narrowed her brows. "Dr. Evans, are you trying to make a name for yourself with this God Gene?"

Rosalind searched Senator Farthing's face, eyes and body language for any hint that she was being facetious, that perhaps she was trying for a little levity in a room burdened with pomposity. But no. No, the woman was serious.

"A *name* for myself? Really? I am heading a multi-million dollar research project at one of the most prestigious research institutions in the world. Our work holds the promise of a cure for leukemia. Why in the world would I risk that by fudging data? This is my life's work, to make sure no other child suffers like my daughter did and thousands of other children do each year. The problem is I can't get any work done because I'm too busy defending myself against outrageous, self-serving politicians who don't know squat about science."

Rosalind didn't dare look at David. He had warned her to stay on point and to not, under any circumstances, insult the Senators. She could feel his stare boring into her.

Senator Farthing slammed the table with her open hand. "I DON'T know about science, but I sure do know a faker when I see one. Like everyone at this table, I have given years of my life to serving the American people. I care deeply about my country. And I will NOT sit here and let anyone trample on the Constitution!!"

"Senator Farthing, do you have any more questions?" Bosch gave Farthing a stern sideways look. She sat back.

"Senator Tanner, you are next," Bosch said.

The barrel-chested, bushy-haired man from Virginia sat forward. He spoke in a slow, gentlemanly drawl.

"Miz Evans, please do not mistake our purpose here. We appreciate your dedication to finding a cure for leukemia. Laudable, certainly. But we have to get to the bottom of this business about God and the Constitution of the United States. Are you or are you not saying that our DNA contains the Ten Commandments?"

"For the hundredth time, I'm saying that the code I analyzed spells out the Ten Commandments."

"The same Ten Commandments that are in the Bible, The Koran, and The Jew Bible?"

"Yes."

Tanner took a sip of water and glared at Rosalind. "Then I guess you, Miz Evans, think you have an open line to the Almighty! You think you can stand there and tell the rest of us that your God is *thee* God! You take *our* money and establish a religion based on *your* God. You have ground your heel into the establishment clause of the First Amendment! How in tarnation, Miz Evans, is that not tyranny?"

Rosalind cleared her throat and took a breath, never taking her eyes off Senator Tanner. "You have summoned me, a law-abiding citizen, from my home and my job, upon threat of prison, so you can sit up there and point the finger of blame at me, publicly mock me, impugn my integrity and accuse me of something I wouldn't dream of doing. How in tarnation, Senator, is *that* not tyranny?"

Tanner slammed his open hand down on the table. "This is the United States Senate! Show some respect young lady!"

"You've got it backwards, Senator. You're the one who needs to show some respect because in case you've forgotten, you work for *us!*" Rosalind gestured at the crowd with both arms. She pointed at the Senator sitting next to Bosch. "If I remember correctly, Senator Langran, you are up on ethics charges, something having to do with a female intern. You, Senator Collins, have taken umpteen January junkets to warm climates at taxpayer expense while you vote for every tax increase that comes down the pike. You, Senator Raymond, fly home to the coast every weekend in a military jet that *we* pay for. And you, Senator Alfred, how do you explain the fact that the feds found half a million dollars stuffed in your freezer? You sit up there and accuse *me* of tyranny? How stupid do you think we are?"

There was a brief, stunned silence. And then the audience erupted in cheers and applause. Bosch banged the gavel. "Silence! Dr. Evans! Senator Tanner! That's enough!" Bosch waited, his gavel hovering over the desk like a guillotine, until the crowd was quiet. "Senator Lattimore, do you have any questions?"

The short blonde woman from Florida looked sideways at Rosalind. She was glossy-lipped and wide-eyed, like a child startled from its nap. "You bet I do. With all this talk of God planting messages in our DNA, there's one thing I don't understand: Why the Ten Commandments?"

Rosalind laughed out loud, a blurting, uncontained chortle.

Bosch banged the gavel and glared at her. "Answer the question, Dr. Evans. You are on thin ice here."

"You would have to ask God about that, Senator. Personally, I think it makes perfect sense. What other set of rules is more fundamental? The Ten Commandments are shared by the three major world religions. They form the foundation for the laws of most of the world's civilizations throughout history. At the same time, what other set of rules is more flagrantly and frequently broken than the Ten Commandments? They are broken billions of times every day all over the world. They're probably being broken by half of us in this room right this very minute!"

The Senator's head flew back. "How dare you? I think you owe everyone in this room an apology for that."

"I'll apologize. But only if one of you up there can recite the Ten Commandments. Anyone?"

Bosch lowered the gavel once again. "Dr. Evans, I'll have to ask you to limit your comments to answering the—"

"I am the Lord thy God!" Rosalind leapt to her feet. "Thou shalt have no other Gods before me!" The words rang out loud and clear. The room was electric.

"Thou shalt not make unto thee any graven images!" The nineteen senators looked around at each other as if, for the first time in their political lives, they didn't know what to do. David was about to tell her to sit down when her voice rang out again.

"Thou shalt not take the name of the Lord Thy God in vain!" There was a smattering of applause. The gavel banged and banged.

"Remember the Sabbath Day and keep it holy!" Rosalind's voice rose in volume. The audience was now applauding loudly. David smiled in spite of himself.

"Honor thy father and thy mother!" Louder applause. More cheers.

"Dr. Evans sit down!" Bosch yelled. His face was livid. "I said sit down!"

Rosalind stood her ground, tall and composed. "Thou shalt not kill!"

Bosch stood and looked at his fellow Senators. They stared back, at a complete loss for what to do. Bosch brought the gavel down hard, over and over again.

Audience members leapt to their feet, cheering and clapping. They recited with her. "Thou shalt not commit adultery!"

"Thou shalt not steal!" The volume rose. Reporters were making calls on their cell phones. Cameras flashed.

"Thou shalt not bear false witness against thy neighbor!" The entire audience and most of the Senators were now on their feet. The words of the tenth commandment rang out loud and clear.

"Thou shalt not covet thy neighbor's wife nor anything that is thy neighbor's!"

Rosalind turned around and faced the audience. She gestured at the array of Washington elites behind her as if to say 'Shall we have a show of hands on that one?' The audience went wild.

Even some in the media were smiling. Bosch banged the gavel. Senator Farthing jumped to her feet. "Shameful, Dr. Evans! You blaspheme! You blaspheme!" She pounded her fist on the table and yelled at Rosalind, but it was useless; the crowd noise completely drowned her out.

Bosch stood and banged the gavel over and over. "Quiet! Order!" He yelled into his microphone. "I'll have this room cleared! I will not stand for this. Quiet!" The crack of the gavel reverberated through the sound system. Rosalind faced the dais, standing stock still as the crowd cheered behind her. Their energy surged through her; she felt lightheaded, but she kept her eyes focused on the space between Senator Farthing and Senator Tanner, making eye contact with no one and hoping that now, finally, this might be over. After a minute, the crowd settled back in their seats. All was quiet.

"I am going to ..." Before Bosch could finish his sentence, the door at the back of the room burst open.

"FBI! Rosalind Evans, you are under arrest!" Two armed men came rushing up the aisle, grabbed her by the arm and slapped handcuffs on her.

David grabbed her other arm. "On what charge!" The FBI agent pulled her one way, David the other.

"Treason!"

The audience came unglued. The Senators sat there wearing shocked expressions, all except for Bosch, who calmly stood and watched as the agents led the struggling Rosalind out the door with reporters and photographers following close behind.

David tried to protest, but his words were lost in the pandemonium.

"You have the right to remain silent ..." The agents quickly steered Rosalind out the door with David close behind.

Bosch brought the gavel down one more time. "This hearing is adjourned," he said to no one in particular. He quickly headed for the lobby where the TV cameras were waiting.

Ron Vaniere rushed out the hearing room door. He sprinted to the stairway and bounded down, two at a time. The main floor lobby was filling up fast. Each time an elevator door opened, a dozen reporters spilled out, shouting questions at Rosalind and the agents, who were nearing the front door to the building. The agents seemed bent on getting her out as fast as possible. Vaniere elbowed his way to the front of the pack.

"Rosalind! Rosalind!" Vaniere shouted as loudly as he could. She turned her head and for a brief moment they made eye contact. She didn't say anything at first, but the look on her face surprised him. She was calm. The fear he had seen in her eyes over the past week was gone. Something in her had changed. The agent muscled her toward the door.

Rosalind raised both hands high in the air, fingers spread wide. "Just tell the truth, Ron!" she yelled to him. "Always. And don't be afraid!" And then she was whisked out the door, into a black SUV, and swallowed up by the yellow D.C. morning.

Chapter 44

AT THE VERY hour that Rosalind Evans was led away from the Dirksen Senate Office Building in Washington, US Attorney Thomas O'Roarke was standing outside the Everett M. Dirksen Federal Building in Chicago. The irony of the building names was not lost on him; both were named for the loquacious late Senator from Illinois, whose philosophy could be summed up in his most famous quote: 'I am a man of fixed and unbending principles, the first of which is to be flexible at all times.' O'Roarke could not agree more.

O'Roarke had spent many hours orchestrating the events taking place at both Dirksen buildings today, timing his appearance to occur just after the shocking sight of Evans being dragged out of the hearing, which was broadcast live all over world.

O'Roarke stood at the microphone for a brief moment before he began, savoring it all: the mass of reporters, cameras and lights, the suave image he projected, and the collective anticipation of what he would say.

He believed that the indictment of Rosalind Evans would go down in legal history as the most brilliant example of expedited justice in American history. Armed with the evidence provided by Bradshaw and Morrison, he had quickly convinced the Grand Jury that Evans was giving aid and comfort to the enemy in a time of war. The arrest warrant followed quickly, and now he had a dangerous woman in custody. With Bosch's help, the nabbing of Evans had gone flawlessly, a true media extravaganza. The Holy Father would be gratified. The endorsement of Bosch was assured, and already he could smell the cherry blossoms blooming outside his office at the Justice Department.

He had crafted the perfect speech for the occasion, and his navy pinstripe suit and sparkling white shirt were smashing. With a solemn nod to the cameras, he stepped up to the microphone.

"Ladies and Gentlemen, who of us has not laid our head on the pillow at night and thanked God in heaven for the wisdom and vision of our founding fathers, who gave us that shining beacon of light known as the First Amendment, that most profound amendment, brief but powerful, which guarantees our freedom to worship as we please and not be told by our government how, where, when, or even whether, to worship? Sadly, that First Amendment is under attack." O'Roarke took a breath. He could feel it; he was touching patriotic nerves all over America.

"Rosalind Evans conspired with a sworn enemy of the United States to topple the very foundations of our American way of life. She has trampled on our Constitution with both feet. But fear not, a national disaster has been averted. Just a few moments ago, under my orders, Rosalind Evans was arrested and taken into custody and charged with treason!!"

O'Roarke looked out at his audience as if waiting for applause. Of course there was none from the reporters. But it was OK; he knew that viewers at home were applauding.

"Allow me, if you will, to describe the sequence of events that led to her arrest. Two years ago, Evan's daughter was diagnosed with leukemia. Evans began spending her days doing Clearbrook work, and her nights working with a Jordanian scientist, Samir Okar, ostensibly testing DNA samples in hopes of finding out why her daughter was not responding to treatment. At the same time, co-workers said she withdrew and became elusive and hard to communicate with. When her daughter died, witnesses say she came unglued. We know now that she was working with Okar not to save an innocent little child, but to create a deadly bio-weapon to be used in a terrorist attack on American soil.

"Months later, Evans visited Syria. She said the trip was for medical research. But I have in my hand a photo of Evans and a Syrian man, innocent looking enough, but in actual fact, this man is Hassan Hussein,

AKA Hussein Nomynatu, a known al-Qaeda operative. What's more, a string of e-mail messages has been recovered from Evans's computer that indicate she had a close relationship with this man.

"Then Evans took another dark turn," O'Roarke continued. "She began research on the top-secret PharmaGen project, and that is where she manipulated the genetic code to make it appear to spell out the Ten Commandments. She claimed that her research proved that God exists as a physical certainty rather than as a matter of personal faith and personal choice. The computer Evans used to sequence the God Gene was funded by the National Institutes of Health, a division of the Federal Government.

"Evans violated the establishment clause of the First Amendment by using Federal funds to establish a religion based on God as *she* defines him. She violated the free exercise clause of the First Amendment by denying atheists their right to *not* worship God. She conspired with al-Qaida to create a deadly bio-weapon. Remember that our enemy is motivated by religious conviction. They want to destroy our government and replace it with Sharia law. Rosalind Evans obviously believed the best way to start was to cripple our religious freedom. She gave aid and comfort to our enemy!

"Some say Rosalind Evans is brilliant, some say she's a nut case, and others say she is evil incarnate. She is brilliant without doubt. And what she attempted to do to our country can only be described as evil. And clearly she's nuts. So what we have here is an evil, brilliant nut. Take her behavior at the Senate hearing a few minutes ago: Reciting the Ten Commandments? Bizarre."

"Are there co-conspirators besides al-Qaeda?" a reporter yelled.

"We are investigating PharmaGen, Clearbrook Institute, and Rutherford University as co-conspirators."

"How did you get an indictment so fast? The God Gene discovery happened just eight days ago."

O'Roarke smiled his best self-deprecating smile. "It was a ton of work. But I have no higher calling than to bring to justice anyone who would harm our nation. I worked around the clock to secure this indictment, and I am proud to say that because of that, we are safer today than we were yesterday."

"Is this case eligible for the death penalty?"

"Treason? Of course!"

"Will you ask for the death penalty?"

"You can take that to the bank, my friend."

Chapter 45

THE NEXT MORNING, Vaniere was in his office at InfoNet trying to sort out the incomprehensible events of the previous day, when Claudia Moray sashayed in.

"Hello Claudia. You're looking fetching today."

"Fetching is for Barbie Dolls. I was trying for delicious, ravishing, or wood-producing." She put on a little pout and sat down on the edge of his desk, her tight little tush facing toward him. She twisted around and leaned down close. "I had dinner with a friend of yours last night."

"I didn't know I had any friends."

"Mick Morrison."

"Who?"

"He works in tech support at Rutherford. I figured you knew him since you're so hot on the Rosalind Evans story. He was in the room when she discovered the God Gene, and he is the one who leaked the story to Starry Messenger that night. He said he did it to impress Starry, who he thinks is a chick."

"Starry Messenger? A woman?"

"Mick thinks so, but Mick's brain is about this big," she said, forming a circle with her thumb and fingers. "But that's beside the point. He says Evans was so upset when he leaked the story that she got him fired. But now Benton Bradshaw has hired him back. He and Bradshaw talk every day."

"Nice work. You angling for my job?" Vaniere said.

"You're a riot. But I would consider a finder's fee."

"I bet you would."

She pouted again. "Not even for the piece I did on the Convocation of Manifest Souls?"

"You did a piece on it?" Vaniere's hackles were instantly up.

"It's all the rage. Everybody's going there now. My piece airs at six tonight."

"Now you're trying to steal my story?"

"We needed the story and you were in D.C. Besides, I like spas."

"Your piece won't air unless I say so. If it does, it will be with *my* intro."

"Hey, who do you think you're talking to? I'm an anchor."

"My point precisely. Stick to your teleprompter and stay off my story."

"I've got news for you, buddy. Mick told me some things you'll find very interesting. But you have to be nice."

"Nice? Me? I'd only be pretending. What did he say?"

"He told me that Bradshaw hired him back and that they are working on a project together. And then he told me that Rosalind Evans planted the God Gene herself and she is in league with al-Qaida."

"Was he trying to impress you to get you in the sack?"

"Yeah, and when I asked him about it—you know, during—he said he and Bradshaw were working on a project that was going to save the United States from a terrorist attack planned by Rosalind Evans. It doesn't add up."

"Why?"

"How could he have known all that before O'Roarke's press conference?"

"He told you this *before* the press conference?" The Shovels hackles were really up now. "Thanks, Claudia. I'll take it from here."

"About that finder's fee ..."

"Maybe later." Maybe never, he thought. "You scoot along. I've got work to do."

"Ingrate. Oh, I almost forgot. Mick told me one more thing. They've called off the hacking investigation at Clearbrook. They couldn't find any evidence that anybody broke into the system."

* * *

Alan Dyer drank orange juice from a crystal glass, savoring the cool sweetness. It had been an exceedingly good eight-mile run this morning, almost effortless in spite of the 95 degree heat. He coveted the time to himself every morning; it reminded him who he was. Every other minute of the day was spent flying the rocket-ship that was his life, dodging obstacles, overtaking challengers, eye always on the goal. He needed his daily run as a time to refuel his engines and clear his mind for new ideas. Others would cut their run short on a hot day, but not Alan Dyer; when the thermometer read 85 degrees or above, he extended it from seven miles to eight. The sweat and pain opened new pathways to inspiration and sharpened his focus.

If there's one thing the President and CEO of PharmaGen had in spades, it was the ability in times of turmoil to filter out the noise and capitalize on an opportunity to make money. Right now, all over the world, people were embracing, cursing, celebrating, denouncing, fleeing from, speculating about, laughing at, and crying over one thing—the God Gene. Everyone everywhere was engaged with God, whether for Him or against Him. No one was neutral. After just one week of watching the world react, he saw with crystal clarity two things: the God Gene was the hottest fad in history, and he wasn't going to make billions on it—he was going to make trillions. He was going to be the richest man on the planet.

His patent attorney looked at him across the desk and smiled. "Of course the provisional patents are secure, Alan. What are you worried about?"

"I am not worried. I'm in a hurry. The God Gene is a world-wide sensation and this is a very volatile time. I want you to move as fast as you can to finalize the patents on them globally."

"OK. So what are you going to do with them?"

"Make trillions."

The lawyer thought it must be a joke, except that in all the years he'd known Dyer, he had never once heard him joke about anything.

"Trillions?" The lawyer laughed. "Then I guess my fees won't be of concern to you?"

"Don't get smart."

"How does one man make trillions? It's never happened. The math doesn't work out."

"Well, let's start with the fact that we're talking about the gene that controls response to the major leukemia drugs. I own the gene, therefore nobody else can test for it, analyze it, develop any product or service relative to it. Nobody can touch it."

The lawyer looked at him for a long moment, drumming his fingers on the table and thinking about how little he knew this man after all these years. Dyer's demeanor today wasn't normal. There was a wealth of subtext in his expression.

"Alan, the patent only lasts twenty years. Even the best leukemia drugs in the world won't make you trillions before the patent runs out. Billions maybe, but not trillions."

"You're not thinking big enough, Jack. Come on, buddy."

The lawyer looked at him with a blank expression.

"The Ten Commandments. They're mine now. I own them. You said yourself that the patent on a gene carries with it an airtight patent on the arrangement of the code. The code spells out the Ten Commandments, ergo, I own the Ten Commandments."

"I'm good, Alan, but not that good. Nobody owns the Ten Commandments."

"I want you to look into copyrighting the Bible, the Torah and the Qur'an. All three contain the Ten Commandments. Once I own the rights to all three, I will issue cease and desist letters to every publisher in the world. I will own the rights to printing all three, and I will own the content of all three. Can you imagine what kind of money I will make on book sales alone?"

"You are out of your mind, Alan."

"How can you say that? You're my lawyer. You're supposed to believe in me."

"C'mon Alan."

"I'm serious."

"Really? OK. Those books are in the public domain. It is easy to put something into the public domain, and almost impossible to take something out. Forget it."

"Are you saying you won't at least try?"

The lawyer didn't like the way the conversation was going. He couldn't afford to lose Dyer as a client; he was a pharmaceutical genius, an intellectual property jackpot. But copyright the three major holy books?

"Next you'll want me to patent God," the lawyer said.

"Yes! Brilliant! Jack, you are one in a million. Why didn't I think of that?" Dyer jumped up and slapped the lawyer on the back. He threw his head back and laughed like he'd seen a reindeer fly. "When I have a patent on God, won't I be able to license the use of his picture and his name?"

"God doesn't have a picture, Alan. C'mon." The lawyer ran his hand through his hair and looked around for a cigarette. "I'm seriously worried about you. Please tell me you're not serious. Please tell me this is a joke."

"I have never been more serious in my life," Dyer said. The expression on his face ratified the declaration.

"What about your investigation into a hack job?" the lawyer asked.

"Well, Jack, the truth is we can't find any evidence that anyone hacked in. We've been looking non-stop for almost two weeks now, and there is no evidence. That's why I'm moving ahead as fast as I can. I can't make trillions on a hack job." Dyer downed the last of his orange juice. "We need to nail these patents immediately."

"OK, but look, Alan, your gene patent will probably be thrown out by a judge."

"Why?"

"Because a federal judge threw out the patent on the breast cancer genes. He said you can't patent something that exists in nature; you can only patent something you invent. You didn't invent the God Gene."

"I spent millions to find it, though. I deserve something for that, right?"

"I doubt it. You need to prove you have created something useful with it."

"What's more useful than the Ten Commandments?"

"Don't you think there will be some push back? Say, from every Mullah on the planet? These guys don't have a sense of humor about their religion, you know."

"The law is the law, Jack. Do I have to tell *you* that? Either we have intellectual property protection or we don't."

"Alan, I've seen people all over the world who believe this is a message from God himself. They are happy. They are sure that God is looking out for them. The God Gene has given them hope. All it's done for you is make you crazy."

"Crazy like a fox, my friend." Dyer winked at him.

"What the hell? Do you think it is fair that you own a gene? Isn't my God Gene *my* God Gene? Or is my God Gene *your* God Gene?"

Dyer laughed and slapped the lawyer's shoulder. "It's mine, but you can borrow it!"

* * *

US Code—Section 2381:

Whoever, owing allegiance to the United States, levies war against them or adheres to their enemies, giving them aid and comfort within the United States or elsewhere, is guilty of treason and shall suffer death, or shall be imprisoned not less than five years and fined under this title but not less than $10,000; and shall be incapable of holding any office under the United States.

Vaniere read and shook his head. The whole thing defied comprehension. One minute Rosalind Evans was showing incredible grit in standing up to the Senate Judiciary Committee; the next minute she was being hauled off in handcuffs, branded a traitor. Furthermore, Mick Morrison knew about the government's case before it went public. He and Bradshaw are working on a "project" to save America from a terrorist attack being planned by Rosalind Evans. And then there was O'Roarke grandstanding at the press conference about a plot too bizarre to be believed. Today, the Feds said she had been released to return to Chicago where she would be on house arrest, confined to her home, until her treason trial.

Vaniere's head reeled from the incongruities. The woman described by O'Roarke bore no resemblance to the woman he'd talked to in New York.

Of all the images from yesterday, the most indelible of all was the sight of her calling out his name as she was being led away by the FBI, holding her hands in the air, fingers splayed, thumbs touching. Ten fingers. Was it some kind of salute? Ten Commandments? The last thing she said to him was to always tell the truth.

What was the truth?

The Shovel knew on a deeply intuitive level that Rosalind Evans had not perpetrated a conspiracy. But something told him she might be the victim of one.

His thoughts were interrupted when the news director slammed open his door and flew in like a freight train. He grabbed the remote on Vaniere's desk and turned up the sound on one of the three flat screen TVs arrayed across the wall. Vaniere had them muted, and he had been so deep in thought about Rosalind that he hadn't noticed breaking news banners across all three.

"Ron! Holy shit. Hitchcock has been rushed to the hospital. AP is saying he took an overdose of sleeping pills. Steele's on the air right now!"

There was Reverend Joseph Steele, grim-faced and disheveled.

"I don't have words to describe what a tragedy this is. It didn't have to happen. Bill was prepared to own up to his transgressions, to reconcile with his family, his God, and the American people. He was preparing to do that when his fate was willfully *seized* from him by a reporter who didn't have the decency to give the man that chance. That reporter, Ron Vaniere, could have waited two hours, but he chose to run the story because it was an *exclusive. An exclusive!* When in God's name did TV ratings become more important than a man's life? A man's soul?" Steele was shaking with anger. His face was tear-streaked and his bloodshot eyes bore holes through the camera. He waved his arms in the air as if wanting to land a blow, then dropped them in frustration. "My heart is sick to death! I pray to God almighty that we find a way to turn our priorities around. We are worshipping the wrong God! We are so consumed with desire for the sensational, the outrageous, the tawdry, that we can't hear God when he is yelling in our faces!" Steele turned and walked back into the hospital.

The news director looked at Vaniere. "That's bull, Ron. This is not your fault."

Vaniere felt a wave of dizziness. "Is he dead?"

"No. He took pills, but not enough. He'll recover." The news director waited, but Vaniere stared at his desk. "Come on, Ron. Steele is a blowhard. He doesn't know what he's talking about. He's wrong."

"No. He isn't."

"But, you didn't—"

"Get out of here."

The news director walked backwards slowly, trying to gauge Vaniere's mindset, but to no avail. He walked out and closed the door.

Vaniere sat for a long time staring at nothing. The lies about Hitchcock's black market scheme were soaring at the speed of light, sucking up irrational adherents by the thousands as they sped through cyber-space and across the airwaves. All I wanted to do was expose the lie. I dug. Along the way I found something from Hitchcock's past. I reported it. It's what they pay me to do. Vaniere felt emotions roiling inside him, unaccustomed feelings that he'd kept in check for years, things that did not serve him well as a reporter. He felt remorse. And sadness. What if I had waited? What if I had held the story until Hitchcock had his chance to tell his wife? He pictured Hitchcock lying in a hospital bed, the victim of his own anguish. It was a vision that sickened him. I didn't want to run the story. The news director made me do it. It's his fault.

Vaniere shook his head. That's a lie and you know it, he told himself. The kid on the plane was right; you're a lame goddam tool.

Chapter 46

"YOU CAN'T TAKE my laptop away!"

Rosalind hugged her computer and stood her ground. David grabbed
for it, but she held firm. The two of them squared off in the living room of
their town house. They had been home just 24 hours. After her arrest in
D.C. there was a flurry of administrative activity aimed at making official
Rosalind's status as an accused traitor. David had secured her release under
conditions of house arrest, along with permission to return to Chicago. A
U.S. Marshall accompanied them on the flight back, and was now
conveniently stationed outside the house, presumably until she was cleared
of the charges, whenever that might be.

Rosalind was dressed in yoga pants and an oversized t-shirt, and her
hair was piled on top of her head in a big pouf. Since she was confined to
house arrest for the foreseeable future, forbidden from stepping so much as
a toe outside except for court appearances, she saw no point in primping.
She would spend her days on the couch with her laptop, surfing the net and
reading about herself. What she'd read so far was stranger than fiction: in
less than two weeks, she had evolved from a mad scientist to a national
threat to a cult hero. The ranks of the Godgeners were growing, and a half-
dozen Israeli and Middle Eastern leaders were calling for a series of talks to
discuss new peace initiatives based upon the common bond they all shared
in the God Gene. Churches, synagogues and mosques were working
overtime to serve the hundreds of thousands of pilgrims all over the world
who were seeking to draw nearer to the God they now knew was real.

Much of the world was embracing the God Gene; the Cynical Messiah was in shackles.

Meanwhile, the media held their own pilgrimage in Rosalind and David's front yard. Their vigil, as solemn and pious as that of the religious pilgrims, had little to do with God and everything to do with the voracious airwaves they needed to feed. The public's appetite for the God Gene story seemed insatiable. Other stories emerged, like the recent troubles that had befallen presidential candidate Willard Hitchcock, but they wouldn't come close to the fervor surrounding the God Gene. There were several dozen reporters staked out at her house, from many countries around the world. Satellite trucks littered the street, and the constant drive-by traffic from curiosity seekers had finally caused police to barricade both ends of her block, allowing in only media and residents.

The situation between Rosalind and David was tense, owing to their newly-defined relationship as accused felon and counsel. The latest point of contention was over her laptop, which David was trying to confiscate. He grabbed for it again.

"You went online. You promised you wouldn't do that," David said.

"But all I did was read. I didn't write anything to anybody. What's the problem?"

"You are the problem. If you say something online, even something as innocuous as 'happy birthday,' it can and will be used against you in court." He held out his hand. "Give."

"Back off! I'm a prisoner here. This is my only link to the outside world. I know you are a good lawyer, David. I believe what you say. But I need to do my research so I can defend myself!"

"Wrong! *I* have to defend you. Give me the computer." David chased her around the room, his bare feet slapping on the oak floor. He was dressed in jeans and a t-shirt that belonged in a dumpster. The bed-hair didn't help the look. He popped open a beer and downed half the can in one gulp. Already the pressure to protect her was wearing him down.

Rosalind sat down on the big leather sofa and crossed her legs. This room, so light and airy, full of green plants and overstuffed comfy furniture, had always been her sanctuary. Now, it was her prison.

"These charges against me are not true, but you and I are the only ones who seem to know that. I have to know what's going on out there. This is my lifeline. Please David!"

"It could also be your death warrant if you say the wrong thing and put it out there."

"David, I had another epiphany."

"Oh? I hope God gave you a defense theory."

"No. I woke up this morning with an idea about why my results were different from Flemingham's, even though we used the same sequencing software. It has to do with the number of samples I sequenced. They tested fifteen. I tested seven thousand."

"How could that make a difference?"

"I think it has to do with the number of SNPs, the number of Xs in the code. That's what I need my computer for; to figure it out. Please."

"OK, I give up. Just don't post anything or e-mail anybody. I'm begging you."

Rosalind had no fear about the charges against her. She and David knew from the moment they read them that they were specious and wouldn't hold up in court unless somebody was willing to lie. What she did fear was the iron-fisted control that the feds exerted over her. It didn't seem to matter anymore who she was, or what she had or hadn't done. She was prisoner #49898-762. She had few rights, no freedom, and not a scintilla of respect. Months and perhaps years of imprisonment weighed on her like wet concrete. It was not like the self-imposed exile she'd endured for the last two years. Forces outside her influence were now in charge of her life. She had no doubt that she would overcome the injustice of the false charges, but she was powerless against this outrage of false imprisonment. The GPS ankle bracelet was her ball and chain. In a brief appearance before the judge in Chicago, he admonished her to 'wear the GPS ankle bracelet at all times. You might be able to remove it with bolt cutters, but we'd know, and then you'll find yourself in that lovely looking high rise over there.' He was referring to the Chicago Metropolitan Correctional Center, a white, triangular skyscraper with ominous-looking vertical slits of windows that distinguished it from every other building in the city. Rosalind had seen it many times from the freedom and relative normalcy of a passerby's perspective. She had often wondered what kind of people were locked behind those dreadful, inescapable windows.

Already she was playing mind games, searching for ways to distract herself from the reality that she could not even take a walk in her own back yard. A day of this was torture; months of it were too much to think about. A pall of gloom hung over her like Pig Pen's cloud.

The doorbell rang. Rosalind lunged at the door, knocking David out of the way. A visitor, even Lucifer himself, would be a welcome diversion.

"Roz! Baby girl!"

Edie Dawson swept into the room with her usual panache, dressed to the nines in denim, leather and turquoise. "I couldn't let you go through this alone." Edie hugged Roz for a long moment, then flew to David. Their hug was long and heartfelt. The last time Edie had seen him was Claire's funeral. A lot had happened since. She loved him like a brother and knew the feeling was mutual. For a short time, she'd feared he was out of her life, but that fear, thank God, was gone.

"I didn't want David to tell you I was coming because I didn't want you to be disappointed if the feds said no. But they said yes! I got the first flight out from New York."

"It was a legal tangle, but I convinced the judge that you were essential to Rosalind's mental health and well-being. I didn't bother to go into details with him about your girl talk, gin consumption and reality TV marathons."

"Oh, David, this is wonderful! Edie, how long can you stay?"

"Till it's over."

"That could take a year or more!" Rosalind said.

"Honey, I make more money than I can spend in this lifetime and the next. I took a leave of absence. So come on, show me the kitchen. I'm fixing us dinner." Edie had a bag of groceries and several bottles of wine. "If we're going to be in jail together, then we're going to make the most of it. Chicken tetrazzini!"

While Edie and Rosalind cooked together in the kitchen, David made one phone call after another with his closest advisors. He no longer had his old firm; he would have to work from home to put together the best legal team he could find. He would soon be consumed with court motions, questioning of witnesses, and late night strategy sessions. Treason was not an easy case to make, which was why despite five wars, there hadn't been a treason trial in the U.S. in over 60 years. What would have prompted O'Roarke to bring these charges? What facts could he possibly have?

Around the table at dinner, the three held their glasses high and toasted their out-of-body strange circumstances.

"David, I want you to tell me how I can best serve the cause. The sooner I get my girl out of hock, the better I'll feel," Edie said.

"Well, as a matter of fact, there is something you can do. I need someone to monitor media coverage of Rosalind and of the case. I need to know what the pundits and the blowhards are saying."

"Stop it! You're killing me. What do I love more than watching TV and reading my blogs and newspapers? You're on!"

* * *

The hospital in Sioux Falls, South Dakota was mobbed with media, Hitchcock supporters, and curiosity seekers. They had been carrying on a round-the-clock vigil since the Governor was admitted 36 hours ago. Ron Vaniere stood on the fringe of the activity, trying to screw up the courage to go in. On the flight to Sioux Falls, he'd rehearsed what he would say to Hitchcock if he got in to see him. But no matter how hard he tried, the words were shallow and morose, in no way conveying the mix of emotions in his heart. He couldn't find the words to express his regret that his pitifully warped sense of self-importance had nearly cost this man his life.

He was petrified. He had always been able to summon strength from the latent rage inside that supposedly made him strong. But not now; the fearless Ron Vaniere was incapacitated by the fear that he had finally done something he couldn't undo, something so egregious as to doom him to hell. What good is your righteous anger now, big man? What oppressor do you blame for this? He walked toward the hospital entrance, grim-faced. Just go in and do it. Tell him you are sorry. Own up to your mistake and pray you get out alive.

Without warning a man lunged from the crowd and punched him in the face, a massive, rabid punch that knocked him flat on his back. The man kicked him in the ribs. "Get up, you chicken shit son of a bitch!"

The man, who was shorter and smaller than Vaniere, reached down and pulled him up like a rag doll. Vaniere instinctively brought his arms up to defend himself, but the man was superhuman with anger. "Did you think it wouldn't *matter* what you did? The great and powerful Ron Vaniere had to tell the story before anyone else? You snake. You hurt a good man! For what?" The man landed another angry blow to Vaniere's midsection. "For *what?!*"

Vaniere countered with a blow to the man's stomach. It knocked him backward, but he charged again at Vaniere. Several other men came at him, punching and yelling. He took a gut punch and doubled over in a burst of white hot pain. In a fog of adrenalin and fear, Vaniere had the sure sense that this was how it would end; overpowered, beaten bloody and kicked to death by an angry mob, with a glut of media there to record it for the world to see. Another punch to the gut, and suddenly the air went white and quiet. He felt himself falling, but he never felt his head hit the pavement.

Chapter 47

Who Needs to Know?

Well, my kittens, is there anything more fun than a breaking news flash? Doesn't it make you want to drop everything to watch and listen? Did you find that hearing the details of Governor Hitchcock's trespasses and seeing photos of his love child made you nobler, wiser and more in tune with the universe? Doesn't that make Ron Vaniere a hero? Did you feel a sense of awe as he revealed the dark secret of Governor Hitchcock's past, and feel a deep sense of relief that the deception was finally over? After all, what horrors would befall our country if we elected an adulterer?

And didn't you rise to all new heights of spiritual bliss when you saw Vaniere being beaten bloody by an angry mob? Didn't he get what he deserved?

We are told that Governor Hitchcock was planning to tell his wife about the child, and to reconcile with the American people, but he didn't have time to do it before Vaniere broke the story, but so what? Surely the public has a sacred right to know the very minute a truth is uncovered, and not the minute after?

Seriously, my kittens, where is the righteousness in all of this?

* * *

When Vaniere came to, he didn't know where he was. He tried to focus. Bright lights. White walls. In a hospital. It took him several minutes to gather the courage to try and sit up.

"Slow down, there, cowboy. You're not going anywhere," the doctor said.

"What happened?"

"I don't know how it started, but I know how it ended: you lost. How do you feel?"

"I have to go and ... I don't know."

"The only place you're going is upstairs. I'm admitting you."

"Why?" Vaniere tried again to sit up, but he couldn't even draw a breath without pain.

"You have some bruises and lacerations, nothing serious, but your head hit the ground pretty hard. I need to run some tests and keep you for observation."

"Where am I?"

"Sioux Falls, South Dakota."

Vaniere remembered; he'd flown out here to talk to Hitchcock and his wife. To apologize. He remembered angry people coming at him, but not much more.

"Is Governor Hitchcock here?"

"Yes."

"Is he—alive?"

"His doctor just announced on TV that he's going home tomorrow."

"I need to see him."

"You are in no shape to see anybody, Mr. Vaniere."

"I can do it. Just tell me what room he's in."

The doctor shook his head. "I can't tell you that without his permission. I can let him know you're here."

"Tell him I ... I'm sorry."

The doctor left. Vaniere tried to piece together the events that led him to this place but soon gave up, his head throbbing, and fell into a dark, dreamless sleep.

"Mr. Vaniere?"

Deep sleep, voices, slight nausea, pain.

"Mr. Vaniere, can you hear me?"

Vaniere slowly opened his eyes and seeped into consciousness. The room was dim; he couldn't make out who was talking.

"What?" Vaniere's voice was thick and dry. "What?" He thought he recognized the man standing over him. He blinked a couple of times. "Gov—Govnor Hitchcock?"

"Yes."

"What ...?"

"They told me you were here. I wanted to see you before I left to go home."

Vaniere reached for the bed control. He raised the head of the bed until he was in a sitting position. The two men looked at each other, each waiting for the other to speak.

At last, Hitchcock shook his head. "You look like hell."

"I'm sorry. I should have waited."

"Yes, you should have. You should have given me the chance to tell my family. You hurt us all very badly."

Vaniere looked down and shook his head. He could hear the blood rushing in his ears. Tears fell, but he didn't have the strength to wipe them away.

"When you ran that story, you had to know how badly it would hurt us, didn't you?"

Vaniere didn't look up.

"Did you think you could do something that blatantly selfish and there wouldn't be consequences? Why did you come here, Mr. Vaniere?"

"To tell you I'm sorry. To ... I don't know."

"Do you want me to say I forgive you?"

Vaniere stared down at his bruised hands. He nodded.

"Look at me."

Vaniere looked up.

"Say it."

Vaniere felt his throat constrict. I can't, he thought. How can I look at this man and ask him to do the impossible? He will mock me and say hateful things. True things. I thought I was great, but I'm the lowest of the low … Vaniere took a breath. His voice was hoarse and tentative. "Will you forgive me?"

Hitchcock paused and looked at Vaniere's bruised face and puffy eyes. He smiled. "I took those pills because I couldn't bear the pain. Thank God I didn't succeed, because now I know how wrong I was. I'm alive. And because of all this, I have reconciled with my family. Of course I forgive you. It's what we do. Besides, I can't carry the burden of hating you. Good luck, Mr. Vaniere." Hitchcock turned and walked out the door.

Chapter 48

ROSALIND, DAVID AND Edie were spending the evening just as they had since Edie's arrival: sitting in the living room, each with a laptop, seldom talking, totally engrossed in their research. On this, the third such evening, their concentration was interrupted by the ringing of Rosalind's cell phone. David dove for it, but she snatched it up before he could reach it. He gave her a look of utter frustration.

Rosalind listened for a moment. "Why are you calling me?" There was a long pause on her end as she listened. "OK, I'll see you then." She hung up. "Ron Vaniere's coming over."

"What?! You can't talk to him! Have you had a stroke?"

"I don't think so, but the headache you're giving me makes me wonder. He said he had something important to tell us. David, it sounds serious."

"He's the enemy! Why on earth would you invite him here? He chewed you up and spit you out in that report last week."

"Everything he said was true. I don't know, something in the tone of his voice …"

"You are out of your mind," David said.

"He's the only one who told the truth about me."

"They wrote a book about you once. Pollyanna."

"He'll be coming in the back way."

"Great. He sneaks in the back looking guilty, someone sees him, and this whole thing blows up in our faces!"

"Come on, honey. Have a little faith." She smiled at the irony: now she was the one telling him to loosen up, and he was the mad man thinking he needed to control everything all by himself. They had come full circle since the night of the storm. She put her hands on his shoulders and began to massage. "Things aren't so bad. It's quite calming, actually, facing death."

"Knock it off!" David said. He was half worried and half angry with her. You never knew what a jury would do; they could fry her. And then there was O'Roarke; he was as dangerous as black ice. "You drive me nuts with your flippant attitude! Don't you know how serious this is?"

"Of course I do, dammit! I'm doing the best I can. What do you want me to do, take to my bed?"

He rubbed his face as if to erase the past few minutes. "I'm sorry."

"David, I know you feel like you're all alone right now, but you're not. You're the one who taught me that."

"I wish I felt that way. When Vaniere gets here, I'll tell him to leave. You can't say *anything* to him. And I'll take you up on that bed thing later."

"I can hear you, you know," Edie said.

"I hear tapping on the back door," Rosalind said.

David raced to open it before she could.

"I'm afraid you'll have to leave Mr. Vaniere."

"Please. I have something important to tell you. I won't stay long."

David was shocked by Vaniere's appearance. His face looked like a pan of burnt biscuits, swollen and bruised. But the expression in his eyes clearly said that he had something he wanted to say.

"All right, but I have instructed my client not to speak to you unless I say so."

Rosalind laughed. "From now on, Ron, you and I will communicate like card cheats. When I raise my right eyebrow ..."

"Enough," David said through clenched teeth.

"Ron, I heard you got into a scuffle. It's all over the news," Edie said.

"Yeah, welcome to my world!" Rosalind said. David glared at her.

"I hear you. It is no fun being in that world." Vaniere said. He was amazed at how quickly every network and blog in the universe had made him the top story of the day. They really seemed to love showing the news footage of him being beaten like a little boy.

"Looks like you got the bad end of the deal," Edie said. "What happened?"

"Let's just say I met the strong arm of retribution," Ron said with an attempt at a smile. "Luckily we have make-up experts at the studio. They'll make it look like it never happened."

David pointed to a chair and Vaniere gratefully sat down. "I'll make this quick because the longer I'm here, the more likely I am to lose my nerve. I wanted both of you to hear this. I didn't know Edie was here." He smiled at her and shook her hand. "It's fine with me if she stays."

Edie hoped she wasn't blushing. Ever since meeting Vaniere in New York, she had made it a policy to keep InfoNet on every minute she was home, just in case he came on screen. Now, standing next to him and shaking his hand, even though he looked like Ali after the Thrilla in Manila, she was beginning to hyperventilate.

"Let's hear it," David said.

"Mick the Tech told a colleague of mine the night *before* your arrest that you are affiliated with al-Qaida."

David, Edie and Rosalind stared at him, wide-eyed.

"O'Roarke was the first one to say that publicly," Vaniere said. "So how could a guy like Morrison have known that the day before? He also said that Bradshaw hired him back and the two of them are working on a project together to save America from a terrorist attack that you are planning. And he said that the hacking investigation has been called off by Alan Dyer because you planted the God Gene in the code."

David shook his head in disbelief. "Mick knew the government's case before it was publicly announced?"

"Yes."

"Do you suppose he and Bradshaw are in cahoots with O'Roarke?" Rosalind said.

"I think so."

"Why are you telling us this?" David said.

"Let's just call it penance. I want to help you," Ron said. "It might cost me my job, but I have to do it"

"Penance for the Hitchcock thing?" David said.

"Yes." Vaniere looked at his watch. "In fact Hitchcock's press conference should be coming on about now. I hate to interrupt, but I really need to see this. Do you mind if we watch?"

David picked up the remote and turned on the TV. There, full-screen, was Wild Bill Hitchcock. He was standing at a microphone, with his wife and children on one side, and Joseph Steele on the other.

"... of these ridiculous charges about a black market scheme. They are not true, but I can't prove a negative. It is up to those who accuse me to provide proof. They will never be able to do that because there is no proof. As for the child you've heard about, it is true. I am the child's father, and I have been supporting him since he was born. He did not know until the other day that I am his father, and I want to say to him, Jackson, I am proud of you. You are a fine boy. I hope one day you can forgive me for how I've handled all this. I am not proud of myself for what I did. I am here tonight to apologize to you, and to the American people, and to ask your forgiveness. Right now, my political rivals and the media are putting my life through a scanner, looking for things to malign me. That is to be expected. That is what presidential elections have become. They are exhausting for everyone, and especially damaging to our souls. Watching candidates bring out the worst in each other is painful. I think we all long for our leaders to act nobly and truthfully. For a return to authenticity in a process that has become poisonous. That's why I have decided to save everyone the trouble, and to come clean with you, the people I so deeply want to serve. On my web site you will find a list of everything I've said or done in my life that could possibly be used against me. It is my confession, and it is a long list. When you read it you will know the worst of me, but I also want you to know how I overcame my past mistakes and changed my life for the better, how I dedicated myself to public service and embraced a life of fidelity to my wife and to God. I wrote about that on my web site, too. I am certainly not perfect, but if you want to know me, read it all. America ought to know the man who wants to be their next President.

"Friends, I am grateful to be alive. By the grace of God and with the love and forgiveness of my family, I am staying in this race. I want to serve as your President because I think I can help lead us to a place of grace and prosperity. My friends, when the lights of all the televisions and computer screens and electronic gadgets go out at the end of the day, each of us is left alone with the musings and yearnings of our own heart. I hope you can find in yours forgiveness for me and reconciliation for us as a people. Thank you."

Annie hugged Willard and smiled warmly at him. The children did likewise. Joseph Steele turned toward the camera and raised his hands in the air. "Can I have an AMEN?!"

The scene cut to Claudia Moray in the InfoNet studio. "Well, that was a stunner. While our staff finds out what is on the website, here to debate the Governor's remarks are former Democratic strategist during the 2000 Gore campaign, Sam Sperling, and Maryann Moore, assistant chair of the Republican National Talking Points Coalition ..."

David shook his head. "He put his confession of past sins on the Internet? Who told him *that* was a good idea?"

"I don't know," Edie said. "As your media consultant, I have to say it's gutsy. Either he soars to the top of the polls or he dies in 48 hours."

Rosalind stared at the TV. "That man just opened his soul for the whole world to see," she said in a soft voice. "He did it with a smile on his face. And then he walked away. Where on earth did he find the courage to do that?"

"I think I know," Vaniere said. "It's a God Gene thing. It's why I'm here to help you."

"Ron, how can you help us and still do your job? A TV reporter can't take sides; you have to be objective, don't you?" Rosalind said.

"It's impossible to be objective and human at the same time. I tried it. It almost cost Hitchcock his life."

"So you want to make up for Hitchcock by helping me?" Rosalind said.

"No. I can never make up for what I did to Hitchcock."

"Then why are you here?"

Vaniere had never let himself see Rosalind Evans as a human being; it wasn't good for business. He looked at the people he reported on as characters in a play, soulless constructs from whom he extracted information. He'd looked in Rosalind's eyes and seen fear, he'd seen her sorrow, her anger, and her courage in facing down a line of United States Senators, but he'd never let himself feel empathy. Now, as he looked in her eyes, he saw reflected in them his own salvation. "I have to help you because you are innocent and I know something that might save you from unjust prosecution. I can't stand on so-called journalistic principles and let them fry you."

"For the last ten days, you've been the enemy. Now you're Rosalind's knight in shining armor? Why should I buy that?" David said.

Vaniere smiled as best he could under the circumstances. "Because I have no agenda other than to help. I'm no knight, and my armor is shattered. But I'm here. The Shovel has a lot of digging to do."

Chapter 49

BENTON BRADSHAW GAVE a passing nod to the Foo Dogs as he escorted Vaniere into his office. "This is Scout and this is Ed. Best if you don't get them confused. They're very sensitive." He motioned for Vaniere to sit on the leather sofa. "I have scotch, lemonade, wine, beer, buttermilk, whatever you want. Fridge is full."

"Water is fine. Your office is ... remarkable, Dr. Bradshaw." Vaniere looked around the tasteless room. Absolutely everything was out of scale.

"Designed it all myself. The carpet is custom loomed. You see how all the borders follow the contours of the woodwork? That's not cheap you know. So, you look amazingly good for a guy who got the crap beat out of him." Bradshaw hung a fat, unlit cigar from one side of his mouth and took a sip of scotch from the other.

"I'm fine, thank you."

"TV said you had a concussion."

"I'm alright, really." Vaniere found it odd and unpleasant to talk about himself. It was a foreign concept. The studio make-up artists had worked for hours to cover up any remaining evidence of the blows he'd taken, but there was no erasing the fact that his sorry mug had been all over television and the Internet "If you don't mind, I came here to talk about Rosalind Evans. How long have you known her?"

"Since she was an undergraduate in my molecular cell biology class."

"Was she a good student?"

"Outstanding. Soared like a rocket. Graduated in three-and-a-half years."

"How is she as an employee?"

"Fantastic until her daughter got sick. Then she went off the deep end."

"In what way?"

"She became quiet and withdrawn. She blamed herself. She would cry at the drop of a hat."

"That sounds like normal grief to me. Deep end?"

"She started hanging out with the Jordanian in his lab late at night. They were plotting."

"Plotting what?"

Bradshaw fingered his cigar and rocked up and down on the balls of his feet. "I'm not going to discuss that with you."

"Why not?"

"Why would I trust you? You're the guy who ambushed Rosalind with a camera and a microphone."

"Ambushed? No, I just …"

"You *ambushed* her, and got her to say things that ruined my life!"

"I'm not trying to ruin anyone's life. I'm here to find out the truth."

"This is complicated, dammit! All I can tell you is that Clearbrook's computers were not hacked. Someone tampered with the data, and that someone was Rosalind Evans."

"How can you be sure?"

"Our computer system is the most secure on earth. There was a thorough investigation and no evidence of hacking was found. On the other hand, Rosalind Evans had every reason and opportunity to tamper with the code. She's in league with the enemy. She's nuts."

"But if she tampered with the data, then how did Flemingham and all the other labs get the same base code?"

Bradshaw walked over to one of the Foo Dogs, Scout. He looked it up and down, then reached up and gave it a soft pat on the head. His ring clinked on the porcelain. "First of all, they didn't get the same result. They only found a few words, and there might be a frameshift."

"But as I understand it, the base code at Flemingham was the same as Rosalind's, right?"

"The Ten Commandments are *not* in the code! I don't know why people don't *get* that!" He punctuated his last sentence with a swift kick to Scout's haunches.

"How does Alan Dyer feel about Rosalind Evans?"

Bradshaw downed the rest of his scotch. He belched slightly and walked to the sideboard. He slowly poured himself another drink, held up his glass and sighed deeply. "If she had *just* kept her mouth shut, none of this would have happened. No one would have believed Mick Morrison. It would have been his word against ours. But no, she had to open her fat trap because some sleaze ball of a reporter goaded her into talking. Y*ou*, Vaniere!"

It was obvious to Vaniere that recent events had taken their toll on Bradshaw. The man staring at him through glassy eyes was far from the cocky little rooster who had interrupted his stand-up at the Steele rally. Bradshaw looked like a baby scarecrow with rumpled clothes and a puffy face.

"Do you think she has been conspiring to overthrow the government of the United States?" Vaniere asked.

"Yes I do."

"Why?"

"Because that photo Mick found proves it. Our computers were NOT hacked!! She *used* me! She was determined to ruin me, and she succeeded. The entire planet thinks I run the world's most expensive al-Qaida training camp. Get out of here!"

"Mick?"

"What?"

"You said the photo Mick found."

"I said they. The photo they found."

"Oh, I could swear you said Mick."

"Get out of here!"

Vaniere rose and headed for the door. "Thank you Mr. Bradshaw."

"Screw you!" Bradshaw turned to Scout the Foo Dog and swung his foot as hard as he could, landing a blow that put a jagged hole right where Scout's lung would have been. "And screw you, too!"

* * *

"So you work with Claudia Moray? Dude, how do you get any work done?" Mick dipped a chicken wing into a bowl of barbeque sauce and stuffed it into his mouth. He sloshed it down with draft beer from a frosty mug. "I knew she'd be a screamer, that one. Come on, have some." He thrust the plate at Vaniere.

"No thanks. So Rosalind Evans was upset after the code was found?"

"Yeah, because she thought somebody hacked in and messed up her code. At least that's what she *said*. That night, I scanned the code sheets and sent them to Starry Messenger. She wrote me back! In person!"

"She?"

"Yeah, Starry's a chick and she's hot."

"How do you know that?"

"I can tell. Just like I can tell Rozzie is hot for me."

"Hmm, someday you'll have to tell me the secret of your success with women."

Mick sat back and scanned Vaniere up and down. He flipped his long blond hair and shook his head. "Nah."

"Why were you fired?"

"I'm not supposed to talk about that."

"Why were you rehired?"

Mick looked around the restaurant and leaned in close to Vaniere. "Bradshaw asked me to go through her computer files and find something that would make her look bad. I found the smoking gun."

"What?"

"The photo of her with the al-Qaida guy, Hussein Nomynatu."

"But it takes more than a photo to indict somebody."

"A lot more. It takes a paper trail. She's trouble, man. I don't know why I ever wanted to boink her. Now her goose is cooked, huh?" Mick stuffed another wing into his mouth and smiled.

"So you found this paper trail?"

"Oh, I found it, alright," Mick said with a chuckle.

"No reason to worry about her any more I guess, right?"

"Right. Once I tell the jury she cooked up the God Gene code herself and was making bio-weapons in the lab, she's toast."

"How do you know that?"

"Well, it's complicated. Let's just say I found it in her paper trail."

"And you shared that evidence with Mr. O'Roarke?"

"If you saw a picture of a hot babe with an al-Qaida operative, what would you do? I'm telling you, she's dangerous!"

"Thank you, Mr. Morrison. You have been very helpful."

"Hey, I have a question for you. Dude, who taught you how to fight?"

* * *

Vaniere rode the elevator to the 54th floor of Lake Point Tower. When he suggested to O'Roarke that they meet off the record, he'd quickly suggested the safe-house at Lake Point Tower. It was the place O'Roarke often used to conduct his under-cover investigations, clandestine meetings with sources and potential witnesses—anything he didn't want the prying eyes of the press or anyone else to see. How ironic, Vaniere thought, that O'Roarke was willing to reveal the location to me of all people.

The iconic building stood like a sentinel at the foot of Navy Pier, its curvy black glass exterior undulating in the summer heat. It seemed to Vaniere the perfect paradox, putting a discreet safe-house in a building everyone in Chicago recognized on sight.

O'Roarke opened the door with a smile. "Come in, Ron. I guess I expected your head to be bandaged or something. You really took a beating the other day. How do you feel?"

"I'm fine really, thank you."

"Did they find those guys? They ought to go to jail for what they did to you. You were just doing your job, for God's sake."

Vaniere was beginning to understand on a cellular level what Rosalind Evans must be going through, to be so exposed yet so misunderstood. He had less than zero interest in engaging with O'Roarke on this.

"I'm sure the right thing will happen," Vaniere said.

"Good. Well, Ron, I don't have to tell you how critical it is to keep this absolutely confidential. We cannot afford to lose this case. That would be unthinkable."

"I assure you we are off the record."

"Ron, I've admired your work for years. You didn't get to your level by ratting out sources. Neither did I."

"If Senator Bosch wins the Presidency, you will be his nominee for Attorney General, is that right?"

"Yes. And I believe he will win, for sure."

"The Pope's endorsement will certainly help, won't it?"

"Absolutely."

"How does the Pope decide who to endorse?"

"I don't know."

"Certainly he would be influenced by his advisors, right? Like Cardinal Christopher Duffy?"

O'Roarke turned and looked out the window at the magnificent view of the Lake Michigan. He took a sip of his drink. "You would have to ask the Cardinal about that."

"You are friends with him, aren't you?"

"Yes, since we were boys."

"How does he feel about the God Gene?"

O'Roarke gave Vaniere a sideways look. "He's concerned."

"How much of a threat is Rosalind Evans to the Church?"

"She could destroy it."

"So she's out to destroy the Catholic Church *and* the United States of America? That's a big load for one woman, isn't it?"

"Don't forget, this is a conspiracy; there are others involved."

"What are her motives?"

"Why don't you tell me, Ron. You are pretty close to her."

"I came here to learn, Tom. So tell me, how could one woman tear down this country *and* the Church of Rome?"

"She conspires with known terrorist enemies. She causes a Constitutional crisis. She maneuvers people into thinking God exists for real. She destroys the mystery. If there is no mystery, there is no faith, and if there is no faith, who needs the Church?"

"That would certainly be a concern for the Pope, wouldn't it?"

"I assume so." O'Roarke again turned toward the window. "There's a storm brewing out over the lake. Look at those clouds. Awesome."

Vaniere made notes as fast as he could. Like the spokes of the giant Ferris wheel outside the window, the elements of the story were beginning to converge.

"When do you think the Evans case will come to trial?"

"These things are very complicated. It will take the defense years to develop their strategy."

"Well, Tom, I want to thank you very much for speaking with me. You have helped me very much."

"You're leaving? But—"

"Sorry, deadline."

* * *

A black-robed priest poured coffee from a silver carafe and proffered cookies from a tray. Vaniere declined. The office of Cardinal Christopher Duffy was a place he never thought he would find himself, especially as a reporter. He looked around at the richly appointed room. What about that vow of poverty, he wondered. I mean, under those elaborate robes beats the heart of a humble servant of God, right?

Cardinal Duffy smoothed his robes, straightened his zucchetto and smiled beatifically.

"I'm glad you've come, Mr. Vaniere. I didn't think you would be at work so soon after your unfortunate clash with those men. The image they've created for you is not one you relish, I suppose, that of an opportunistic, amoral media personality? Not so easy having to take what you dish out, is it my son?" The Cardinal smiled in lordly fashion.

"Not something I sought, Your Excellency, I assure you."

"Anyhow, I am glad you've come. I am always glad for an opportunity to clarify the Church's position on matters of great importance."

"Your Excellency, do you believe the God Gene is an act of sabotage, a hoax, or a message from God?"

"It's a hoax. I'm not a scientist, but I know her work doesn't add up."

"If there is no message from God in the genetic code, is that good news or bad news for the Church?"

"Good news. The truth is always good news. Whatever is going on with the woman, whether she is hallucinating or just lying, there are no Ten Commandments in the DNA. That much you can quote me on."

"I would think the Church would rejoice at finding proof that God exists."

The Cardinal's eyes widened. "We don't need proof. We have faith."

"You don't *need* proof, but what if you *had* it?"

The Cardinal's eyes flashed and his voice went deep and intense. "You are on dangerous ground, Mr. Vaniere. This woman is promoting a disastrous false theology that comes from Satan himself. Be careful." He looked at Vaniere over the tops of his glasses and toyed with his ring, a gold and ruby-encrusted barrel of a thing that he slowly rolled around his finger.

"Satan himself? Really?"

The Cardinal's eyes drilled holes in Vaniere. "We cannot prove God! Anyone who says we can is playing the devil's hand, I tell you! She must be stopped!"

Vaniere could see the flash of fear in Cardinal Duffy's eyes, as if he had seen the gates of hell. It sent a shiver down Vaniere's spine.

"The Holy Father must be very worried about the effect of her discovery on the future of the church."

"Leave the Holy Father out of this ..." The Cardinal was breathing heavily and his face was flushed. He paused. "The authorities have told us how dangerous this woman is. Thanks be to God she is in custody. All we can do now is pray that justice is swift."

"Cardinal, forgive me, but Rosalind Evans has said repeatedly that she just wants all this to go away. What if she is not what you say she is?"

"Then what, pray tell, would she be?"

"A victim?"

"Of what! You don't know what you are talking about!"

"So the church's official position is …?"

"Rosalind Evans is a sick woman who seems determined to harm our country. That's our position." He stood and turned toward the door.

Vaniere did not get up. "You were boyhood friends with U.S. Attorney Thomas O'Roarke, weren't you?"

Duffy turned around and looked at Vaniere. He said nothing.

"You are still friends, aren't you?" Vaniere said.

Duffy forced a slight smile. "Why, of course we are. Mr. Vaniere, I would love to continue the conversation, but I'm afraid I must go. Duty calls, you know."

"Have the two of you discussed the Rosalind Evans case?"

Duffy forced a slight smile and gestured toward the door.

The Shovel knew the signs. The tilt of the Cardinal's head, the slightest hint of forced nonchalance in his voice, the smile that was just a hair too controlled—Cardinal Christopher Duffy's non-answer was all the answer Vaniere needed.

* * *

"You need boxing lessons, Ron. Those guys had you for lunch." Senator Bosch laughed and shook Vaniere's hand.

"They certainly did. How are things in Bourbonnais, Senator?" The two men were sitting in the back seat of Bosch's limo in a parking garage in downtown Chicago.

"Great. We are breaking ground for the new Intercontinental Communications Hub there. Information runs the world, and no one should be denied access to it for lack of a wireless signal. No one left in the dark, that's what I say."

Bosch poured drinks from the limo bar. The sound of the ice tinkling in the crystal glasses was incongruous to Vaniere. It was a lighthearted sound in an increasingly ominous situation.

"How do you feel the election is going?" Vaniere asked.

"I am ahead. I plan to stay ahead. I plan to get the nomination and I plan to win. What else do you want to know?"

"How did you get the Pope's endorsement?"

"The Holy Father believes in the same things I believe in—fairness, social justice."

"Have you ever spoken with the Pope?"

"No."

"Will you nominate Thomas O'Roarke for Attorney General?"

"He is a great man. All of America agrees with that. He is doing great work on the Rosalind Evans case, and I'm sure that if it comes to trial, he will prove his case."

"If?"

"Well, these things are complicated. The important thing is that she is now in custody and we are all safer because of it. It will take a long time to prepare the case. Long time."

"I know you are not a scientist. Neither am I. But I am interested to know what you think the God Gene really is. Is it a message from God?"

"Let's hope not!" Bosch said, laughing. "Would you want someone looking over your shoulder watching everything you do? Who could stand that kind of scrutiny?" He raised his eyebrows and took a big gulp of Jack.

"Will the Judiciary Committee hold any more hearings regarding the God Gene?"

"No, that won't be necessary. Now that she is in custody, the threat is over. I have taken steps to make sure this kind of thing never happens again. It's dangerous to have all that genetic information out there for just anyone to use. I know a lot of good is done with it, but if even one bad person gets hold of it, we could be in a heap of trouble. It is only fair that we screen everyone and put safeguards in place. That's why the Senate and the House passed the American Freedom of Genetic Information Act."

"When did that happen?"

"Late last night."

"I didn't hear anything about it."

Bosch laughed. "My plane is waiting to fly me to DC so I can be with the President for the signing this afternoon."

"Your plane?"

"Well, it's not really mine. It belongs to my foundation."

"The P.P. Bosch Fairness for America Foundation, right? You must be doing very well."

"On behalf of the *people* we are doing well, yes."

"Was there any debate on this Freedom of Genetic Information bill?"

"No time. National security was at stake."

"What's in the bill?"

"Don't worry. I know what's in it, and I guarantee you it is spot on. It keeps nuts like Evans from having access to sensitive genetic information. Total protection where we need it most. And a ton of revenue to boot!"

"*Freedom* of Genetic Information? It sounds like *Restriction* From Genetic Information," Vaniere said.

"That's where you're wrong. It's regulation. Only with regulation are we truly free."

Chapter 50

AFTER THREE DAYS of digging, Vaniere was back in Rosalind and David's house. Rosalind paced around the room, her anger flaring. "Are you telling me that O'Roarke, Bosch, Duffy, Bradshaw and Morrison intentionally cooked up a scheme to get me indicted and arrested for treason?! All *five* of them?!"

"That's what I'm saying," Vaniere said.

"Are you kidding me?! Why?!" She looked at Vaniere, David and Edie with big eyes and a face that was growing redder by the minute.

"The irony is that they don't care whether you are convicted. They simply wanted to shut you up, to discredit you in order to protect their territory. It wasn't personal," Vaniere said.

"Oh *really*? Not personal? Bring them over here and let me have them alone for an hour. I'll show them personal!"

Vaniere reached into his bag and handed David a sheaf of papers. "Here are all my notes."

David read for several minutes, looking at one page after another. He regarded Vaniere with a look of amazement. "This is absolutely incredible."

"I interviewed them all. These five men are perpetrators of a conspiracy to silence you. They framed you for the crime of treason."

"Why would they do that?" Edie asked.

"As I piece this together," Vaniere said, "the Vatican needed a way to shut down the media frenzy and put an end to speculation that this is proof of God's existence. They're afraid that people might start to believe it, which would undermine the authority of the Church. Duffy and O'Roarke are friends, and together they decided that the way to solve the problem was to discredit the woman who claimed she proved the existence of God."

"But I never said that!"

"I know. I know. Meanwhile Bradshaw was motivated to protect Clearbrook Institute. He had to discredit you, so that no one would think Clearbrook had been hacked. So he got Morrison to snoop through your computer files, where he found the photo of you and the al-Qaida guy in Syria."

"Hassan? No! He's not a terrorist!"

"But he is a dead ringer for an al-Qaida operative named Hussein Nomynatu."

"It has to be a case of mistaken identity. Or a ginned up photo." David said.

"That's what I intend to find out." Vaniere said.

"I have Hassan's DNA sample. If the CIA has Nomynatu's DNA, we could compare the two," Rosalind said.

"Sure," Vaniere went on. "So Bradshaw gave the photo to O'Roarke hoping he would make it public. He also told him that you know how to engineer bio-weapons. Remember that O'Roarke needed to discredit you so that the Pope would be happy and endorse Bosch, then Bosch would win and name O'Roarke Attorney General. So O'Roarke took the evidence to the Grand Jury and got an indictment. The Senate hearing was Bosch's way to get in on the act and look like a hero to voters. He knew the arrest would come during his high-profile hearing. Political theater at its best."

"Can the government do that? Gin up a case for *treason*?" Edie said.

"It happened to Tokyo Rose," David said. "Her case was based on circumstantial evidence and lies. The government had to make a statement to the public about their high-level security and intelligence. She was eventually pardoned, but not before she served 10 years for something she didn't do."

"Lovely," Rosalind said.

"Ron, are you absolutely sure of all this?" David said.

"Yes. I saw it, I heard it, and I felt it. They all kept saying this was complicated. Very complicated. I think what they were really saying that this was complicated to conjure up."

"If it's true, we'll get a dismissal." David said.

Rosalind stood tapping her foot, arms folded. "If you do that, what happens to the five conspirators?"

"It would be up to the US Attorney to investigate."

"Except that the US Attorney is one of the conspirators!" she said.

"Well, I suppose the Attorney General might appoint a special prosecutor—"

"If we get a dismissal, O'Roarke walks. They could all walk." Rosalind said.

"Who cares? Our only goal is to get you cleared." David said.

"I care, dammit! I'm sick and tired of cowards and liars who think their actions don't have consequences. I'm not going quietly. The way to clear my name and shine a light on the conspiracy is in open court. I want a trial!"

"The last thing you want is a trial," David said.

"I want to show these bastards that they can't get away with what they've done. I want the people to see their deceit first hand, not through the distorted lens of the media!"

"You don't know what you're saying," Vaniere said.

"Yes I do. The evidence they have against me wouldn't convict a jaywalker. I want a trial!"

"Don't talk crazy," David said. "I'm going to file a motion tomorrow morning to get this case dismissed."

"Don't mess with me, David. I'm going to have my day in court. It's the only way to get the truth out. After you make mincemeat out of O'Roarke and his witnesses, I'll take the stand and tell my story like it should be told!"

"OK, Pollyanna, picture this: We go to trial. O'Roarke pulls his dirtiest tricks out of his bag. He gets people to lie on the stand. The press turns on you. The public turns on you. You testify. O'Roarke makes mincemeat out of *you*. The jury convicts you. You get life. Or death. Boom. Over."

"You can't scare me, David! If you try to get this case dismissed, you're fired. I'll defend myself." The three stared at her like they didn't know her. She raised her eyebrows and shrugged her shoulders. "So? Who do I see about a speedy trial?"

"I'm your lawyer and I say no."

Edie put her arm around Rosalind's shoulder. "Come on, baby girl. Let David make a motion to end this thing! You have a life to live; go do it. Those bastards will rot in hell."

Ron nodded. "These guys really aren't worth it, Rosalind. You don't need to prove anything. The dismissal will vindicate you in the eyes of the public."

"We're your team, Roz," David said. "We all love you and want what's best for you. Write a book; tell the world your story." He gave her a shoulder hug. "You've been through enough, love. It's time to let the God Gene go and get on with your life."

"Get on with my life? Write a book? What's the matter with you people? Let's call their bluff! We have an opportunity to beat them at their own game. Ron, you keep digging. David, you and your brilliant legal team put together the defense. Edie, you help me package a message. Now let's get busy. We've only got three months!"

"Three months? Why?" Edie said.

"We can't take a chance that the American people will unknowingly elect a criminal like Bosch! We have to get this done before the election!"

Chapter 51

"YOUR HONOR, MY client wishes to exercise her right to a speedy trial."

David glanced over at Thomas O'Roarke and smiled. Rosalind smiled, too. US District Court Judge Elwood Baumgartner was impassive. He looked back and forth between the two men.

"Your client has only been in custody for two weeks. I'd hardly call that an undue amount of time," O'Roarke said with the slightest hint of derision.

"My client is the subject of a world-wide public phenomenon called the God Gene. Since the discovery a couple of weeks ago, the world has been in an uproar over the cause, meaning and veracity of it. The uproar is not dying down; it is heating up by the day. Your Honor, never in history has there been a cause, religious or otherwise, that has so captured, no, *riveted* the public imagination. Never have millions of people marched in the streets demanding to know whether the God Gene is an act of sabotage, a hoax or a message from God. How long will it be before we see violence, mayhem, panic? There are people, millions of them, who believe the end of the world is near."

O'Roarke swallowed hard. "Don't mess around, Evans. You can't put together a defense in anything under a year."

"Not only can I, I feel I must. These are unprecedented times. Not in times of war, nor times of natural disaster, nor times of great unveilings and discovery has the world been so desperate to know the truth. The heart and soul of humanity longs for an answer."

"They know the answer! Your wife—I mean your client is a danger not just to the United States, but to the whole civilized world. She is aiding and abetting Al-Qaida in their attempt to kill us all!"

"Your Honor, we ask that you grant us a trial date of October 15."

"Are you out of you freaking mind?!" O'Roarke came dangerously close to revealing the panic lurking just beneath his skin. He quickly caught himself and closed his mouth.

The judge cleared his throat. "You object, Mr. O'Roarke?"

"It's absurd, Your Honor. He can't put together his defense in three months. We're talking treason here!"

"We're talking world-wide panic here!" David said. "We're talking about *God*!"

"God is not my concern!" O'Roarke yelled.

The judge was clearly irritated. "What's the matter? You sounded supremely sure of yourself at that globally-televised press conference of yours the other day. You said some things that I wouldn't have said if I were you, but I'm not you, thank God, so what's your worry?"

"Three months, Your Honor? It's unprecedented," O'Roarke said.

"I know it is unprecedented, but I'm inclined to agree with Mr. Evans; these are extraordinary circumstances. The God Gene is a global phenomenon unlike any in human history. Until the issue of Rosalind Evans's guilt or innocence is settled, there is great risk of social unrest, even panic. We cannot wait for the sluggish wheels of justice in this case; we have to take the bullet train. Trial is set for October 15."

* * *

Thomas O'Roarke sat down heavily in his desk chair and put his head in his hands. He had to suppress the urge to throw open the window and scream. The Evans case was *never* supposed to come to trial. There was supposed to be an indictment, an arrest, and a ton of negative press against her, but never a trial. Trials were dangerous. Risky. A witness could flip, the defense could throw in a surprise, the judge could get irritated with you. And you never knew what a jury might do. Worst of all, you never knew when the media might turn on you. Any of which meant you could lose. Now, that weasel David Evans had put the screws to him. What is he up to, asking for a speedy trial? What does the man *know*? O'Roarke picked up the phone and dialed with a shaking hand. After several agonizing moments, the Senator answered.

"P.P., the judge just granted Evans a trial date."

There was an ominous silence on the other end of the phone. O'Roarke waited, afraid to say anything. He could hear Bosch breathing in shallow drafts. He could hear ice tinkling in a glass and the sound of Bosch gulping, then clearing his throat softly.

"When?"

"October 15th."

Another pause. "Of what year?"

"This year."

Another long silence. O'Roarke looked around for a place to throw up.

"Not good, Tom. That's three weeks before the election. You really screwed this up."

"There was nothing I could do. Evans asked for a speedy trial. If the defendant wants a speedy trial, there's nothing I can do! It's not my fault!"

"Oh? Really? I'm sorry, but I was under the impression that you were the U.S. Attorney for the Northern District of Illinois."

"I am, P.P., listen, why don't I just drop the charges? Make it all go away?"

"And look like the minnow you are? No! Not a chance in hell!"

"This is a treason trial, dammit! He can't come up with a defense in three months. That's not enough time to grow a mustache, for God's sake. He's bluffing."

"Obviously Judge Baumgartner disagrees with you. What did he say?"

"He said I sounded supremely sure of my case at the press conference, so what am I worried about? Of course I was confident—I knew it would never come to trial."

"You *knew* nothing."

"Come on P.P. I still have some tricks up my sleeve. I'll have my guys make pre-trial motions. Ask for continuances. We can have witnesses go missing. Evidence disappear. Delay. Delay. Delay. There's lots we can do. Evans won't get away with this."

Bosch tried to keep his voice level. "All you had to do was make sure this never came to trial. You blew it. Now that it's coming to trial, you better make sure it lasts until after the election."

O'Roarke felt the chill through the phone. "Look, don't worry, P.P. I have a great team and they will do a great job trying this case. I will coach them every step of the way. They will do a great job, I promise."

"Tom, grow a pair. You have to try this case. If you pawn it off, you look like a weenie. In the Bosch administration, there is no room for weenies. Oh yeah, did I mention you have to win? In the Bosch administration, there's no room for losers either. You better find a way to improve the pitiful fairy tale you call a case."

"Uh, P.P., there's one more thing. Evans got a court order to have his wife's 7000 DNA samples re-sequenced." There was another long silence on the phone. Judging by the intensity of the silence, O'Roarke knew that Bosch fully comprehended the ominous implications of this. If the results were released before the election and vindicated Evans, it was game over.

"Get Bradshaw to delay."

"Well, that's the problem, P.P. The work isn't being done at Clearbrook. It's being fast-tracked at Flemingham."

Chapter 52

Will She Testify?

Kittens, are you aware that there is a theory among some astrophysicists that what we perceive as reality is nothing more than a wrinkle in time/space, and, assuming we ever existed at all, that we are now long dead? What if that were true? What if string theory were true? What if some of us are moving through time/space faster than others? Makes your head swim, doesn't it? Why would God create a universe so chaotic and then populate it with creatures like us, who are so ill-equipped to understand it?

Or are we?

It has been said that the most appalling thing about the Rosalind Evans story is the speed of her descent from acclaimed cancer researcher to accused traitor in just one week, but I ask you: how could it have happened any other way? Now it has been six weeks, and judging by the world's reaction to the God Gene, might her dramatic fall be part of a larger cosmic event, something truly life-altering for millions of people? If so, is it any wonder it happened so fast? How could we expect something this momentous merely to amble along? Even amid the wailing and gnashing of teeth, is it possible that the speed of her fall is not a negative, but a positive? After all, what else but high drama could possibly keep our attention these days? Didn't Willard Hitchcock go from frontrunner to suicidal disgrace to his party's nominee for president in just one month? And didn't P.P. Bosch win his party's nomination just two weeks after a federal investigation was launched into the financing of his charitable foundation?

Instead of the incomprehensible chaos we *think* we see, might we all be moving together through time/space in perfect harmony? Might this be exactly where we are *supposed* to be on our journey together? Could we be witnessing, dare I say it, perfection?

As we stretch our brains to contemplate that, we can't help but wonder, who is Rosalind Evans? As the world holds its collective breath in anticipation of her trial, and as we speculate and theorize and wonder what it all means, what is the one thing we all agree on? Don't we need to know the truth about Rosalind Evans? Is she a liar, a traitor, a hero or a mystic? In the end, there is only one person who can tell us, but will she testify?

Chapter 53

October 15th

THE HISTORIC COURTROOM on the twenty-fourth floor of the Dirksen Federal Building in Chicago was filled to capacity with spectators, lawyers, and media. Reporters bathed in white TV lights at the rear of the room carried on a constant stream of commentary. Amid a barrage of camera flashes, spectators carried on cell phone conversations with babbling speculations on what would ultimately happen to the woman standing tall and silent in the front of the room.

The oak-paneled room featured an imposing tiered dais at the front, with the judge's bench highest, jury box a bit lower on the left, and the witness stand just below it. On the floor level were long wooden pews for the spectators, the media gallery, and two tables at the front, one for the government and one for the defense.

"All rise!"

The admonition went unnoticed by the majority of the people in the room. The din continued as Judge Elwood Baumgartner swept up to the bench, reached for his gavel and brought it down with a crack. He looked slowly from right to left and back again, holding his gavel like a night stick, smacking it tensely into the palm of his left hand. Fixed in his mind was the memory of the most notorious trial ever held in this room, the Chicago Seven, a trial more famous for its circus atmosphere than its outcome, with defendants slouching in their chairs yelling epithets, and a judge who demonstrated by word and gesture his open contempt for them and their lawyers. The most enduring image was that of defendant Bobby Seals, gagged and bound to his chair. Judge Baumgartner wasn't about to let that kind of mayhem mar his trial-of-the-century. He waited until the din began to ease, and then brought the gavel down like a sledge hammer, again and again, each succeeding blow bringing another wave of people to attention until finally, under his fulminating glare, the last echo died. The Judge sat down, folded his hands and eyed the crowd intently.

"If you think the presence of cameras is a license to misbehave, you're wrong. I know the temptation to mug is strong, but get over it. This is a court of law. Now turn off your cell phones and let's get this show on the road." He set his gavel gently down on the bench.

There had been little debate about whether to allow cameras in the courtroom. A recent change in federal law left to each Judge's discretion the decision about cameras. David had argued, with Rosalind's full approval, that this trial was important enough that the American people had the right to see and hear every nuance of the arguments for and against Rosalind Evans, to look her in the eye so they could judge for themselves.

The U.S. Attorney had found no reason to disagree. For Thomas O'Roarke, the opportunity to be seen in action by millions of people was the only saving grace of this whole sorry scenario. If he had to try this case, he might as well get all the visibility he could. He knew the risks, given that the election was less than a month away, but he also knew that with his ability to craft language and choose clothing, the American people would fall head over heels in love with him. His confirmation as Attorney General would be a breeze. That is, if he could find a way to make this thing last until after the election.

Judge Baumgartner had always been in favor of cameras in the courtroom. His philosophy? There is nowhere to hide any more. This is the Twenty-first century. Everyone carries a camera—everyone is going to end up on YouTube sometime in their life. Why fight it? The only question was how many cameras to allow and where to place them. In the end, he reasoned that if he were to err, it would be on the side of more coverage, not less. The people had a right to see it, and see it well. As a result, there were enough cameras and lights in the courtroom to make a feature film.

No one—defendant, lawyer, witness, judge or spectator—was safe from close scrutiny of every gesture and facial expression.

The live, high definition, gavel-to-gavel coverage would be managed by a director and a team of technicians in the room next door, which had been converted into a fully equipped control room, complete with a large glass window looking directly into the courtroom. This was the most important trial of the new millennium, and the Judge wanted the world to see it in stark detail. It's all about the details, Baumgartner always said. That's where the devil hides.

Standing at the defense table, Rosalind Evans was all too aware that there were a half-dozen TV cameras trained on her at that moment, and would be for the duration of the trial. Her orders from David were to show no emotion, and the best way to do that was to avoid eye contact.

David Evans leaned over and whispered to his wife. "How was your omelet? Mine was overcooked."

Rosalind smiled at him. "You're trying to distract me. Mine was great, and no, I'm not nervous. I am eager. This is our moment, David."

He smiled at her and resisted the urge to give her a peck on the cheek. If she wasn't nervous, then he couldn't afford to be either.

Thomas O'Roarke sat at the prosecutor's table going over his notes, calculating the impact of his verbiage and orchestrating in his mind the movements and gestures he would bring to bear as enhancements to his performance. A recent poll showed that 68% of Americans thought Evans was guilty. The media had meticulously reported the details he'd given them of the government's case and the shady circumstances of her mental and emotional past. They had spent countless hours showing and re-showing the tapes of her running from Vaniere in front of Clearbrook Hall, of her attacking Joseph Steele, and of her smirking at reporters on the dock at DuSable Harbor. When they showed snippets from the Judiciary Committee hearing, they were cleverly edited to make her look sinister. The media knew that a heroic Rosalind Evans wouldn't bring the ratings that an out-of-control, dangerous, evil one would. O'Roarke didn't have to make his case to the American people; the media made it for him.

The public had marinated in her guilt for three months; it was in their cells now, a part of their DNA. O'Roarke's experience told him that there comes a point when the weight of public opinion in high profile cases simply can't be overcome. With cell phones and other gadgets, there is no way to completely sequester a jury. They hear things, no matter what.

"Bailiff, call the case," Judge Baumgartner said, sounding more like a man ordering an egg salad sandwich than one presiding over the first treason trial in over 60 years.

"The United States versus Rosalind Fanning Evans!!"

Rosalind stood stock-still. It sounded like the punch line of a bad joke.

Next, O'Roarke was called upon to deliver his opening statement, which was merely a rehash of his press conference. Having predicted as much, David kept his opening brief and to the point: the Government's case was pure, unadulterated fiction from bottom to top.

Obviously pleased with the brevity of both, Judge Baumgartner rubbed his hands together. "Mr. O'Roarke, call your first witness!"

O'Roarke stood ceremoniously and buttoned his coat.

Rosalind did not look at him. She didn't have to. His visage was projected many times life-size on the ten-foot tall Jumbotron situated on the wall above Judge Baumgartner's head. Rosalind could watch the whole spectacle without so much as turning her head. In fact, on cutaway shots, she could see the entire gallery. Edie was in the front row behind her, dressed in a lavender mini dress and black cowboy boots. Every once in a while, Edie would smile and give Roz a subtle little wave, as if to indicate that all was well. Also present was Cardinal Duffy, in his black suit, red sash and red zucchetto. He constantly toyed with his ring and chewed his lower lip each time O'Roarke spoke. Bradshaw was there, and Mick the Tech, but Dyer and Gleason were nowhere to be seen. Nor was Bosch. Ron Vaniere was seated in the press gallery. Lex, Summer, and Stefan sat together near the front. And there in the middle was Boone Wilkes, the street preacher.

Next door, the director was busy switching from one camera angle to another. As the judge spoke, there were cutaway shots, as in a dramatic film, showing reactions from the defendant, audience members, and the lawyers. He couldn't understand why he wasn't allowed to shoot the jury—they were the ones whose reaction counted most, right? The people who make the rules around here don't know about dramatic tension, he thought. But still, he was in his creative glory, exercising his talent for pacing and his penchant for high tension in the Trial of the Century. He just knew that viewers were dialed in, popping beers and popcorn all over the world. This was entertainment!

"The Government calls Dr. Benton Bradshaw!"

There was a slight shuffle of feet as Bradshaw rose from the gallery and made his way down the long center aisle and up into the raised witness box. He looked around with satisfaction. It was rare that he was able to look down on people, and it felt good. He made sure his father knew the date and time of his appearance; it was bound to be a barn-burner. *I know you're watching me. From up here I can see the top of your ugly head.*

A dour-looking man approached him and stuck out a Bible. "Do you swear to tell the truth, the whole truth and nothing but the truth, so help you God?"

Crap, Bradshaw thought. *Do they have to start with that? Of course I tell the truth whenever I can. I value the truth, I believe in being honest. But these are extraordinary times. When O'Roarke made 'helpful suggestions' for my testimony, I couldn't turn him down. This is my chance to be the star witness defending justice in a court of law!*

The bailiff cleared his throat. "Well?"

"I do."

O'Roarke quickly made his way through the required questions to establish who Bradshaw was, what he did, and how he was related to Rosalind.

"Dr. Bradshaw, your PharmaGen research studied two genes, CLAIRE and DZPro2. Did Rosalind Evans have access to the CLAIRE and DZPro2 data before the Ten Commandments were found there?"

"Originally, she had complete access to the CLAIRE data, but not the DZPro2."

"Why not?"

"The CEO of PharmaGen wanted to keep the two sets of data separate so that no one person would have all the data. It was a matter of protecting proprietary information."

"Did she ask to see the DZPro2?"

"Yes, she begged to see it. And eventually she did see it."

"How?"

"She stole it."

"Objection!" David's voice was loud and clear.

"Overruled," Baumgartner said.

"How do you know she stole the data?"

"She told me several times that she was desperate to see it. She logged in through Clearbrook security the night it was stolen. There was nobody else there because the computers were all shut down earlier that day. According to the security logs, nobody else was in the building except janitorial staff and the security guards."

"How did you become aware that it had been stolen?"

"The logs for the ANSR 1000 showed that data had been copied that night."

"If she had access to both sets of data, then would she have the scientific skills to rearrange it to make it appear the Ten Commandments were written there?"

"Easily."

"What motive would she have had to do such a thing?"

"As I said before, she was unstable."

"Objection! The witness is not qualified to judge the defendant's mental state."

"Sustained. The jury will disregard the answer."

"Did the forensic investigation find evidence of hacking or tampering?"

"No. Our computers are totally secure."

"How else might the data have been manipulated?"

"The only way was to do it herself. I've studied the data and it is clear to me that she created the code that spells out the Ten Commandments."

"Is Rosalind Evans a good employee?"

"She's a good scientist, but since her daughter died she's been what I would call—erratic."

Rosalind sat stock still. What she wanted more than anything was to look Bradshaw in the eye to let him know she was listening to every word he said. Instead she focused on his farcical image on the tron, five times life size. Erratic? Nothing could be further from the truth. She told herself not to worry. David had warned her that Bradshaw was off the reservation.

"Can you elaborate?"

"Talking to herself. Coming to my office and crying, saying she was to blame for the little girl's death. I've known Rosalind for 15 years. She was always happy, loved her work. Then something snapped. You should have seen her at the funeral. She went crazy and told the pastor to go to hell, for God's sake. The *pastor*."

"Objection!"

"Sustained. The jury will disregard. Mr. Bradshaw, please don't make statements as to the defendant's mental state. You are not qualified to do so," Judge Baumgartner said.

Bull, thought Bradshaw. I know a loon when I see one.

"Did she ever mention a trip to Syria?"

"Yes. She said she was a volunteer on a mission trip. She said they were studying people who suffered from retinitis pigmentosa," Bradshaw said.

"Did she tell you anything about the trip after she got back?"

"No, she didn't want to talk about it."

"Objection!" David said. "Speculation."

"Sustained."

"Could the God Gene be used to make biological weapons?"

Here we go, Bradshaw thought. Father, be prepared to wet yourself!

"Yes. The CLAIRE gene has markers for drug resistance. With the proper splicing, inserting it into a pathogen such as anthrax would result in a new, vaccine-resistant strain. Put the new strain of anthrax into some kind of mass delivery system like a cold bomb—and poof, millions dead in a matter of days. No way to stop it."

"Has anyone ever made vaccine resistant anthrax?"

"Yes, the Russians. What makes it doubly disastrous is that the perpetrators make a vaccine to protect themselves against the new strain of anthrax. They live, everybody else dies. It's just a matter of time before something like this gets into the hands of people who want us all dead."

"Objection! Speculation."

"Sustained."

"Does Dr. Evans know how to do this splicing?"

"Of course," Bradshaw said.

"Objection!" David was on his feet.

"Sustained! The jury will disregard the question and the answer!" Baumgartner stared daggers at O'Roarke.

O'Roarke paced across the room for a moment, lost in thought. Bradshaw took the opportunity to glance up at the tron behind him. I'm huge, he thought. I'm bigger than you, Father.

"In your opinion as the Director of the Clearbrook Institute, would a scientist of Dr. Evan's talent and expertise have a working knowledge of the process you just described?"

"Of course."

"Where would she have done such a thing?"

"Clearbrook has dozens of laboratories," Bradshaw said.

"Isn't it very dangerous to work with anthrax?"

"Oh, no, they weren't actually culturing anthrax. That would require a level of containment we don't have at Clearbrook. They were just designing the genetic profile and the mechanism for transferring the genetic information into the anthrax. Typically by electroporation."

"When would she have had time to do this?"

"For several months in a row, she worked all night."

"You saw her?"

"Yes. I saw her working late at night with Samir Okar, a post-doctoral fellow. He is Jordanian."

"You saw them working together at night?"

"Yes, on several occasions."

"Is Okar still working at Clearbrook?" O'Roarke said.

"No. One day he left suddenly."

O'Roarke picked up a file folder from the evidence table and handed it to Bradshaw. "What is in this file?"

Bradshaw took the file and looked at it. "These are files from Okar's computer. They clearly show that he and Dr. Evans were working on a mechanism for creating vaccine-resistant anthrax."

O'Roarke then proceeded to slowly, painstakingly question Bradshaw about every detail of what Evans and Okar doing, and his scientific conclusions about it. It was highly technical and detailed and designed to take up as much time as possible.

In the control room next door, the director was having a minor conniption. This was the most brutally boring thing he had ever seen. He could hear TVs clicking off by the millions. He turned to his assistant director. "Hey, Cal, can we get a live feed into the system from outside?"

"Sure. What do you want?"

"How about a live feed of the Sox-Yankees game at the Cell? Anything would be more interesting than this."

"Just give me the word, and I'll get the feed. Or any feed you want. Technology, baby," Cal said.

O'Roarke continued his questioning of Bradshaw. "Did the defendant ever display to you any feelings of resentment about the United States?"

"Yes. She often complained that Americans were close-minded about the Islam. She said America was full of religious bigots, and that she was sending money to support a local mosque. She told me she was considering converting to Islam."

Rosalind leaned over and whispered to David. "There it is, the pure lie."

"No further questions," O'Roarke said, wishing it weren't so. Bradshaw had only eaten up two hours.

Bradshaw smiled, relishing his triumphant moment. He pictured the repentant look on his father's face.

David stood and approached the witness stand.

"Dr. Bradshaw, did Dr. Evans ever tell you that she knew how to do the procedure you described?"

"No."

"Have you ever seen her doing it?"

"No, but—"

"Creating a new strain of anthrax, is that something a person could do alone, in secret?"

"Possibly."

"How long would it take?"

"Months."

"If Dr. Evans had been engaged in this kind of activity, could she have done it at night at Clearbrook?"

"Maybe ..."

The director snapped to attention. OK, he said to himself, now we're talking. Snappy. He liked this guy Evans; he understood show biz. He began switching back and forth between Bradshaw and David like a tennis match, zooming in on their faces, working to capture for his audience the obvious discomfort that was beginning to show on Bradshaw's face.

"Could she have avoided detection for the months it would take to do it?"

"Maybe."

"Dr. Bradshaw, are you saying that security at Clearbrook is so lax that a person could be there at night with a team of people working on a secret biological weapon, and you *wouldn't know it?*"

Bradshaw glared at David. "I beg your pardon! Our security measures are second to none. But Dr. Evans is very clever and devious. And she had Okar working with her."

"How many times did you hear the defendant say that Americans were religious bigots?"

"She said it all the time."

"How often?"

"At least several times a week."

"Where did she say it?"

"In my office."

"Anywhere else?"

"Not that I remember."

"Was anyone there when she said it?"

"I don't remember."

"Not one other person witnessed her saying it to you?"

"I don't know."

"No further questions."

David turned and walked back to the defense table. Rosalind folded her hands and forced herself not to smile. Smiling made her look smug, David said. Juries want to see humble, not smug.

Judge Baumgartner leaned back in his chair. "Any redirect, Mr. O'Roarke?"

"No, Your Honor."

"Mr. Bradshaw, please step down," the Judge said.

Bradshaw looked thoroughly disappointed that his time in the spotlight was over. "Your honor, may I just say—"

"You may not. Step down."

Bradshaw made his way out of the witness stand and down the aisle, smiling for the cameras, taking as long as he could.

O'Roarke stood, and the director groaned behind his one-way mirror.

"The Government calls Mick Morrison."

Mick stood and shook his hair back. This was his moment on the world stage. He'd dressed in his best jeans and muscle shirt and he felt totally ready for the cameras. He sauntered to the witness box and stepped up. He put his hand on the Bible and waited for the question, looking at the camera the whole time.

"Do you swear to tell the truth, the whole truth, and nothing but the truth?"

"I most certainly do," he said with a big smile. He turned and looked at himself on the tron, then back at the camera, back at the tron, back at the camera.

"Sit down, Mr. Morrison," Judge Baumgartner said.

"Mr. Morrison, did you give the translation code with the Ten Commandments on it to Starry Messenger on the night of July 1st?" O'Roarke asked.

"Sure did," Mick said proudly.

"Did anyone tell you to give it to Starry Messenger?"

"Ole Rozzie over there. She told me to send it to Starry."

"Why?"

"She didn't say."

"So you didn't question her, you just did as she said?"

Mick smiled and chuckled. "Oh yeah. I figured there would be some percentage in it for me, you know what I mean?"

"What kind of percentage?"

"Well, I don't want to actually say with her husband being here in the room, but it would fall into the bodily contact category."

In the control room next door, the director sat bolt upright. He flew into action. "We're back! Woot! Ready camera two!"

"Did she tell you to do anything else?" O'Roarke said.

Mick paused and tried to remember the exact wording O'Roarke had given him. Gotta get this right, he told himself. Go slow, and get it right.

"She said not to tell anyone that it was her idea to give it to Starry, that it would be our little secret."

"I have no further questions," O'Roarke said.

David walked to the witness stand and stood as close to Mick as he could. "Mr. Morrison, when exactly did Rosalind Evans ask you to send the translation code to Starry Messenger?"

"After the meeting where they found the words in the code." Mick looked sideways at David. I know this dude hates me, he thought. I would hate me, too, if I was him. How did he get a hottie like Rozzie? There's no comparison between him and me.

"What exactly did she say?"

"She comes up real close to me and she says, 'Dude, this is a gold mine. Send it to Starry Messenger but don't tell anyone I told you to do it. It will be our little secret.'"

"Does she always call you Dude?"

"Dude, no. Just sometimes."

"Like when?"

"Well, you know, in those magic moments."

"Magic moments? What does that mean?" David leaned in close to the witness stand and gave Morrison an intense stare.

Mick looked up at the Judge, then over at O'Roarke. I'm all alone here, he thought. This guy might take a swing at me. "Nothing. I never meant to say that."

"So you never had a romantic relationship with Rosalind Evans?"

"No, Man, back off."

"When you sent Starry Messenger the translation code sheets, did you say they came from Rosalind Evans?"

"No."

"You never mentioned Rosalind or wrote her name in your posting?"

"No."

"Was her name on the translation code sheet?"

"No."

"When Starry Messenger wrote back to you, what did he say?"

"She. Starry's a she. And she's hot." Mick raised his eyebrows and smiled coyly for the cameras.

With that, a loud, gravelly voice emanated from somewhere in the back of the room.

"Do I look hot to you?"

Judge Baumgartner squinted out at the gallery, not quite sure whether or not he had heard something. The TV lights were so bright that he couldn't see anything.

A man slowly rose to his feet. "Do I look like a woman, Your Honor?" he said.

Judge Baumgartner banged his gavel. "Order! Who said that?"

Spectators turned around to get a look at the man who had spoken out. A TV camera zoomed in on him and his face popped up on the tron, looming behind a bewildered-looking Judge Baumgartner. The man looked to be about 75 years old. His gray hair was parted in the middle and hung in two long braids down the front of his denim shirt. His leathery face was deeply lined, the color of iodine, and beneath his bushy white eyebrows glistened sharp hazel eyes. A smile slowly spread across the old man's face. "Your Honor, may I comment on this man's testimony?"

"You may not!!" Baumgartner shouted. "Who do you think you are!?"

The man paused. He tilted his head slightly, as if weighing his options. He smiled again. "My name is Rowan Glass, but would you believe I'm also known as The Starry Messenger?"

There was a rumble in the spectator gallery. In the control room, the director sat bolt upright. He pushed his headphones onto his ears, not sure he had heard right.

"Silence!" Baumgartner yelled. "The jury will disregard this. I want to see this man and both counselors in my chambers right now! Fifteen-minute recess!" Baumgartner crashed his gavel down and exited in a swirl of black robe.

In chambers, the Judge faced the old man squarely. "What makes you think you can march into my courtroom and interrupt these proceedings? I should cite you for contempt of court!"

"I'm sorry Your Honor, but won't you please forgive an old man for standing up for his manhood when it was impugned in open court?"

O'Roarke looked at the man with contempt. "Do you expect us to believe *you* are the Starry Messenger? Look at you."

The old man ran a rough-hewn hand over his stubble of a beard. "What is so unbelievable? That my name is Rowan Glass, and I used to be a Professor of Theoretical Psychology, and now I'm a full-time blogger working from a Barcalounger in my bedroom in Past Tense, Illinois?"

The three stared at him in silence. The old man smiled like a kid caught mooning the neighbor lady.

"No way," O'Roarke whispered.

"No? Think about it; why would I leave the comforts of Past Tense to sit in a stuffy courtroom all day, blow my cover, and risk a contempt of court citation if I didn't have a very good reason?"

"Past Tense?" Baumgartner said.

"Pastens, actually, which you may know is the Potawatomi word meaning 'people of the lost land'? For that reason alone, is it any surprise that we locals have always called it Past Tense?"

David regarded the man carefully. "If you are really Starry Messenger, then you know that I posted a question to you yesterday," David said. "You e-mailed me a private response. Can you tell me what I asked and how you answered?" David had a hunch that this might really be Starry Messenger; there was a simple, straightforward authenticity about him.

"You asked me whether our world would ever be rational again, didn't you, Mr. Evans?"

"Yes. What did you say in response?"

"Has it ever been rational?"

"That's exactly right," David said. He stuck out his hand. "No one else could have known that. It's a pleasure to meet you, Starry Messenger."

The old man took David's hand and shook it firmly. His efforts at maintaining anonymity for the past four years had been so successful that no one had ever addressed him in person as The Starry Messenger. "A pleasure, indeed," Glass said. "Your Honor, may I please stay in the courtroom if I promise not to say another word? Forgive me, but surely you understand that it will break my heart to miss this?"

"Why?"

"Is there anything else more *important*?" Glass asked with wide eyes.

Baumgartner briefly considered the legal and ethical ramifications of allowing the man to stay, then quickly reminded himself that there was nothing about this trial that aligned with anything in the known universe. "You may stay."

O'Roarke suddenly felt a sense of anticipation unlike anything he'd felt in this or any other trial. He was standing in the presence of the one and only Starry Messenger. This was the chance of a lifetime. "Your Honor, I know this is out of the ordinary, but I'm going to request a recess until tomorrow morning so that I may question Mr., uh, Messenger as a potential witness for the prosecution." O'Roarke was utterly amazed at his own brilliance. Not only would this cause a delay in the proceedings, which was good, but it would be the biggest television event of all time. This is once in a lifetime! Starry freaking Messenger. On the stand. Under oath. All mine to question for as long as I want. And the whole world, literally the *whole world*, watching!

David couldn't believe his ears. He bit the inside of his cheek to keep from smiling. "No objection, Your Honor."

Chapter 54

THAT EVENING, ROSALIND circled the dinner table and poured wine for David, Edie, Vaniere, and the Starry Messenger. This was a dinner party she couldn't have conjured up if she were John Irving.

"David, call me Rowan. That way I can revert to my much less glamorous self and speak in declarative sentences. I have no idea why Mr. O'Roarke asked me to be a witness. We talked for several hours this afternoon, so he knows that I have nothing to say that will help him."

"Does he still intend to call you as a witness?" David said.

"Yes. And I'll be happy to testify that Mick Morrison misstated the facts about giving me Rosalind's name. The question is why did Morrison think he would get away with it? I have everything on my web site archived. It shows without doubt that he told me Rosalind's name."

"Either he's that dumb, or someone made it worth his while to lie. I'm guessing both," Rosalind said, laughing.

"So Rosalind, tell me why you would take the risk of testifying?" Rowan asked.

"Because I need to tell the world the truth."

"Bravo, but do you think they'll hear you?"

"I've been working on this for months. I'll tell it straight. There will be no way for them to misunderstand."

Rowan laughed. "There will be a billion ways. We all listen through filters because the truth can be painful."

"I'll risk being misunderstood by some if it means being understood by most. I have to try."

Glass smiled and raised his glass. "I admire your courage, Rosalind. Most of us hide from big truths. They're very scary."

Rosalind regarded the man with a mix of curiosity and admiration. She had always pictured The Starry Messenger as a late 50s male, brilliant yet reclusive, sitting in a candle-lit attic with his laptop, drinking mead and exuding God-like wisdom. Rowan Glass in no way fit the image. He was much older, but beyond that, he was much more humble than she'd imagined, a plain-spoken man with not an ounce of arrogance despite his fame. His dress was simple: blue jeans, a white cotton shirt, and sandals. He had a sweet smile and his eyes sparkled with curiosity.

"Rowan, why did you decide to become the Starry Messenger?" Rosalind asked.

Rowan took a sip of wine. The delicious smells of Edie's cooking permeated the softly lit dining room. He smiled. "Money. My teaching pension was not enough, so I needed to supplement it. Now, the Starry Messenger website makes me way more than I ever dreamed. Enough that I can really retire."

"How did you build such a large following in such a short time?"

"Bloggers blog because they think they have something important to say. Most don't. I knew I had nothing to say, so I decided to just ask questions. It caught on."

"Isn't that hard to do, to end every sentence with a question mark?" Vaniere asked.

"Very. We are wired to declare, even though it gets us nowhere. Socrates said 'Wisdom begins with wonder.' He knew he didn't know anything. And he knew that nobody else knew anything, either. So he taught by asking questions to help people recognize the errors in their thinking. I thought it might work in today's world."

Vaniere nodded in agreement. "You've put into words what I hate about my job. The roar of assertions is deafening."

"Precisely!" Roz said. "Edie and I have examined literally thousands of articles and news clips about me and the God Gene, and no one, *no one*— except you, Rowan—ever stopped and asked what was really going on."

Vaniere laughed. "Too bad we can't hit the refresh button on this whole God Gene dialogue."

"That's exactly what I intend to do when I testify!" Rosalind said. "Rowan, there's one more thing I've always wondered about: why do you call your readers kittens?"

"Because I truly love them. What's more loveable than a kitten?"

Edie was in the kitchen putting finishing touches on the main course, Chateaubriand, which she had spent hours preparing. It had become her routine while at Rosalind and David's, after researching the media all day, to spend a good part of each evening in the kitchen with her laptop, the TV, the fresh groceries she'd purchased earlier in the day, and a good bottle of wine. A veteran multi-tasker, the woman could knead dough, take notes on news stories and get pleasantly breezed by dinner time. Never drunk, just zoned to a blissful level, doing the things she loved most: cooking, catching up on news, and helping her baby girl. Keeping the mood light for Roz and David was her top priority. More and more, though, her afternoons were also taken up with thoughts of Ron Vaniere. He'd been around a lot lately, working with Rosalind and David, and she was increasingly preoccupied with thoughts of him. Seeing Rosalind and David back together and happy again was kindling her desire to settle down and find Mr. Right, who in her mind was looking a lot like Mr. Vaniere. Tonight was a magical evening, with the unexpected presence of the Starry Messenger at the table, and her signature dish was ready to serve. Tossing back the last of her third glass of wine, it suddenly seemed like a great time to make her move. She peeked her head out the kitchen door.

"Ron, would you mind helping me for a minute?"

Ron quickly joined her in the kitchen. She was carving the meat. "I just need you to tell me whether this is OK," she said, holding up a succulent hunk of beef wrapped in flaky pastry. She didn't know about the meat, but Ron was looking luscious.

"Ooh, I'd be delighted." He shot her a crooked smile that sent a little flash of lightning through her. He opened his mouth and she put the meat in. He raised his eyebrows.

"You like it?"

"It's outrageous. You made this?"

She smiled demurely at him and nodded.

He made a gesture for another bite.

"That good?" She put another juicy piece of meat in his mouth. Her fingers touched his lips slightly and she thought for an instant that she might faint.

Ron smiled again, "Amazing. This crust—you'll have to show me one of these days how you did this."

She was feeling dizzy, and it wasn't the wine; it was the overwhelming charisma of this gorgeous, tall hunk of a man. She looked in his eyes and tried to focus. "You cook?"

"A little. I'd like to get better at it."

"When do you want to do it?" she said, licking the juice off her fingers.

Ron laughed. "Do what?"

Edie couldn't help herself; she was at the full mercy of the wine and the nearness of Ron Vaniere. "You know—get together."

"Are you asking me out?"

"Yes." She fought to keep her equilibrium. "Yes, Ron, I definitely think I am."

"Are you of sound mind at this very moment?"

"Almost completely."

"Then the answer is yes."

She smiled and leaned in with the vague notion that they should seal it with a kiss. He took her gently by the shoulders.

"Let's save that for dessert. What we should do right now is serve this dinner before it gets cold. Come on. I'll help you." He picked up the serving platter and headed for the dining room.

Edie slumped a little against the wall. This is the guy I've been waiting for all my life, she thought. He's gorgeous, he likes to cook, and, maybe I'm a little drunk, but I could swear the world is wrong about him. This man actually has a soul.

"We were beginning to think you two left," Rosalind said with a smile as they walked back into the dining room.

"We did," Ron said. "But we're back now."

As the meal progressed, Starry Messenger studied Vaniere's demeanor. This was a hard-bitten reporter, a man whose stock in trade was digging dirt and bringing down the powerful. But that image didn't square with the man he met this evening. He saw in Vaniere a kind of moral steadiness and genteel charm that was unlike his media image. How does that happen? He made a mental note to find out.

Chapter 55

THE DAY DAWNED crisp in Chicago, a glorious, golden Indian Summer morning. Outside the Dirksen Federal Building, Dearborn Avenue was jammed with people buzzing about the events of the previous day. Was the old man really The Starry Messenger? Meanwhile, the Starry Messenger Ticker scrolled the question of the day: Are you listening with filters? Are you listening with filters?

Up in the courtroom, Judge Elwood Baumgartner gaveled the room to order. "Mr. O'Roarke, call your next witness."

"The government calls The Starry Messenger."

It was a bombshell. The spectators, who had figuratively bound and gagged themselves since the trial began, looked at O'Roarke as one, not quite sure they had heard him right. They were unable to overcome their urge to whisper to each other.

Baumgartner cracked the gavel. "Order in the court. You heard the man."

Rowan Glass rose and slowly made his way toward the witness stand. He put his hand on the Bible and smiled. The room was absolutely silent.

"Do you swear to tell the truth, the whole truth and nothing but the truth?"

"Don't I always?" He sat down.

"No freakin' way!" Mick the Tech was on his feet. "You are not Starry! Starry's ..." Mick stopped. He looked around and saw that everyone was staring at him, including the Judge. "... blonde." He slumped down into his seat.

O'Roarke was so excited that he actually had butterflies. This was his big moment. He had concocted a series of questions that would get the man to talk; not to offer any evidence of course, or insert any facts, but rather to take as much time as possible and just ... talk. "Please state your name."

"Which one?"

"How many do you have?"

"My legal name is Rowan Glass, but might you better know me as The Starry Messenger?"

"Certainly. Mr. Glass, do you believe the God Gene is an act of God?"

"What does my opinion matter?"

"Well you have been blogging on the subject for months. Is it an act of God?"

"When I ask my readers whether it is an act of God, what do you think they say?"

"Mr. Glass, if you don't mind, I'm the one who asks the questions," O'Roarke said.

The Starry Messenger tilted his head and gazed off into the distance. "Do you know how difficult it is to watch a man lie on the stand?"

"Who lied?" O'Roarke said. A bolt of adrenalin shot through his stomach.

"Why don't you ask me if Morrison told me that the code came from Rosalind Evans?"

"Your honor, please instruct the witness not to lead counsel," O'Roarke said.

The Judge thought about it for a moment. "How can the witness lead counsel?"

"By telling me what questions to ask?" O'Roarke said.

"Tell?" Glass said. "Don't you know that I never tell, only ask?"

"Mr. Glass, you are not allowed to speak except to answer questions," the Judge said.

"Why not?"

O'Roarke scratched his head. "Let's pretend that it's illegal for you to ask questions. Using a sentence that ends in a period, can you please tell me whether you think the God Gene is an act of God?"

Starry leaned back and laughed a deep, lusty laugh that went on and on.

"Can you speak without asking a question?" O'Roarke asked.

"What do you think?"

"Why do you put everything you say in the form of a question?"

The old man ran his hand over his grizzled stubble. His face filled the Jumbotron, dominating the scene in the courtroom. His eyes scanned the ceiling for a moment, and then he shrugged.

"Because I don't have any answers."

All at once, as if someone had changed the channel, Starry Messenger's face on the tron was replaced by a shot of two young Asian men on the steps outside Clearbrook Hall. The raspy voice of the Starry Messenger was replaced by a blaring, loud, younger voice. Everyone in the room was startled. It looked like a totally unrelated feed had been mistakenly plugged into the Jumbotron. The young men appeared to be holding some kind of press conference. Judge Baumgartner craned his neck around and looked at it. "What the ...?" He turned and looked at his bailiff. "What is that?"

In the control room next door, the director was beside himself. His buddy from a local Chicago station had tipped him off that there was a major announcement going on at Clearbrook Hall about Rosalind Evans and the God Gene. How perfect! He could feed it right into the courtroom where everyone was focused on the Starry Messenger. Zowie! One bombshell on top of another! This was killer TV!

In the courtroom, all eyes were on the tron. Mick the Tech was once again on his feet. "It's Kew and Wu! My grad assistants! Those guys clean my office!"

Danny Wu and Sammy Kew were grinning from ear to ear, dressed in ratty blue jeans and sneakers. Wu had on a wrinkly Chicago Bears t-shirt, and Kew's t-shirt had the faint remnants of a Harvard logo.

Baumgartner pointed his gavel at the tron as if it were a gun. "Get that off of there! Get it off!"

The volume increased as Wu spoke. Everyone in the courtroom was riveted on what he was saying.

"We couldn't let Rosalind Evans be punished for something we did," Danny Wu said. "That's why we are speaking out now. We put the Ten Commandments in the code."

O'Roarke stared at the tron, open-mouthed.

"But *why*? Why did you do it?" a reporter shouted at Kew.

"To promote our new Internet security company."

"How did you do it?"

"We used data from the project Dr. Evans was working on because it was close and easy to get. We altered the sequence just enough to have the Ten Commandments spelled out in the amino acid code. Our plan was to bugger it into the Global Genomic Access software. It's the one software that every sequencing facility has to use if they want to get into the GGA site. We created an algorithm to replace the real DNA sequence with our altered one, whenever it appeared in any database anywhere in the world. Then we were going to use our proprietary 'Banishit' algorithm to erase all past versions of the sequence, everywhere they appeared in any database. Then, of course, we would bring out our new security system to show how foolproof it is, even against the best hackers in the universe—us! But when it looked like Evans might be convicted for what we did, we decided to call the whole thing off." Wu and Kew raised their fists into the air in a victory salute. "Anyhow, we have created the most secure, fool-proof, hack-proof computer security system in the world. Click on our website, InfoTaze.com for more information on how to buy our security system or invest in our company." Kew smiled and pumped his fist in the air. "Woot!"

"Mr. Kew, can you prove that this is not a publicity stunt?"

"Of course I can."

"How?"

"I could show you our exact methodology and our computer files that show the timeline, but then I'd have to kill you." Kew let out a snarky little laugh.

Any semblance of order in the courtroom was gone. O'Roarke felt like if he tried to stand, he'd wet his pants. This is perfect, he thought. These two hot-shot computer geeks just gave me my exit strategy! He looked over at Cardinal Duffy, who had his hands in prayer position and his eyes heavenward. They could be lying, O'Roarke told himself, but *I'm not going to wait around to find out. I have to act now!*

O'Roarke stood and tried to get the Judge's attention. The room was pandemonium. Baumgartner was banging his gavel, trying to restore order.

Rosalind jumped to her feet. "No! It's not true!" she yelled.

David grabbed her arm and motioned to her to be quiet.

"It's a stunt," she told him. "It has to be."

"Keep quiet and let me handle this," David told her sternly.

"Your honor! Your honor!" O'Roarke yelled at the top of his voice. Baumgartner banged his gavel over and over again, glaring at the spectators. They began to quiet down.

"Your Honor!" O'Roarke finally could be heard. "This admission by these two men casts grave doubt on this case. If this is true, these men have violated Section 1030(a)(5) of the Federal Code and almost caused an innocent woman to go to prison! In light of this new development, and in the interest of justice, the Government has no choice but to drop the charges against Rosalind Evans!"

"No!" Rosalind leapt to her feet and faced O'Roarke. "You can't do that! I haven't testified yet!"

"Mr. Evans, control your client!" Baumgartner looked sternly at David.

"Yes, Your Honor." David gave Rosalind the dagger eyes. She slowly sat down, and as she did, she caught the eye of Starry Messenger, who was still sitting in the witness stand. He was smiling and giving her a thumbs-up.

Judge Baumgartner banged his gavel again and again. Finally he yelled into his microphone.

"Case dismissed! Dr. Evans, you are free to go." He gaveled the proceedings to a close.

David turned to Rosalind, his eyes wide. He let out a whoop and started to scoop her up in his arms, but she wasn't paying any attention to him. It was all so sudden that she couldn't completely grasp what just happened. Ever since her arrest, she had been living for the moment when she could take the stand in her own defense and tell the world the real truth.

"No! Your Honor, please. You can't do that!" Rosalind yelled.

Baumgartner looked shocked. "Of course I can. I just did."

"I want to testify."

"You can't. It's over. Go on home and hope the Government doesn't change their mind."

"All rise!!!" the bailiff shouted, even though everyone was already on their feet. Judge Elwood Baumgartner took one last look around the historic courtroom and with a disappointed shake of his head, he walked out.

Rosalind turned to David. "It's over? Just like that? I don't have my day in court?"

"No, and you should be very happy about that. You are a free woman!"

Rosalind was suddenly surrounded by well-wishers. Edie grabbed her and gave her a long hard hug, followed closely by Lex, Summer and Stefan. Boone Wilkes, the street preacher, took her hand. "I told you that you were a good girl, Rosalind," he said with a smile. "God bless you!"

His sincerity touched her, and she thought it was possible that this man of poverty and humility might be the most Godly she had ever met.

Ron Vaniere waited patiently until it was his turn, and then picked her up and twirled her around, giving her a big celebratory kiss on the cheek.

In the control room next door, the director was celebrating the blockbuster ending of the story. It was not an ending anyone could have predicted, but it was an attention-grabber. On one of the monitors, he heard Mick the Tech talking to Starry Messenger, who was still sitting in the witness chair with a live microphone.

"Dude, I can't believe this," Mick whined. "How do I know you are the real Starry Messenger?"

"Well, you don't, but what does it matter?"

"I *know* you are not her! You can't be!"

"Why did you think I was a woman?"

"I *know* Starry is a woman." Mick was sorely agitated, bouncing from one foot to the other like a prize-fighter waiting for the bell.

"Son, what are you so worked up about?"

"Dude, please tell me you are not Starry Messenger!" Mick's lower lip was quivering slightly.

Glass could see that he was wasting his time with this young man. He was obviously one of those few for whom the Starry Messenger simply did not compute. Ah well, he thought, I've blown my cover, but no regrets; the last few minutes were worth it. I'm ready to retire anyway. The pressure to be God-like is wearing me down. Time for somebody else to take over. "Ok, young man, I'm not the Starry Messenger. Feel better?"

"Dude! I knew it! That's what I'm talkin' about! So you *were* lying up here on the stand?" Mick leaned in closer. "So was I! Bradshaw, too. O'Roarke said it would be worth our while to help him out. But I guess it doesn't matter now. It's over!"

In the control room next door, the director sat upright. "Hey, Cal! I think this guy just said he lied on the stand. You got that recorded?"

"Sure do, Boss."

"Replay it on the tron!"

In the courtroom, the screen suddenly switched from Wu and Kew to the image of Mick talking to Starry Messenger.

"More audio!" the director said.

The assistant ramped the sound up so that no one in the room could ignore it. The sound was so loud that even Judge Baumgartner could hear it as he walked toward his chambers.

"Play it again!" the director said. "Camera two, get reaction on O'Roarke. Look at that! The guy looks like he's been tased. Camera one, get reaction on Bradshaw. Ha! Nailed. This is fabulous! Oh, man, Emmy Award here I come!"

Curious about the commotion coming from the courtroom, Judge Baumgartner turned and walked back in. He looked at the tron. For the third time, the entire confession was playing out, bigger than life. He walked up to Mick, who was staring at the tron.

Judge Baumgartner tapped him on the shoulder. "Excuse me, Mr. Morrison. Did you just say that you and Bradshaw lied on the stand?"

Mick was dumbstruck. "You weren't supposed to hear that, Dude!"

"Bailiff, please escort Mr. Morrison and Mr. Bradshaw into my chambers. Mr. O'Roarke!" Baumgartner yelled across the courtroom. O'Roarke was staring at the tron, open-mouthed.

"O'Roarke!"

He turned and faced the Judge.

"My chambers, now!"

David couldn't believe what he was seeing. "Well, it looks like our co-conspirators are going to find out what justice really feels like."

"How sweet is that?" Vaniere whooped. He and David patted each other on the back.

"David, I can't let this end here!" Rosalind said. "I still have something I want to say!" She looked at the media section and saw that it was empty. "Where did all the reporters go?"

"My guess is Clearbrook Hall. That seems to be where the action is."

Edie was scanning the breaking news feed on her iPhone, as she had done almost continuously since arriving in Chicago. She was grinning from ear to ear. "Hey, you're story is number one. Government drops charges! Cool. And those two hot-shot computer guys are number two. Ha ha!"

All of a sudden she stopped in her tracks. She read for a moment, then looked up with wide eyes. She handed the phone to Rosalind. David and Ron leaned in so they could see it.

FLEMINGHAM REPLICATES EVANS STUDY. FULL TEN COMMANDMENTS FOUND.

Rosalind read the first two paragraphs of the story. "They did it," she whispered. "Dear God, they did it. It took them three months, but they re-ran all 7000 of my samples using Deep X and they got the full Ten Commandments."

"What does it mean?" David asked.

"The Deep X might be faulty," Rosalind said. "But there is something else trying to happen here. Something much bigger." David, Ron, and Edie looked at each other with wide eyes. "Let's go."

Chapter 56

THE FRONT STEPS of Clearbrook Hall were filled with press and spectators. Wu and Kew were still at the microphone, not answering reporter's questions anymore, but reciting what sounded like marketing copy for their new company. Rosalind jumped out of the cab and bounded up the steps with David close behind, and Edie and Ron right behind him.

"Roz, slow down," he said, trying to keep up with her. "Let's give this some thought before you say anything. What are you going to say?"

"I'm going to tell the truth," Rosalind said. "Those guys didn't put the Ten Commandments into the code."

"But you don't want to say that! O'Roarke thinks they *did* put it in there. Can't you leave well enough alone?"

Rosalind gave him a sideways look.

"OK, let me rephrase," David said. "Please leave well enough alone. You don't want the government to change their mind."

"I'm a free woman, remember? I don't need a lawyer anymore." She continued to the top of the steps and walked right up to the microphone.

There was a murmuring from the crowd. "It's Rosalind Evans!" somebody yelled.

She leaned in between Wu and Kew. "Ladies and Gentlemen, these men did not plant the Ten Commandments in the genetic code."

Kew gave her a shove. "Hey, this is our press conference. You've had your fifteen minutes of fame. You should be happy we saved your hide.

Come on!" Wu made a move to grab her arm. She pulled away from him and kept on talking.

"If you will allow me, I'll explain. From what you gentlemen said a few minutes ago, you were going to send the altered code out to the Global Genomic Access site, but then you decided not to. Is that right?"

"Yes," Wu said, looking at Kew out of the corner of his eye.

"Did you alter the code on any other computer at any other facility besides Clearbrook?"

"No."

"Then you cannot possibly have done what you say you did."

"Are you saying they are lying?" a reporter from the crowd yelled.

Rosalind leaned in to the microphone. "I am saying that Mr. Wu and Mr. Kew did not create the God Gene. I know it, and *they* know it."

Kew shoved her. "You won't get away with this! That's slander! I'll see you in court, lady!"

Ron Vaniere calmly stepped between Rosalind and the two men and stared down at them. The scruffy pair were no match for the ex-jock. They turned and angrily walked away.

Rosalind looked out at the reporters. They wore confused expressions and, for once, said nothing. They looked at her with big, dumb faces and closed mouths. Gone was the arrogance and silent the tongues that had maligned her for so long. The sight of them made her laugh out loud. "Well, this is sure a turn of events," she said.

"What's so funny?" a reporter yelled. "Are you all right?"

Rosalind looked up at the soaring gothic spires of Clearbrook Hall glittering in the sunlight. The splendid architectural embellishments and bas relief motifs made a singular statement about the soul of the man who designed it, and about the noble—some would say sacred—work going on inside. Clearbrook Hall was the symbol of all that mattered to her as a scientist, the glory of scientific exploration and the satisfaction of contributing to mankind's understanding of the world. She was a scientist to her core. Nothing could change that. But she was a far different woman from the one who analyzed 7000 DNA samples for Alan Dyer.

"I'm fine. In fact, I'm wonderful. The government dropped the charges. I'm free."

"Why did the government drop the charges?" a reporter asked.

"They said it was because of what these two young men were claiming. But the truth is, their conspiracy to silence me and discredit the God Gene was coming apart at the seams."

"Conspiracy? Why?" a reporter asked.

"Because it threatened them."

"Who?"

"The men who are right now answering to Judge Baumgartner. It's going to be a big story. You might want to check it out."

"Dr. Evans, what is the God Gene? What does it mean?" a reporter asked. This was the question Rosalind had been waiting to answer on the witness stand. It looked like she would have her day in court after all, on the steps of Clearbrook Hall.

"For several reasons, the PharmaGen study was different from any ever done. First of all, we were working with two of the largest genes in the genome, CLAIRE and DZPro2, which have more SNPs than any other genes. Second, we had 7000 samples to analyze, more than other studies by an order of magnitude. Third, we had the brand new Deep X software, which is unique in that it allows us to combine 7000 sequences and look at all the SNPs at once. In trying to replicate my work, other labs looked at only a few samples at a time. They found a word or two, but not the entire Ten Commandments. I was able to look at 7000 samples at once. Picture the translation code from each of the 7000 samples printed on an ultra thin transparency. If you stacked them one on top of the other and held them up to the light, you would see all the SNPs at once. Only when we looked at *all 7000* at once did we see the full text of the Ten Commandments," Rosalind said.

"Why 7000 samples? Is that number significant?" a reporter asked.

"In scientific terms, no. But I've learned that it is significant in religious terms. In the three major holy books, the number seven is God's number, a perfect cycle, the seventh day, the Sabbath. The number 1000 signifies a millennium and eternity."

"Did you intentionally set out to analyze exactly seven thousand samples?"

"No. I didn't choose 7000. 7000 were given to me."

"But how can you be sure Wu and Kew didn't hack in and put the Ten Commandments in the code?"

"Because I just learned that Flemingham has re-sequenced all 7000 of my samples using the Deep X software. They got exactly the same result I got: the full Ten Commandments."

The audience fell silent, as if they didn't quite grasp the magnitude of what she said. After a long moment, the voice of one reporter piped up. "But ... Flemingham's computers could have been hacked, right? This could still be a hoax, right?" Some in the crowd nodded and murmured in agreement.

Rosalind laughed again. "You guys need to start asking the right questions! Put your cameras on wide-angle because you are missing the point. When people learned that the Ten Commandments were written in our genetic code, it caused a global sensation. It shook the earth off its axis. *Why?*"

Rosalind looked out at the reporters. She paused a moment, waiting for someone to answer. By now, hundreds more people had joined them, and more were streaming toward Clearbrook Hall from all directions. Three more satellite TV trucks pulled up, and the cameras were rolling.

"It's not a rhetorical question. *Why?*" Again she waited. No one spoke; they were totally focused on her.

"Because it resonates! It echoes an ancient reminder that God cares about us. Like a good parent, He knows that when we play by the rules, we are happier than when we don't. Look, how does a lab error in Chicago capture the attention of a Syrian peasant, a French politician, and a Brazilian fisherman? How does an act of sabotage in America cause people the world over to fall weeping to their knees in gratitude? How does a cheap publicity stunt on the steps of Clearbrook Hall cause all of you to be here right now, listening to a woman you've been ripping to shreds for three months?"

The plaza was full now, and she could feel the anticipation in the crowd. This was the day in court she so desperately wanted. She no longer had to fight the media and the mobs; everyone was listening.

"The God Gene is so powerful, so filled with potential for good, that it has to be more than a lab error, an act of sabotage, or a publicity stunt. Don't you see? *Regardless* of how it got there, the God Gene is REAL!"

Again the plaza was quiet. The sound of the carillons rose up from Rutherford Chapel. A gentle autumn breeze blew Rosalind's auburn hair away from her face as she reached in her pocket and took hold of Claire's marble.

Suddenly a reporter yelled out in a loud, snide voice, "I suppose you think it's a miracle?"

"I don't know. But let's not miss the point. It's not about what the God Gene *is*. It's about what it's *done*!"

"Ruined your life?" The reporter sneered at her. She could see that he was, indeed, missing the point.

"No! Gave me *back* my life! I have hope again, I have faith, I want to follow the rules laid out for us. And so do millions of others! Can you imagine what the world would be like if we *all* obeyed the Ten Commandments?"

The reporter clearly was agitated. He climbed to the top of the steps and confronted Rosalind head on. "Aren't you angry about all that has happened to you? Losing your job, being charged with treason?"

"No."

"Why not? Don't you think it was unjust?"

"I lost my privacy, my security, my job. But I've gained something far more important. We all have. The God Gene reminds us that we're not alone, that we don't have to be afraid anymore. What could be simpler? The God Gene reminds us who we *are*."

The reporter raised his voice. "You're telling me you are not angry with all those religious leaders who called you a heretic? And the politicians who called you dangerous and a liar?"

"And the media? You belong at the top of that list. You beat me to a bloody pulp. No. I am not angry. To be angry is to miss the point. The question isn't what I think. The question is what do we do with this gift we've been given? Let's open our eyes and ears and hearts so we don't miss what's trying to happen here."

"I thought you were an atheist!" the reporter shouted. "Now you're talking about God like you believe in him. You lied!"

"I changed. Atheist is a state of mind. Faith is a state of the heart. The God Gene opened my heart."

"Are you actually saying the God Gene is proof that God exists?"

"Now you're starting to ask the right questions! The God Gene is a *reminder* that God exists. What else could it be?"

"A software glitch?"

Rosalind laughed out loud. "A glitch that caused the code to rearrange itself into the Ten Commandments? I want to meet the programmer who made that mistake!" The sound of the carillons rolled through the plaza, rising to a crescendo. As the last note died, Rosalind looked at the angry reporter. "The God Gene resonates." She paused and cocked her ear upward. "Can you hear that?"

Again, all was silent. The crowd, twice as large as the one that gathered for the Steele rally, stretched as far as the eye could see in every direction. All eyes were focused on her. She looked out at the assembled multitude. "What about you? Can you hear that?"

A group of people on the steps began to nod and look around. A few began to clap. Then more. The clapping spread out to the edges of the crowd. The crowd began to cheer, and the cheering spread, and the applause grew until the entire plaza shook with the cheering and clapping of thousands of people.

Rosalind leaned into the microphone. She put both hands in the air, fingers spread wide. "Can you *hear* that? Our Creator is telling us something!"

The cheering intensified. People raised their hands in the air. Rosalind turned and took David's arm. Followed closely by Ron and Edie, they walked down the steps of Clearbrook Hall and into a waiting taxi.

The city sparkled in the autumn sunlight. As their taxi swung onto Lake Shore Drive, Rosalind rolled down her window and breathed in the cool air. Lake Michigan shimmered deep blue and inviting. The four of them rode along for several minutes, quietly taking it all in.

"Let's take *Proteus* out and celebrate," David said. "This might be the last good sailing day of the season. At least this time we won't have the media chasing us. They're probably on to something else already. That's how the news cycle works. By next week, the God Gene will be old news, and by next month, it will be forgotten."

Roz smiled and shook her head. "I'll never let that happen."

"You two want to join us for a sail?" David asked.

Ron, seated in front, turned around. "I'll have to take a rain check. I have a date." He smiled and winked at Edie.

"Ron, is there still a chance you could get fired over all this?" Rosalind asked.

"Not if I quit first."

"Edie, you're not going to New York right away, are you?" Rosalind asked plaintively. After three months together, she couldn't bear to think of her leaving.

"I'm looking at options," Edie said with a coy smile and a wink at Ron.

The cab pulled over to let Edie and Ron out. They waved as the cab drove out of sight.

"Well, finally, it's over," David said.

"It's far from over."

"What do you mean?"

"I have to analyze the Deep X software. If there's a glitch I have to find it."

"But you just said a glitch doesn't change anything …"

"It doesn't. The God Gene is real either way. But I'm a scientist. I have to know if there was a glitch."

"Then can we get back to life as usual?"

"Whatever lies ahead, I doubt it will be life as usual."

"That's what worries me," he said, giving her a squeeze.

"David, I want to go sailing, but there's one stop I need to make first."

"Where?"

"The cemetery."

"Are you serious?" David searched her face. He saw no fear, only a calm look of determination.

She sat silently for a moment, staring out at the lake but seeing the cemetery in her mind. Deep emotion welled in her, but it was not despair, not the pit looming. She was infused with a new kind of energy, as if a secret door within her had unlatched itself and swung wide.

"David, I thought my redemption would come from finding out why Claire died. But I was wrong. I was the one dying. I want to live again. Do you remember the last time we went to the cemetery and you said you wanted us to hold each other and cry for our daughter, *together?*"

David nodded.

"I'm ready."

Chapter 57

Where do we go from here?

Well Kittens, it's been two months since the God Gene trial abruptly ended, so what have we learned?

As the world eagerly awaits the results of the Deep X software investigation, newly elected Pope Innocent XIV announced that he will issue a statement clarifying the church's position on the God Gene as soon as the study is complete, but what does it matter? As the Archbishop of Chicago, he denounced it, but even if he changes his mind and embraces it, will the God Gene be any more or less real?

There were many memorable moments at the Evans trial, but who could ever forget the accidental public confession of Mick Morrison? The question now is, will the special prosecutor find evidence that the conspiracy to frame Rosalind Evans goes beyond Morrison, Thomas O'Roarke, and Benton Bradshaw? Might Senator P.P. Bosch be involved, as some are suggesting? His indictment for fraud in the operation of the P.P. Bosch Fairness for America Foundation came just days after his humiliating defeat in the presidential election, and we have to ask ourselves, is this just the tip of the iceberg?

How long do you think the current rash of kindness and generosity will last? Will the Godgeners' peace address at the United Nations resonate? How long will the cease-fires in the Middle East last?

Doesn't it seem like Chicago has become the center of the Universe? Have you ever seen so many images of the Windy City burned into the global consciousness in one six-month period? Who can forget the image of Benton Bradshaw, the day after he was brought up on perjury charges, burning a huge portrait of his father on the steps of Clearbrook Hall and shouting through the smoke and flames, 'Die, you bastard, die?' Or the sight of 300,000 people at the refurbished Decker Tower in the South Loop, the new home of the 50 story Convocation of Manifest Souls?

And of course, who can forget the image of Rosalind Evans smiling and waving to reporters as she returned to Rutherford University after a four-month absence to become the new Director of the Clearbrook Institute? Will the PharmaGen leukemia project continue, in light of the untimely death of Alan Dyer? We may never know whether it was murder or suicide, but did the rejection of his God Gene patent application have anything to do with it? How will the new CEO, Peter Gleason, cope?

So my Kittens, where do we go from here? Will the God Gene era launch us to new heights of spiritual clarity and enlightenment? Will we love each other more? Or will we rebound to new lows of moral confusion? What does it mean that Willard Hitchcock tried to commit suicide, yet won the presidential election in a landslide? Or that his first official act was to create a new cabinet position, Secretary of Reconciliation, and appoint Rev. Joseph Steele to the post? Can the American political system cope with the concept of reconciliation? Were you surprised when Steele dissolved the First Light Campaign and donated all the assets to charity? What are the lessons in that?

Finally, won't you join me in a tip of the hat and a fond farewell to Rowan Glass, the first Starry Messenger? Where would our collective consciousness be without him? Who else could have consistently asked the right questions at this momentous time in human history? For if we don't ask the right questions, how can we possibly expect to find the truth?

As ill-prepared as I am, I nevertheless have been called to take up the mantle as the new (and completely anonymous, of course) Starry Messenger; a daunting task, wouldn't you agree? So, won't you please join me as we wield our collective shovels in a never-ending search for truth?

P.S. I almost forgot; have you heard the news that Rosalind Evans is writing a book about the God Gene and dedicating it to the baby girl she and husband David are expecting on April 3rd?

The End

About the Author

Jaymie Simmon is a native of the Chicago area. She is an avid sailor, cyclist, news junkie and cook. She has a Bachelor's degree in theatre from Northern Illinois University, and for several years produced and hosted the Emmy-nominated local TV show "Kankakee Valley Prime Time." Jaymie and her husband, Harry, live near Chicago. *The God Gene* is her first novel.

CPSIA information can be obtained at www.ICGtesting.com
Printed in the USA
BVOW032126040613

322462BV00002B/71/P